Offspring.

Being A Tale Of Friends, Unplanned Children, and Unwanted Adventure.

George R. Mead

E-Cat Worlds Press

This is a work of fiction. All the characters and events portrayed are creations of the imagination, nothing more, nothing less.

Comments and questions? –> gmead01@gmail.com

Offspring

LCCN 2009929087

Mead, George R.
Offspring: Being a Tale of Friends, Unplanned Children,
 and Unwanted Adventure./
George R. Mead.
p. cm. – (From Grandeville, a tale; Tale 8)
 ISBN-13 978-0-9817446-0-5
          1. Fantasy. I. Title. II. Series.

E-Cat Worlds established its publishing program as a reaction to the large commercial publishing houses currently dominating the book industry and the smaller intellectual clones. It is interested in publishing works of fiction and non-fiction that are often deemed insufficiently profitable or commercial or that are not necessarily reflective of literary trends and fads.

E-Cat Worlds, 57744 Foothill Road, La Grande OR 97850
www.ecatworldspress.com
SAN 255-6383

In the middle of nowhere - Creativity.

First Edition:
Printed in the United States of America

From Grandeville.

Tales Told

Portal
Lair
Search
Not Again
And Again.
Magiwitch
Rebirth
Offspring

Tales Yet To Be Told

Holiday
Treasure
Two
Seemna
Choice

Chapter One

Just Another Day, So To Speak.

Grandeville. Tinker's Place. Early Morning.

She sighed.

It was a long, soft exhalation of breath.

And stretched.

And relaxed.

Even more. Or maybe just a little.

And laughed.

It was a soft, happy laugh.

It was a most unusual sound to make.

Even for a happy witch.

Especially for a happy witch.

"Tink?"

"Ummmm?"

She turned her head. "Tink?"

His eyes opened. A little. Mere slits. Looking up, he saw reflected light on the ceiling, outside coming into the room, reflected light. On the ceiling.

"Ummm?"

"I have been destroyed."

He smiled. "I doubt that."

MindMate, it snowed. It was Smoke. Speaking inside his mind.

"Again?"

Yep.

R-Bar sat up and threw the covers to one side. And looked at him. And laughed.

His eyes opened, fully opened, this time. And looked at her. This time.

She pouted, lower lip poking out. Just a little. "I don't think that you can."

He sighed. "Smoke just said that it had snowed last night. And I said, again. See?"

"Oh." She grinned. And laughed again. "Sure." And rolled her eyes at him. "But we could ask the Vander for one of their potions. A stiffener of some sort."

"Knock it off," he grumbled.

She turned and flopped on her side, facing him, and dragged the covers back up and around them. "Just trying to be helpful." And blew warm into his ear.

He rolled toward her, slid one hand across smooth, moon pale skin. "Don't want that kind of help. Never again. We do not want to do that sort of thing, ever again? BrenBand, that ring of Ancient Magic, was more than bad enough."

Smoke banged the snow from her boots, yanked them off, and left them sitting by the back door, the back kitchen door. She then hung several layers of clothes on the row of wooden pegs mounted on the wall for that purpose. And began to prepare breakfast. As she worked at the large range, Ran wandered in and peered over her shoulder. "Cold."

"Then put on your pajama top. I just came inside."

Ran stepped back, untie the sleeves knotted around her waist, and swung the garment into place.

"My elseplace did not have this snow stuff weather."

"Fix the other coffee pots."

Ran nodded, turned away, and stared intently. The pot she was staring at wobbled through the air, filled with water, and finally made it back to the coffee maker. The filter cup floated over and gathered up the correct amount of coffee grounds before heading back.

"It was so easy when I was Tanpak witch," grumbled Ran.

Smoke turned and waited. Until everything was done moving around. Then she hugged Ran. "Past is past, Sister Self." The great orange-gold eyes swallowed Ran's yellow and brown eyes. "You are lovely, just as you are."

Ran nodded.

"Fry the sausage." Smoke released her.

"Morning, morning, morning," bubbled Messenger, popping into the kitchen, yanking open the refrigerator. "Let's have pancakes. Lots and lots."

The rest of them began to arrive from their bedrooms.

"Snow bound," mumbled Chantal, pouring her cup full and shuffling toward the large living room. Her cup had a cartoon of an insulted cow sticking out its tongue.

Another coffee maker began gurgling harshly.

"Ghastly noise," observed Fair Morn, looking at the thing through slitted eyes. '"Why is it so bright in here?" And turned toward the living room, taking the first coffee pot and her cup. That cup had butterflys all over it.

"Huge snow drifts," giggled Messenger, standing on her tip-toes, peering out the kitchen window over the sink. "Really really big. One ate the garage." She nodded violently. "Really really did."

In the living room, Tinker collapsed into one of the chairs, and slumped, taking the cup offered to him by R-Bar.

She took the emptied pot and headed back to the kitchen and met Chicken.

"Pray tell, Sweet Witch," asked Chicken, leaning against a counter top. "How do it pass that Our Lord this morn so early rise?" She turned and looked at the coffee maker in its gurgling last stages of being done, and then carefully looked at R-Bar. "Most sudden and fierce do be this winter."

"Just woke up," grumbled R-Bar.

"Toast," commanded Smoke.

"Oh aye, Our Verra Own Commander Sister Self Boss." Chicken jabbed at a loaf of bread with one finger. Then after checking for freshness, she began to drop slices into the large toaster. R-Bar ducked into the dining room and began to set the table.

"Eeeeeek!"

Smoke had slipped past and pinched her before stopping at the wide arched opening into the living room and leaning forward. "Anyone alive enough in there to eat some breakfast?" She walked in, over, and ruffled his hair. And looked at the others.

"Gumpf," he said.

"We get lots of snow?" Fair Morn still had her eyes shut.

"Just lots and lots," beamed Messenger, leaning around Smoke, the top of her head just level with the top of Smoke's shoulder. Messenger's eyes twinkled. "But no gumpf."

"Shhhhhh," snarled Chantal in Messenger's general direction, squinting a little.

Messenger dropped into the couch next to her. "Do you know that you are even slower than he is?" she whispered.

"Nothing worse than bubbly in the morning," mumbled Chantal as she held out her cup.

Messenger filled it. "To wake up," she amended softly.

Tinker stretched and yawned, "Let's eat." And stood. And ruffled Smoke's hair in return. "Well?"

She kissed him on the cheek. "Ready when you are." And spun and headed back toward the kitchen.

As they finished breakfast, he looked around the large dining room table and nodded at them. "Lots of work waiting out there."

"OOG GLUK," announced Messenger.

"Huh?" He stared at her.

She laughed happily. "It means 'you betcha' in Eskimo." Then she ducked her head. "I made that up."

"Really?"

She hit him with a well thrown muffin. Blueberry.

They dug a tunnel into the woodshed and carried and stacked large quantities of cord wood onto the deck near the front door. Then they tunneled into the generator shed and checked everything in there. Just in case.

Chicken, Fair Morn, and Ran headed for the barn to take care of the animals.

Then he realized that this snow fall made very good snowballs. And caught Chantal just as she bent over to look at a snow pattern on one of the snow drifts.

So, of course.
The war commenced.

In the large living room.
Wet clothes hung everywhere.

In the living room.

    They sprawled.

        Wearing thick white robes.

In the room.

    They drank hot cocoa.

And warmed themselves with the heat from the wood stove.

And then, one by one, they fell asleep, right where they were.

The wood stove crackled into the silence, the sleeping quiet of the room. Outside the wind began to blow. Again. The house creaked. Talking to the wood stove. The wood stove muttered back.

And it started to snow. Again.

His eyes popped open. Someone had just entered the living room.

"Hi, Pop. Boy, did you ever get a lot of snow."

It was Sedeem. And Farth, her husband. She stared at the bodies and the scattered clothing. "What have you been doing to my moms?"

Farth fizzled and nudged her. It didn't sound like a proper question to him.

"Nothing," replied Tinker. "We just had a little snowball fight and got kinna wet. And cold. There is probably still some cocoa in the kitchen." He stood. "I'll make coffee. You two staying? Or just passing through?"

She looped her arm through one of his as he passed. "Staying for awhile. Can we use the corner room?"

"Sure."

She pointed at one of the shelves. "Funny looking ring."

He smiled. "Souvenir. Want to see?"

"Sure." She released his hand . He carried the ring to the kitchen, gave the rewarming cocoa a stir, and punched the on button on another coffee maker, and said, "Come out, Dat."

"What do you want me to do to her?" asked the tiny figure standing on the counter top. "Is she making trouble?"

"Nothing. No. This is my daughter, Sedeem."

Dat smiled up at her. "Pleased to meet you."

"She is very pretty," said Sedeem as she bent to take a close look. "Do you ever become our size and get to mess around." And laughed, looking over and up at her father.

Dat shook her head slowly. "I can't maintain that size long enough."

"She is an indjinn," he explained as Sedeem straightened up. "The ring is her home."

Sedeem smiled at her. "Want some cocoa?"

"Yes." Dat sprang onto Sedeem's shoulder and sat, kicking her legs, one hand clenched in Sedeem's hair. "It is good to be outside." She looked around.

"I am Farth," said Farth, who was standing behind Sedeem, looming large.

"Does it hurt?" asked Dat.

Tinker laughed.

"It is his name," explained Sedeem. Farth looked puzzled. Tinker reached around and handed him a cup. Dat held out her's.

"Maybe you ought to dip from Sedeem's," suggested Tinker as he poured his daughter's cup full. "It might be easier."

Dat did and took a sip. "Tastes just like boodle."

They all headed back to the living room. Tinker took the cocoa pan and the coffee pot. He felt the others waking.

"Hi, Moms." Sedeem hugged Smoke, the only one standing.

Farth stood and looked out a window at the storm swirling around the house. His elseplace didn't have this kind of weather, not this much.

Sedeem dropped heavily into it. "Nice couch." And looked at Smoke. "Relaxed. Happy."

Smoke winked at her. "Very good. Your eyes are barely noticeable."

"Learned how to control it."

Messenger leaped to her feet. "REALLY? Really really? Show me!" She walked over and peered into Sedeem's eyes. Sedeem's eyes glowed brighter and brighter blue and then faded away.

"Daughter, you will teach that to me."

Sedeem smiled at her. "Yes, Mom."

"Oh boy, oh boy, oh boy, oh boy," gurgled Messenger. "Now I can get rid of those yucko sunglasses." She kissed her daughter of the forehead.

Dat squeaked.

Messenger had almost set one of her hands on the indjinn sitting there on Sedeem's shoulder. "Didn't see you. Sorry."

"Well, all right," said Dat. "If you mean it."

Messenger looked round-eyed at the indjinn. "Oh I really do."

Sedeem laughed softly.

"What is funny?" demanded Dat.

"Ummmm," replied Sedeem. "Messenger."

"I'll get more cups." Messenger hurried from the room.

Tinker sat next to his daughter and looked at Dat. "Pretty tough for a shrimp."

"What is a shrimp?"

Smoke sat on the other side of Sedeem and explained shrimp and shrimp cocktails and other types of cuisine utilizing shrimp.

"I am not," stated Dat, very firmly.

"Tough?" suggested Tinker.

"A slimy thing," grumbled Dat.

"They are not slimy," said Tinker. He stared at her. "Maybe I'll go get the cocktail sauce. Give you a dip in it."

Dat leaped to her feet and glared at him. "I do not work for cannibals."

"Fee fi fo fum," he replied.

Chicken leaned over the back of the couch. "My Lord, do cease thy jesting. Fair Dat do most a'vexed be."

"Fair Dat," he sighed.

"Most fair," agreed Chicken. "For most petite indjinn."

"Was threatening Messenger," he mumbled.

"She almost mashed me," stated Dat, all indignation.

"Cups, cups, cups," announced Messenger, carrying a tray into the room.

Tinker poured. Chicken served, Everyone arranged themselves. Chantal fetched the cookies. Sedeem let Dat dip into her cup and then set a cookie fragment on her shoulder.

Dat sat and kicked her legs back and forth. "A very nice daughter, Great Master." She crunched on the cookie fragment and smiled at him.

"Thanks," replied Tinker.

"Thanks," said Sedeem.

"Thanks," added Smoke.

"Indeed," agreed Chicken.

"Right," said Messenger.

"Pass the cookies," said Fair Morn. "We think so."

"Yep." R-Bar shoved the cookie jar at Fair Morn. Ran

nodded.

Chantal and Ran stood and headed for the kitchen. Ran nudged Chantal as they made more cocoa. "I am glad that his Dat can not be our size."

Chantal nodded. "So is he, I think."

Day was fading toward night. Outside the house, creeping across snow drift and snow dune came blue shadows, creeping. Inside the house, people were scattered, doing things, here and there.

Tinker was in his office, working on the computer, editing. Dat was on the shelf above the computer, lying in the narrow space between the edge of the shelf and the book spines, sleeping.

Chicken, Chantal, and Sedeem were making the evening meal. Chicken had insisted that Sedeem ought to learn more of this skill even though she had some previous experience. But she needed to add to her knowledge.

In the shower room, Fair Morn was sprawled on the floor while Messenger and Ran scrubbed her great butterfly wings. The air was steamy. The floor ran with soap suds.

Outside, admiring the blue and white, Smoke clumped around the house, accompanied by Farth, just getting a little exercise.

R-Bar set the dining room table and then went into the kitchen to help with the salad. She worked next to Sedeem, who asked, "Mom, you ever visit Faro Tan?"

"Nope." R-Bar knew which mom was being addressed.

Sedeem slipped closer and grinned. "I think that Dad would like it."

"Oh?" Chantal dumped a few more ingredients into the pot.

"I think so." Sedeem looked sideways at her. "All the younger females, younger beautiful females, do not wear anything above the waist. Farth fizzled a lot." She laughed. "He didn't like the males staring at me."

"Hum," said R-Bar.

"MOM! That is not nice. We just dressed that way because it is the local custom. A very strong custom."

"Indeed?" Chicken chewed on one corner of her mouth.

"Yep. It was a warm and sunny elseplace. A nice one to visit. Very relaxed, little villages here and there."

"Praps," grinned Chicken. "We might Ourselves do be Faro Tan this even a'meal?"

"Hum, hum," murmured R-Bar.

Sedeem blushed.

"Not a good idea, Princess." Chantal wacked her, lightly, on a rear pocket. "Her husband would fizzle and he would do worse."

"Piffle," suggested Chicken.

"Have to wait until our house guests are gone." R-Bar nodded. "Chantal is correct. Keep your shirt on."

Chicken turned back to the large kettle and gave the contents a thoughtful stir. It was sauce. They were having spaghetti for dinner.

Dat woke, sat up, stretched and arched her back, and checked to see whether he was looking at her.

He wasn't.

Looking at her.

He was staring at the computer screen and making changes to his document.

She jumped down and sat on the top edge of the monitor. "You are not nice, Great Master."

"Huh?" His eyes rose. "What?" One hand reached sideways for his coffee cup.

"Not nice," she restated.

He leaned back, took a sip, and stared at her. "Now what?"

"I am very beautiful and you did not notice."

"Oh." He leaned close and leered at her. "How's this?" Then he flapped his lips at her, and sang, "OOOOOWWEEEE!"

"Nix nix bik tik."

"That sounds pretty bad and nasty. For a cute indjinn."

"I am not cute."

"Ahhhhh, lovely?"

"Of course."

"I see." He leaned way back, the swivel chair creaking loudly. "Well, your language sounded pretty bad to me. For a lovely indjinn."

"You were making fun of me."

"Sure. Tell me something?"

"Of course."

"How come all you lovely females need to be observed and complimented upon all the time?"

"Because we are there."

"Ah, ha."

Dinner, My Lord.

"Let's go, gorgeous. Time to eat."

Dat jumped down and ran up his arm and kissed the side of his face and sat on his shoulder. He turned off the computer, after closing down everything, and headed downstairs.

They were all sitting around the table by the time the two of them arrived, Tinker and Dat. He bent over Chicken and kissed her. "Beautiful."

Dat leaped to the table top.

Then Tinker repeated himself six more times as he made a circuit of the table. "You, too, daughter." And dropped into his chair. "There." And looked satisfied at a job well done.

Messenger looked at Smoke who shrugged. And began to heap spaghetti on her plate.

And then served the rest of them.

Chantal ladled on the sauce as the plates were passed.

Dat stood next to Chantal's plate and poked her finger into the sauce and tasted it. "Strange." She walked over to watch Tinker. He dropped a strand of uncoated spaghetti over her. "Have some."

"ZIK, ZIK, ZIK." Dat spun around and around, finally flinging the wet strand away.

"About as much fun as a cat."

She glared at him.

"My Lord, do be not so."

"Sorry, Dat."

Dat walked over and kicked the back of his hand.

"Really," he said. "I am. Just not used to having an indjinn of my very own. Especially one so beautiful." He rolled a big knot of spaghetti on his fork. "Want something else to eat?"

"Indjinns do not need to eat. We just do it for the experience." She huffed and walked down the table to check out the cheese.

The light flickered as they began to clean off the dining room table. "I'll do it," said Chantal. "Come on, Ran."

They hurried away to dress and to head out to the generator shed.

The lights went out.

Chicken knelt and began to take out the boxes of candles kept for just such occasions. "Me'Lord, let us this night enjoy most soft golden glow."

"Sure."

"And watch a movie." Smoke headed for the large living room.

Two figures appeared.

And sank out of sight in a puff of white.

They had landed on one of the new large drifts, not yet consolidated. The wind blew over their heads and began to drift white flakes down upon them.

"WHERE ARE WE?"

"Calm, calm. This is the correct elseplace. However, no one ever mentioned this kind of thing." She yanked a silver wand from somewhere. All around them the snow disappeared as a yellow glow illuminated the spherical space carved by the wand.

He poked one finger into a wall. "Very cold stuff. What magic does this?"

"Doesn't smell of magic, Dear. Take my hand."

He did.

They floated slowly upward, the snow receding around them as they did.

"It is everywhere!" he gasped.

"A strange noise. That way." She drifted them toward the sound.

He squeezed her hand tightly. "It is a dragon."

They could see heat shimmering from one spot in the heaped up whiteness. It was coming from a small, dark opening in the white.

"If it is, it must be sleeping under these white lumpy

hills."

Then they could see the structure looming up in the dimness of swirling clouds of white.

She nodded. "Much larger than described."

"Should we go inside?"

"Much better than staying out here, Dear."

They settled and pushed open the door. And walked inside. Into darkness.

"It's a whiteout!" Chantal shouted into Ran's ear and tugged her toward the house, back toward the rear door of the house, as the storm roared around them.

Chantal slammed the door shut behind them as they lurched onto the back porch. She tugged on the knob. "Well, it's staying closed this time."

"This elseplace has terrible terrible storms." Ran stomped her feet, imitating Chantal. "Terrible."

Chantal laughed. "I think that this is going to be a winter to remember. Let's make some cocoa."

Stepping into the kitchen, she flicked on the lights and yanked off her boots. "I wonder who tracked up the floor?" Wet spots were heading down the hallway.

Shucking their outer clothes, the pair started making the cocoa. For everyone.

Messenger popped from the dining room into the kitchen, candle in hand. "We're going to watch a movie. By candlelight. Oh boy, I'll get the marshmallows."

The two small figures peered into the large room. At the people sitting there, talking. In candlelight.

She leaned close to her companion and whispered, "This is the correct place. That is him." And stepped into the room.

"Greetings, John Tinker. May we visit?"

His head snapped around. "What?" Then he stood and squinted into the dimness. "Plum Duff?"

She stepped into the candle glow, tugging the other with her.

"Yes. This is Tears Trimblechin, Sorrowful's grandson." The tops of their heads were just even with the back of the couch.

"ELF-TRANG!" screamed Ran, hurtling into the room, thrusting herself between Tinker and his visitors, dropping the bag of marshmallows on the floor.

Tinker threw his arms around Ran as Duff shoved Tears behind herself. "WHOA. That is Plum Duff, a friend of our's."

"What are Elf-Trang?" asked Tears, peeking out and around Duff.

"Stunted wizards," hissed Ran. "In mind and body."

Dat stood on Tinker's shoulder, one hand clenching his hair, growling.

"Relax, relax, relax," he grumbled. And smiled at Duff. "Kick off your shoes and try the couch." As the pair did, everyone who didn't know someone made introductions.

Duff grinned at him as she looked at the others and then back to Tinker. "You have certainly been busy."

Tinker shrugged. "Not any more. So, why are you here? Without $1.98?" He sat back in his chair. Ran moved to one side and carefully watched their visitors.

Duff told him. Of the search for the disturbance, about The Zedar red jewel-like creatures, and the death of Sorrowful Mistidings. And the final attempt by the $1.98 Magician to destroy that thing and the blast that almost killed the three of them.

Chicken sobbed quietly. Smoke looked grim.

Messenger huddled next to Smoke and wept silent tears. The rest folded around them and their sorrow. Tinker slumped and glared into nothingness. Sedeem sat by his side, on the free arm of his chair and gently set one hand on his shoulder.

"'It is hard to bring bad news," said Duff, one arm around Tears' shoulders. "But we came for help, not to cause sorrow."

Tinker's eyes shifted. "What kind of help?"

"$1.98 remains ill. Nothing I can do changes the damage. He is slowly fading. I am here to plead, if I have to, for help, for him. He was barely able to tell me how to find your elseplace. Please? Chosen One?"

It was a long, slow, weary sigh of breath. It came from Tinker.

Sedeem's fingers tightened on his shoulder. "Dad?"

"What?"

"We'll go, Farth and I. We'll visit the Vander first and I'll get Sa'ar to come as well. Between us, we ought to be able to fix whatever kind of magical damage has been done." She smiled at Duff. "Let's you and Mom R-Bar and I talk in the dining room. I need to know everything that has been tried."

Chapter Two

Medicine Is Medicine.

Magevern. Soft Dim Light.

"This desolation is the correct place?"

Duff looked at the stark environment, bare rock stretching to horizon greyness in all directions.

Tears clenched the hilt of the dagger on his belt, his weaponkin, with his left hand. And stayed close to her side.

Sedeem nodded and pointed. "Everything is below ground. The entry is just there."

Farth scanned their surroundings. He knew that there would be nothing here to fear. But it was a Silver Ranger habit to check. So, he did.

Sedeem nudged him. "Lets go." And led them down into a narrow crevice, the entrance, and the seemingly long stairs.

Farth followed Duff and Tears.

Pushing open the door, Sedeem stepped inside, waited, and then closed it behind them.

"I thought that someone would be here to greet us."

It reached out.

And grabbed them.

Grandeville. Tinker's Place. Afternoon.

He was taking a nap.

Several days after they had left.

He was trying to take a nap. Soft classical music was

playing inside the house, in the living room. A blizzard of blizzards was howling around the house, on the outside.

The wood stove muttered.

The house creaked.

It was their usual conversation.

Messenger sat on the couch, next to his sprawled form, and was lightly ticking him.

He decided to ignore her.

She caught his thought, and giggled.

"No privacy," he mumbled.

Her mind slipped in. *Peek-a-boo, I see you.*

Go away.

Tickle, tickle, tickle.

His eyes popped open. "I was taking a nap, I was." He stressed the 'was' part.

"No, you wasn't."

"Was to."

"You were not sleeping. Yet."

He pushed, so he could sit up, and sighed. "O.K. Now what?"

"Ran got trapped in the barn."

By your white terrible stuff, Amtar. It was Ran. She showed them the white wall outside, as she peeked out the chicken coop window at it. *I can not see anything out there, but that stuff.*

"Whuff, whuff." Smoke came into the room from the hallway, dressed in several layers of heavy clothes, and carrying coils and coils of bright yellow rope.

"St. Bernard's," explained Chantal. She was dressed the same way. "We're going to string a guide rope from the corner of the rear deck over the drifts and out to the barn."

Tinker reared up and glowered at them. "You're not going out there."

Chantal shoved him back down. "Don't get in an uproar, Cowboy, of course we are. Ran is trapped inside the chicken coop."

"Straight out, straight back," said Smoke. "No problemo, Dude." She turned and clumped through the dining room.

"You could make some hot cocoa." suggested Chantal as she turned and followed.

Tis in process, My Lord. Chicken and R-Bar had already started.

The front door banged open and a snow crusted figure stumbled inside, turned and heaved the door closed. She scraped snow from her face ,and yanked away her goggles. "I had to crawl," said Fair Morn. And grinned at him. "But the generator is fine. And so is the fuel supply." She began to peel away layer after layer. And hang the garments on the line of wooden pegs near the door. "Oh boy, I smell hot cocoa."

Messenger hurried away to collect cups.

Fair Morn removed the last layer and walked over and dropped onto the couch.

"Everything is cold."

He admired her goose bumps and yanked a comforter from the couch back, and tucked it around her, up to her chin. "There."

"Here." Messenger handed her a steaming cup.

Clenching the cup in both hands, she smiled and looked from Messenger to Tinker. "Thanks. Have a good nap?"

"NO. Go soak in the hot tub, when you finish the cocoa. I think I'd better check the wood supply."

"No need, we did it this morning. Early."

Messenger refilled Fair Morn's cup. "While you were

sleeping. Before this storm really started."

"You did?"

"Yep."

Fair Morn stood, dumped the comforter over him, handed her empty cup to Messenger, and left. "Cold, cold, cold."

"Nobody said anything," mumbled the comforter.

"She said, cold, cold, cold."

"Kitten!" The comforter flopped to one side.

"OH." Messenger giggled. "Want some cocoa?"

"Sure." He followed her into the kitchen, leaving the comforter on the couch in an untidy heap.

Magevern. Deep Below.

"Sorry, sorry, sorry, Deem." Sa'ar laughed as she began the release. "We were traveling and left a warding. Just in case."

She hugged Sedeem and kissed her. And gave Farth a friendly pinch, then finished releasing the rest. "I didn't know that you had children. Why wasn't I notified and invited to the Naming?"

"I AM NOT A CHILD!" Duff glared up at Sa'ar.

Sa'ar stepped back and looked at Sedeem. "I didn't think that your Mother could have more but that certainly sounds just like what I heard about her."

"And, I am not her mother's offspring either. Neither is Tears." Duff threw an arm around Tear's shoulders.

"This woman," said Sedeem, stressing the, word 'woman' very hard, "is Plum Duff, the $1.98 Magician's consort. Tears is the grandson of Sorrowful Mistidings. She is a powerful magician and he is a Teller of Tales from The Six Lands."

"I see. Small folk." Sa'ar waved at the entry. "Let's go

inside and get comfortable. The rest will be here shortly."

She led the way, slipping an arm around her cousin's waist. "Nice of you to visit. How are your parents?" And glared at Duff. "Don't get too close to me. Yet."

Grandeville. Tinker's Place. Cold and White.

"COLD," chattered Ran as the three of them clumped stumbled into the house, shaking brushing snow from themselves.

Smoke and Chantal quickly shed layers and headed for the hot tub to join Fair Morn.

Ran stopped fumbling with her clothes and stared at Tinker who was standing behind Chicken and R-Bar, his arms thrown around their shoulders, peering at whatever they were cooking.

He kissed Chicken on the ear. "A chicken crossing the road is poultry in motion."

She jerked her head sideways. "Most ferle, My Lord," said Chicken. "Your Ran do require some assistance."

His head turned. "What?"

"Rip her clothes off, Tink." R-Bar nudged him.

"My fingers do not work. Much." Ran held her hands up and peered at them.

Tinker stepped over and began to undo her coat. "Didn't you wear gloves?"

"No." She shrugged off the jacket and watched as he began to unfasten her shirt. "This elseplace of your's has strange weather, Amtar. Will it ever be warm again? Outside?"

"That's all you wore? In a few months."

"Yes."

He scooped her into his arms. "O.K., it's hot tub time for you."

Yanking her trousers down, he said, "O.K., get in there."

As Ran slipped into the steamy water, joining the others, he pointed at Smoke. "She needs weather memories. She could have frozen out there."

Smoke's minds reached out, found the appropriate memories, and slipped them to Ran. She goggled at Smoke. "Normal? This is normal weather here." She sank up to her neck.

Chantal smiled at her. "Welcome to Eastern Oregon in the mountainous northeast corner, Ran ourself. But this is really one of the worst winters that I've seen. And I grew up here." She looked up at Tinker and stared.

"What?"

"You just going to stand there ogling our bodies? How about some of that hot cocoa?"

"With marshmallows," added Fair Morn.

"Anything else you want, Boss?"

Chantal grinned. "We'll talk about that later, Simba Leader."

Magevern. Deep Below.

"So you think that I might be able to do something about it?"

Sa'ar sat on the long cushioned bench, one arm thrown around Sedeem's shoulders. She had directed her comment at Duff. She and Tears sat on chairs facing them.

"I have no idea," replied Duff. "Sedeem thought so. They would not leave home."

"Big winter storm blowing," explained Sedeem. "For the moment they are isolated from town and then some. When we're done, come visit. We can all play."

"Hum, hum," said her cousin, a soft smile coming and going.

"Don't be crude, Shar," chided Sedeem. "In the snow."

"Just a passing thought." Sa'ar laughed. "But I don't think your father wants us to visit."

"You can leave the others home. He wouldn't mind just you coming. And you know that."

"It would be no fun." Sa'ar stood. "Anyone hungry? We can eat and then go see this ailing magician of Duff's." She led them from the room.

A young woman flowed through the door as they finished the light meal and stopped just beyond the door and to the right side of Sa'ar. And fastened pale violet eyes on Sedeem.

"Imdar," said Sa'ar. "This is Sedeem, my cousin, Farth is her's, Plum Duff, a powerful magician, and Tears Trimblechin, a Teller of Tales. Imdar is our newest sister, a healer, a specialist in cures. She is coming with us."

Imdar slowly licked her lips, a slight flushing under the deep tan barely visible on her high cheek bones. "Sedeem Cousin, we are deeply honored to be of aid to thee."

She bowed formally. "My Vander sisters told me of all you did during our Great Final Battle. While I came after that event, I also stand in debt." One corner of her mouth puckered. "To you. And to your Father. And to all the others."

Sedeem laughed, quietly, noting the look in her eyes when Imdar had mentioned her Father. Farth fizzled softly. He'd seen it also. She nudged him with an elbow. "I'll tell him. He already knows about the rest, um, and their debt."

Grandeville. Tinker's Place. Cold and White.

The storm had finally ended The sun had come out. Now the drifts were wind packed hard.

So.

They dug a tunnel through the big one and cut notches through others as required for access to the wood pile and the generator shed.

Again.

"If the weather holds, we should get power back on soon enough and get the road plowed."

Tinker stood on top of a drift and looked down and out into the valley. It was a white, silent world out there. The valley had been transformed. Everything was now winter beautiful.

Chantal leaned against him. "Pretty nice, huh?"

He ran thick gloves over the many layers of thermal wear. "Certainly hard to tell. You're just one big lump of quilting."

She kicked his boot. "I was referring to the view, Cowboy. Of the environment down there." And waved one arm. "And all around us."

Chicken jumped up and down on a snow cornice and sent herself sliding, along with Ran and Messenger, and loads of snow, down the steep face of a gigantic drift. Laughing and giggling, they collided with Smoke and Fair Morn.

And soon.

Snow and vile curses flew.

In all directions.

As the combatants attacked anyone in sight.

R-Bar peeked from the tunnel and ducked back inside, came out the other end and headed for the house.

"Good idea," said Tinker. "Before that mob expands their interest area." He leaped, tugging Chantal with him.

At the base of the slope, he wound up on the bottom.

She dumped two mitts full of snow on him. "Smart guy."

Sitting up, he wiped the snow from his face, and glared at her. "Grumpy butt."

"Don't you slander my anatomy."

"NEVER."

"Better not." She stood close. And kicked snow at him.

He leaped to his feet. A very clumsy move. "Let's go inside. And check it out."

"What?"

"All that anatomy."

"Smooth talker." She batted her eyes at him. "Do we get hot cocoa first."

Tinker laughed and wacked her with a load of snow as she turned away. He lumbered for the back door.

"PAYBACK, COWBOY, PAYBACK." The snowball whizzed past his ear as he banged the door open, spun and slammed it shut. Something heavy thumped against it. And shouted unkind things.

He clumped down the hall and into the living room, shed and hung the many layers up to dry. Then he went into the kitchen. Humming happily. Content. Relaxed.

"Not ready yet," said R-Bar. She was stirring the pot of cocoa.

"Yum, yum." He peered over her shoulder, and breathed in the aroma of her hair.

"It is just cocoa."

"I wasn't referring to the cocoa although it does smell pretty good also."

"LECH!" Chantal banged into the kitchen. "First you are after my anatomy. Now you are staring down her shirt."

"Very stare able," he mumbled.

"Thanks," said R-Bar, giving the cocoa another stir.

"RAT FINK." Chantal headed down the hall.

"Shouldn't have dumped snow on her," suggested R-Bar.

"She started it."

"They are all going to get cold and wet."

Their minds looked out at the group now engaged in an outright brawl.

"Right," agreed Tinker. He headed back toward the living room. And leaned in. "Pacem winterae, chickie-poo."

Chantal looked over from the couch where she was spreading a thick down quilt. "What?"

"It means winter peace, gorgeous babe."

"Oh." She lifted thick blue layer and slipped under it, leaning back against the arm rest, pushing the pillows into place behind her back. "If you were dressed properly, like in your pajamas, you could join me, chickie-poo."

"I will rush off and do that."

"Do."

He did.

But first he put more wood into the stove.

Clear Bandler. A Sunny Day.

Sedeem stared up at it. "WOW."

The 'wow' was Duff's home. It hung from gossamer threads that were strung from three tall spires of greenish blue stone. Clouds drifted lazily across the sky. Some passed under the structure.

They had arrived. And were standing in a meadow. Tall flowers poked their heads waist high on Sedeem. They grew in a widely spaced singularity. One here, one there.

"This is my home." Duff pointed at a mountain range. "$1.98 lives far over there. But I have been keeping him here. It has quiet and peace. Ready?"

Sedeem nodded.

They stood in the open, airy living room. Farth shifted from foot to foot and stared out one of the large open windows. At one of the distant spires. He just couldn't get used to traveling this way. Suddenly here, suddenly there. Sedeem gently touched his arm.

Gesturing for them to sit, Duff walked away. "I will bring him."

Tears excused himself and headed for his room.

And soon, Duff returned, holding his hand, gently guiding the tall shuffling figure wearing the tattered multi-colored robe. She pushed him onto a couch, made him sit on the edge.

Imdar stood. "I am Imdar of the Vander, often called the Purple Magicians. I am the one who cures among our guild. May I approach, Magician?"

"Yes." $1.98 watched her carefully. Duff moved to one side.

Imdar stepped close, and stared at him. "You have been badly damaged."

"Yes."

"By angry evil."

"Yes."

"Show me your rings."

He slowly lifted his hands.

Imdar reached out and turned his hands back and forth, carefully not touching the rings.

"The red ring is keeping you alive. Nothing else. You are almost shadow."

Duff gasped.

Sa'ar frowned at her.

"Remove all the rings," commanded Imdar. "Except for the red."

"Give them to me, Dear." Duff moved close enough to reach her hand out. One by one the rings were twisted and pulled and removed.

"There," said $1.98. "Done."

"And the wand up your sleeve."

He slipped the long black stick free and handed it to Duff.

Imdar nodded. "Sa'ar and Sedeem will aid me." Her eyes flicked at Duff. "No one interfere. Or he will die for sure."

Duff walked to the far end of the room, and watched. Tears returned and stood by her side. She whispered in his ear and threw an arm around his shoulders. He watched carefully. Tellers of Tales did this, recorded everything in their memories.

Then Imdar waved the pair, Sa'ar and Sedeem, over and purple mist seeped across and around them and $1.98, and she began to explain what she wanted the others to do.

Grandeville. Tinker's Place. Cold and White.

"When did you get silk pajamas?"

"Surprise, Cowboy."

"Pretty erotic."

Chantal smiled. "I'll say." And snuggled closer.

"My, my, my."

Chantal grabbed him. "We had better head for the closest bedroom, Simba Leader."

"What?"

"They are headed inside. And this Lady Lion is not an exhibitionist. Nor are you."

Messenger sat on the couch cradling her hot cocoa. "Someone left their pajama top out here. OH." She ran her fingers over the garment and tittered. "Where did she find silk pajamas? They are sooooo smooth."

Chicken reached out and stroked the material. "Praps when roads do open becomen we all shall to town go."

"May we buy?" asked Ran, sitting next to her.

"Indeed," answered Chicken. "Our Lord do have treasure near uncounted. For this elseplace. T'was gift from most fierce Macabre." She half-turned and brushed back Ran's hair. "Now that thee do be most healthy, Fair Ran Ourself, a'shopping we shall go."

"Oh, boy." Messenger smiled. And licked the cocoa from her upper lip. Shopping was always fun.

Dinner was started.

The dining room arranged.

And every one who hadn't already done so changed into appropriate attire.

Men's pajamas.

Clear Bandler. A Fairly Pleasant Day.

The recoil knocked them rocking backwards.

Farth leaped from his chair, the gleaming silver sword in his hand ready to hack things to pieces. But there wasn't anything there.

Duff shoved Tears behind herself and plucked a loudly crackling bronze wand from somewhere, calling down protection.

Imdar sagged against Sa'ar, who hastily threw one arm around her waist. Sedeem quickly supported Imdar from the other side as the Healer wobbled badly.

$1.98 sat straighter and looked more alert and watched Farth sheath his great sword.

"Am Do Chat," mumbled Imdar as she was gently lowered into a chair.

Duff stepped over to $1.98 and looked into his face. "Dear?"

"Feel much better." He stretched and smiled at her. "Who are they? How did we get here? And what happened?"

Duff handed him his black wand, carefully holding it by two fingertips. "Here, put this thing away."

He did. Then she handed him his rings. One by one. He put them back on the appropriate fingers.

"Sedeem," said Duff, introducing him to the others. "Lord John Tinker's daughter. Farth, her consort. Sa'ar and Imdar of the Vander Mage Guild. Sa'ar is Sedeem's cousin. Imdar fixed you with their help."

"Gurg," sighed Imdar as she toppled from the chair.

"We better get her home," snapped Sa'ar.

Farth picked her up, cradling her in his arms, and nodded at his wife.

"Done," answered Sedeem as she turned them away.

Tears blinked his eyes and stared around at the mostly empty room.

"What is his daughter?" asked $1.98.

Duff sat next to him and dragged one of his arms around her waist. "She said magiwitch."

"Never heard of anyone like that."

"Me neither, Dear, But she is more powerful than most." And kissed him. And felt the cure spreading through him.

Grandeville. Tinker's Place.

Chantal sighed. "OOO . . . my . . ."

"Ummm?"

She rolled onto her side and kissed the corner of his

shoulder. "Yum, yum." And bit him.

Just a little. A little more.

Just for fun.

And laughed.

And nipped him again.

"Hey!"

"Straw."

"How would you like it if I bit you?"

"You did."

"Did not."

"Ha."

"Nips. Those were just playful nips."

She sat up. "That is what I did. Nip."

"You win. Beautiful."

"You want to go and get my pajama top?"

"Huh?"

"Before you dragged me here and assaulted me, you were frantically tearing off my pajamas. Back there, on the couch."

"You could go get it."

"Nope."

"O.K." He stood and headed for the door.

"John?"

"What?"

"Better put on your p. j.'s." She winked at him. "We have guests."

He grabbed his pajamas and yanked them on. "How'd you know that?"

"Smoke told me."

"Damn voyeuristic cat."

"She knew that we were . . . done."

"How'd she know that?"

"Feminine intuition."

He hurried into the living room. Mumbling to himself

"OOP."
They stood there and looked at him.
"Hi, Dad."
"Hello, Uncle."
"Great Lord." Farth was cradling a slack form in his arms, her head hung back, one arm dangled loosely.
"Sedeem." Tinker squinted. "Sa'ar? What are you doing here?" And began to button up his top. "And what is going on?" He pointed at Farth and his burden.
Sa'ar nodded at Farth. "Put her in that side bedroom."
"WHOA." Tinker grabbed the top from the back of the couch where Messenger had placed it. "Room's occupied. Stay right there, I'll be right back." He spun around and headed for the bedroom. Sedeem covered her month with her hand and stifled her laughter. R-Bar poked her in the side with a finger. "Do not make fun of your father, Daughter." And stared at Farth's burden.
Sedeem bent and kissed her mother on the forehead. Sedeem was a full head taller. "Who's he got in there, Mom?"
"Chantal."
"Oh." Sedeem grinned as she straightened up. "Thought maybe I had a new mom."
"That is nasty, Daughter." R-Bar's eyes glistened. She poked the burden Farth held in his arms with a fingertip. "Hum, hum, hum. Is that what this is, a gift from you, for your Father?"
"What?"
"Think your Father needs a bed present?"
"MOTHER!"
"Heh, heh."
She frowned at R-Bar. "That is not funny. Imdar is sick.

Sa'ar said home. And here we are."

"I meant my home." Sa'ar looked at R-Bar. "But we will have to stay here now, Aunt. Imdar should not travel again until she recovers."

Tinker and Chantal joined them. As did the rest of the household, coming from various directions.

"Hi, Moms." Sedeem nudged Farth into motion. "Be right back."

She was. Then the Moms took turns hugging and kissing their daughter.

Sa'ar stepped close to Tinker, murmuring softly, "Aren't you glad to see me, Uncle?"

"Sure."

"Gimme a hug, then."

He did. Cautiously. She leaned back in his arms, and grinned. "When you going to come and visit us? Everyone wants to thank you. All of us."

"Just forget it. I am not interested in Vander magicians leaping in and out of my bed."

"Or, on and off."

"Enough of that."

"Sorry." She leaned close and slipped one hand inside his top. And whispered, "But we really want to." And gently caressed his ribs.

He whispered back, "If you don't behave, I'll have R-Bar call your mother, Ramp, to come and get you."

She pouted. Just for him. "Vander Lord, I am older than you want to admit." And pinched his side. Gently.

He decided to ignore that and asked instead, "So, who was she?"

"Imdar She came to us later. She is a powerful curer. You haven't met her yet." She grinned. "But she knows all about you."

Tinker sighed. "But you, and she, will behave in my home, won't you?"

Sa'ar nodded. "Of course. We wouldn't do anything that you didn't want to do." Her smiled broadened. "But if you wish . . ."

Chicken nudged him. "My Lord, if thee do be finished a'fondling Sweet Niece, praps do we sit and hear what do be a'going on?"

"I am not," sighed Tinker.

Sa'ar looked at Chicken. "May he?"

"I told you," snarled Tinker, yanking his arms away.

Sa'ar winked at him.

Sedeem nudged from the other side. "Oh, Dad, you are so easy to tease."

Then they all settled in chairs and on the couches. And Sedeem and Sa'ar took turns telling them what had happened.

"So, she is staying here until she recovers, is that it?" He looked at Sa'ar.

"Yes. It would be dangerous for her to travel until she is much stronger."

Ran sat on the left arm of his chair, watching this magician in the lavender clothing very, very carefully. She remembered her from before. And from her now collective memories.

Sedeem sat between Farth and Sa'ar. He was wedged into the end of the couch. There was plenty of room at the other end.

Chicken poured cocoa and announced, "Great Smoke will make additional preparations for dinner, for tis near time to dine."

Sa'ar grinned. "I certainly do not understand why you

are so uneasy around us Vander. I mean, after all, we were only five at the end of The Great Battle."

He jumped up and cautioned her, "I know. Ah, ah, ah, I know. Let's eat."

As they were eating dessert, Smoke looked at Sa'ar. "She is waking up."

"Excuse, please." Sa'ar hurried from the room.

Chantal yanked the cake plate over, away from Fair Morn. And smiled at Tinker. "We'll protect you, Simba Leader." And cut another slice before pushing it back in front of Fair Morn, who also took another slice.

"I do not need protecting," he mumbled. "Pass the cake, please."

Ran nodded and lightly touched his arm. "The Vander magicians are said to be iron-willed and dangerous."

Smoke stood. "She needs to eat. A little. I'll take a tray in." She left. But passed the cake first.

"And predatory," said Ran. She whispered harshly, "And they steal men."

"No, they do not." Sedeem rapped on the table top with the butt of her knife. "OH!" She blushed. "Sorry, Mom. But it is just not true."

"Well," said Tinker. "They are a determined bunch."

R-Bar nodded. "The purple magicians are dangerous. Just like any other set of magicians, or witches. As you well know, Ran."

"And they are sorta predatory," added Tinker.

"Oh, Dad. You just say that because they all want to drag you into their beds."

Farth began to fizzle, loudly. Sedeem nudged him in the ribs with her elbow, gently, and said, "Well, it is true." Then she looked at Ran. "But they do not go around stealing men."

Sa'ar came in and knelt by the side of Tinker's chair. "Vander Lord?"

"Oh, oh, What?"

"I thought that I would visit my parents and my brother and his wife for awhile. Is it all right with you? Leaving Imdar here? In your care?"

"Of course," said Chicken.

"Good." Sa'ar jumped up, kissed him on the cheek, and disappeared.

"No," said Tinker. And looked around the table at them. "For all the good that it does to try and make a decision around here."

"Smoke do require Our Own assistance." Chicken ruffled his hair in passing. "Grumble Lord."

Messenger headed for the kitchen. "Going to give Imdar a sponge bath."

R-Bar leered at him. "You could go help, check her out."

"DON'T START," snarled Tinker.

R-Bar grinned.

Sedeem covered her mouth.

Farth frowned.

Fair Morn winked at Tinker.

And ate the last of the cake.

Then they all headed for the living room. To watch a movie.

Fair Morn sprawled happily alongside him.

On the couch.

Both were propped up by stacks of pillows.

"Hi there, Long Moth."

"Hi. Want some popcorn?"

"Already?"

"Small snack."

"Right."

She had the largest mixing bowl from the kitchen heaped with popcorn. "She is sick. So you are safe."

"How come I do not feel safe?" He took a handful of popcorn. "Huh?"

"Heh, heh, heh."

"Eat your popcorn." He took another handful. "You guys are all getting goofy."

She did. Grab another handful of popcorn. "We're not the ones that ripped Chantal's top off and hauled her into the bedroom and . . . "

"STOP."

Fair Morn batted her eyes at him. "Welllllll, you did."

"Pointless discussion." He grabbed some more of her popcorn. Smoke and Messenger continued to debate which movie to watch, shoving their choices in and out of the cabinet.

"You going to assault me, pajama top snatcher?"

"Nope."

"Spoil sport." She munched louder.

He sat up straighter. "O.K., Butterfly, speak! What is going on? This time?"

"Nunin," mumbled Fair Morn.

"I'll wait."

She swallowed. "Nothing."

"So how come I do not believe you? All?"

Setting the bowl on the floor, she dragged the blanket up and over them. "Just thought that you might want to take advantage of me while we are isolated in our little cabin in the woods by this terrible winter storm."

"No one can ever take advantage of you guys. Some

little cabin. Some isolation." He yanked the blanket down off their heads. "Some woods."

Smoke leaned on the back of the couch. "It will be a few days before she is on her feet."

"I want you to check everyone right now."

"For what?"

"Vander urges. One or the other of them seems to be having some sort of effect on you all."

Smoke's minds reached out.

"Eeeeeek." Fair Morn twitched.

There, MindMate. I think that Imdar did it. And I do not think that Sa'ar knew she did it.

Her mental presence faded from his mind.

"Thanks."

"Anytime, Dude." She ruffled his hair with one hand.

Messenger started the movie. It was science fiction. A compromise. Smoke moved around and sat on the floor. And looked at the empty bowl.

R-Bar ran for the kitchen. "I'll make some more."

Clear Bandler. The Land of Magicians.

"OUCH!"

"I didn't do anything. Did I?"

"You touched me."

"I meant otherwise."

They were in their room. Duff had just dimmed the lights. And $1.98 had reached out for her. He did it again.

"OUCH!"

He frowned at her. "This will not do."

"ABSOLUTELY." She grabbed a garment and yanked it on. "Get dressed, Dear. We have to visit and get you fixed." She waved on bright light. "I will get Tears."

"Ohhh . . . " She dragged the covers up and over his head. "You have stabbed me clear up to my heart."

"Not . . . possible . . . "

"What they say in all the romances." Fair Morn wrapped her arms around his waist and hugged him.

"OOOOOOF." He gasped as the air was forced from his lungs.

"Forgot." She released her grip, some. "Um?"

"UMM?"

"We have guests."

"What?"

"Why I covered us, us being on the couch, and everything."

"Bad timing. Where are they?"

"Outside. Headed for the kitchen. Smoke says."

"Who?"

"Tears. $1.98. And Plum Duff. Let's run for your bedroom."

"Umm?"

"I'll take a raincheck, One." She gave him a quick kiss.

Chicken met them as they entered the kitchen. And kept them there for the required time, until Fair Morn and Tinker joined them. He was glowering. Fair Morn folded a piece of paper and tucked it into her pajama top pocket.

"Raincheck," she said to Chicken. "It is the middle of the night," she said to the others.

"We will speak with your daughter and her cousin," said Duff.

"Do it in the morning," grumped Tinker.

"NOW!" demanded Duff.

"Morning. Sedeem is sleeping and her cousin went

home to visit her parents, etc."

"What time is it?" Sedeem yawned widely as she walked into the kitchen. "You look pretty good, $1.98. Why are you here." She bumped past Tinker. "I felt the disturbance. Dad." And got a drink of water from the sink tap, turned and yanked her robe closed, cinching up the belt.

Duff pointed at $1.98. "He is not right."

"Huh?" said Tinker, snapping on the lights.

"Looks all right to me," said Fair Morn, squinting her eyes against the kitchen brightness. "Ratty robe though." She opened the refrigerator and began to take out things. "Snack?"

"What's wrong?" asked Sedeem as she leaned back against the counter top, crossing her arms over her chest.

"If I touch her she gets a shock," explained $1.98.

"Most strange that," observed Chicken, joining them, tying her robe shut with its belt. "Cease thy glower, Our Love." She patted him on the hip. "This do be most serious a'thing."

"Certainly is." Duff glared at Sedeem.

"We ought to wait until morning. Sa'ar gets pretty growly about being woken up like this." Sedeem glared back.

"Now," stated Duff, quite firmly.

"Well. O.K." Sedeem did something with her wand. "But you were warned."

"HOW DID I GET HERE? IT IS STILL DARK OUTSIDE! I WAS SLEEPING!" The silver wand she held flashed anger. Purple mists flowed and eddied around her.

$1.98 threw his hood over his head. Tears squeezed his eyes tightly shut. Tinker yanked off his pajama top and handed it to Sa'ar. She was only wearing a pair of shorts.

"Morning, Vander Lord," she breathed at him, smiling a slow knowing smile. And slowly pulled on the offered garment. And slowly buttoned it. The bottom two buttons. Her eyes watched his all the time.

"Wench," snapped Chicken.

"$1.98 needs our help," explained Sedeem.

"Now what?" Sa'ar walked over and stared at the hooded magician. "You may look at me now, bashful. What kind of help?"

They told her.

"Strange," said Sa'ar. "Deem?" She buttoned the rest of her buttons.

"Yep. Strange. Shall we look?"

"Yes."

"Do not move," said Sedeem to $1.98.

"Move away," said Sa'ar to Duff.

"Aahh . . . haaaa," observed Sedeem.

"Some sort of protection. Tastes Imdar," said Sa'ar. "Push right there."

Sedeem did.

"OUCH!" $1.98 jerked sideways.

"Go over there and poke your short, cuddle magician," ordered Sa'ar. "Let's see what happens."

$1.98 did. Duff smiled at him. Then at Sa'ar and Sedeem. "Many, many," she said.

"Might as well stay for breakfast," grumbled Tinker, looking out an east facing window. "Sun is coming up."

Ran walked into the kitchen from the hall and handed one of the thick white robes to Tinker and one to Sa'ar.

"Put it on," ordered Chicken.

Sa'ar did. But left it open to the waist and unbuttoned the top button on her pajama top now that they were done with $1.98.

"You could go home," suggested Tinker, yanking on his robe, flapping the belt into a loose knot.

"I accept your invitation to stay for breakfast." Sa'ar smiled broadly at him. "What are we having?"

"Ask the cooks."

Bahn Duhr Tohr. The Royal City.

The five of them sat at the large table in the Royal Advisor's rooms. Three sat on one side, two on the other. They all sipped at their beverages, waved in by Ripple, who stared at one of her visitors, the air shifting and grumbling dark around her. She just stared at that person.

"Rbat, is that really you?"

The woman nodded. "Witch true, sister. I am need of great healing, however, to be all myself." She laid a hand on the shoulders of the pair sitting on either side of her. "Motaiss and Turintor were of great aid. I owe debt beyond counting."

Turintor shifted her shoulder. "No debt is owed this witch. She, in some manner unknown to me, sent us out of that trap."

Motaiss nodded. "I merely helped them find aid."

The air darkened around them as Ripple leaned forward. "I would know who, or what, and where. All is about to not exist." One did not trap witches and expect to survive. For very long.

Pulling her hands down, Rbat waggled one hand at her sister. "Already done." She smiled, a true witch smile of death and destruction. Then she told Ripple all that she had seen and had done and the final solution to those who would trap witches. "Nothing there for you, Ripple."

Ripple nodded. The air cleared. "You two make room, much room." The pair shoved away and quickly made room, carefully watching the spell gather as Ripple worked.

It flashed out, wrapped around Rbat, and vanished.

Rbat surged sweat from all pores.

"At last," she sighed. "I am myself again."
"Welcome, Rbat."

Chapter Three.

She Wants What?

Grandeville. Tinker's Place. A Sunny Day.

"Imdar shouldn't have done anything like that. I will speak to her." The air crackled around Sa'ar.

"Relax."

"Yes, Vander Lord," she said softly. And did.

He smiled. "I suspect that she did not know after what she had been doing when whatever you guys were doing whatever it was that you did. Look at the shape she was in when she arrived."

"Oh. I thought that you were speaking about what we did to $1.98."

"Nope." He shook his head. "I was speaking about what she did to us." He crossed his arms over his chest.

"Ummmm. Lord?" She stepped close and fiddled with the belt around his waist.

"What?" It was a very cautious question.

She smiled, very warmly she smiled. "Probably wouldn't have happened if you had accepted the Vander debt." Her eyes watched his, very carefully.

"Forget it."

"Ummm?" She bumped against him, causing him to unfold his arms.

"No."

"Errrm?" She slipped her arms inside his robe.

"NO!"

"Compromise?" And held him. Staring deep into his eyes. Her fingers began to rub up and down his back.

"What kind of compromise?" His frown was getting deeper and deeper, rapidly turning into dark glower.

"Just one for the many?"

He sighed. "I will have to think about that."

"Good." She lifted onto her toes and kissed him. And hurried toward the dining room.

"For a long, long, long time," he mumbled, tugging his robe closed, tightening his belt.

"You really are a sneaky dog." Chantal nudged his side.

He grinned. "Think twenty years or so is long enough to ponder an offer like that?"

"Maybe just a quickie would settle the problem." One corner of her mouth was having a hard time keeping control of the smile wanting to push out.

"Merde."

"Tsk, tsk, tsk." She turned to stand in front of him. "Such a foul Lord it is."

"Humbug and stuff like that there. I am awash in females as it is." He was leaning forward, glaring. "And I do not trust the Vander either."

She nodded sagely. "Probably right."

"They can all take long cold showers." He grunted.

"Doesn't work." She yanked his robe further closed.

"Huh?"

"Took one the other day." And yanked his belt. Tighter.

"What?"

"Just before I lost my top and you tossed me here and there and yonder and back again, etc., etc., etc." She grinned as he mumbled something. "Bounce, bounce, bounce," she laughed.

"Run," shouted Messenger, leaning into the kitchen. The shout was not all that loud. "He is going to explode."

They all crowded in to watch.

The explosion.

He didn't.

Explode.

He looked from merry face to merry face, and grumped at them. "O.K., O.K. I know . . . when I'm beat. Again." He took the cup of coffee offered by Chicken. "Maybe they'll get the road plowed tomorrow, or even today. You guys need some exercise, running to town and back."

Smoke tickled his ear with one finger. "If you would go into the living room with most of your pliant female selves, I could get breakfast started. The Princess and Messenger can help. R-Bar can make cocoa and start more coffee. OUT."

They went.

Those that could.

After breakfast, they said goodbye to Duff, $1.98, and Tears. Then Sa'ar. Tinker told her to bring the robe back, later.

"Peace and quiet." He slumped in his chair in the living room. "At last! It's wonderful." He cradled his coffee cup, which was resting on his stomach, in both hands. And sighed.

"We still have one of them," said Ran. "In there." She didn't look happy.

"Forgot." He stared toward one of the large windows. "Looks like a nice day, even if we did start awfully early."

Smoke yawned and stretched. "We could go back to

bed."

"I think I'll soak first." He handed his cup to Messenger, who was collecting, and headed down the hall.

"We will with thee come," said Chicken, hurrying after him, grabbing an arm.

He grunted.

And sighed as the hot water lapped just below his chin. "Just you and me, kid."

"Indeed, My Lord." Bright blue eyes fluttered at him.

"You up to something?"

"Nay." She crept closer, moving slow, not making waves on the surface of the steaming water. "Howsomever," she said, nestling against him.

"Pretty sneaky. For a Noble Princess."

"Thee do be most ready. So We this sneak do."

"Ahhh."

"Waste not, want not, Heart of Our Hearts."

"Did Smoke clean out that Vander urge?"

"Indeed. Tis naught but this Thy Verra Own Most Pliant and Willing Queen. As Dark Smoke do say We all do be." Her arms slipped around his chest. "Soon, we will nap, thee and Us. But not too soon, not too soon, Our Prince."

They were lightly dozing. Not really asleep, minds blended together.

Someone fell into the hot tub.

Four eyes popped open.
Minds broke apart.

"WHAT?"

"MY LORD, she do drown." Chicken ducked below the water. *Lend us thy hand, Our Own, tis Imdar.*

Bending, crouching, he grabbed an arm, heaved her up and glowered at her. "What do you think you are doing?"

Chicken draped Imdar's other arm around her neck and smoothed Imdar's hair back from her forehead. "HIST, Fierce Prince. Ease off thy most fierce a'snarling. This fair maid do bedazzled be."

Pale violet eyes wobbled in his direction. And focused on his face. She coughed. "Who?" And sagged. Tugging Chicken sideways.

Tinker let go, surged from the tub, reached down, and dragged Imdar from the hot tub, to lay her sprawling limply on the wooden slats.

Chicken climbed out, hurried into the walk-in closet and returned carrying robes, wearing one herself.

"Here, My Lord, clothe thyself. This one requires no distracting." She draped a robe over Imdar. "Nor do thee." And helped her sit up. Tis most pretty a'package do this one be."

He dragged his robe on. "She'll need to wear something besides that robe."

"Yum, yum, yum," said Chicken.

"Stop that."

"T'wert naught but thy thought, My Liege."

He sighed. "Must mean that she is feeling better. To come this far from her bed." He knelt by Imdar's side. "Still looks pretty pale." And stood.

Fair Morn ran into the room. "Need some help?" And stopped as Imdar managed to stand up and begin to pull the robe on. "Wowee. A mod bod."

"You too?" mumbled Tinker.

"I caught your thought, One." She winked at him.

"Worse and worse," he said. "How about you get her some pajamas and another robe? You and the Princess can dry her off." He lightly touched Imdar's shoulder. "You hungry?"

She looked in his direction, eyes more or less aware of him.

"I'll take that as a big yes." He headed for the kitchen, announcing over his shoulder "TEN MINUTES. FIFTEEN, TOPS!"

He set her breakfast in front of her. Imdar was wearing dry pajamas and a dry robe, and had a towel wrapped around her head. Color had returned to her face. She watched him carefully.

He stared at her eyes. He didn't remember ever seeing eyes colored like that before.

"Your minions were rough. They forced me to wear these eccentric garments, and dragged me to this table." She plucked at her robe and pajama top. "It would be best for you to contact my guild and release me. I will not be held prisoner."

He filled her cup, then his own and set down the coffee pot. And took a chair. "You may leave whenever you wish, and are able to. And the next time that you fall into my hot tub, I will let you drown." He shoved her plate over. "Eat your food, Imdar," he grumbled.

She carefully tasted it. "How do you know my name?" And began to eat. "Why did you kidnap me? And I do not like your manner."

"Don't talk with your mouth full," ordered Tinker. He half-turned away, leaned one elbow on the table, and took a sip from his cup. "We did not kidnap you. They are not my minions. They are myself, ahh, my, um, my wives." And too damn bad, he thought to himself, what you happen to think.

"Oh." Imdar's eyes darted around the room. "OH," she said around her toast. "Well, they were rough."

"Vigorous," said Fair Morn, entering the room, sitting next to his free side. Followed by Chicken.

"Hi, Father, Moms, Imdar." Sedeem joined them. "Farth's still sleeping." She shoved a cup at him so he could fill it.

Imdar frowned at him. "Father?"

"Yes. My daughter." He emptied the coffee pot into Sedeem's cup.

"Our daughter," amended Chicken.

"Mothers?" said Imdar, her eyes darting from Chicken to Fair Morn.

"Yep," replied Sedeem. "Fair Morn and Princess Chicken."

"YOU?" Imdar stared harder at him, her face flushing redder and redder. "Are him?"

"Ta dah," said Tinker.

She gasped and fell back in her chair, sagging limply. "Om dagar om." And closed her eyes.

"My Lord." Chicken leaped up and placed one hand on Imdar's forehead. "Most feverous."

"'Finish your breakfast," ordered Tinker. "They will help you back to your room." Chicken took her hand away

"I will be punished," whispered Imdar, peering at him through slitted eyes. "Severely."

"Nope." He looked at Sedeem. "Right?"

"Sure, Pop. Someone cooking?"

"Let's do it." Fair Morn stood. "I'm hungry."

R-Bar wandered in, poured a cup full and joined them at the table. "What have you been doing to her? She is all flushed. Hum?"

Sedeem leaned in from the kitchen. "That is nasty, Mom." And popped back.

"Heh, heh," said R-Bar.

"Nothing," mumbled Tinker.

"She do near drown in great warm hot tub," explained Chicken.

"Fell in," muttered Tinker. "Warm hot is redundant."

"Nay, Picky Lord, for thing hot tub do be most a'filled with water warm."

"What are you doing out of bed?" demanded R-Bar, reaching over, poking Imdar.

"Gooba," he said.

"Piffle," replied Chicken.

Imdar shrugged a shoulder, and said, "Mom?" And looked at her.

"That's me," said R-Bar.

Imdar rolled her head and looked at Tinker.

"Yep," he said. "We all met you when they carried you in. But you were mostly out of it. This is R-Bar."

"I wasn't in anything," stated Imdar.

"Morning, morning, morning," bubbled Messenger, carrying in a fresh pot of coffee. "They are making just lots and lots of pancakes." She dropped into a chair. And looked at Tinker. "How come she is wearing your pajamas?" And turned red. "OH. Sa'ar thought that she'd be the one." And covered her face with her hands. "OOOOOPSIE."

"Nothing happened," snapped Tinker. Chicken hastily shared her memories with them.

"Oh, dear," said Messenger. "Sorry." Then she grinned. "But she is very, very pretty."

"Never mind," he grumbled.

"Damn bright in here," mumbled Chantal, fumbling with the wall switch, dimming the lights over the table.

Messenger shoved a quickly filled cup in front of Chantal as she thumped down, and slumped, and took a sip.

"Chantal," said Tinker to Imdar.

Messenger passed the memory before Chantal could ask.

"Certainly a beauty." Chantal sat straighter as Sedeem set a platter of pancakes on the table.

"Morning, Mom." Sedeem reached more plates from the cupboard.

Fair Morn joined them, carrying the syrup. And another platter of pancakes.

Smoke and Ran came in. Ran sat opposite Imdar and watched her. Smoke touched Imdar in passing and winked at Tinker.

"Smoke, and Ran," said Tinker. "That's the bunch of them."

"Seven?" Slowly Imdar looked around the table. "My sisters misjudged and knew not."

"Smoke," said Tinker. "You may explain when you tuck your patient back in bed."

Smoke nudged Fair Morn as she reached for one of the platters.

"He didn't," said Fair Morn, taking a few more. Then passed the platter to Smoke, and to Ran.

"He may pounce on her when she is healthier," said Smoke, pouring syrup on her stack. "Pass the jelly, please. And the toast."

Sa'ar walked in from the living room. "I came for breakfast. I left your robe in there." She glared at Imdar.

"She fell into the hot tub. Nothing else. Sit down." He banged his cup down on the table top and glared at everyone. "And I do not want to hear any more about Vander debts, mod bods, or pouncing. Either."

Messenger hurriedly refilled his cup.

"You guys," he glared at everyone, "have worn out that line of thinking and, or, conversation. Way out. And beyond."

"Damn right, Cowboy," growled Chantal. She took a couple pancakes, and smiled at Fair Morn. "These are pretty good." Then she looked at Tinker. "And you can just forget about dragging that piece of luscious into a closet. Anyone gets dragged around here, it is going to be one of us."

"Hear, hear," said Chicken, thumping on the table with her cup.

"Gerk," snarled Tinker.

"That, too," mumbled Chantal around a mouthful of pancake.

Messenger looked at Smoke. She shrugged.

Sedeem pulled at her lower lip and glanced at R-Bar.

"I do not know," said R-Bar.

"We are never going to have house guests again," grumbled Tinker.

Ran tentatively held up her hand. "Amtar? Tinker Lord?"

"What?"

"You may if you wish."

"What?"

"Gerk me."

Laughter rippled around the table, including Sa'ar and Imdar.

"Is this a party?" Farth had just joined them.

Sedeem shoved back her chair. "Husband mine, just breakfast." She piled a plate high and pushed it at him as he sat. "Just teasing Dad."

"It is improper for a dutiful daughter to tease her Father."

"Damn right," agreed Tinker.

"Fiddle de dee," said Messenger, reaching over and topping up Tinker's cup. "Dee dee."

"Dee dee, it is," he said, knowing when the game was lost.

"Hum," said Sa'ar softly.

"Shar!" cautioned her cousin with a glance. "Shhhhh."

"Hi, everybody."

Sa'ar and Sedeem leaped up and grabbed this newcomer and wrapped her in a hug.

Szaifeh looked across the table at Imdar. "He add another one?"

"We having open house?" Tinker asked no-one in particular.

"No," hissed Sedeem to her cousin.

"Nope," said Chantal to Tinker.

"Have some pancakes." Messenger beamed at Szaifeh. "We have lots."

"My cousin also." Sa'ar nodded to Imdar. "Szaifeh, this is Imdar, the Healer, our newest Vander sister."

Szaifeh sat down and looked at Sedeem who whispered in her ear, "Don't say anything. Pop's getting testy about her, so to speak. I'll tell you later."

"Here." Smoke grabbed the platter from in front of Fair Morn and shoved it over toward Szaifeh. "Have some."

She nodded. And did. "I just came to visit."

"Roaming over?"

"No, Uncle. Not yet. Mom said that they might come by in a few days. Dad's been working on a large project. She's been keeping an eye on him." She popped a forkfull into her mouth. "Mmm."

"Thanks," said Fair Morn.

"Oh," said Sa'ar. "Mother said that they would come

as well. When Uncle is done."

And then.

Soon.

Everyone scattered, here and there. To dress. To do chores. And other tasks.

Tinker went up to his office. To edit. To rewrite. To work.

Smoke, Chicken and Sa'ar took Imdar back to her room. Then they went back into the living room to talk, having tucked their patient in.

"To consult," said Sa'ar.

Sedeem, Szaifeh, Messenger and Ran went outside to admire the snow drifts and to slide and wave happily at Chantal and R-Bar as they trudged out to the barn. Fair Morn floated overhead, soaring happily in the cool crisp air.

"For just a little bit," she called down. "They are starting to itch."

"That is just not fair." Sa'ar glared at Chicken.

"Thou art daughter of close friend. As is Szaifeh." She smiled at the deeply pouting magician. "There do be the others. What one do receive, all may receive."

"Will not do," stated Sa'ar.

"This is a great debt?" asked Smoke.

"Greatest. We must satisfy it," stated Sa'ar. "He, and you, aided us in our Great Final Battle. We would have all died, our Enemy would have triumphed."

Chicken slipped an arm around Sa'ar and tickled her. "Let us away to Mine Own Bedroom go, Vander Heart. There we will satisfy this debt."

Sa'ar shook her head. "NO. It must be him!"

Smoke's eye widened as she pushed gently with her minds. "I think that I see more than debt here. What are the

Vander trying to do?"

Sa'ar carefully checked her Aunt's face for expression. There was none. "We need a male."

"It do seem a'me, it do," suggested Chicken, nodding. "That Vander do be tightly focused so."

Sa'ar shook her head. "We need a male. Offspring."

"A male kitten? Born to one of your order?" Smoke leaned closer. "And he is to be the sire?"

"Our body pleasure, freely given, pays our debt, the Vander way."

"And thus Our Lord do impregnate a Vander in return?" Chicken frowned.

"Yes," answered Sa'ar ever so softly.

"And it would be a male?" Smoke stared at her.

"Yes," came the whisper. "It would be so."

Chicken sat back. "Thee can do this?"

"Yes."

Smoke leaned ever closer, the space between them shrinking. "A male? And he would not know?"

"Yes."

"I do not think this is a good idea. And you should know better."

"The Vander must pay their debt. The Vander must have a male." Sa'ar straightened up and peered deep into those orange gold eyes. "We must."

And Smoke looked back and beyond.

"Don't," hissed Sa'ar.

"Dark Sister?" Chicken laid her hand on Smoke's arm.

Smoke's eyes shifted. "Princess?"

"Praps he might be a'willing. Do we so present this Vander need most delicately. He might."

Smoke shook her head.

"Please," said Sa'ar. "Please." Her voice cracked. "It is

our very survival, the Vander." She leaned back, hands clasped around knees. "Aunts. I beg for your help."

And returned Smoke's stare through tear glistening eyes. "If we must, we shall steal him, charm him, and have our way. Even if that means he would hate us for the rest of his life." She shook her head. "We, I, do not want it to be that way. Help me. Help us."

Smoke stood, grabbed Sa'ar by the forearms and casually lifted her to her feet. "Why don't we just go get Imdar, take her to Big Darlene's Pub. She can pick any male there and get impregnated eagerly."

"AUNT." Sa'ar looked shocked.

"Well?" Smoke waited, And released her.

"No. Won't do." She shook her head.

"Why not?"

"Ummmm . . . "

"Me'thinks that there do be layer pon layer of secret here in this thy umm." Chicken frowned and tapped Sa'ar on the side of the thigh. "Niece Vander Heart, praps t'would be best do thee tell us all of this conundrum or t'will be solved never."

Sa'ar dropped heavily back into her chair. "You may never tell him. Never, never, never."

Chicken looked blank. Sa'ar looked at Smoke. "Can you really hide a thought from each other?"

"Yes. It may be done. I can make sure that the proper block is in place." She smiled. "Even now he can not hear what we discuss."

Sa'ar sucked in a deep breath, and slowly let it back out. "O,K., here is why it must be The Vander Lord."

"Tink?"

She carefully poked her head through the open

doorway. The floor inside the room was strewn in some sort of order with papers.

"Huh?" He looked up and over at her. "Oh. Come in."

The small witch slipped in, stepping cautiously over piles of papers to a place near where he sat. She was carrying a tray set with a pot, two cups, and some cookies.

"It is almost ten." She set the tray on the desk top.

"Never noticed." He filled the cups, handed her one, and munched on a cookie. "Have a seat. Thanks."

She looked around and frowned. "Hike up your knees a little." He did. She sat on his lap, and draped her legs over one arm of his chair. And made herself comfortable.

He set the cookie down and slipped his arm around her back. "Pretty hard to hold a mug, a cookie, and you.

"Here." She shoved the cookie at his face. "Bite."

He did. And sipped. "Pretty cute. For a witch."

"I'd like to talk about that."

"Cute?"

"Witch."

"I suppose. What?" He took another bite. And wondered, now what is going on?

"Witches understand other magical folk better than plain folk do."

"What did Ran do?" He smiled.

"Nothing."

"Umm?"

"The Vander are magical."

"Oh, oh."

She pushed the cookie at him. "Bite." He did. And chewed, watching her very carefully.

"They need your help, Tink. Even now Sa'ar is in the living room with Smoke and Chicken, begging for help. She sounded desperate."

"How do you know that, kiddo?" He reached out. But he couldn't feel anything. "They're blocked."

"I know. But I was coming down the hall. And I heard them talking."

"Ah, ha. Kinna sneaky."

She frowned. "It was an accident."

He nodded. "Accident."

"Well, it was. An accident."

"And?"

"What?"

"Drop the other shoe. The suspense is killing me. What is the plot this time?" His fingers tickled a rib or two. "Now what is going on?"

"Wellll?"

"That is a pregnant well."

She nodded vigorously. "Exactly." And beamed at him.

"Huh?"

"Imdar," she said softly.

"Imdar?" He frowned. And became very still.

She waited.

"IMDAR?" Coffee sloshed over them as he jerked violently. She almost slid from his lap.

"Don't be angry. Please?" She waved the mess away and the coffee pot over, and refilled their cups.

"Imdar?" He stared at her.

"Yep."

"She wants to be pregnant?"

"The Vander."

"Want her to be pregnant?"

She nodded. "Yep"

"Me?"

"Yep."

Coffee sloshed again. "Damn them. Damn all magical folk."

"TINK."

"I didn't mean you. It is just that they are always assuming that whatever they might want they ought to get. And too bad for anyone else."

She nodded. And said slowly, very sagely. "They are like that. Certainly are." Everyone knew that. So he ought to know that as well.

"Got another cookie, cookie?"

"Bite."

He did. "Sa'ar behind this?"

She shrugged. "Tink?"

"What? NO!" He looked down. "There are coffee splotches all over my papers."

"Sorry."

"Not your fault. Even if you are a witch." He smiled.

"TINK," she warned.

"A little short kid witch." He smiled broader.

"AM DUK TAK TAK," she growled.

"My feelings exactly." He kissed her.

She bit his lip. Gently.

"Making lunch?"

"Yep." Chantal bumped Fair Morn sideways with her hip as she sliced the cheese. "Wait!"

"I am hungry."

"You are always hungry."

"Not really. I just eat a lot. Often." She snatched another piece of cheese.

"And no weight problem."

"Very high metabolic rate. Way I was made." She took another slice.

"Toast the bread and stir the soup."

"What's for lunch?" Tinker entered the kitchen on silent, bare feet.

"Soup and sandwiches. You're down early."

"I got distracted."

"Heh heh." R-Bar followed him in.

"You have time to take a shower," said Chantal.

"A quick shower," amended Fair Morn.

"Right." He spun and headed down the hall. R-Bar was already ahead of him.

"Quick," she cooed back over her shoulder. "But not too quick."

LUNCH. Chantal shouted to all their minds.

Outside the snow warriors stopped their combat and headed for the house. And pelted Farth with snowballs by way of telling him and Sedeem that it was time for lunch.

The living room cabal went to help Imdar to the dining room.

"A day or two," said Smoke, passing the platter to Fair Morn. "Maybe less."

"For what?" Tinker blew on his soup spoon. "Hot."

"Until Imdar is ready, MindMate."

Chicken's eyes popped wide.

Ran tapped him on the elbow. "Pass the pepper, please."

"To?" he asked

"Me," replied Ran.

"Travel," answered Sa'ar.

"Couple more days, umm?" He chewed on his sandwich. And passed the pepper to Ran.

"Yes," replied Imdar. "The Transformed One said that it is so."

"That's me," explained Smoke to his puzzled look.

"Ummm," he said, spooning up more soup. "Good."

Sa'ar gasped.

Imdar looked crushed.

He looked up. "What?" And laughed. "The soup. I was referring to the soup." And frowned. And sighed. "Eat your soup." Then he looked over at Imdar. "So, how are you feeling?"

"I am feeling much better, Forever Vander Lord."

"Good," he said. "That's good. Too." And pushed his bowl in the general direction of Chantal. "May I have some more, please?"

"Sure, Oliver." She took it and filled it. "Eat hearty, Simba Leader. It's full of good stuff. Nourishing."

Halfway through the meal, Messenger announced, "Road's open."

"That's good," said Tinker. "Also." He grinned. "Now all we have to do is dig out the van, put on the chains, open two drifts across the driveway, and you can go to town."

"Right after lunch," said Fair Morn. "After we finish."

And that is what they did.

Everyone.

Except for Imdar.

Who rested.

But no-one went to town.

By the time they were finished working outside, it was too late. To go to town.

So. They stayed up late.

And slept late.

Chapter Four

One of These Days.

Grandeville. Tinker's Place. Morning.

He wandered into the kitchen, yawned, stretched, poured a cup of coffee, and felt the mental emptiness, the quiet hollow silence, that told him that they had all gone somewhere. Probably to town, he decided. It was a frequent event, them all going off together into town.

He paused in the dining room, read the note propped up on the table, against a salt shaker, written by Chantal, which told him that they had all gone to town. He smiled to himself. The note said that they would all be back by dinner time. And that he should fix it, dinner.

He wandered into the living room, plopped into his chair, and said, "OOOOOP."

She was sitting on the couch, thick quilt pulled up around her chin.

"Morning," he mumbled, slumping deeper into his chair, taking a sip, then holding the cup on his stomach. "Been up long?"

She nodded.

His eyes closed. He began to slowly come awake, taking a sip now and then. And listened to the quiet. And the wood stove's soft muttering. The house didn't creak. There was no wind blowing.

And, by the time the cup was almost empty, his eyes

opened. He took the last sip, yawned, stretched, and sat up. He was awake. "You hungry?"

She nodded.

"Let's make some breakfast."

She watched him. "You know how to do that?"

"Sure."

"Don't your minions see to your wants, first?"

"Not my minions," he grumbled. "And no, they did not." He stood. "Coming?"

She nodded. "I do not know how to do this cooking thing."

He smiled. "Toast is easy." And headed for the kitchen.

She followed.

Quilt covered.

Quilt enfolded.

Quilt enwrapped.

As the last bite was chewed and swallowed, he refilled their cups and rose. "Might as well sit in the other room. Enjoy the wood heat."

And he did, dropping back into his chair. She sat on the couch and watched him.

One of her hands clenched the quilt tight just below her chin. The other held her cup. She watched him carefully.

"What's the matter?" He stood and added more wood to the stove.

"Chosen One, Great Hero, Mighty Warrior, Vander Lord?"

"That the problem?" He laughed. "You heard all those stories and believe them, right?" He sat.

She shook her head.

"You wanna tell me what it is then?"

She nodded.

He waited.

She cleared her throat.

He waited.

She took a sip from her cup.

He waited.

"In your eyes, am I pleasant to peer upon?" She looked past her cup, at the floor, head tilted down.

"Sure."

"True speak?" Her eyes looked up, watching his face, watching his expression.

"Beautiful."

"You vigorously enjoy your minions? All of them, everyone?"

He frowned. "Not my minions. Ahhhhh, yes."

Her head rose. "They are slaves?"

"NO. Didn't Sa'ar tell you anything about us? Didn't any of the other Vander?"

She shook her head. "Only of the Great Final Battle. And of our Great Debt to The Vander Lord. Which must absolutely be paid." Her face started to flush.

His frown deepened. "I see. So to speak." He nodded. More to himself than to her. And cleared his throat.

"O.K., let's see if I can explain, umm, everything. They, the ones you call my minions, all of them, are really me. I am them. We are one, a single being. All linked together, umm, mentally. A sort of complicated organism of eight parts, eight independent parts, all of which can, if they wish, merge in, erm, any combination we chose. You follow that?" He slumped deeper in his chair.

She nodded.

"Then you can see why no-one could be anyone's slave, or minion, or anything else. We are all . . . us, ahh, if we wish to be."

"Strange."

He laughed. "Certainly is, at times. Takes a lot of getting used to." He laughed again, softly. "Really and truly it does. But I think that we have finally done it, gotten used to it."

She nodded. And took a sip. And looked at him over the top of her cup. "Is that why?" And straightened up, releasing her grip on the quilt.

"Why what?"

"You will not enjoy me. Because all your female parts do not want to?"

He choked on suddenly inhaled coffee. And managed to croak out, "NO." And hastily waved at her to remain seated as he sat straighter and vigorously cleared his throat. He swallowed. "Ummmm, let me explain that, also. Umm, when we, ahhh, do . . . that, there is only the two of us. No one else involved. Very private. Definitely not a group activity."

She nodded slowly. "Then you could, if you wished? With me?"

He sighed, heavily he sighed. "Errrrrm, I suppose, I guess." He was starting to worry.

"Then?" She smiled a small smile.

"Hard to explain, I suppose."

She frowned. "Did not your min . . . others explain?"

"What?" He frowned back. "What? Explain what?"

Her eyes grew rounder. "If I tell you a secret, does it remain a secret?"

"Of course."

"Sa'ar told them."

"Which them?"

"The Princess one. And the Transformed One with the

overwhelming orange gold eyes."

"Smoke."

She nodded. "The Smoke."

"Yes?"

"She, Sa'ar, Our Heart, told them, that if you did not, she would have you taken and charmed, and we, the Vander, would get what we wanted. Even if you would hate her, Our Heart, and us, forever and forever and forever."

"For a long time, huh?"

She nodded. And blinked away a tear.

"Please don't cry."

"We are very enjoyable, the Vander."

He sighed, a long drawn out very slow sigh. "Tell me, exactly what did Sa'ar explain to them, Chicken and Smoke?" And slumped deeper into his chair, setting his cup on the floor, legs sticking straight out, frowning darkly, fingers laced over his stomach. He knew that he really didn't want to hear this.

So she sat straighter.

And told him.

They had taken a large table and now sat huddled around it, eating hamburgers. Mostly.

All of them.

> Except for Sedeem and Farth. They were elsewhere in town.

All of them.

> Except for Sa'ar. She had gone to her family home in Grandeville to visit with her parents and her brother and his wife.

All of them.

Around the group rattled and banged the usual noise and bustle of fast food being served and eaten, fast. They were eating slow.

Chantal squinted across the table at Chicken. "That is why we are in town? So he can jump on Imdar?"

"Indeed," replied Chicken, prying the lid off her coffee container.

"Crude," said Fair Morn to Chantal.

Chantal sucked in a deep breath. "We going to collect stud fees?"

"Really crude," added Messenger. "Really really."

Chantal snorted. "Well, that is what it is, isn't it? These two," she waved her hand at Chicken and Smoke, "are putting our stallion into the pasture with Sa'ar's filly. That is your MindMate, Smoke, not some dumb animal." She took a bite from her sandwich. Fish.

Messenger looked worried and poked her finger around in her fries.

Ran looked at R-Bar.

Fair Morn started on another hamburger. "Sa'ar said that they would kidnap him."

"And charm him, too," whispered Messenger, passing some of her fries to Fair Morn.

Chantal shook her head. "Somehow I really believe that R-Bar and Sedeem could keep that from happening."

R-Bar nodded. "True."

"So, what is really going on, then?" Chantal frowned at Chicken. "That is also me you are screwing around with, if you'll pardon the bad pun."

"I do not like it either," said Ran. "His Chicken and his Smoke should have let us all know why this is going on."

Smoke rolled her eyes at Chicken.

Chicken's face flushed. "True, most true. We will speak to all that Sa'ar do say. Then we will memory share."

So, she told them.

They boiled into the house, laden with groceries, and other purchases. And, after shedding jackets and boots, put everything away, and then checked to see that he had started the dinner. And what he was cooking, if he did.

He had.
A roast, large.
And many potatoes.
In the ovens.
Cooking. Baking.

They headed for the living room. They knew that he was taking a shower.

Imdar sat at one end of the large couch. Sa'ar was sitting next to her.

Sa'ar stood and smiled at them. "Have a nice day?"

Chantal took one look at Imdar, two quick steps forward, banged Sa'ar around by one shoulder, and punched. "BITCH!"

Sa'ar rocked backward, looked confused, and collapsed.

Imdar screamed, curled into a ball, and yanked protection crackling down around herself.

Smoke yanked Chantal back before she could kick Sa'ar in the side of the head.

Tinker hurtled in from the hall, yanking on one of the thick white robes, shedding water everywhere. "WHAT'S HAPPENING?"

Imdar pointed a quivering finger at Chantal. "Your other killed Sa'ar, Our Heart."

Smoke shoved the glowering Chantal into Fair Morn's arms, knelt and checked Sa'ar.

"NO. She will wake in a moment."

"Someone want to tell me what is going on?" He stared from face to face.

Chantal snarled at Fair Morn, who held her tightly wrapped in her arms. "Let me go, dammit." Fair Morn did.

"I punched her," snapped Chantal. "Once. And she deserved it."

"We do at lunch, Me'Lord, this dilemma discuss." Chicken nodded at Chantal. "And she do feel most put upon, for thee, Our Love."

"Ahhhhh," said Tinker, looking from Sa'ar, wobbling into a sitting position, to Chantal, still glaring darkly at Sa'ar. "Defending my virtue."

"Such as it is," growled Chantal.

Sa'ar looked at Imdar. "You are safe?"

The crackling stopped. Imdar nodded.

Sa'ar looked up at Chantal. "Am I safe? Aunt? May I rise?"

"Get up."

Sa'ar half stood and sat next to Imdar. "We will leave."

Tinker stepped over, tapped Imdar on the shoulder. "Move over, make room." And sat in the space created between her and the end of the couch, and slipped an arm around her waist. "Nobody leaves, just yet." He looked at the others. "Everyone out. The Vander and I need to talk."

They all headed in various directions.

And as soon as they were alone, he tickled Imdar. "Now we have serious matters to discuss."

Imdar blinked, her eyes moving between Tinker and Sa'ar. The Healer gently touched Sa'ar's jaw, taking away the pain and the redness.

"Vander Lord?" Sa'ar twisted around, tucking her legs up and around.

"Imdar will have my son, right?"

Imdar nodded.

"Yes," said Sa'ar, taking one of Imdar's hands in her's.

"Do I get visitation rights?"

"Ohhhh, yes," replied Imdar.

"Here?"

"Vander Lord, we will visit. Here."

"Name?"

"Rorx," replied Imdar.

"An ancient Vander name," explained Sa'ar. "From our very early beginnings."

"It has great meaning," added Imdar.

"One . . . more . . . thing."

"What? Vander Lord?"

"No more talk of debts."

"BUT." Sa'ar leaped up and crashed to her knees in front of him.

"NO BUTS."

"Vander Lord . . . But . . ."

"NO."

She glared up at him. "You will now listen to me." It was a command, The Heart of the Vander now speaking. Imdar blanched, sucked in her breath.

Tinker nodded. "Shoot."

"In The Great Final Battle you helped us survive. From those moments till now. Your son guaranties that we will survive from these moments into the future. This is a debt beyond payment. The Vander owe their lives, their future, and their existence, to you. This cannot be altered. Nor denied. Not by you. Not by us."

"Ummmm."

"We are very willing," said Imdar softly, gently, leaning against him.

"My point exactly. O.K., this way or not at all."

"What?" asked Sa'ar.

"I decide how the Vander repay their forever debt, not you. Or any other of them. All right?"

Sa'ar blinked. And chewed on one corner of her lower lip.

"Well?" he asked.

She nodded, slowly. "You win." Then she grinned. "What do you want to do?" And sat back, straightening up, shoulders back, square.

"Ah, ah, ah, ah, ah, ah, ah, slow down, slow down. I need to think about it. I'll let you know, umm, during one of your visits."

Sa'ar leaned toward him. "Will Aunt remain angry with me, with us?"

"No." He smiled at her, The Heart of the Vander. "It was just a momentary thing. No one felt it, or they would have grabbed her fist, first. How's your jaw?"

"Imdar healed. Where did she learn to do that?"

"Her father. Taught them all."

"All?" asked Imdar.

"Her other sisters. She has three. They are all sorta alike."

Sa'ar sat back. "We should leave."

He nodded. "Then you had better say goodbye." The rest had silently joined them. "I called them in."

They stood. And he wrapped Imdar in his arms. "Take care of my son, O.K.?" She nodded.

Then they all said their goodbyes. Sa'ar and Imdar stepped to the center of the room. And disappeared in a soft flash of violet.

Tinker grabbed Chantal and threw an arm around her shoulders. "Hi, Slugger." And kissed her on the cheek.

"Sorry."

"One good thing though."

"What?"

"I am now in control of the Vander debt. I decide what it is. Tee hee."

"Sneak."

"Have to be. Now how about you all show me what you bought in town?"

Everyone whirled away to fetch their purchases.
Including their gifts for him.

"A popcorn popper?"

"Sure, Dad. The old one is ugly." Sedeem and Farth had joined them.

"Ugly, ugly, ugly, ugly, ugly," chanted Messenger. "Greasy, grimy, black and eeeeevil." She cackled wildly, sounding just like the wicked witch from the Wizard of Oz, the one Dorothy had all the trouble with, curling her hands into claws.

"Not nice," grumped R-Bar, who felt that this elseplace had some very bad ideas about witches. Ran nodded.

Chantal handed him an envelope.

Messenger stuck her tongue out at R-Bar.

He took out the card, looked at it. "Ha. Ha. Ha. Not funny." The card said 'Happy Father's Day.'

"I couldn't find one for stud service," grumbled Chantal.

"A real grump, huh?" He kissed her on the side of the face and gave her a little pinch.

"YES. As a matter of fact, I am."

"But they would have all died." Messenger looked at Chantal as a single tear wandered down her cheek. "Even Sa'ar."

"Well," growled Chantal. "They didn't have to weasel

around like that. Should have just laid it right out."

"Drool pun, that," observed Chicken.

"Witches like to do devious. So I suppose do magicians," suggested Tinker.

"BOO TAK!" snarled R-Bar.

"Boo tak yourself, shorty," replied Tinker.

"Mom, that is nasty, really, really nasty." Sedeem laughed and shoved Farth toward the hall. "Let's take a nap."

"I am not short," snapped R-Bar.

"O.K.," said Tinker. "Vertically challenged."

R-Bar hurtled her package into his arms. "HERE."

"OOOOF." He ripped it open. "Wowee, paisley pajamas."

"If I still had all my powers I could make you taller," said Ran to R-Bar.

"Maybe the Vander could do something?" suggested Messenger.

"Hold it," said Tinker.

"They said that they are in our debt," stated Ran.

"HOLD IT. STOP. CEASE," demanded Tinker.

"What'sa matta?" asked Fair Morn, anxious to hand over her gift. It was a rather large chocolate cake. And she felt like a snack.

He glared at them all. "Nobody changes anything. Nuthin. No how. Not a hair. Not a . . . anything. No way we are going to have somatic chameleons running about the place, changing their shapes. My life is crazy enough already."

"Here." Fair Morn jabbed the cake box against his chest. "I'll get the plates."

"I will get your gift, Amtar. Your Messenger said that you liked neopreme." Ran hurried after Fair Morn into the kitchen.

Tinker stared at Messenger, who had started giggling. "Neopreme?"

"Ice cream," explained Messenger. "Neapolitan."

He laughed as he opened the box. "That is the largest chocolate cake that I have ever seen."

Chicken looked inside. "Indeed, My Lord, tis most grand."

He kissed her on the forehead. "Like you all."

Smoke edged closer and leered at him, and the cake.

"All. I said all."

"I was admiring the cake. You were admiring her anatomy."

Chicken's eyes popped wide. "True?"

"Certainly was," stated Smoke. "Of course, you have managed to unbutton your shirt down to your gut."

"Fair Navel, Dark Sister. Gut do be most crude."

Smoke took the cake box from his arms. "Before you drool on it, MindMate."

"I am not drooling. And exactly what is wrong with admiring her anatomy?"

"Naught," stated Chicken.

"Of course not," added Chantal. "He is supposed to."

"What?" He stared at her.

Messenger turned around slowly, and winked at him.

"Let's eat," yelled Fair Morn from the dining room. "You can drag the Princess into a hall closet and work your wicked ways upon her later."

Chicken slipped her arm around him and bumped him with her hip. "Truly a'wicked ways, Sweet prince?"

"Let's eat," he mumbled, starting toward the table. "You guys have one-track minds."

Smoke breathed on the back of his neck and kissed him. "Nothing wrong with that, Our Mate."

Ran looked up from where she sat. "Everyone want some creamed ice?"

"Neopreme's my favorite," said Tinker dropping into his chair. "You better cut the cake, Princess, before Fair Morn drools on it."

"I do not droll."

"Me neither," he said, looking pointedly at Smoke.

Sedeem walked in, yanking the belt around her robe a little tighter. "May we have some?" She smiled. "I'll take it to our room."

Chantal handed her two plates. "Here." And dropped two forks into Sedeem's robe pocket.

And then, they all settled down and enjoyed the cake and the ice cream, gently joshing Ran about the neopreme flavor.

Suddenly R-Bar sat up and gasped.

He jerked. "What?"

She stared at him, just stared and looked blank.

His eyes jerked. "Smoke?"

Smoke shrugged. "Shock of some sort."

"She is alive," whispered R-Bar.

"Who?"

"Rbat, my sister. All thought that she had gone far."

"Huh?"

R-Bar sucked in a deep breath and exhaled slowly. "I just felt it. Suddenly she was there." She dragged over her ice cream dish. "Ripple will tell."

Everyone settled back down. To eat the cake and the ice cream.

And winter followed the usual pattern.

    For a very heavy winter.

And eventually melted into spring.

Mostly blue skies.

And sunshine.

"The crocusesssss are up. They're up."

Messenger clumped into the kitchen, eyes sparkling, boots muddy, arms clenching the mail which she had just retrieved, and which, in the act of doing, she had stopped, here and there and everywhere, to admire the bunches of bright flowers popping up among the scattered few remaining patches of snow.

"OUTSIDE." Chantal pointed a wooden spoon at her. "Your boots are mucky."

As Messenger backed out the kitchen door into the entry room, she grinned. "You dripped something on the floor. Right next to the mud."

"Spaghetti sauce," grumbled Chantal, wiping up all the mess, sauce and mud.

Messenger shot past, bare feet hopping over the wet spot, and down the hallway, delivering. "Mail, mail, mail," she sang.

"Certainly is," said Sa'ar as she stepped aside and caught Messenger hurtling from the hallway into the living room.

"Ooopsy." Messenger grinned. "Oh. It's Sa'ar. Who, what?"

"Male," replied Sa'ar.

"You didn't get any." Messenger thumbed through her bundle.

"His son," added Imdar, her arm wrapped protectively around the shoulders of a young boy.

"MY. You are Rorx?"

He nodded. And tugged at Imdar's trouser leg. "Her eyes just flared green."

Messenger giggled. "He is coming downstairs. I told him. Bye." She dropped the mail in a heap on a table, ducked down the hall and headed for the rear deck.

"Snookered again."

Tinker entered the living room and nodded at them. "Eight? Nine? Ten?"

"Nine years your time, Vander Lord," replied Imdar.

Sa'ar stepped to his side, leaned, and kissed his cheek. "First Greetings, Vander Lord."

"Father?" Rorx took a tentative and careful step in Tinker's direction.

"Yep." Tinker held out his arms and gently wrapped Rorx in them. "Mind if I pick you up?"

"No, Father."

Tinker did. "Ump. You know, I never got a chance to do this to your sister. By the time that I saw her, she was already nineteen years old."

He glared at Sa'ar past Rorx's head. "I suppose that this is an improvement."

Imdar stepped close. "Do not be angry with us, Great Vander Lord."

"Not angry," grumbled Tinker. "It is just that with you guys, it is always little surprises, little unexplained, unwelcome surprises. Or unexpected, surprises. How long are you staying?"

"A week," said Sa'ar. "I also want to visit my parents and my brother. And Szaifeh is also home."

Tinker nodded. "Sedeem and Farth are traveling." He jiggled Rorx up and down. "Too had. You'll meet your sister one of these days. Just a little better planning, and you will." He stared pointedly at Sa'ar.

Rorx twisted a little and whispered in his ear. "Did you

really do all those things? May I see your weaponkin? Touch it?"

Tinker laughed. "I'll bet that a lot of what you have heard is just fancy stories. We can talk about all that while you are visiting. You wanna meet the rest? They're sorta your mothers also. They are keeping out of the way, but are beginning to fidget."

"My Lord," snapped Chicken, standing right behind him. "We do fidget Us not."

"Princess Chicken," he said by way of introduction. Then he named each one as they stepped close.

Rorx tightened his grip on Tinker's arm when Smoke slipped up.

"She doesn't bite," said Tinker.

Smoke winked at Rorx. "May I hold you, our male kitten? His arms are getting tired."

Rorx thought, for just a moment, then nodded. Smoke easily lifted him from Tinker's arms.

Rorx's eyes grew round as he leaned close to her chest. "She is making rumble sounds."

"Purring," explained Tinker. "It means that she is very happy. Maybe we'd all better sit down."

"I'll make hot cocoa," sang Messenger, heading for the kitchen, grabbing the mail and dumping it on the dining room table, having popped back into the house to see their son.

"I'll get the marshmallows," said Fair Morn, following her.

As they settled down, Tinker nodded at his visitors. "Use whatever room you wish."

"I'm staying with my parents."

"I will use The Bedroom," stated Imdar.

"Ahhhhh, whatever." Tinker smiled at them. "So,

how's everything?"

"We progress," said Sa'ar. "Imdar mothers."

"And Rorx trains," added Imdar, smiling at her son.

"It is hard work," whispered Rorx very, very softly into Smoke's ear, causing lots of smiles as all listened to what he said.

Rorx noticed and touched Smoke on the side of her face. "It is true. You are one."

"Yes," she said. "We are one. Did not your mother tell you this? Or the other Vander?"

"I don't think so." Rorx frowned. And looked at Imdar. "Mother?"

Imdar looked at Tinker. "Not totally."

He moved over and sat next to her. And slipped an arm around her waist. And said to Rorx, "Some things are pnvate. And not shared." And tickled her. "We are very private when we wish to be." And did it again.

This time, Imdar smiled, a little.

"HOT COCOA." Messenger carried in a tray with two pots on it followed by Fair Morn with another tray loaded with cups and a bag of marshmallows.

Fair Morn smiled at Rorx. "You'll like this. Especially the white things." And handed him a cup. He was content to remain sitting on Smoke's lap.

"May I come in?" asked a disembodied voice.

"Grand Central Station," mumbled Tinker.

"Sure," said Sa'ar, recognizing the voice.

"Oh," she said. "Hi, Shar." She nodded at Tinker. "I was looking for Deem."

"She left yesterday," said Tinker. "Have some cocoa."

"Thanks, Unc." Szaifeh took a cup and held it out to be filled. "Cute kid."

Then she grinned at Tinker. "Wowee."

"Rorx," said Sa'ar. "This is Szaifeh, my witch cousin. Szai, Rorx is his son, Imdar is the mother. We can talk later."

Szaifeh stepped over and kissed Tinker on the forehead. "Bet that Deem was surprised."

"Will be when she finds out," he grumbled.

She squirmed into a place next to him. "Still collecting babes, huh, Unc?"

"No."

Szaifeh frowned and looked over at Chicken. "Princess?"

Chicken laughed at her puzzled expression. "As thy cousin do just now so say, pon this we shall ourselves be'speak later."

"Hum hum," said Szaifeh.

Sa'ar laughed.

"Not at all," snarled R-Bar, the air crackling around her.

"Oop." Szaifeh ducked her head. "Sorry, Aunt, sorry."

"She is pretty," observed Rorx.

Szaifeh smiled at him.

Sa'ar frowned at her.

Szaifeh wiggled against Tinker. "As long as you are branching out." And jerked.

"OUCH."

"Behave," snapped R-Bar.

Szaifeh jerked again. "I was. That hurt."

"Not as much as it could have." R-Bar stood. "Szaifeh, Sa'ar, come with me. We shall talk. Now."

The cousins followed her down the hall. They knew a command when they heard one.

He was oozing into morning, coffee cup cradled on his stomach, slouched on the couch.

Sunlight came creeping sharp edged across the floor toward him.

A small figure slipped into the room, onto the couch, and dragged a blanket up around them.

"Morn," mumbled Tinker.

"They said that I could," explained Rorx.

"Who?" Tinker took another sip, having rearranged things so that he could.

"Smoke and Fair Morn."

"Umm."

"Mother said that they are really all my mothers as well. Is that true?"

"Umm."

We are, they all stated.

He nodded. "Yep. True."

"The others are not."

"What others?"

"The Vander."

Tinker's eyes opened. He was awake. "What are they?"

"Teachers."

Chicken slipped in, refilled his cup, and handed Rorx one filled with hot cocoa. "Fair morn, Sweet Prince."

Rorx blew on his cocoa and looked up at her. "Are you really a Princess?"

"Indeed. As this thy Father do be Our Verra Own King, as We do be His Verra Own Queen. And as thee do be Our Verra Own Fair Prince."

Rorx grinned at her. "A Prince." His smiled faded. "Can a Warlock be a Prince?"

R-Bar joined them "Of course. Come and eat."

Tinker sat up, carefully swinging his legs around. "Well, she ought to know."

Ran leaned over the back of the couch and tickled the back of Tinker's neck. "I agree with your R-Bar."

Tinker stood. "That's two votes from the witch contingent." He winked at Rorx. "I don't think that you will have any problem if the Princess wants you to be a Prince."

In the dining room, Imdar kissed Tinker on the cheek. "First Greetings." And pulled out a chair for Rorx.

Szaifeh and Sa'ar came from the kitchen, eyes twinkling, and set large platters on the table.

As they sat, Tinker looked at the pair and grumbled, "Run for your lives."

Under the table, Chicken kicked him, gently on the side of the leg. "Whish, Me'Lord."

Messenger set two wicker baskets on the table. "Cinnamon rolls." She dropped into her chair. "They're hot."

Chicken banged a basket against Tinker's elbow and took a roll. The other basket started around the table in the opposite direction. And the rest joined them for breakfast.

Rorx sat, ate, and carefully watched. And listened.

And then they were done with breakfast.

Or almost done.
Mostly.

Fair Morn was finishing whatever was left.

Rorx was trying not to stare at her. He looked at Tinker.

"Bottomless pit," said Tinker.

"Where does it all go?" whispered Rorx.

"One of life's little mysteries." Tinker winked at him.

The explosion shook the house. A window rattled.

"Sonic boom," said Tinker.

"No." R-Bar jumped up and ran for the back door. "I will check."

Tinker looked at Sa'ar. "Now what?"

She shrugged a shoulder.

DRAGON, shouted R-Bar in their minds. LOOK.

Tinker peered from her eyes as she looked around the corner of the house.

Out in the meadow, beyond the edge of the rear deck, beyond the flower beds, the creature stood, poking its snout in the tall grass.

Doesn't look like any kind of thing we have ever seen before, said Tinker. *Sorta looks like a dinosaur.*

Slarsia, said Ran.

"Lord?" Sa'ar rapped her knuckle on the tabletop, next to his hand. "LORD?"

His eyes snapped sideways as he pulled away. "What?"

"What is it?"

Szaifeh nodded.

"Visitor. Ran said it is a Slarsia, whatever that is. Anyone have any idea what that thing is doing here?"

Ran frowned. "Your R-Bar must be careful. They cough deadly."

I will, said R-Rar as she slipped across the rear deck and out into the flower beds, a long silver wand clenched in her right hand. She was keeping trees and shrubs between herself and the creature.

Chicken, Chantal, Messenger and Fair Morn hurried away to get their weapons. Smoke slipped out the front door and circled around the house and the garage and the generator shed.

Tinker looked at Ran. "Why is that thing here? Any idea?"

Ran nodded.

"Well?"

All eyes watched her.

She looked only at Tinker. *It has come for our son.*

WHAT? He surged up violently, shoving his chair backward.

Wait, wait, wait, screamed Ran through their minds.

The attackers froze in place.

The Slarsia ripped up more clumps of green, and chewed. And looked at R-Bar. Swallowed and blew. At her.

In spite of her protection, it tumbled R-Bar backwards, over the flower beds, crashing into the still empty swimming pool along with shrub and tree parts.

PAN DO THROP, snarled R-Bar as she scrambled toward the shallow end of the pool and the ladder.

Ran walked around the table and stood behind Rorx, setting her hands on his shoulders. "Among my folk, Amtar, it is said that when the Slarsia comes, then it is time to travel. They are sometime warlock companions."

"He is too young," gasped Imdar. "Too young."

"We are not finished." Sa'ar jumped up, eyes flaring angrily. The air snapped and popped around her.

Szaifeh hastily shoved away from her. "Careful, careful," she hissed, witch nervous at flying magician magic.

"What kind of travel?" asked Tinker.

Rorx wiggled. "Your hands tingle."

"Residual magic," explained Ran. "Discovery."

"Huh?" Tinker looked back outside. Everyone was staying carefully still. The Slarsia was looking at the house. Deep crimson fumes curled from the corners of its mouth and dripped puddling into the grass around it.

Ran stepped away from Rorx and looked at each one of them in turn. "It is time. Our son will now make The

Travel of Discovery. To find strength and weakness. This is a Mage Warlock need."

Imdar slipped an arm around her son's shoulders. "Too young."

"I will kill it," snapped Sa'ar.

"You may not," stated Ran.

"Witch," snapped Sa'ar.

"He will die."

Imdar wrapped protection around them.

Ran walked back, reached through and touched Imdar. "It will do no good."

Imdar gasped.

Ran nodded. "I borrowed from Rorx. I am Slarsia touched."

Tinker screwed his mouth to one side. "You guys wanna sit down?" He refilled his cup. And took a sip. "Will he be safe?"

Ran gently stroked Rorx's hair. "As safe as one may be when they travel. Some die."

"Just him and it?" Tinker nodded toward that side of the house.

She shrugged. "He may find other companions."

"Do we have a choice?"

The answer came soft as soft. "No." Ran gently touched Rorx and then Imdar.

"When?"

"Soon."

"Merde."

Chicken charged into the room. "Tis most strange this beastie." She banged her sword into its scabbard. "Our Witch Sister did swear most vile a'oath and did a'threaten thing most fiercely. It did naught but blink one great eye thusly." She turned her head, looked wall-eyed at him, and slowly blinked.

"You heard what Ran said?"

"Indeed, My Lord. Most unsettling." She nodded at Rorx. "Young Prince Our Own, it do seem thee and yonder green beastle be soon a'traveling." She walked around and knelt next to him.

"Our Fair Son, your magical folk have ways most strange for this simple Princess a'grasping." She reached around and yanked a dagger from her boot. And handed it to him, sheath and all.

"On thy belt do hang this. But most careful be. Tis wickedly sharp."

R-Bar ran in, disheveled, dirt smudged, and angry still. She glared at Ran.

Ran winced. "I did not call it. No one does."

R-Bar handed Rorx a short black-green wand. "Keep this up your left sleeve. But be very careful with it, it has three magics."

He carefully looked at the wand. "Three magics?"

"Yes. Faan, Ancient, and a little something from my Father, also a warlock. Wild magic."

"May I?" asked Sa'ar reaching for the wand.

"Sure," said R-Bar.

Sa'ar took the wand, turned it over and over, and handed it back. "Here Rorx. Now it has four. Vander. For Vander."

Tinker stared from R-Bar to Sa'ar. "You sure you want to do that? Mix witch and magician like that. It is like giving a kid an atomic bomb to play with."

"It is our son," stated R-Bar.

"That kid knows how to handle it," snapped Sa'ar.

"He has been well trained," added Imdar.

"Rorx. Catch." Fair Morn had entered, her space

cannon, a gift from Macabre, riding in its thigh holster. The small object flipped end for end through the air.

Rorx caught it and looked at the small wafer. "What is it?" He held it by two fingers.

"Help," replied Fair Morn.

"Macabre's signal?" Tinker shook his head. And smiled. "I suppose."

"Who is Macabre?" Rorx looked at Tinker.

"Let me get dressed. Then we, you and I, will hide your, ummm, companion in the barn. And then we, you and I, will have a long talk. O.K.?"

Rorx nodded.

They sat on the edge of the huge depression, on the dry spot. The sun had taken away the snow from this place earlier than most. An annual event.

"You don't think that you are kinna young to go wandering through the elseplaces?"

Rorx nodded.

"You do?"

"Yes."

"Well, maybe we can find a place to keep that . . . Slarsia until you are older."

NO. It was Ran. *It is a call. He must go.*

Tinker's shoulders sagged. "Sorry. Looks like you, we, have no choice. Again." He felt Ran began to sob. Smoke blocked her emotions away from him.

"Father?"

"Umm?"

"For just a moment, you felt not-there."

"Ran just told me that you had to go, that it was a call of some sort."

"Why can't I do that? Be not-there?"

"Special trick. You have to be a person like Smoke to do that. To give it to others."

Rorx frowned. Then he carefully studied his father's face. "If I visit her elseplace, do you think that someone there would help me to learn how to do that?"

Tinker fought back his smile. "Ahhhh, I don't know. Ummmm, maybe they might eat you first, before you could ask."

MindMate, growled Smoke. *That is not nice. My batarlan would know better. They share my memories from before.*

And the others?

Smoke snorted. *Well, maybe.*

Tinker looked at Rorx. "Doesn't matter. No one knows how to find her elseplace."

"Would her folk really eat me?" He edged closer. "Really?"

Tinker slipped his arm around his son and said, "Let me tell you about Smoke. She comes from a long line of telepathic carnivores and . . . "

And he told Rorx all about her. And how she had been physically transformed by Big Red. And what she had looked like prior to that.

"Now you know."

"The stories were all true?"

"Oh, probably not." Tinker laughed. "'From what we have heard, they get pretty far-fetched. But Smoke is Smoke Ask her to show you what she looked like before. You'll see."

And then Tinker told him about the others.

As they stepped up on the rear deck, Rorx stopped. "Father?"

"What?"

"I am really your son, am I not?"

Tinker nodded. "Yep. Sure are." And laughed. "Unless your mother was messing around and didn't tell me."

Sa'ar gasped. "VANDER LORD!"

"OOP. Didn't see you sitting there." She sat at one of the tables. In plain sight. She had been reading a book.

"Hi."

They looked up, at Fair Morn, leaning over her balcony railing, three stories up.

"Hi," answered Rorx. "May I see them?" Fair Morn grinned at Tinker. "Isn't he rather young for that. Oh well, like father, like son. I suppose." And ducked back inside, laughing gaily.

"Pay no attention," mumbled Tinker. " They are all like that." He sighed. "Most of the time."

Imdar stepped from the side door. "Ran is in her room."

"I'll go up." said Tinker.

Fair Morn burst out the door, grabbed Rorx under the arms and lifted him up until his face was level with her's. "I'll show you mine, if you show me your's." She winked at him. "Just kidding."

And headed out into the pasture beyond the flower beds, still holding him off the ground. "Not so heavy. And there is a slight wind. I am sure that we can do it."

"HEY?" yelled Tinker. "What are you up to?"

"Not much"

She faced into the wind. And unfolded and unfolded and unfolded her great multi-colored wings, the great butterfly wings. And lifted up. And up.

I will be careful, One. She rocked from side to side and then spiraled down to land gently on the spot she had left a moment before. And set Rorx down. The wings folded and folded and folded.

Rorx turned and hugged her. "Oh, Mother. None of the tales mentioned them or how colorful they are."

"Thank you. They are only used in private, that's why."

"Mother?"

"Yes."

"Does Smoke really eat people?"

"Nope." Fair Morn winked. "But, I think that she bites him once in awhile. Just for fun."

Smoke followed him through the tub room. "Now Our male kitten thinks that I devour people."

"Oh well. He'll learn."

She jerked him to a halt. And bit him. On the shoulder. Gently.

"What are you doing?"

"Practicing."

He sighed. "This isn't going to be some new thing you guys get into, is it?"

"Turn about is fair play."

He started for the door to their chamber. "One carnivore is more than enough." And headed up to Ran's room.

"Did you see them?"

Rorx sat on the arm of her chair.

"I did." Imdar smiled at him, enjoying his excitement. "I am beginning to understand how very different they really are."

Then she spoke very softly so just he could hear. "Between us, I think that Big Red is very much involved in their being. This makes them very special, very powerful, more than they know. And it makes you special also. And I think I now know why we have that strange creature out there." She indicated the barn.

Rorx frowned at her. "Why are there tears in your eyes?"

"Because my only son, my only ever son, I am happy. And proud."

"Mother?"

"Yes?"

"It makes you special, also, doesn't it?"

She wrapped her arms around him. And held him.

"Knock, knock."

He leaned through the open door. "Anyone home?"

"Yes." Ran sat on the bed, back propped against the head board. It was a thick cedar headboard that she had spent months carving into an ornate design of swirls and blending images.

"May I come in?"

She nodded.

He sat, and slipped an arm around her. "What's the problem?"

She told him

Far Corner. A Rather Nice Day.

Turintor stepped sideways, the air shimmering in wild patterns around her. "Sorcerers?"

Her companions just stared.

He nodded.

"Here?"

"Newly arrived. Some or sort."

She handed him the sack and took the offered scroll and sent it elsewhere. "Newly arrived?"

He nodded. And pointed. "Up at the many tower."

"Hum," mumbled Rbat.

The trio turned and headed for the door. They had come here after an extended wander, resting here and there, spell searching, and, in general, doing the normal things witches did when they were on a wander. Or when they were resting.

They weren't sure that they had been told the truth. Sorcerers were thought to be child tell tales. But, maybe it ought to be looked into, just a small bit of curiosity.

After some discussion as they walked along, they decided that it was probably some strange witches doing strange witch things with the local population.

They stood, a very discrete distance from the main entry of the structure and watched. The trio were wrapped in deep shadow. Now and then someone left from there or returned from somewhere, walking. Apparently unconcerned, apparently secure in themselves.

All these folk wore the same dark almost black attire: baggy pants, loose smocks hanging free.

Motaiss cleared his throat. "There is a miztak feel to those."

"True?"

"Witch true."

A woman walked from the entry door and strolled down the gentle slope into town.

The trio drifted silent soft shadow after her. They followed her around town and into a bustling bazaar and watched her sit at small table near a food booth and order something to eat. The three split into three directions and approached that table and sat, all with one motion.

The woman's eyes jerked from face to face. "Witches?"

"Yessss," hissed Rbat.

Turintor stared at her. "You are a sorcerous?"

"Who asks such a thing?"

"Potri witch Turintor."

"Faan witch Rbat."

"Talair warlock Motaiss."

Turintor waved over a server and ordered for all.

The woman picked up her cup and sipped. "I am Abadoda, Three Rank Anaza sorcerous. What seek three black hearts here?"

Turintor looked at her companions. Rbat looked at Abadoda. "New met. Never met. Sorcerers are said to be myth hidden creatures."

"Azba," hissed Abadoda. These three must be part of The Great Change foreseen and prepared for.

Rbat tapped the table top with a long black wand. It crackled softly. "We have heard that sorcerer stands shadow form to witch."

Abadoda frowned at her.

Turintor held her hand over the table top, casting a shadow over Abadoda's hand. "Shadow form."

"No sense," growled the sorcerous, casting swift.

Turintor grunted. Motaiss spun from his chair, looped an arm around and under Abadoda's neck, the snarling green wand tip depressing the material of her smock.

"No harm!" snapped Rbat.

"No harm," gasped the startled sorcerous.

"True?"

"Sorcerous true."

Motaiss released her as Turintor grumbled, "This one needs small teach."

"No," said Rbat.

Motaiss waved in a large jug, filled all their cups, and set his wand on the table top and sipped, eyes watching carefully.

Abadoda stared at them.

"No harm," repeated Rbat, casting vile.

Abadoda jerked, stared at her smock front, then at her. Rbat nodded. "No harm."

Turintor sipped and looked across the table. "It was told by an Under Parq on Three Down Over that long before before there did begin this tale of origin." She began to narrate.

The witch clan Fanikta, now extinct, now long vanished long ago into the forever gone, gathered all in one spot to cast a great spell that they had worked long over. This spell would forever protect the Fanikta from all witch magic. To cast this thing they did gather all in an empty spot. For many days and for many nights, the spell worked and grew, the air shimmered, the spot shivered, until, finally, the spell was released.

The spell glare etched their shadows in the very stone they had gathered upon and sucked that clan away, ending the Fanikta.

Long after after, a wandering thing crackling weird found this very spot, the shadow marks, and a ring that flashed dark. Taking the artifact, it tried to leave. The ring ate it. And exploded, spraying cross-tied weird Fanikta magic over all.

And the shadows stood and looked around.

And became real.

"As you. As us," stated Turintor.

"Puska!" stated Abadoda, filling her cup and looking at her with a lopsided frown. "Small tale for the young and untrained."

"First clan of sorcerer folk met," said Rbat. "Shadow witch."

"Phylota," hissed the sorcerous. "Not clan." She held

her hand over the table and peered at the shadow she cast. Then she grabbed Rbat's hand. And stared down. "Nothing happened."

"Most brave," observed Rbat. She knew that direct contact between unlike magic users often resulted in destruction for both. There were ways around this problem. But these required great effort. And there were cultural taboos against it. Most of the time.

Turintor reached out and ran a gentle fingertip over Abadoda's hand. "Safe touch, shadow witch."

Abadoda jerked her hand away. "Sorcerous," she whispered. She lurched to her feet. "I must speak all this with Netanada."

"Who?"

"The Elixa of the Anaza."

"What?"

"Witches call clan head." Abadoda spun and wobbled away through the throngs in the bazaar.

"Safe safe," suggested Turintor.

"All true?" Motaiss looked at her.

"Yesssssssss."

"And?"

"Never before met."

Rbat nodded, and smiled.

"What?" gasped Turintor.

Picking up her wand, Rbat waggled it, and held the tip close to her face. "Magic isn't always needed to kill a thing. Shadow or other."

"Um ah."

"Hum hum."

The trio stood and returned to their lodgings to discuss things.

Grandeville. Tinker's Place.

There were a number of bales of hay in the barn. The Slarsia, after inspecting them, ate half of one of them. It decided that this dead plant material was rather dull stuff and tasted bland, but that the strange colored cording wrapped around it added an interesting taste touch.

It waited patiently. The Selected One had said to do that. But it knew. Soon they would travel. Then the boy Rorx would become the man Rorx. The Elders had assigned the Slarsia name called D'tarr. And D'tarr had spent many years training. Not all warlocks were so assigned. Only those with Special Purpose.

They lay side by side, stretched out on the bed. He held her gently. Her arms were folded between them.

"So, you are worried, right?"

"Yes, Amtar, I am. I am worried that your son Rorx, our son Rorx, will not return."

"Sa'ar promised frequent visits."

Her voice was barely audible. "I meant that he might die. Many that go, do not return."

"He is pretty well armed. The Vander have been training him. And he has that wand. It must be the magical equivalent of an atomic cannon. And Fair Morn gave him Macabre's device. If he calls Macabre, nothing will survive, except Rorx and his pet thingee. I'd say he is about as safe as one kid can get."

"Perhaps." Her arms slipped from between them. "Hold me, Amtar."

He did. And kissed her on the tip of her nose. "Now that I have you in my clutches? Here? On the bed? What do you want to do?"

"Hum, hum, hum."

He kissed her again. "You witches are all alike." And tugged her shirt loose.

"Where is Father?" Rorx stood and looked around the rear deck.

"Busy, busy, busy," sang Messenger.

"Kitten," cautioned Smoke stepping through the side door.

Messenger ducked her head. "I didn't say anything. Much."

Smoke stood next to Rorx and looked down, great orange gold eyes seeming to grow larger and larger. "So, you think that I eat people."

Rorx looked up. "Father said that you would show me."

"I know." Smoke beckoned Messenger over. "Kitten, stand next to him. We can't have magical stuff flying all over if he gets excited."

Messenger did, slipping an arm around Rorx's shoulders.

And the Velvetmist peered down at him. The great saber canines gleamed white in the sun. Her jet fur absorbed the light, reflecting little. To the top of her shoulders, she was twice as tall as he was. Her paws were as wide as his chest. The tall rabbit ears swiveled in his direction as she watched him down the length of her dog-like snout. The long tail swayed to its own rhythm.

Messenger grabbed his hand as he whipped the wand from his sleeve. "Stop. It is only Smoke."

Then Smoke stood in front of him, smiling. "That was before Big Red changed my form." She rolled her eyes. "And we did not eat people." And laughed. "There weren't any in my elseplace. We are the people, the sapient species." She stroked her hair back from her forehead.

And Rorx realized that it was as thick and as dark and as light absorbing as her fur had been. He slipped the wand back into his sleeve, looking sheepish.

"LUNCH TIME." Fair Morn carried a large tray of sandwiches to a table. She winked at Rorx. "I got hungry."

"Coffee and cocoa," stated R-Bar, setting down her tray.

Chicken slid a tray of cups on the table top. "They will eat later."

"Who?" asked Rorx.

"Our Prince, thy Sire, and Fair Ran."

He frowned.

Chicken laughed and handed him a cup.

R-Bar rapped a knuckle on the table top. "Come and eat."

He did.

They all did.

And then.

The days slipped past.

And they stood in the back pasture, saying goodbye to Rorx and the Slarsia.

Ran leaned close to Tinker and said, "It looks very capable."

"Think so?"

"Yes." She hooked her arm under his. "It is strange to loose a son we have only had for a few many days."

He nodded. "At least I met this one before he was full grown. You witches and magicians have a peculiar way to raise children."

She tightened her grip. "We turn out well, do we not?"

He shrugged. "Don't know about that. Only have close relations with a couple, mmm, three. Pretty bad, ahh, small sample."

"Sample?" She kicked him in the ankle.

"What's that for?"

She glowered at him. "Your Ran does not think that you should think about witch or magician sampling."

"Not what I meant," he grumbled, and threw his free around Rorx who had walked over to say his goodbyes.

"Gonna miss you," said Tinker. "Son."

"I will visit. Soon." Rorx wiped at his eyes with one hand. "Father." Then he hurried to each of the others. And was hugged and kissed. And he promised each one that he would be careful, very, very careful.

And then.
He stood next to the Slarsia.
And they were gone.

R-Bar stomped over. "Tink . . . you are not dragging any more witches to bed. Or magicians either." She grabbed his hand.

He sighed.

Imdar leaned against his back, hugged him, and kissed the back of his neck. "That is correct, Father of my Son. Sa'ar and I are leaving now. Also." She let go.

Sa'ar bounced over. "Bye, Vander Lord." And kissed him. And whispered, "One of these days." And laughed, hurrying over to where Imdar was standing a proper distance away from everyone. Sa'ar waved goodbye.

"Hold it." Tinker freed his hand, walked over to Imdar and wrapped her in his arms. "My, my, my, quite an armful. Stay in touch." He looked sideways. "Goes for you too." He kissed Imdar. "When he returns, come and visit, ya'hear?"

Imdar smiled. "Yes, Vander Lord. To hear is to obey."

"Fat chance of that," he grumbled.

And stepped away.

Imdar nodded.

And they were gone.

In a soft puff of violet.

Smoke rubbed against his back, wrapping her arms around his waist. And murmured, "Well, Great Lord Lech, wanna take a nip? Here and there?"

He sighed. "Now what?"

She laughed.

Chapter Five

Nothing But Surprises.

Grandeville. Tinker's Place. A Fairly Pleasant and Warm Day.

"Hi, Dad."

Dad was sitting slumped in a chair, a pile of papers stacked next to his right side, on the rear deck. There was another stack in his lap. A cup of coffee also sat on the deck next to his left side. His feet were propped up on a bench pulled over from one of the tables.

It was warm.

It was almost noon.

It was late July.

They, as Tinker often referred to the rest of himself, were mostly in Grandeville, at the local college, taking more course work, Summer Session, in various subjects. Except Chantal. She was, as always, working at her Veterinarian Clinic, with her partner, added to her practice not all that long ago.

He looked sideways as his daughter came clumping down the deck toward him. Farth followed. He didn't clump.

"New boots?"

"Yep. Got them on Imp." She picked up and handed him his cup, dragged a chair over and sat, propping her feet next to his. Her boots were a dark green color, soft burnished dark green shine. His feet were white, sorta pink, sorta brown. They were bare.

"Ummm, Dad?"

Tinker carefully set everything, except his cup on the deck, on the side away from her. "Back less than thirty seconds and I am already worried."

Sedeem stuck her tongue out at him. "Poop."

"Tsk, tsk. Sound just like the Princess." He watched her with no small amount of suspicion. Farth went inside the house. "What?"

"When we were on Imp," she started.

"Yes?" he interrupted.

"I met this young man."

"You're married," he grumbled.

"DAD! . . . ummmmmmm?"

"What?" He nodded, just to show that he had been joking.

"DAD . . . ummmmmm?"

"What?"

She took his hand, her thumb brushing back and forth over its back. And looked at him. A steady, firm stare.

"What?" He frowned at her. Now he was really worried.

"He said that his Mother was Vander." She watched his face.

Tinker sat up, feet banging on the deck. "Young man? How young a man?"

"Ohhhhh, eighteen, twenty, around there." She grinned. "Good looking. Sort of."

"Damn those Vander," he growled.

She jerked her hand away. "Dad?"

Tinker blinked. And reached over and gently covered her hands with his. "Did he have some sort of strange lizard looking thing with him?"

Sedeem gasped. "Do you know this person?"

"Yep. He is your brother."

She stared at him. "Brother? I have a brother? True?"

"Yep. Rorx. He come with you?" Tinker looked around.

"No. . . No . . . He said that he was going to visit Xarp."

He sighed. "Figures. So, tell me about him. He look healthy? Things like that."

She nodded. "Very healthy. Strong. Powerful. And we got along. Right away." Her eyes carefully scanned his face. "Now I can see the resemblance."

Tinker nodded.

Sedeem winked. "He was alone. Other than having that beast with him."

"Huh?"

"Not . . . married, . . . Dad."

"Good. Too young."

"Daaaaaad?"

He frowned. "What?"

"Wanna tell me? About Rorx? My brother?" She grabbed his hands. "You branching out? What do my Moms think about you doing that? Who is the mother? Did you get Sa'ar? Did Sa'ar finally get to you? She really wanted to, you know."

"HALT." He wrestled his hands free and stood. "How about I get a cup of coffee first?" He chucked his cold stuff into the flower beds.

She walked with him as he headed for the kitchen, snaking an arm around his waist. "Hum hum hum."

"Don't get nasty, Daughter."

"Not me having children by any handy magician I can get my hands on, any Vander babe." She laughed as he glowered.

In the kitchen, he glared at the clock. "Fast story. They're due back soon. Let's sit in the living room. It's not much of a story."

So they did.
　　　　With Farth.
　　　　　　And he told them.

"We do returned be," announced Chicken,　quoting her version of Arnold, as they poured into the living room, and as she flopped next to Tinker on the couch.

"Oh?" he said.

"Hi, Moms."

"Sweet Daughter, Greetings."

"I'll make lunch." Messenger headed back toward the kitchen. Fair Morn went along.

"She met Rorx," said Tinker. "He is eighteen, or twenty, more or less."

The air crackled loudly. "May we come in?"

"Of course," said R-Bar, recognizing Szaifeh's voice.

They appeared.

"Look what I found on Sandern," announced Szaifeh, eyes sparkling. "Isn't he gorgeous?"

"RORX," snapped Tinker.

"OUR PRINCE," stated Chicken.

"Oh . . . oh," murmured Szaifeh, looking from face to face. "This is that Rorx, Uncle?"

"Hello Father, Mothers," said a subdued Rorx. "Szaifeh said that she had a surprise."

Szaifeh fell into a chair and stared at them, at Tinker. "Uncle?"

"Ummm," replied Tinker.

Sedeem stood, walked over and kissed Rorx on the forehead. "Hi. I am your sister."

Rorx twitched. "Sister?" He looked from a dazed looking Szaifeh to a dazed looking Tinker.

"Uncle."

Tinker stared at Szaifeh.

"I found him," she said, staring back. "Unmated."

Smoke nudged Rorx. "You had better sit down, you feel wobbly."

Rorx sat. In the chair that was shoved into the back of his knees. He looked at Chicken. "We were just traveling together. Sort of."

"Mine," gurgled Szaifeh.

"Oh, no." Tinker sank deeper. And lower. Sliding down. "No. No, no, no, no, no, no."

"Rah-ther complicated, that," observed Chicken.

"Understatement of the year," grumbled Tinker as Sedeem dropped back onto the couch, on her Father's free side.

Ran leaned on the back of the couch and breathed on top of Tinker's head. "He is Vander tied."

"Weellll," sighed Tinker, shoving his legs straight out, settling about as low as he could get. "Life does get complicated in a hurry around here, at times. Ummm, let's try it this way. R-Bar can explain Rorx and the, errrrrr, Vander problem to Szaifeh. The Princess can talk to our son. And I will get a cup of coffee." He lurched to his feet, beckoning to Sedeem. "Everyone else may worry about making lunch."

"So, what do you think?" He leaned on the table, one of the several on the rear deck, and stared across the soft grey wood at his daughter.

"Szaifeh is a lot like her mother."

"Uh huh."

"And a lot like her father."

"So?"

"So," said Sedeem, clinking her cup against his. "I think that she is strong-willed, determined, and clever enough to find a satisfactory solution. For all concerned."

"Perhaps. But witches are very narrow-minded about their mates. And Rorx has, emmm, duties he must perform, ahhh, do, to see to the survival of the Vander. And they are magicians. And he can't escape that. Neither can she."

She grinned at him. "That doesn't seem all that much different than my parents."

"CERTAINLY IS!"

"Coffee? Cookies?" Messenger hustled up to them, carrying a tray. "What is?" Sliding it onto the table.

"What?" he asked, taking a cookie.

"Certainly."

Tinker stared at her. "Kitten, what are you talking about."

"Certainly is," she replied, refilling his cup, and starting to eat a cookie.

"Sit down," he growled.

"Join us, Mom. Please?" Sedeem slid the tray down the table. "What do you think?"

"They're pretty good," said Messenger, refilling Sedeem's cup, and sitting next to her, waggling the remains of her cookie.

Tinker sighed.

"About Rorx and Szai," said Sedeem.

"Oh." Messenger giggled. "I think that they're pretty good, too."

"Mom?"

Messenger smiled at her daughter and poked her arm with an elbow. "She is Sa'ar's cousin also. They ought to be able to work it out." She looked at Tinker. "Does it run in your male line?"

"Don't start," he warned.

"Mom?"

Messenger whispered to her. "Harems. Seraglio."

"Hum," said Sedeem. "Must be a male thing. I am quite content to have just Farth."

"Knock it off," hissed Tinker.

"Exactly," agreed Messenger, nodding at him. Sedeem burst into peals of laughter.

Chantal walked down the deck and joined them, slipping onto the bench next to Tinker.

She was wearing grey coveralls. "Came home early." And took a cookie. And his cup.

"Smell like a barn yard," grumbled Tinker.

"Hi, Mom."

"Deem," mumbled Chantal around a mouthful of cookie.

"Rorx is going to marry Szaifeh and take care of the Vander too," said Messenger.

"WHAT?" gasped Chantal, choking and coughing.

"Drink some of my coffee," suggested Tinker. "And don't talk with your mouth full."

"I think," said Sedeem. "That it is some sort of a male thing."

"What?" asked Chantal after clearing her throat and drinking some of his coffee.

Tinker hissed.

"Shhhhhhhh," said Chantal.

"Rounding up a covey," said Sedeem.

Messenger nodded sagely. "Like father, like son."

"Merde," observed Tinker.

"Right, Cowboy," agreed Chantal. "Got it on my boots and coveralls. Why I smell like a barn yard."

Tinker grabbed his cup back. And took another cookie. And thought, to himself, that this conversation wasn't making a whole lot of sense. Not to him, it didn't.

"So, young witch, you have a problem. He is bound to the Vander. Their very survival is at stake."

They sat facing each other, knee touching knee.

R-Bar took Szaifeh's hands in her's as they leaned toward each other.

Szaifeh bobbed her head. Once. "Aunt? You seem to not mind."

"It is different. We are One. And together. You are separate beings, entities. The Vander are out in the elsewheres. We are not."

R-Bar shook her head, stopping Szaifeh's comments from starting. "Your's is a warlock of some power." She smiled. "Mine is just a man from an isolated backward elseplace."

"Sa'ar will understand."

"Probably," replied R-Bar. "But will she agree? Do you agree?"

Szaifeh stared into her Aunt's eyes, and pulled her hands free. "I will speak with her." And disappeared in a sharp swirl of black.

On the front porch, sitting side by side, Rorx jerked and banged his shoulder against Chicken's.

"OUCH."

A dark ring had appeared on the index finger of his right hand.

"Sorry Mother." He held up his hand. "It was hot."

"Passing strange."

"Szaifeh put it there."

"Sweet Our Prince, do thee most sure pon this matter be?"

Furrowing his brows, looking at her from the corners of his eyes, Rorx sighed. "It is what she wants."

"Yes."

"She is attractive."

"Most pleasing a'morsel."

"Very pleasant."

"Indeed."

"For a witch."

"She did learn much."

"She told me about that."

Chicken patted his thigh. "This Prince has duties and obligations."

His head slowly turned. "I know. It is almost time. I feel the call. Soon the rituals will start."

"And thou art the survival of their race. My Lord, and we, did fight for this survival." Yanking her sleeve high, she pointed at the jagged white lines. "All who were there do now wear such marks pon fair bodies. All."

He turned and hugged her. "I know. Mother told me, over and over and over."

"Imdar do teach thee well?"

"Yes." He tightened his arms around her. "But you, and them, are my mothers as well."

"Then, Our Son, listen thee to this one, to this thy also mother. Witch lust must wait."

"She is very determined."

A slow smile crept across Chicken's face. "We do believe Us, We do, that R-Bar and her most strong sister, mother of thy most eager package, will see a'that. Thy witch mother, R-Bar, and thy witch mother-in-law, Reep, both fiercely powerful, have no equals. Sweet Niece will see the wisdom of patience."' She kissed his cheek. "Add then . . . "

"Then?"

She smiled. "Why, then, thee may drag her into thy fair bed and . . . "

"PRINCESS . . . MOTHER!" His arms dropped as he jerked back.

"My Prince?" She pushed her smile away.

"I . . . I do not think that is proper."

"Ripping fair raiment asunder from Thy Bride-To-Be?"

"She has a bawdy streak." Smoke tostled his hair and sat down next to Chicken. "Don't pay attention to her." One elbow nudged Chicken in the side. "Rorx is rather like his father, that way."

Chicken nodded. "This Prince do have other traits as well, me'thinks."

Rorx stared at Chicken who suddenly squeaked. Smoke had pinched her.

"Most unkind," snapped Chicken.

Smoke did it again. Chicken jerked. "Szaifeh said that she would speak to Sa'ar," said Smoke to Rorx.

"What?"

"Most Father like," observed Chicken, slapping at Smoke's hand.

"She left," continued Smoke. "To visit Sa'ar to work out various details."

"Heh, heh," said Chicken, winking slowly at Rorx, who leaped to his feet.

"I think that I had better speak with Father."

"On the rear deck," said Smoke. "With your Sister."

"Better get used to it," said Tinker, as Rorx hurtled from the side door and plopped onto the bench across the table from him.

"Face is flushed," said Sedeem.

"Chicken got out of line," said Tinker. "S'what happens when you have more than one to, mmm, account for."

Sedeem grinned. "There are ten Vander now, I think." She turned to her half-brother. "Hum hum hum."

Rorx jerked. And hissed at her. "That is coarse, Sister, very, very coarse."

She frowned him. "You had better pace yourself, Brother . . . or you will never be able to get Szaifeh."

"COOL IT!" snapped Tinker. "Chicken gave him enough of that kind of conversation." He looked toward the far end of the deck. "Company's coming." He had heard a vehicle park, doors slamming.

J. C. and Reep strolled around the corner and onto the deck.

"Aunt!" gasped Sedeem. Rorx stared, mouth open. His face flushed, flushed even brighter. Reep was wearing a pair of shorts and a pair of very large sunglasses. And, as she came closer, and as it became apparent to all the staring faces, a flesh-colored t-shirt, a very pale flesh-colored t-shirt.

"R-Bar told Szaifeh was here," sighed the feather soft voice. "I came."

"Interesting garment," said Tinker.

J. C. dropped onto the bench next to him. "Her idea. Does startle ya, doesn't it?"

"Yep."

Tinker nodded at Rorx. "These are Szaifeh's parents. Reep and J. C." He nudged J. C. "Your daughter has the hots for Rorx. My son."

"Son?"

Reep stared at Rorx.

Tinker nodded. "I'll explain in a bit." He stared at Reep. "Problem?"

"Hum hum," breathed the summer air. "Hum."

Sedeem clamped her hand over her mouth, eyes crinkling at the corners. Rorx looked uncomfortable.

Reep settled next to J. C., pushed at him, and settled under his arm as he swung it around her. "A powerful warlock. Vander?"

Rorx nodded.

"Magician and witch," breathed the air. "Strange. Unusual. Not often done." Reep propped her sunglasses on top of her head. J. C. tickled her ear with a finger. And laughed.

Tinker smiled. "There are ten Vander, all females. His mother's, ummm, guild sisters."

"Holy Cow," said J. C.

"You don't know the half of it."

R-Bar joined them. "We need to talk," she said to Reep.

J. C. quickly yanked his arm away as Reep stood, and drifted to the end of the deck with her sister. "What are they up to?"

"Beats me," said Tinker. "But I am sure that we will find out, sooner or later."

Szaifeh and Sa'ar appeared. Szaifeh walked over, touched Rorx on the shoulder. "Mine." And ran down the deck. "Mother!"

Sa'ar sat next to Tinker and pressed against his side. "Hello, Vander Lord." She leaned and peered around him at J. C. "Hi, Uncle."

"Sa'ar," mumbled Tinker.

"Hi, Gorgeous Babe," said J. C., winking broadly and

lewdly at her. "My, my, my, my."

She pinched Tinker. "See."

He sighed.

"Good thing that I am married," said J. C. "And that you are a niece."

Sa'ar leaned further and stared at J. C. "What does that have to do with anything?"

"Well, Me Fine Beauty," drawled J. C., rolling his eyes dramatically, and smacking his lips. "Reep, my one and only wife, would kill me, us. But single, or married, one does just not mess around with their nieces, no matter how gorgeous or willing they might he."

"Q.E.D." stated Tinker.

"I . . . I . . . I disown you both."

"I'm crushed," said Tinker.

J.C. nodded. "Me too." And looked properly sorrowful.

Sa'ar hissed at them.

"Rah-ther snaky, My Dear," drawled J. C., being very British, looking solemn and wise down his nose. "Won't do, ya know, hissing about the place. Frightfully startling, having young ladies popping off like steam radiators."

Sa'ar looked at Tinker.

"Don't ask me," he said. "He's your uncle." He slipped an arm around her shoulders. "Besides, we did agree on Vander debts, didn't we?"

Sa'ar pouted. And smiled. "Yes. But."

"Behave. For a little while? Please?"

She kissed his check. "Sure." And slipped her arm around his waist. "Umm?"

"Yes?"

She looked from Tinker to Rorx. "Szaifeh and I agreed."

Rorx stared back. "To what?"

Sa'ar stared harder. "Vander warlock Rorx, as long as you perform the annual re-creation ritual, the Vander will not interfere. If you want my cousin, take her. But if we send a call, you must come, no matter what." She held out her free hand, palm facing him. "You must come whenever called. No exceptions! The Vander will survive. Do you agree?"

Rorx slowly nodded. "Of course. I understand the survival needs."

"Good. Szaifeh understands as well."

"Let's have a big blow out," said J. C. "I like big weddings. Even if I didn't get to have one for myself."

Chapter Six.

Some Wedding.

Grandeville. Tinker's Place. A Nice Day.

It was a big blowout.

It was a large wedding.

With lots of guests.

With lots of food.

With lots of drink.

All the Vander guild came. Dressed in flowing silk-clinging lavender garments.

All the Faan sisters came. Dressed in variations of black Faan witch garb, jet black figures.

Ripple, Hanred and their daughter, Shitar, arrived early.

J. C. and Reep, and Szaifeh were already there. As were Hard and Ramp, Sa'ar's parents. And Shem, her twin brother. With his wife, Tajaar.

Ripple, Reep, Ramp, and R-Bar greeted each of their sisters as they arrived. The two magical groups eyed each other. Magicians and witches each giving the other ample space, other than those that had traveled together before.

Sa'ar, being Ramp's daughter, was also Faan. R-Bar mingled and greeted warmly the Vander she had met before.

And this core group of the Vander, one by one, walked over and greeted Tinker, standing close, brushing against him, murmuring softly to him, grinning wicked grins. And then they spoke to Rorx using formal gestures, nodding to Imdar who stood proudly by his side.

Each Faan Aunt approached Szaifeh, offering some small gift, casting sideways glances at her choice. And discussing this binding of Faan witches with Vander magicians, and what this meant for the clan future.

Tinker's group bobbled around meeting and greeting all those they had met before in the many elseplaces they had visited.

Shem stood and talked with Rorx, warlock to warlock. Tajaar stayed close to Shem's side and kept a watchful eye on the Vander.

The three cousins, Sa'ar, Shitar, and Szaifeh, split away and formed a small group of their own and told each other all the things that had happened since last they had been together.

Sedeem joined them, sending Farth to help Fair Morn and Messenger organize the food and drink while she talked with her cousins, Some of Ran's sisters arrived, causing no small stir among everyone. Her clan was known by name and reputation. The Faan eyed them cautiously, even though they were also linked with the Tanpak clan.

Ran brought them over to Tinker. And made introductions. "My sisters, Windfer, the eldest, Ardan, and Reslar, the youngest. This is mine, the Great Lord Tinker, called Chosen One, called Vander Lord, called Amtar, called John. Ergle, he prefers being addressed as Tinker, his clan name."

Tinker nodded. "I remember Windfer and Ardan. From before, at Red and Sandy's wedding."

Ran pointed here and there. "Each of those are his. The short Faan also, called R-Bar. She and I bound us." She pointed at Ripple. "My sister Windfer, the tall haughty one is

Faan Clan Head Ripple. And that one is Sa'ar, Amtar's Niece, Vander Heart."

Ran moved close and dragged Tinker's arm around her waist. "The Vander warlock Rorx, his son, is binding to that Faan witch Szaifeh, his niece also."

The sisters stepped close and closer. Reslar eyed Tinker, eyes squinting, head tilted to one side. "Are you responsible for our Ranfer sister's damage?"

"No," snapped Ran. "He is not. We will speak later. And I am called Ran now."

"Umle."

Windfer headed toward Ripple. Ardan walked away to inspect the food being set on the tables by Farth and the rest.

Reslar ran her hand over Tinker's chest and smiled at Ran. "Ooom?"

Ran hissed and kicked her in the ankle. "INT AK DUR PRAK."

Reslar pouted. "Unkind."

"Ahh?" asked Tinker.

"Never mind," said Ran.

"I would not hurt your's," said Resler.

R-Bar slipped up to his side and growled.

"Now what's going on?" He curled his free arm around R-Bar's neck. "Huh?"

"This young witch wants to drag you into bed."

"Never," snarled Ran.

"Really?" said Tinker.

Reslar plucked at a button on his shirt. The air crackled softly. She hastily yanked her hand away.

"Umm," said Tinker. "I appreciate the thought, but, ummmm, it is not done, eerrrr, not my clan custom. Thought that you might have heard that."

"I was not here met before." Reslar kissed him. "But I may do this, Ran mate?"

"Not very often," snapped R-Bar.

"Let us talk." Ran towed her sister out onto the lawn.

"Im dur pok pok," gurgled R-Bar deep in her throat.

"Relax kiddo. I'm safe."

R-Bar looked up, and grinned. "From them, Tink, from them."

"Think that I'll go talk with Hard and the others, drink something." He did.

R-Bar headed over to talk with Chantal.

J. C. handed him a cool can. Hanred nodded at him. Hard smiled.

"I'd say that we are outnumbered, pard," said J. C. He grinned at Tinker. "Sorta reminds me of my long ago Southern California days."

"Oh?"

"Yep. Babes everywhere. Sorority picnic."

Hard turned to look, hooked one foot on something, and lurched sideways. "Pity the frat rat that would make that error in judgement."

Hanred carefully watched Hard. "It is an amazing sight. That many witches and magicians milling around. Peacefully."

"Reminds me of the Foregather," said Tinker.

"Maybe I ought to go to one," said Hanred. "I'll have to talk Ripple into it. Let her suggest that we go. Rorx your son?"

Tinker nodded. He beckoned a passing Vander over. "Imdar, this is Hanred. Hanred, Rorx's mother."

She stared, eyes going rounder and rounder. "You are Hanred, The Old Hanred, Illusionist?"

Hanred smiled. "Yes. You have heard of me?"

"Many times. Many elseplaces speak of Old Hanred. Ripple's?"

"All mine. Every black-hearted part." He indicated the four cousins standing and talking and laughing. "Our daughter, Shitar, the one in the baggy pants."

"Very pretty."

Hanred nodded. "Takes after her mother." They watched as Reep led her daughter from the small group out into an open space.

R-Bar stood there already with Rorx.

Then Ripple, Sa'ar, and Windfer walked over to them, joining hands, forming a tight circle around the pair as R-Bar and Reep hurried away.

"What are they doing?" Hard bumped Hanred.

"Fair Youth, I have no idea. I have never seen this behavior before."

Inside the circle, Szaifeh turned and faced Rorx as he wrapped his arms around her.

Bright white flashed into bottomless black.

My Lord?

I don't know, Princess.

The three jumped back as the black faded back into day. Crackling orange poured from the pair, puddled around their feet, and seeped into the smoldering grass.

Tinker felt them all tingle as adrenaline surged. Chantal snatched up the only knife on the table.

Easy, easy, cautioned Tinker. *No one seems disturbed.*

Chantal turned and sliced a sandwich from corner to corner and began to eat half.

"The pair are cross bound," breathed the sunlight. Reep nudged J. C.'s side and waited until he had his arm draped around her. "They are unharmed."

Tinker slowly let out his breath. And felt the rest relax.

Rorx and Szaifeh walked toward Tinker. Her eyes sparkled, an arm tightly wrapped around his waist.

Rorx smiled.

"Father?" began Rorx.

"We would like to stay here, Uncle," continued Szaifeh.

"For awhile," finished Rorx.

Szaifeh looked from Tinker to J. C. and Reep. "May we?"

J. C. laughed. "If he can put up with you."

Tinker leaned forward and gently touched a tiny round spot on his son's left cheek bone. It was a dull orange color.

"Me too, Unc," said Szaifeh. Her mark was on the right side. "May we? Stay?"

Tinker nodded. "Sure."

"The private bedroom in the office building?"

"Oh ho," said J. C. "Ouch!" Reep had pinched him.

"Sure," said Tinker.

Imdar kissed his cheek as she rejoined the small group.

"What's that for?" asked Tinker.

"I have a Right, Father of my son."

He touched her check. "You too?"

R-Bar nudged him. "Everyone, Tink."

"Me too?"

"No. Clan members," said Ramp, slipping her arms around Hard as she leaned against his back There was a small orange dot on her face. "The several clans are linked and relinked. The indot appears in the presence of a member of the linked clan."

"Witch work," explained Imdar, snaking an arm around Tinker's waist and patting his hip.

"Hum," grumbled R-Bar.

"He has a Right, a Claim," stated Imdar firmly.

Szaifeh giggled.

Rorx looked uncomfortable.

Ramp looked carefully blank. "Beauty and I are leaving." She was leaning heavily against his back, arms wrapped tightly around him.

"We are?" Hard settled his hands over his wife's hands kneading his stomach.

"Yes." They disappeared.

Reep was slowly pulling J. C.'s shirt loose.

"Ahhhh heeee hooooo," he said. "Looks like it is time for us to go. Congratulations." J. C. shook Rorx's hand. And kissed Szaifeh. "Lose a daughter, gain a son." Reep nodded at the couple. She and J. C. disappeared.

"Im tark," murmured R-Bar, startling everyone except Tinker, who merely nodded.

"Now what, Short Stuff?"

R-Bar frowned. "Her claim is first."

"What claim? Who?"

"Unc?" Szaifeh tapped his arm. "See you later, O.K.?" She led Rorx to the end of the deck and around the end of the house, toward the office building.

"Imdar," stated R-Bar.

Tinker swivelled his head. Imdar kissed him. R-Bar bit his hand, more or less gently.

"OWWWWW." He stepped back, dragging his arms loose. "All right. One of you is going to explain what's going on, now." And stepped a little further away. "Well?"

"The binding affected the mates," explained R-Bar. "And I am not short. Or stuff."

"The mated ones. Of the clans. And guilds." Imdar smiled at him. And tugged her blouse loose.

R-Bar spun on her heels and stomped off, to speak

with Ripple, who was draped around Hanred.

Imdar stepped close and began to unbutton his shirt. "Your room," she purred. They disappeared.

Sedeem kissed Shitar. And grabbed one of Farth's arms.

"You also?" asked Shitar.

"Heh heh," replied her cousin.

They disappeared.

Then it just started.
They left.

They left.
One by one by one.
Witches and magicians.

Blink.
Blink.
Blink.
Blink.

Each in her own fashion.
They left.

Blink.

Ran's sisters stepped close, touched her cheek, and were gone.

Shitar, sitting in a chair on the deck, watched them leave. And was joined by R-Bar.

"Most restless Aunt."

"Dur zar m'pak," grumbled her Aunt.

Shitar nodded. "Wonderfully coarse. Who dares bother you so?"

"Tink's Vander Mage."

Shitar gasped. "Shar?"

"Of course not. Imdar."

Shitar grinned, a pure witch grin. "Fix her, Aunt." She plucked a long silver and black wand from somewhere. "May I? Help?" Black crackled up and down the length of the wand.

"No," hissed R-Bar. "We may not."

"Oh?" One corner of Shitar's mouth puckered. "Is this one so powerful?"

"Of course not."

"Then?"

"That Vander is the mother of our son, Rorx."

"Hum hum."

R-Bar frowned. "Behave yourself. And put that thing away."

The wand disappeared. "Aunt?"

"What?" A palm banged into her forehead. "OOOOOF. Oh. Ahhh, thank you, clever young witch."

"It will hold until first light next."

R-Bar grinned. "Long enough. Then he is mine."

"Did this happen when you took him?"

"No. This binding, this new special binding, this never before ever done before binding, is an arcane thing. I do not think anyone realized this would happen."

"Aunt?"

"Yes?"

"What did all the rest . . . of you . . . think . . . about her?"

R-Bar looked at Shitar. "Everyone agreed. It was necessary. The Vander guild would have died. Otherwise."

Shitar stared into R-Bar's eyes. Black into black. "And all agreed it was acceptable?"

"Yessssss. Say it!"

"Ummmmmmmm."

"Speak!"

Shitar leaned toward her. "Perhaps I could?"

"NO."

"I would not hurt him."

"He would not agree. A value of this elseplace."

"Erem."

"Do not grumble."

Shitar glowered, the air crackled around them. "I want mine. Shar has the Vander guild. Deem found that Silver Ranger Farth. Now Szai has his son."

R-Bar's mouth twisted. "Each finds their own. If they do. Some do not. Many of your Aunt's have not. Yet."

Shitar growled. Deep in her throat.

R-Bar laughed.

"Gur TAK," snarled Shitar.

R-Bar tried to look shocked.

It didn't work.

Chapter Seven

Things Keep Happening.

Grandeville. Tinker's Place. A Fairly Nice Day.

It was long after the binding together of Rorx and Szaifeh.

It was September.

Mild early morning.

Sunlight poured steep angled sharp light across the fields turning golden fall.

Black agony inched through hip deep grass slow moment after slow movement, rasping breath, crawling.

Toward the building not all that far away.

Smoke snapped upright, tossed bed covers in all directions, jumped from the bed, and ran.

"Whazzit?" Tinker rolled and lurched up, eyes popping wide as adrenaline banged everything awake. "DAMN." He charged out, down the hallway, toward the living room.

And felt them all waking, running, grabbing weapons, pouring outside.

Converging on the thing in their pasture.

They saw Smoke bend over. And lift something in her arms. *Still alive. No one else around.*

R-Bar hurtled up to her. "Far corner room, far corner room." She ran back toward the house.

Chicken banged open a hall closet snatching more blankets down while Chantal carried the first aid kit past.

Tinker, tightening the belt of his robe, met them in the room. And as soon as Smoke had set her burden down, handed her a robe. "Here. Who is it?" He stared at the body.

The woman had a heavy black cloth wrapped around her head, only her eyes showing and a bit of forehead. The hood was tight around her face. Everything she wore was torn and dirt covered and scorched. Heavy dense odor seeped from her clothes.

"Shitar," said Smoke.

"Magical conflagration," observed R-Bar as she began striking away spell fragments, neutralizing the gar strokes.

Chantal carefully cut away the hood and head wrapping to expose the pale skin dappled with gray blue welts pulsating with inner life.

"UGGGGG," gasped Messenger as she leaned around Chantal and stared.

"Never saw anything like this before." R-Bar plunged a wand into the bed next to Shitar's left ear.

Ran hissed sharply. "Ur-drak, under her shirt!"

Chantal jerked her hands away. "What?"

R-Bar threw down red green powder and began to rip open the mostly torn garment. The thing was coiled tightly around Shitar's chest, multitudes of sucker feet pulling draining life away.

Ran gurgled. "Thrice wound."

"KILL IT!" snapped Chicken, yanking a dagger from her boot. She was the only one that had fully dressed.

Fair Morn nodded, flicking a lever on her weapon.

"HOLD IT, hold it." Tinker nodded at R-Bar. "What do we do?"

"Dark gray, all twisted." Messenger poked at the

magical strands with her wand.

R-Bar looked up. "Dark gray?"

"With muddy brown."

R-Bar looked at Ran.

"No," said Ran.

R-Bar nodded and stabbed the thing with a thin silver wand.

Blue flame flashed bright. The windows blew out. Shitar screamed, heaved, spine arching, arms flying wide, knocking Ran one way, R-Bar the other.

Smoke leaped, crashing down over the thrashing heaving figure, her arms and legs wrapping around, pinning Shitar in place. Smoke's minds plunged inside twisting black shattered.

SHITAR . . . SHITAR . . .

Chicken fell to her knees, clamping her hands to her ears.

And in the quiet still of wreckage settling, a small voice asked, "Aunt?"

Smoke released her and rolled to the floor, wobbled up, and heaved Tinker to his feet.

Chantal twisted off the cap and poured disinfectant over Shitar's torso. "We will worry about the bedclothes later."

R-Bar fumbled with Shitar's belt and began to yank off the baggy trousers as Chicken tugged at her boots.

"Ummmm, I'll go make coffee." Tinker backed toward the door.

Ran went with him. "Amtar, she will heal. Now. Your R-Bar has cast a great protection."

He began to fill the several coffee makers. "Now what's going on?"

"Great evil."

"I'm not in the market for any."

Ran began to prepare breakfast, breaking a large number of eggs into a bowl. "That one, Your Niece, Faan witch Shitar must be very powerful."

"Probably," mumbled Tinker, starting to make toast. "Her mother, Ripple, is."

Ran began to wallop the eggs with a wooden spoon. "Some mage hates her."

"What are you doing? Why?"

"Your Smoke wanted eggs scrambled. The Ur-drak. Only great hate would put one of those on someone."

"Use this." He handed her a wire whisk. "Like this." He demonstrated.

"Ermle." She took it and attacked the eggs. Violently.

"Having a good time?"

"Egg . . . scrambling," she hissed.

Tinker nodded and started the bacon frying. "If you were a piece of bread we could have French Toast."

"Fair lecherous a'thought," said Chicken, leaning her chin on his shoulder, staring at the frying bacon, giving him a pinch.

"Everything from the bowl rim up is coated with egg," explained Tinker.

"Sweet Prince?"

"Yes?"

"Do take most agitated Ran a'showering. We will see to final preparation for this breakfast of our's."

He smiled, pinched her in return, turned, grabbed the bowl from Ran, and nodded. "Let's go, Sloppy. You heard the Boss."

And tugged her toward the shower room.

"We do be Thy Boss not," called Chicken at their backs, cracking and adding more eggs to the bowl.

"I will finish the toast and set the table." R-Bar nudged Chicken in passing. "I wrapped her in heal and cure. She is as rangle as her mother."

"Weird Sister Self?" Chicken shoved the bacon around on the large cast iron grill.

"Princess?"

"Ran do be most upset."

R-Bar started three toasters working. "Saw more than I did. She'll tell us after we eat, I suspect."

"Our Love do just now calm most agitated near-witch."

"Never heard it called that before." R-Bar stacked the toast on a large plate and walked into the dining room.

Chicken poured the eggs onto the grill. *Near time, one and all.*

"Hear that?"

They had rinsed her pajama top, dropped everything into the clothes hamper, taken a quick shower, and settled into the hot tub up to their necks. Ran nestled inside his arms.

"I did. Your Princess was quite clear."

"She can be. Well?"

"Amtar?

He kissed her forehead. "Is my Ran calmed down and ready tell me what is really going on?"

She nodded. "After the meal."

"See. I told you," called R-Bar from the dining room. "Table's set."

Time. Chicken called in all their minds.

They gathered and sat.

Ran and Tinker in thick white robes. The rest in pajamas, more or less, in their usual manner.

It was a hurried meal.

And then, they settled in the living room.
He sprawled in his chair, and nodded at Ran.

And they became one.
      And she spoke to the one.
            And told them of the Ur-drak.
      And of what magic evil it had to be.
        They separated.

"What was she doing?"

R-Bar looked at Tinker and shrugged.

"The Ur-drak only live on Erh Takk Terh," said Ran.

"Never heard of it," said R-Bar.

"It is a blocked elseplace." Ran looked at her, face blank.

"BLOCKED." R-Bar leaped up and stared at Ran.

"Ummm?" said Tinker.

"WHAT?" R-Bar whirled around, bristling.

"I suppose we could contact Macabre."

Chicken sat up. "My Lord?"

"What?"

"Praps t'would be best do we ourselves first bespeak with Shitar err we do loose such destruction pon some elseplace."

"Probably right." He set his empty cup on the floor next to his chair.

Messenger hurried toward the kitchen, carrying the empty pot.

Smoke's head snapped around. "She's up."

He jumped to his feet and caught her as she sagged through the doorway, stumbled, and fell.

He managed to get an arm under her legs and hauled her up into his arms. "OOOOOOOF."

Head wobbling loosely, she managed a grin, a faint grin. And mumbled, "Too much beauty for you . . . Uncle?"

"Damn right. What are you doing out of bed?"

Shitar tried to leer. "Pretty nice, though."

"Wonderful."

Smoke stepped around and easily lifted Shitar from his arms. "You belong in bed."

"Don't want to," grumbled Shitar. Her dangling hand clenched one of Tinker's. "Please?"

Tinker heard R-Bar stifle a gasp. He nodded. "O.K., put her on the couch. As long as she is up, she might as well have something to eat."

Chantal hurried to the kitchen. "I will get it."

Fair Morn hurried into the hall and fetched a blanket from a closet.

Chicken poked pillows behind Shitar's back as Smoke set her down. "From where came these fair pajamas?"

"I created them," said R-Bar. "This young witch has no sense of modesty."

"I have lovely skin." Shitar looked up at Tinker.

"Show it to someone else," snapped R-Bar.

Shitar continued to look at Tinker. "You sure you don't want to see?"

"Nope," he replied. "Seen one witch, seen 'em all."

"Tink!"

"AMTAR!"

"So to speak." He winked at Shitar.

Ran sat on the arm of his chair, slipped her arms around his shoulders, and leaned against him. "Your Ran does not think that it was funny what you said."

"Aunt?" Shitar's lower lip was pushing out.

"What?"

"Do not be mean to him."

"Heh, heh, heh," replied R-Bar.

"Now what?" He looked from one to the other.

"Altered the pajamas," said Ran.

Tinker looked. Shitar now wore a one-piece garment. No buttons. No way to take it off.

Chantal returned, carrying a heaped plate with food and a fork and sat next to Shitar. "Open up." And began to feed her. "Really unusual pajamas you've got there."

"Heh heh," said R-Bar, changing them back. Then, one by one by one they left to change into their daily clothes.

Chicken slipped up behind him, wrapped her arms around his waist, and leaned against his bare back.

"Kinda hard to put my shirt on this way," he grumbled.

"Me'Prince, We do believe Us that thee do lust pon that thy Sweet Niece."

"I did not. And she is not sweet, she is a witch."

"Thee do drool."

"I did not."

"Ogle some."

"Some. All witches like that. To be ogled."

She patted his stomach.

"Princess?"

"My Lord?"

"How come you are not wearing a shirt?"

She cleared her throat. "All the better for to rub Our Verra Own Self pon thy back."

"You been reading Little Red Riding Hood, or something like that?"

"Nay."

He tried to turn around. She wouldn't let him. "Hey."

"Ein moment. Now."

He spun around. "You put your shirt on."

"Indeed. Nay distraction enow."

"How come?"

"We must counsel."

"Ummm."

"This thing must a'killed be."

"What?"

"Most terrible monster do Shitar attack."

"Perhaps."

"My Lord." She banged his hands away.

"She might not remember where."

"Praps."

"Well, let's go." He stepped back, grabbed his shirt, and yanked it on.

"Whither?"

"Living room. Might as well check out all that pale skin."

Chicken leaped, blocking the door.

He laughed. "A joke."

"Most poor a'jest."

"Tat for tit." He grinned at her.

"Most feeble a pun that, Our Love."

"Oh, well." He stepped close, hooked his hands under her armpits and lifted her up. "How about a cup of coffee? First?"

"Randy Lord, that we might do."

He set her down, kissed her, did it again, and allowed himself to be towed to the kitchen.

"So? You wanna tell us?"

He slumped in his chair and sipped from his cup. The rest gathered around.

"Damu Targh," said Shitar.

R-Bar shrugged her shoulders. Ran shook her head.

"A small out of the way elseplace." Shitar hitched herself more upright. "We went there, Szaifeh, Rorx, and myself. On our way to the Vander home elseplace."

Chapter Eight.

All Problems Tend To Reappear.

Damu Targh. Warm and Pleasant.

It was as they had been told.

A small, isolated, out of the way elseplace.

The local population was sparse, mostly living in scattered hamlets. They were a friendly folk, mostly curious about their infrequent visitors. But polite enough not to stare, very much. Or pry. They were short and stocky. And glad to have an influx of outside currency.

Szaifeh discussed their lodging arrangements with the Room Keeper, who assured her that they had adequate facilities for large Ardu, that the local cuisine was excellent, and that they would enjoy their visit. She paid for their stay, including their meals. And waved to the others.

"Let's go look at our rooms." And dragged Rorx up the stairs. "Watch your head."

Shitar followed them.

"Two rooms," said Szaifeh. "Ours is left, your's is right." She threw open the left door and banged it closed behind them.

"If you jump a little, your head will bump," observed Szaifeh.

Rorx touched the ceiling with his hand.

"About a double, I'd say." Szaifeh pushed on the bed

with one hand and smiled at him.

"Let's eat," said Shitar, pushing open their door. "All those Vander tired me much."

Rorx stared at her.

"Hum hum hum," said Szaifeh.

Shitar snarled at her. "Don't be coarse."

"Kettle calling."

"Dip tur," suggested Shitar.

"Now that is coarse, Tar."

"I am hungry."

"Shall we go eat," said Rorx, tugging Szaifeh toward the door, nudging Shitar into the hall.

He suppressed his smile as he herded them downstairs and into the restaurant. Ducking their heads on the way down.

Shitar slumped in the booth, lingering over her drink, staring into nowhere. Szaifeh and Rorx had retired to their room.

"Lovely Witch, may I join you?"

She looked up, not moving her head. An extremely elderly man stood there, across from her, looking expectant. Her eyes scanned the otherwise empty room.

He nodded. "Exactly. Quite empty."

"You may." Shitar slid her outstretched legs to one side.

"Many thanks to you. It is nice to have company." Pulling out a chair, he sat.

"Mmm."

"For some." He waved over the waitress. And looked across the table at her. "If I may?"

"You may."

He ordered for himself and another of whatever she

had been drinking.

And after their orders arrived, and the waitress had left, he peered sharply at her. "I thought that witches did not associate with magicians."

"Don't. Mostly."

"The young man looked mage to me."

"Special case."

He took a long swallow. And wiped his mouth on a gaily decorated cloth. "Very good. The drink. Special case?"

"Yes."

"Mighty special case." He burped gently. "In all my travels, long and wide, I have never seen such a thing as that particular kind of pair. Before. Most curious."

"Special case." Shitar's mouth pulled, the right corner puckered. Dark flickered deep, deep in her eyes. She wasn't sure that she felt kindly toward her visitor.

He leaned forward. "Do you know his clan name?"

"He has no clan."

His eyes popped wide.

"Ummm," said Shitar. "Clans are witch. He is mage guild."

"Guild? Which? If I may ask?"

"Vander."

Hastily wiping his mouth, again, he stared at her. And shook his head. "There are no Vander. All died. Long, long ago." And took a drink from his mug.

"What he is." Shitar yanked her legs back and stood.

"Staying long?" asked her table sharing companion.

She shrugged her shoulder and started up the narrow stairs.

He sat, cupped his chin in one hand and stared at the wall. "I thought that they were all dead," he mumbled to himself.

In the morning, after eating breakfast, after sitting and waiting, and waiting, and waiting, Shitar stomped from the dining room and headed outside. And tromped down the first path that she saw. Witches were not good at waiting. With a few exceptions.

And after walking some distance she decided that this wasn't all that unpleasant an elseplace, this Damu Targh.

She smiled to herself and thought that this was true for such a small, isolated, out of the way elseplace where there was nothing to do except to sit and stare at the walls. And, eventually, as she walked along the winding, twisting path, she calmed down. More or less. At least as calm as a witch ever got. She knew that sitting and waiting was not something that she did very well. But knowing that didn't really change anything. The black swirling around her faded away.

At the top of the hill, she stopped and looked down and out and over a broad, very deep, green valley. And relaxed just a little more. And for a witch that was not much. Especially for a Faan witch.

"A pretty view, is it not, Young Witch?"

Her head snapped around.

The old man's eyes twinkled at her.

"Very silent," she replied.

"One learns many things if they live long enough."

She turned and drifted a light check spell over him.

He smiled. "Very clever."

"What guild are you, Ancient Mage?" Shitar watched him carefully, hooking her thumbs in her belt. She had the normal witch distrust of magicians.

"Tak'Dir."

"Never heard of it."

"Very small."

"But long lived."

He nodded. "We are that."

"Why are you here?" Shitar began to layer silent protection. And to ready herself. "Long lived ancient mage."

"May I tell you a short story?"

"If you wish." She called deep dark stuff up beneath her feet.

"A very short story."

"Tell me," she ordered, turning to face him squarely, dropping her arms to her sides. "Your very short story." She gathered soft, quiet magic around herself.

"Do you have any brothers?"

"No. All female relatives." She bounced a warning message off Szaifeh.

"I had a brother, once. No sisters."

"Ummmmm." She jolted Szaifeh awake with urgent.

"And long ago my brother . . . " And he told her his very short story.

And attacked.

Her counter spell blew him far, out and down. Into the deep green and silent valley.

Spinning away, she ran. From the shattered, smoking hilltop. Toward the inn.

As she charged around the last twist in the path, he appeared, between her and the inn

"Very strong, Young Witch."

Without slowing down, she hunched her shoulders, bowled him over and charged inside the inn. And screamed, "SZAIFEH! RORX!"

They banged down the stairs toward her.

Szaifeh stared at her. "Tar, what's . . . ?"

"RUN! JUMP OUT! NOW!"

Shitar whirled, cloak wrapped, and pulled as the old

mage's spell took them.

Everything within reach collapsed and billowed into dust. She collapsed.

The old man stood there, leaning heavily on a long staff. He wheezed at them. "Very strong." And kicked Shitar in the side. "I am Iztam of the Tak'Dir." And looked around.

Rorx lay crumpled in a heap. Szaifeh was struggling to sit up. All around them, the ground was ripped and smoking. The inn was gone. All living things, except them, were gone.

He hobbled over and peered down at Rorx. "A Vander Mage that young, newly mated, means that they are not yet complete." And bent and plunged an ornate dagger into the still form.

"And never will he." He turned and hobbled back to Shitar as her eyes opened. And kicked her again. "Tell me your name before I kill you."

"Dar par tak ram," snarled Shitar.

"What a wonderfully vile witch you are." He twitched. And wrapped his free arm across his chest. "You nearly did it."

The air near them exploded.

"NOOOOOOOOOOOO," screamed Iztam. Szaifeh had twisted herself and Rorx elsewhere. He glared at Shitar as she lurched to her feet. "Where did she take the body?"

"Unknown." Her bolt shattered his staff and arm.

Pulling up all his remaining strength, he dragged one in and threw it around her. The Ur-drak. "A gift. Wear it in health." He tried to laugh. But only managed to gurgle red liquid from the side of his mouth.

She screamed.

"A slow death," he said. "Tell me your name."

"I am Shitar," she growled, fighting with the thing digging into her.

The dark stuff reached up and sucked him down. Slowly. Into the beneath.

Her eyes watched him sink. "Of the Faan."

Then she slowly, painfully fought herself into the inbetween.

And out again.

And fell searing into tall grass.

"And you found me." Shitar managed a smile for Tinker and the rest of them.

"Most vile a'beast, this Iztam," said Chicken.

"But dead," said Smoke.

"Did he die?" asked Ran.

Shitar nodded. "I heard cracking."

R-Bar smiled. "Good. I sent a call to Shem."

"Why?" Tinker looked at her. Shitar nodded at her Aunt.

"He knows more mage and witch history than most. I wish to know of this Tak'Dir Guild."

The shadows whispered to them as she drifted wraith silent into the room to stand and to stare at her niece.

"What have you been doing, most rangle daughter of Ripple? I felt your arrival but waited," whispered soft darkness.

"Aunt," gasped a very startled Shitar.

"Reep." R-Bar leaped up and grabbed her sister. "We have to find Szaifeh and Rorx."

"Really, really, really," added Messenger.

"The Vander Mage is almost dead," explained Ran. "We think."

"Whoa!" shouted Tinker. "She doesn't know what happened."

Reep stared at Shitar with eyes going darker and

darker as death began to peer out. "Where is my daughter and her's?"

"I do not know, Aunt." Shitar told her of the end on Damu Targh.

Reep's clothes shimmered. And became. A thick dark robe, heavy hood over her head, covering her face. Only black shadow looked from the deep recess. She slipped her hands in opposite sleeves. "I will go look," breathed nothing at all. She was gone.

Shitar exhaled loudly. And shuddered violently.

Ran dropped beside her and wrapped her arms around Shitar. "You must rest. Or become as I, a near-witch."

"Too rangle for that." R-Bar stepped behind Tinker and looked at her niece.

"Hold me, Uncle," mumbled Shitar.

"You are already being held."

"I want to be held by you," she demanded.

"Pretty pushy for such a beat up person," he grumbled.

"Pure witch," said R-Bar, massaging his shoulder muscles. She leaned close and whispered in his ear, "We will protect you. She is witch weak nervous."

"My Lord, do sit thee pon great couch and comfort this thy poor niece."

He stood and glared at Shitar. "You gonna behave?" And yanked pillows and blankets and settled them around her as Ran moved away. Then he walked over to one wall, selected a tape and shoved it into the VCR, and grabbed the remote control, sat, yanked off his boots, and settled next to Shitar.

"All right, come'mer."

She did.

Ran pushed the pillows and yanked the blankets

around until she was satisfied. "A badly damaged witch feels very insecure, Amtar." And kissed his forehead.

"You done squirming around?" he grumbled at Shitar.

"Yes, Uncle."

"We will enow take our leave of thee and thine," said Chicken, heading for the dining room. "Do make her rest."

"Thought that I might as well watch a movie," he grumbled.

"I will bring coffee and stuff back," said Messenger, hurrying toward the kitchen behind the rest.

He clicked on everything.

"Lots of blood and guts?" asked Shitar, snuggling closer.

"Yep."

"Good." She managed another smile. And managed to tickle him. A little.

"Just watch the movie," he grumbled at her. "And no witch wiggling."

"Yes, Uncle."

Smoke slipped predator silent into the room. And turned off the equipment.

Chicken joined her, on quiet bare feet. "Sweet Niece do in Orpheus arms sleep."

One of Orpheus' eyes popped open. "Shhhhhh." And closed.

Messenger peered around Smoke. "Zonked."

Both of Tinker's eyes opened.

"Ooops." Messenger ducked back.

Chicken took a blanket from the floor, draped it over the pair, knelt and tucked one edge around Tinker. "Our Prince, wouldst have lunch late?" she whispered.

"Sure," he whispered back and winked at her. "If I can slip out of the clutches of sleeping beauty."

Shitar's eyes opened. "I did not think that you had noticed, Uncle."

"What?"

"That I am a beauty, sleeping or otherwise."

"Go back to sleep." He frowned. "And unwrap. Now that everyone is awake, we might as well have some lunch."

She grinned at him. "How can you tell if I am beautiful when I am wrapped in blankets and clothed and you have not. OUCH!" R-Bar had walked into the room.

Shitar frowned up at her. "Not nice, Aunt. In my weakened condition."

"Sounding healthy to me," replied R-Bar.

"Im dip," snarled Shitar.

"Right," agreed Tinker, shedding blankets, shoving Shitar more upright.

Smoke picked up the cups and cookie jar. "Her rest was beneficial." She winked at Shitar. "I'll bring you a tray."

"I can walk," snarled Shitar, heaving herself to her feet. And toppling sideways. To be caught by Tinker.

"I will bring two trays," said Smoke, heading for the kitchen.

Ran knelt and pressed her hand over Shitar's eyes and said to Tinker, "Your niece is very weak weak."

"Just strong enough to be a pain in the butt," he mumbled. He hitched her into a more comfortable position. "OK, Sneaky Pete, move it over. We can't eat lunch this way."

"Wasn't being sneaky," gurgled Shitar, easing herself into a more comfortable position. Off Tinker.

"Good," he said. "And button up your blouse, not-sneaky."

Pouting and frowning, she did.

"Hum," said R-Bar.

"AUNT!" snapped Shitar. "I was not."

Chicken dropped onto the couch and wrapped her arms around Tinker. "Protect thee We will, Our Prince."

"Knock it off," he growled.

Chantal charged in from the hall. "Oh no you don't, Simba Leader."

His head snapped around. "What?"

"Not with her." Chantal leaned on the back of the couch and wrapped protecting arms around Shitar.

"Huh?"

Fair Morn came in and sat in a chair, holding one of Smoke's two trays. And said very carefully to him, "Knock up. Vulgar Slang. To make pregnant. Knock it off. Or in this case."

"ENOUGH!"

Fair Morn set the tray in Shitar's lap. "And eat it all."

Smoke thumped him in the chest. With the edge of the second tray. "Here, Stud."

"And eat it all," giggled Messenger heading out the front door with Chicken.

"Heh, heh, heh," cackled R-Bar, going with them.

"You win," he sighed.

Shitar smiled at him. Chantal winked at Tinker and headed for the kitchen.

"Not you," he said to Shitar. "Them." He took a bite from his hamburger.

"Ber tik," she replied around a mouthful.

Ran sat on the arm of the couch nearest Tinker. "She has the largest collection of coarse expressions of any witch that I have ever heard. And she is so young."

Shitar glanced at Ran from the corners of her eyes. And finished her hamburger.

"I suppose," agreed Tinker. "And her just a child."

Shitar growled.

"With a foul mouth," he added.

She hissed.

"And a real sulky pout."

Shitar glared at him.

"A standard witch," he added.

"Not so," said Ran.

"Correct! I am not standard," snapped Shitar, straightening up, shoving her tray on top of his.

He shrugged "O. K. I will concede the point. Kid."

"I am not!" Shitar looked at Ran. "Am I? Aunt?"

"No," replied Ran, reaching over and touching Tinker's shoulder.

"I am as old as Messenger," stated Shitar firmly.

"Really?" Tinker rolled his eyes at her.

"I will take those trays, trouble making Mate." Smoke did. To the kitchen.

"And prettier," stated Shitar, throwing her shoulders back.

"Nope." He shook his head. "Different."

Shitar hiccuped.

"Ate too fast," he said.

Ran shoved at his shoulder. "Amtar, your niece requires rest, not agitation."

"Right." He stood. And, pointed at the couch. "Lie down, Wreck." Shitar glowered at him. And hiccuped.

He laughed. "Down Tiger Witch, you heard Ran."

Grumbling loudly, Shitar shoved the pillows around and stretched out. "Tuck me in." And hiccuped.

He leaned over and did. "There."

"Kiss me."

He did. On the forehead.

"Ger pik." She hiccupped.

"R-Bar says that uncles kiss nieces on the forehead." He smiled sweetly at her.

"Aunt is ik zur," she grumbled to him. And hiccuped.

He brushed the hair back from her forehead. "Go to sleep. Or your eyes will be even baggier. We have work to do." He straightened up. "We will be around. Smoke's watching. Rest. Please?"

She nodded, squirmed, found the correct spot. And fell asleep. After one last hiccup.

Ran and Tinker slipped out the front door.

Chapter Nine

A Small Rescue.

Damu Targh. A Smoke Filled Day.

The silent figure wearing the thick black robe stood there.

And looked at the destruction spreading to all sides of where she stood. She tasted the touch of Shitar. And of something else. Not so pleasant. She looked down at the irregular stain, at the soil, sunken, disturbed. Then drifted to one side.

Great dark eyes hidden in black filled hood searched for the thread, the faint trace thread that would lead her to Szaifeh.

And found it.

She tied it quickly to a glittering silver wand.

And faded away.

Following her daughter.

Grandeville. Tinker's Place. Late in the Day.

"I am hungry."

"Me too." Fair Morn leaned over their patient and nodded at her. "You need a bath and clean clothes." She yanked the blankets away and lifted the startled witch in her arms, holding her easily.

"I can walk," growled Shitar.

"Taking no chances," said Fair Morn.

She set her burden on her feet at the entrance to the shower room. And pointed. "Just toss your pajamas in there."

Fair Morn heaved her own shirt into the hamper and sat down to undo her boots.

Shitar threw her top into the hamper, wobbled over and sat next to her. Heavily. "Maybe I will just sit here."

Fair Morn nodded. And stood, yanking off her trousers. She winked at the witch. "I think that you are losing weight. Better eat more." And walked into the shower room and turned on the shower heads.

Kandor of The Two Moons. A Quiet Day.

She stared at the cave mouth

The entrance was small and narrow.

And twice-guarded.

Drifting close, she tasted it, using one cautious finger. "Szaifeh," whispered the afternoon breeze. "Let me in."

The cave silence said nothing.

Yanking out a glittering green wand, she slashed at the air and called him. HERE!

"Whoa!" J. C. stared at the strange surroundings, and at his wife. "I was working." And grinned at her. "Well, I was about to start."

"Husband," said the darkness. "I require your help."

"Me? Sure. What?" He pointed at his feet. "I will need boots." He had just yanked them off and had walked into Doc's library to start working on a new project, and had been searching for a book when she had grabbed him.

"No." His boots appeared, on his feet. She swept the hood back from her face, floated up and kissed him. "I will explain all, later. Call your daughter."

J. C. looked at their surroundings. "Where?"

"In there." Reep settled next to his side and pointed at

the cave.

"Sure." He stepped forward. And was knocked backward. "Ah ha. Now I understand." And looked back at Reep who stood watching. Sucking in a deep breath, he turned and bellowed into the cave. "SZAI, YOU IN THERE?"

An echo returned.

"Big cave. Can't you just break the spell?"

"Probably," replied the sunshine. "But she might be injured. More."

"More?"

"Call."

He did. After sucking in another great lungful.

"YO IN THERE. ANYONE HOME?"

In between the echoes, they heard.

A voice.

A faint voice.

"Dad?"

"CERTAINLY IS. COME OUT, COME OUT, WHERE EVER YOU ARE."

"Wait."

"LET ME IN. OR I'LL HUFF AND PUFF AND ETC., ETC."

Something crackled faintly.

"Go inside, husband. I will guard."

J. C. slipped into the cave entrance and then carefully edged deeper and deeper. "Dark in here, daughter. Got a light?"

Faint, pulsating light wobbled into existence.

"Over here."

J. C. stepped around a sharp bend and into a side tunnel. And knelt in front of them.

"What have you been doing?"

Szaifeh lay back against the wall, arms wrapped

tightly around the crumbled form of Rorx. They were both very dirty, covered in shades of grey and brown. Her eyes flicked at her father. "He is not dead."

J. C. reached for Rorx.

"Mine," she snarled.

"LET GO. Szaifeh, take your arms away. Do it. NOW."

She did. And sagged sideways. "Sorry, Dad."

"I can spank you later." He grabbed Rorx under the arm pits and managed to get one shoulder under the limp body. "Not too heavy."

And lurched to his feet. "Your mother is outside. Back in a minute." He headed for the outside.

Grandeville. Tinker's Place. Early Afternoon.

Tinker sat at the table.

One of the several

On the rear deck.

And watched.

Chantal had spread newspapers over the top of the table and was cleaning her revolver. It had been in a number of pieces. As each had been cleaned, she had reassembled it.

"Certainly wouldn't want a dirty gun," he said.

"You betcha, Johnny Love."

"What are those?" He poked one finger at the box of cartridges.

"Special loads." She pushed something together. A soft metallic click.

"Oh?"

"Yep. Hit something with one of those and if they are not already dead, they'll certainly wish that they were."

"Planning something, killer?"

She spun the cylinder. Inspected a cartridge, and slipped it in place. "Nope. Just in case. How's she doing?"

"O.K."

"Strong kitten." Smoke dropped onto the bench next to him. "If he stops teasing her."

Chantal looked up and glared at him. "Messin' around with the young stuff, Big Feller?" She slipped her revolver into its holster.

"Not yet. I was going to wait until she's healthier."

Chantal yanked out her revolver, and finished loading it. And winked at him. "I'm pretty healthy."

"That's the problem."

"What?"

"You guys are all pretty healthy. OUCH."

Smoke had pinched his side. It had been just a little pinch.

The air behind them sizzled loudly. Chantal's hand jumped, thumb snapping the hammer back, muzzle reaching past his ear.

"Where are they?" demanded an angry voice.

Chantal eased the hammer down as Tinker and Smoke spun around.

Ramp stood there, the muscle in one cheek jumping. "Tell me."

"Who?" asked Tinker.

"Szaifeh and Rorx."

"We don't know. Reep went to search for them."

Ramp shook her head. "She took J. C."

"WHAT?"

Smoke leaped to her feet and pointed. "There."

Figures had just appeared in the nearby meadow.

Ramp stabbed a finger and nodded and crooked it.

They stood on the rear deck.

"Hi there, Tinker," said J. C. He was carrying Rorx whose arms and legs swung loosely. Reep was helping her daughter stand.

Smoke took Rorx from J. C.'s arms and headed into the house. "Alive."

Chantal ran for her medical kit.

The others poured onto the deck from either end.

"Dim, dim, dim, dim, dim, dim," snarled R-Bar, the air shimmering around her.

Szaifeh shoved tangled matted hair from her face and forehead. "I really need a bath, Aunt." And started to cry, tears cleaning white streaks down her cheeks. It was a most un-witch thing to do. "He killed Shitar."

R-Bar stepped close and swung an arm around her. "Nope. She is inside. Sleeping."

The tears became a torrent down Szaifeh's cheeks as Chicken stepped close. "We will this one clean. In great warm hot tub."

Reep drifted close. "My Daughter," whispered the breeze.

Chicken nodded and watched as R-Bar led Szaifeh toward the tub room, Reep walking with them.

Tinker hurried along and down the hall to see his son.

He heard the showers start.

"Yuck, yuck, yuck."

Messenger hurried through the living room carrying a plastic basin filled with warm water.

Shitar's eyes popped open. "What is happening, Aunt?"

Messenger told her. And hurried away.

As Shitar struggled to her feet, Fair Morn reached over the back of the couch and shoved her back down.

"Tam tik," snapped Shitar.

"Lie down. You'd only be in the way anyway." Fair

Morn handed her a banana. "Here. Have one, have several." She finished the one she was holding and took another from the bunch she had placed on the back of the couch.

"Tell me what is happening," demanded Shitar, slowly eating her banana.

"Sure. Reep is washing Szaifeh's hair, and Szaifeh, in the shower room. Chicken and Smoke are washing parts of Rorx while R-Bar and Chantal and Ramp are working on him. She is mostly fine. He is mostly marginal." Suddenly Fair Morn looked nowhere. "Oh, Oh."

"Aunt?"

R-Bar had just grabbed for Sa'ar and Imdar.

The explosion in the front yard rattled the picture windows. And two very angry Vander stalked into the house through the front door.

Violet light flooded the living room, pushing aside the sunlight.

Sa'ar clenched a deep purple wand in her hand. It was humming loudly. "WHERE IS THAT AUNT?"

"Shhhh," said Fair Morn. "Not so loud."

R-Bar dashed into the living room from the hall. "Bout time." And grabbed Imdar by one arm and yanked her into motion. "Don't just stand there, come on." And nodded as she hustled the startled Vander healer from the room. "Hayou, Sa'ar," she said back over her shoulder. "Sit down. Back in awhile."

They heard the bedroom door slam.

Sa'ar looked from Shitar to Fair Morn.

"Here." Fair Morn handed her a banana. "Might as well sit down."

Glowering angrily, Sa'ar sat, and shoved her wand up her left sleeve. And stared at Shitar. "What's your problem?"

She yanked the peel off her banana. The light returned to normal.

Sa'ar jerked her head around and looked at Fair Morn. "Mother in there?"

"Yep," replied Fair Morn around a mouthful. "And Reep and Szaifeh are still in the shower room." She began to gather up all the banana peels and touched Shitar lightly on a shoulder. "You tell her. I am going to make some cocoa." And headed for the kitchen.

Shitar cleared her throat. "Cousin . . . "

And did

Ramp watched as Chicken sponged their son's face clean. Ramp said something

Rorx jerked.

She said it again.

His arm twitched.

R-Bar began to edge toward the far wall of the bedroom. She didn't like the change she could see happening in her sister's face.

Ramp leaned over the now constantly quivering form, shoving Chicken to one side, grey smoke seeping down.

R-Bar leaped forward and yanked Chicken backward. "Shhhh." And wrapped protection around them both.

Ramp's finger shredded Rorx's shirt open with a just formed talon. She dumped the contents of the basin over his chest. The water splashed and steamed and disappeared.

His eyes snapped open.

Messenger shoved and crowded Tinker into a corner, crouching in front of him, a long black wand held rigidly in her right hand.

Ramp slid her hand over his chest, gently stroking the ugly wounds, closing them, banishing the spells.

The window, hastily replaced, shattered, blowing outward, scattering glass and wood fragments across the rear deck. Dead birds fell from the nearby tree.

"Aunt?" mumbled Rorx.

Ramp said something.

He howled, neck twisting, head snapping back and forth. His spine arched and arched.

And then he fell.

Flat on the bed.

"Szaifeh," he cried.

Ramp collapsed.

Tinker heaved Messenger aside, grabbed Ramp and rolled her off Rorx and the bed.

He knelt and lifted her up, and brushed the hair away from her face.

Messenger and R-Bar leaped to the bed and leaned over to peer at the groggy warlock.

Imdar pushed at them. "Get away, get away. Now I may aid her. And him." They all hastily filed from the bedroom.

"Out, out." Imdar pointed at the door. The room was filling with a violet haze. And other things, dimly seen.

Shitar hit the floor with a heavy thump. She had grabbed the edge of the couch and tried to stand. "I heard a dartar."

Fair Morn hurried over and picked her up and dumped her back on the couch. "Are all you witches this dumb, or are you just an exception?"

"Dit dit a'am tak," spat out Shitar.

Sa'ar laughed. And ate another marshmallow. "My cousin is a little, um, thick-headed."

"Gim dur," commented Shitar, rearranging pillows

and blankets. And frowning at everyone and everything. "Cocoa?" She held up her cup. "Please?"

Sa'ar reached over and filled her cup. "Tar, if our Aunts and Imdar can't do anything, then neither can you." And before Shitar could respond, she stuffed a marshmallow into her open mouth.

Tinker, R-Bar, Chicken, and Messenger banged into the room to be met by Smoke carrying in a tray with two coffee pots and lots of cups.

Chantal joined them from the other end of the house. "Beyond my medical skills."

Ran slipped in from somewhere and forced herself in between Messenger and R-Bar who were now sitting on the other couch. "Anyone alive in there?"

Smoke nodded. "Nothing dead yet."

J. C. ran in from the hall. "Hey, that replaced bedroom window blew all over your back yard. What are you guys doing? There are a lot of dead birds out there."

"Ask Ramp. Later." Tinker shoved a cup into J. C's hand. "Here."

"Hi, POP." Two figures wearing thick white robes wrapped their arms around him. And were kissed in turn. "Much better," said J. C. "Nice and clean." He looked at the deep lines in his daughter's face. "You all right?" And squeezed his wife with his free arm. "And you?"

"Rest. Sleep. Medicine," sighed the slight figure.

Szaifeh pulled away and knelt by the couch, wrapping her arms around Shitar's legs. "Witch debt, Tar, witch debt." And began to sob.

Grumbling and mumbling, Shitar wiped away her own tears.

J. C. leaned forward, Reep nestled under his arm, looked over at Tinker, and frowned. "Tinker, I never thought that I would ask such a question, but I will, now. Do you need any help killing that guy?"

Tinker sat back, and shook his head. "Too late. Shitar got 'em." He looked at Sa'ar. "How much more Vander crap are we going to have to endure?"

"MY LORD! Tis most unseemly." Chicken banged him on one shoulder.

The bedroom door slammed open and Imdar reeled out and into the living room before Sa'ar could answer.

Fair Morn caught the sagging mage and dropped her into Tinker's lap. He wrapped his arms around her as she leaned to one side. "HEY!"

"Hello, father of our son." Imdar leaned heavily against him. "He lives. And the dark mage as well."

"You don't look too good," said Tinker.

He received a weak smile. "I thought that I was beautiful."

"Not what I meant," he mumbled.

"I know." She tickled him.

He looked at Chantal. "Well, Doc, what do you think?"

"I am a vet, not a people doc. Mostly." She stood. "I need help in the kitchen. Making stew. Good food for everybody."

Smoke and Fair Morn went with her.

Chicken stood. "We will Us construct most great and tasty a'salad." She crooked a finger at Sa'ar. "Thee will help Us."

They followed the others.

And then.

From outside.

They heard a car skid to a halt, and the doors slam.

"Now what?" Tinker watched the front door.

It banged open.

Tajaar hurtled into the room, dagger flashing. Followed by Shem and Hard, both of whom tripped over the threshold as they entered.

"Ramp?" asked Hard.

"Where's Mom?" said Shem

"Resting," said Imdar.

"Everything is O. K," added Tinker.

"Right," said J. C. He tugged Reep toward the kitchen, "Guess we better tell the cooks."

Hard dropped into a chair.

Shem sat and started at Shitar. "What are you doing here? And Szaifeh? And, and, everyone?"

Tajaar stood behind him, hands lightly resting on his shoulders, her blade back in its sheath.

Szaifeh and Shitar had arranged themselves on the couch.

"You tell them, Tar." Szaifeh leaned back and cradled her cup in both hands.

Chapter Ten.

Vander and Then Some.

Grandeville. Tinker's Place.

Late afternoon.

Late late afternoon.

In the hammock.

She lay on her side.

And tickled him.

"Ummm?"

And did it again.

Tickle him.

"Huh?"

"Many people went home."

"What?"

She bumped his chin with a cup. A full coffee cup. "Here."

His eyes opened. "You say something?"

"Father of our son, I did. But I will wait."

He struggled into more of a sitting up position. And took a sip. "For what?"

"For you to wake up."

"Oh." He took another sip. "Where is everyone?"

"Shem, Tajaar, Hard, and Ramp went to their home."

"She all right?"

"The magician needs rest."

"And how about this magician?"

She smiled. "I have been resting. Here. In this strange bed. Next to you."

"It is not a strange bed. It is a hammock. For napping. Or reading. Or tickling Vander magicians." He reached over and did.

She wiggled. "I see."

"And?" he asked.

"And," she replied. "Rorx and his witch are also resting."

His ear was tickled from the other side. "What are you doing to our healer, Vander Lord?" It was Sa'ar.

He rolled onto his back, carefully holding his cup so he didn't splash on anyone or anything. "Nothing."

"Looked like something to me."

"Nothing . . . much."

"The Princess said that you should come to dinner. Now. We are eating early." She leaned over and kissed him. And, after awhile, went back inside for dinner.

"She shouldn't have done that." Imdar threw an arm over his chest. "But our debt is growing greater and greater. You may not scold her."

"What?"

Imdar kissed him. "She may be your niece, but she is also the Heart of the Vander, the Brooch Wearer."

"So?"

"So, she needed to thank you."

"O. K. Let's go eat."

Ran made room for Imdar so she could sit at the end of the table next to Tinker.

"What are you growling about?" Tinker looked down the table at R-Bar who was frowning at Sa'ar.

Sa'ar winked at him.

R-Bar's expression darkened. "Nieces kiss uncles on the forehead. And. They do not try to seduce him in the hammock."

"Shame on you," he said to Sa'ar. "Pass the rolls, please." He nodded at Chicken.

"Rim dip ptar gur," snapped R-Bar.

Shitar's eyebrows shot straight up. "Worse than coarse, Aunt." Then she smiled at her. "I've never heard that combination before."

"Corrupting the morals of the youth," grumbled Tinker. "Will someone please rescue the roast from Moth Gut and send it down this way?"

Chantal did.

   Rescue the roast.

Shitar leaned closer to R-Bar. "I wouldn't mind being corrupted."

Smoke nudged Shitar in the side. "He is not going to help you in that endeavor."

"Prak," suggested Shitar.

Sa'ar nodded. "Right."

Imdar handed Tinker the gravy bowl. "I do not think that you can corrupt her."

Tinker looked startled. "Which her?"

"Her."

"He could try," suggested Shitar, rolling her eyes at him.

Tinker gazed longingly at the basket of rolls. Messenger shoved it in his direction,

"I think that she is getting healthier," he said to Chicken.

She smiled. And passed the basket of rolls. "Indeed, Me'Lord. Most healthy."

Shitar coughed dramatically. And slumped in her

chair, her eyes watching him.

"Two dolla," said Chantal.

"Now what?" He decided that a little more beef would be all right. And another roll or two.

"Five?" said Sa'ar, bidding up.

"Leaving soon?" asked Tinker around a mouthful of roll.

"In the morning," said Sa'ar.

Messenger bounced up and down in her chair. "Maybe Imdar should stay until Rorx is much better?"

Chicken nodded sagely, reached across the table, and patted his forearm. "The Mother of thy Verra Own Son ought here stay some while longer."

"In your room?" Ran stared at him.

Smoke smiled. "Easier to pounce upon."

Tinker sighed, a long low sigh.

"Six dolla," chanted Chantal. "The price just went up."

He stared at her over the top of his coffee cup and slipped lower in his chair.

She smiled sweetly at him. "As long as we are selling your services we might as well go for top dollar. STUD! Ten dolla." And looked around the table.

"Merde," commented Tinker.

"Cow dung," offered Fair Morn.

"Pig poop." Messenger giggled.

Tinker looked over at Imdar. "Wanna run away with the gypsies? There's a gang of them just down the road."

Chantal leaped to her feet. "One step toward the door and I will strike you dead." Her right arm snapped back.

Protective spells leaped from R-Bar, Shitar, Sa'ar and Imdar as Chantal's arm whipped forward. They did no good.

"HA!" she cried triumphantly.

The roll bounced from the center of his chest.

Fair Morn caught it. On the bounce. And ate it. "Good thing that it wasn't buttered first. Stain your shirt." She smiled at him. "Stud."

"Bug nuts," mumbled Tinker.

"Take a number and stand in line," said Chantal to Shitar.

"True?" Shitar sat up. "Aunt?" And tugged her blouse down.

"What's the problem? Now? This time?" Tinker also sat up.

Chicken reached over and filled his cup. "Glower not, Sweet Prince." He shoved his chair back, face grim. And struck her. The roll smacked Chantal in the forehead.

"Ha," said Tinker. "HA. HA. HA."

And fired again.

"Ha."

And again.

"Ha."

And again.

"Ha."

Rolls bounced off her chest.

"Watch what you are hitting, Cowboy!" Chantal glared at him.

A whirling crackling mass of air swirled across the dining room ceiling and burst out through the window. Glass and wood fragments bounced and tinkled across the front deck and the front lawn.

"Oh, My," said Messenger.

"What was that?" snapped Tinker.

Two magicians and two witches stared at each other.

Standing, leaning on his hands, glaring around the table, he demanded, loudly, "What just flew out the window, through our dining room window? Taking the window with it?"

"Golly," whispered Messenger.

His head swivelled in her direction. "Kitten?"

"Um," replied Messenger.

Chicken tugged at his belt. "Do seat thyself, My Lord."

He did. Dropping heavily into his chair. "Well?"

Messenger's eyes darted from Imdar to Sa'ar to Shitar to R-Bar.

"It was her fault," snapped Shitar, pointing at Chantal "Uncle."

"Sorry," said R-Bar.

"We were afraid," added Imdar. "Father of our son."

"True, Vander Lord." Sa'ar smiled at him. And unbuttoned the top button on her blouse.

"Clear as mud," grumbled Tinker, looking at the shattered window. The top half was mostly outside.

"It was the protect spells, MyTinker." Messenger sat up and folded her hands together on top of the table.

"What protect spells?"

Imdar reached over and gently touched his arm. "When, ahhh, Chantal, threatened to strike you dead, we cast protection on you, Sa'ar and I did."

"Me too, Tink." R-Bar nodded.

"Certainly did," agreed Shitar. "Can't have anyone killing you, Uncle."

He looked at Messenger. "And?"

She looked down and slowly traced a pattern on the table cloth with a finger tip. "Witch magic and magician spells do not mix very well. Most of the time. The tangle broke our window."

Chantal leaned sideways and whispered to R-Bar and began to vigorously brush at the flour blotches on her shirt front. "You should have known better."

R-Bar's lower lip poked out. "I just reacted because they did." She chewed on her lower lip. "You better stop doing that. He is getting distracted."

"That's his problem." Chantal patted away more white blotches.

R-Bar grinned at her. "You are doing that deliberately."

Tinker rapped on the table with one knuckle. "O.K., gang, settle down." He nodded at the magicians and at the witches. "When we are at home, we are safe. Even if some of us get a little, ummmm, extreme." He hefted a roll in his right hand and looked at Chantal. She snatched over the other basket.

"Thanks, anyway." He broke open the roll smeared jelly on it. And ate it.

Smoke stood. "I'll phone Jona's Wood Works. Again." And headed out through the kitchen. "He can take care of both windows."

Chicken crooked at finger at Fair Morn and began to clear the table.

Tinker stood and crooked a finger at Chantal. And kissed the flour smudge on her forehead when she got close enough. "Need some help, Doc?"

"Something wrong with my chest, Cowboy?"

"Nope."

"Certainly getting stared at."

"Lots to stare at, Cowgirl."

"Uh huh," she said as he slid his arms around her.

He mumbled, "Let's go out back and sit."

She brushed at the flour on his shirt. "Sure."

"Really sneaky," giggled Messenger as she slipped past them.

Smoke took the tray from Szaifeh and made her lie back. She was in the living room. On one of the couches. And had been trying to rest. All through the meal.

"Aunt, I heard spell crackle. What is wrong?"

"Nothing. Button your top and pull up that blanket You are a sick kitten. And not on display."

Szaifeh frowned at her. But did as ordered.

Imdar and R-Bar went into the bedroom to check Rorx.

Shitar sat on the couch, next to Szaifeh.

"Tar, what happened in there?"

"The window broke." Shitar's lower lip pushed out. "We broke it."

"Tell me."

So. Shitar did.

Far Corner.

Natanada sat in long silence and beckoned Abadoda forward. Hatopa, standing by the side of her chair, one hand on the back, watched her approach.

Abadoda knelt at Natanada's feet. "It is all as said, Elixa." She dragged her upper garment open, pointed at a dark spot. "Her wand did this, dagger used."

"Witches?"

"So said."

"And we?" Hatopa cleared his throat. "Are shadow witches?"

"So said."

She stared deep into Abadoda. "Bring them to me. I would so see."

Abadoda backed away, stood, and hurried from the chamber, the building, and down into the town, wondering if the group would be reasonable. The Elixa had no interest in relocating from a greatly irritated local folk, irritated from the great damage to their area if the Elixa had to take these three unwillingly.

The three stood in the room and looked at her. Totally controlled. Absolutely blank faced.

Natanada nodded. "You are obviously witches. What do you here?"

Turintor indicated with her chin. "Abadoda asked."

"In this elseplace?"

"Witches do as they wish. Answer to none." Flame flickered deep in dark eyes.

"Never met before."

Rbat shrugged.

Natanada looked at Abadoda. She indicated the three. "High curiosity. High witch curiosity," said Abadoda. "They have never met one of us before. Witches believed, until now, that we were myth hidden creatures. Things of child song."

"And now they have new thoughts?"

"Just so."

"And?" The Elixa looked from face to face.

Abadoda walked over and dropped one hand onto Rbat's shoulder.

Natanada gasped. "No harm?"

"Just so," stated Abadoda.

"What if mage?"

"Death," stated Rbat.

"Most often," added Turintor.

Natanada leaned back and nodded. "Stay visit? There is much to learn."

The trio nodded.

Natanada pointed. A door appeared. She stood and walked that way. "Come. My quarters. Most comfortable."

They followed her. High curiosity. Witch and

Sorcerers.

Natanada lounged back on the strangely shaped couch and gestured for the trio to sit near.

Abadoda waved in refreshments and handed around ornate goblets. "A favorite of the Anaza." She sat on a wide chair-shaped piece and patted the cushion with a free hand. "Come, Shadow Cousin Rbat, sit."

Rbat looked at Turintor, walked over and did. She poked one finger into her mug, testing the beverage, then took a sip.

Natanada looked at the trio, took a sip. "You are a great, umlaba, surprise."

The three witches shrugged.

"We have heard tales and stories and such of witches and magicians, but our, ubla, fieldwards have seen none." The Elixa smiled. "It seems that the zones have been, until now, mutually isolated." She took another sip. "This is a curiosity." Rbat's eyes flicked to Abadoda.

"There are many phylota," replied the sorcerous. "What they call clans. These tend to be very free and very independent."

"Most witch," stated Turintor. "Most witch."

Abadoda nodded and held her hand close to Turintor. Her hand was a faint brown tinge, noticeable when held near the moonlight pale witch skin. "Some difference." She looked deep into the dark eyes. "Are you happy?"

She shrugged. "I am witch."

"You do not smile."

"At times." Then she explained that smiling witches were most often one small step from doing vile, releasing chaos and terror.

"We frown."

"Hum." She held out her cup. Abadoda tapped the

edge gently with her's, filling it.

"Sooooo ba," murmured Natanada. "Not same, some, not same." Reaching over she touched Rbat. "Touch feel same."

"Magic'd not same." Rbat plucked at the sorcerous blouse. "All color same?"

"No. Witch?"

She shook her head and indicated Motaiss. "Many black, many not. As you can see."

The Elixa nodded. "Rest time. Here? Or there?"

Rbat looked at the others. "Here."

Natanda gestured them to their rooms, and smiled at Abadoda. "That spell works."

Grandeville. Tinker's Place.

They sat on the edge of the deck and kicked their bare feet in the warm water of the swimming pool.

"You gonna tell me what that was all about back there?" He tickled her, It was just a little tickle.

"Grumble, grumble," said Chantal.

"Oh? Really?"

"Growl, growl," she added.

"Oh? Really?"

"You want to take your hands off my anatomy?"

"I do not have them on your, ahhh, anatomy."

"Well, you should have. Just so I can complain."

"Ah, ha." He nodded and reached around. "How's this?"

"It'll do." She leaned against him.

"You gonna complain?"

"Nope."

He sighed. "So?"

"I just don't like people coming here and making

assumptions about you, that's all."

"Ahhhh."

She leaned away and glowered at him. "And what's that supposed to mean? Ahhhhhhh?"

He glowered back. "Just a sage-like noise. I don't know what you are talking about." And kissed her on the tip of the nose.

"Imdar."

"N. C."

"What?" She fiddled with the buttons on his shirt.

"No comment."

"Coward!"

"Yep." He tugged her closer.

She turned a little and slipped a hand inside his shirt. "Well, O.K." And bent and bit his shoulder, lightly. "But she still owes me ten dollars."

He nodded. "I think that we ought to get twenty."

"Braggart."

"Ummm."

She sat back, a little. "But those pneumatic nieces better behave."

Fair Morn carried dessert into the living room, handed around the dishes, and stared at Shitar, then at Sa'ar. "Certainly are." And smiled. *One, I think the witch is more well inflated.*

He laughed. And leaned away. And poked her with a fingertip. "Just checking for air pressure."

Chantal shoved him into the swimming pool.

Chicken laughed and held out her cup so Messenger could refill it.

The three cousins exchanged puzzled glances.

"You are doing it, aren't you?" asked Sa'ar, looking at Ran, who was smiling.

Ran nodded.

He grinned up at her. "You might as well jump in, your water wings are already inflated."

She leaped.

The waves washed over his head.

Chantal slid up against him as she surfaced. "Really crude, Simba Leader. Let's go inside and shed these wet clothes."

Chicken began to collect dessert dishes, cups, etc., on a tray. And winked at Smoke. "Sly Doctor did Fair Imdar out maneuver." And took everything to the kitchen.

Smoke nodded. "Imdar will be here for a week or longer. Rorx will require care for at least that long."

Fair Morn reached over and poked Sa'ar. "Do the Vander use money?"

"Only when we travel, Aunt."

Messenger flapped both hands over her mouth. Then burst out. "I think that she has twenty dollars?" And tried to look serious.

"His Ran does not think that is funny." Ran glared at her.

"Oh my,"said Messenger.

"What does she need money for?" asked Shitar.

Szaifeh pushed herself up into a more upright sitting position. "What are we talking about?"

A slight hand reached over the back of the couch and pressed against her forehead. "You feel well," sighed soft quiet

"MOM!"

"Daughter?" Reep kissed her on the cheek. "How is your's?"

"Improving. Slowly."

Imdar joined them. "It was close."

Reep walked around the couch and sat, slipping an arm around her daughter's shoulders. "I think, as does Imdar, that the monster did not die."

Shitar leaped to her feet. "I saw him sink."

"I looked again. No trace."

"Rak, rak, rak, rak, rak," spit out Shitar. And started to turn away.

Reep grabbed her. "Stay."

Shitar stopped. None dared disobey this aunt.

Sa'ar looked at Imdar. "You heard?"

"Yessssss."

"Guard him well." Sa'ar stood. And was gone.

"Oh my," said Messenger.

Chicken ran into the living room. "We will us leave next fair morn."

Smoke and Fair Morn headed for the hall and storage closets. To ready their gear.

Chicken tapped Messenger on the shoulder. "Thee may disturb them not, kitten."

Messenger's face flushed. "I wouldn't do that." Then she whispered, "He's got her in the hot tub."

Her arms were locked around his neck. "Top dolla," she said in his ear.

"You owe me twenty," he said, running his hands up and down her back.

She leaned back and grinned. "Do I get a refill?"

"Really crude, Doc."

She nudged him into a seat. And sat. "Well?"

"Guess we will have to wait and see."

The outer door banged open.

His eyes flew open. Chantal gasped.

Someone ran past and into their chamber using the side door.

"Who was that?"

"I don't know, John. But she was wearing lavender duds."

He reached out. *SMOKE.*

Vander.

"Now what?" He nudged her. "We better get out of here and go see what's going on. This time."

"Damn them anyway." She slipped from his lap. And surged from the tub, and snatched up a robe from the stack. Jamming her arms into the sleeves, she swung it closed, and angrily tied the belt.

He slipped next to her, shrugging on his robe. "Golly gee, Doctor Lady, you are certainly purty when you get all riled up. Hyuk, hyuk, hyuk." And pushed her hair aside and kissed the back of her neck.

She stepped away and into the walk-in closet. He followed her.

Then they heard footsteps running across the rear deck.

"Um," he said. "We better go get dressed. Sounds like we have a lot of company. "

Chantal leaned back against him. "Smoke isn't worried."

"True." He shoved the closet door closed. And latched it.

Moonda stomped into the living room and announced

loudly, "We are here to protect him."

R-Bar's head jerked around. "We do not need your help."

"We will protect our own."

Messenger looked up. "Rorx?"

"Of course."

R-Bar frowned. "Sa'ar send you?"

Moonda nodded.

Smoke carried in a tray and spoke to Moonda. "Find a chair. There is nothing around here to worry about." She handed a cup to the Vander and filled it.

"What is this stuff?"

"Coffee." She turned to watch the front door.

Three more Vander hurried inside.

"There is nothing around," said Aada to Moonda.

Smoke rolled her eyes and handed the newcomers cups. "Drag some chairs from the dining room in." She filled their cups and returned to the kitchen.

Aada spoke softly to Moonda, who grinned. Then handing Moonda her cup, Aada stood and drifted down the hallway. Monda set one of the cups on the floor.

She bowed her head and hunched her shoulders. Water flooded over them, steam filled the shower room.

He raised a thick lather in her hair and reached around. "Hold this." And handed her the shampoo bottle.

"That was decadent." She laughed.

He patted her hip. "Once upon a time, I was just a normal person pursuing a quiet life. Then you guys corrupted me. So, it is your fault."

Chantal leaned back. "Nope. Your guys corrupted me."

Soft hands slid over his back, a silken smooth voice

breathed in his ear. "You may corrupt me, Vander Lord."

Tinker leaped sideways and spun around. "Damnation."

Chantal hastily rinsed her face and hair under a nozzle, turned and wiped her eyes with her hand. "Who the hell are you?"

The soft lilac blouse and trousers were plastered to her. "I am Aada, most fair one." She smiled at Tinker. "That one was not before. And yet you refuse the Vander."

Tinker's arm flew up as one finger quivered and pointed. "OUT!"

Aada bowed. "To hear is to obey, Vander Lord." She spun on her heels and walked from the shower room.

He leaned in a corner and glowered at nothing at all.

Chantal slipped over and poked him with a finger. "We all agreed that it was all right with Imdar, but how many more babes do you have, Super Stud?"

"G.D. Vander," he mumbled. Then his eyes focused. "I feel like a house over run with ants." He shook his head. "Amend that, not ants, cockroaches. You can't get rid of them. That's what happens when you help someone." His eyes flared. "Time to take care of this little problem."

R-Bar leaped to her feet, snarling at Aada, who had dried herself. "Now you've done it." She was close to panic. A mate-for-life in that state of mind was dangerous. To everything. Her finger jabbed. "You, you, you, and you. Get into that corner. NOW." Things crackled around her. "MOVE!" She grabbed Moonda by the arm and shoved her sideways.

Moonda screamed and yanked her arm free.

The Vander hurried into the corner, unwilling to test a very dangerous witch, eyes darting from face to face.

Moonda stared at the mark on her arm.

"Oh, dear." Messenger looked at Smoke.

"Shhhhh," replied Smoke.

"Most a'riled be," said Chicken, watching R-Bar cast around the Vander.

And Tinker stomped into the room. "All right, where are they?"

Chicken leaped to her feet. "My Lord, where be thy garb?"

"Put your damn robe on, Cowboy." Chantal hit him in the back of the head with the still folded garment.

Fair Morn snatched it from the floor and held it out and open. "One?"

He grabbed it and jerked it on. "Where are they?" And glared at Shitar and Szaifeh. "Well?" And fastened his belt.

Their eyes jumped to R-Bar.

He spun in her direction. "Ah, ha. All right, Short and Sneaky, what did you do with them?"

She hissed at him. "I am not short." Something mumbled overhead.

Chicken stepped to R-Bar's side. "Most Angry Lord of Us All, what plan thee?"

"Look and see."

Chicken shook her head. "Nay, Our Prince, for thy fire do be most fierce and dangerous to a'us. None of these, Thy Most Frail Ladies, would dare do so." Smoke winked at her from behind him.

Messenger hiccuped.

"Amtar?" Ran peeked up over the top of the back of the couch. "What terrible things are you planning to do to those Purple Magicians?"

"Dad?"

"Husband!" Szaifeh tried to rise. And tumbled to the

floor. Rorx lurched from the doorway. And sagged to his knees.

"Merde." Tinker jumped over, grabbed Rorx as Smoke lifted Szaifeh back onto the couch.

"What are you doing out of bed?" demanded Tinker, heaving Rorx to his feet.

"Weak kitten, stay there," commanded Smoke as she pushed a blanket around Szaifeh.

Rorx wobbled toward the couch. "The Vander owe you everything. And anything you could ever wish for. But I cannot allow you to abuse my now guild sisters. Father."

Tinker helped him sit next to Szaifeh. "Who said I was going to abuse them?"

Szaifeh wrapped her arms around Rorx and kissed him on the temple. "Certainly sounded like it to me, Father-In-Law."

Tinker turned and growled at Fair Morn. "Get out of my chair, Mothra." And flopped into it as she leaped away.

She cowered dramatically in front of R-Bar. "If he tries to pull off my wings, will you protect me?"

"BULLY," cried Messenger.

Chantal handed him a filled cup. "Here."

R-Bar nodded.

The Vander appeared. All trying to appear meek.

"Very tricky," grumbled Tinker. He looked from the crowded corner to Rorx. "Do you know how to make them behave?"

Shitar kicked her legs straight out and relaxed.

Rorx smiled. "What were they doing, Dad?"

"They were after his bod," said Fair Morn.

Aada pushed around Imdar and knelt in front of the couch facing Rorx. "There is nothing wrong with that."

Chicken snorted.

The rest of the Vander slipped closer.

Aada grasped one of Rorx' hands. "Your Father, The Vander Lord, who all must obey and honor, refuses to take the Heart of the Vander. Thus, we cannot release our great debt. I thought to substitute."

"Father is a problem." Rorx looked from her to Tinker, and smiled. "You certainly are. For The Vander."

Tinker frowned at his son. "They are all, every one of them, being remarkably pig-headed, deliberately manipulative, and generally all around sneaky."

His eyes snapped here and there. Vander were standing close, smiling softly.

Rorx nodded. "Very Vander."

Szaifeh stroked Rorx' hair, then looked at R-Bar who was beginning to glare at Shitar who was beginning to get a wry smile on her face.

Tinker noticed all this, sighed heavily, slumped lower in his chair, and held his cup on his stomach.

"Moon-eyed wench, make yourself useful." Chicken jabbed Cazor in the side. "Fetch yon kitchen coffee pot. His cup do require a'filling."

"Stay," ordered Imdar. "I know." She left.

Tinker looked around. At them. "You wanna sit down. You are making me nervous with all that hovering."

The Vander sat in place

Princess?

Me'Lord?

What are we going to do?

I could shoot them, offered Chantal.

Me too, One, added Fair Morn.

My sisters could put a sphere around your lands, Amtar. These Vander mage would not be able to enter. Ran looked at him.

Pounce. Smoke's eyes grew rounder.

What? Tinker looked at her.

Pounce, MindMate. When Sa'ar returns, grab her, and drag her into your den.

Certainly solve the problem, Tink. R-Bar nodded.

Oh, my, said Messenger.

Imdar returned and filled his cup. "Father of My Son, is what we ask so terribly unpleasant?"

Tinker shook his head.

She gently touched his shoulder with her free hand. "Aada is very willing." And leaned close to whisper in his ear. "You could pick anyone. If needed, I could cast a certain spell on you?"

Rorx suppressed his smile and cleared his throat. "Sorry, Dad. There isn't anything that I can do. It is a strong cultural value." He squirmed. "The Vander will never be, ahhhh, it is a hard, a difficult to explain term, ummm, free, healthy, calm, complete." And sagged. "Until you do."

"Husband?" Szaifeh tightened her grip and looked at Imdar.

"He is just tired," said Imdar. "Put him to bed," she commanded.

Two Vander carefully helped Rorx stand up and walked with him as he wobbled into his room.

Tinker stood and handed Imdar his cup. "I am going for a walk."

He headed down the hall to change his clothes.

She swooped high in the late afternoon sky, scanning down below for anyone who shouldn't see her. And spotted him. Standing. Alone. Out past the far pasture. On the lip of the great depression, curving down in a steep graceful spiral, she coasted owl quiet. And landed in front of him, wrapped her arms around him as she did, and announced in deep, rolling tones, "Attack of the Teenage Killer Moth." And kissed him. "GOTCHA."

"Not exactly a teenager," he mumbled. "What are you doing out here, Killer Moth?"

"Seeking prey."

"Find any?"

"Sure. Mind if I devour you and leave bits and pieces of almost digested body parts scattered about to gross out the innocent and unsuspecting villagers?"

"I think that this is somewhere below a B-grade movie."

"Pretty low budget all right. One?" Her eyes watched his.

"What?"

"She is back."

He frowned. "Who?"

"Sa'ar. And sorta dirty."

What? SMOKE?

Just a little beat up. They are under siege, We are packing.

Chicken met him on the rear deck as he ran up. He dropped into a chair, sucking in deep breathes.

"The Vander Heart do be but slightly abused, My Lord. We do Us make her pon couch to lie. The rest do be most greatly agitated."

He sucked in another deep breath. "What's going on? This time?"

R-Bar banged outside. "It is the brother of the thing we killed, the one that attacked Shitar, Rorx, and Szaifeh. Avenging his brother's death. Sa'ar said that he managed to break inside before they isolated him in one wing. Sounds like the fool is unleashing urdark forces."

Shitar slipped out the side door, the air crackling

around her. "I am coming."

"No, you are not," snapped Tinker.

She stalked over and glared down at him, hands jammed on hips. "Uncle, that ptar tak tried to kill my cousins. And me. I am coming." Great forms shifted fog soft dark around her. She smiled, a pure witch smile, threatening all forms of vile.

"I was too kind the last time." Nothing should survive that tried to attack a witch, especially one of the Faan clan.

"Behave," snapped R-Bar, punching one of the things. "Cretin." And nodded at Tinker. "She is coming."

He sighed. "Her decision. How's Sa'ar?"

Messenger joined them, a small day pack on her back. "Well enough to travel, MyTinker. We are not taking much." She stuffed the long black wand up her left sleeve.

"Who's staying home?"

"Szaifeh, Rorx, and most fierce Vander guard, My Lord." Chicken bent and rearranged a knife in her right boot. "And Imdar, the healer. Our Princely Son and His Wife do require much care still."

Shitar turned and stared at R-Bar's hair. She had it fixed in an ornate french roll. "Hum."

"Don't be a smart mouth," growled R-Bar.

"Witches do not have long hair, mostly. Or fixed like that!"

"This one does. And likes it."

The woman stepped from the side door and joined them. Her hair was pulled back and fastened by a dark purple band. On her forehead, over her left eye, was a large band aid. She was wearing a corduroy shirt, jeans, and boots.

"Now what? Who is this?" Tinker shifted his gaze to Chicken as she bent close and whispered in his ear. "Tis naught but Sa'ar, My Lord."

He stared at that person who stared back at him. "Really?"

She stepped closer, and smiled at him. The smile did it.

"You've changed."

She edged closer. '"I have." And plucked at her shirt. "The Aunts gave me these clothes. My others were badly torn." She didn't mention that she could have just created new.

"That is my shirt," said Tinker.

"Her apparel do be most dirty, most filthy t'were, My Prince." Chicken nudged him.

"Yucky," explained Messenger.

"Most well befilled enow, Our Gaping Lord."

Smoke joined them. "We are ready."

"Sure are," agreed Chantal, stepping around her. She had her revolver strapped on, a bandana tied around her forehead. And a small pack filled with ammunition.

Tinker stood. "I'm not. Back in a flash." He ran inside to change his clothes, to fetch his great black weaponkin.

Shadow soft he stepped from his room.

She grabbed him.

"Careful, Father of our son. Our enemy fears nothing, including his own destruction." He kissed him. "Guard her well. If The Heart dies, the body dies." And tightened her arms around him. "You, all of you, are as much a part of us as anyone can ever get." Her eyes sparkled wet.

He kissed the tears away. And tugged her toward the living room. "Ummmm, time to go."

Rorx struggled to sit up. Szaifeh frowned at him, and rearranged pillows and blankets.

"Be careful, Uncle," said Szaifeh. "And don't worry, we are safe here."

Ran stepped from behind the couch, and nodded. "My sisters are coming. Also to guard here."

Aada stepped in front of Tinker. "Our Heart is in your care, Great Vander Lord John Tinker, Chosen One. Guard her well."

He nodded. "Sure."

Rorx cleared his throat. "Dad?"

"What?"

"Be careful, be safe."

Tinker smiled at him. "Aren't we always? Son." And hurried to the corner and snatched up the great two handed sword, it glistened darkly as he swung it up and over his left shoulder. It stuck to his back. "Guess we are ready."

He turned, walked back, and took Rorx' hand. "Look, with the company I keep, I am safe." He smiled. And winked at his son. "See you in a couple of days." And looked at Szaifeh. "Make him rest." And hurried from the room.

Ran followed.

Imdar watched them go.

On the rear deck they gathered. He nodded at R-Bar, who grabbed Shitar and Sa'ar by an arm.

Sa'ar nodded. "Careful, Aunt. Not too close."

R-Bar smiled.

And twisted them away.

Magevern. Deep Below.

The walls were slick with grey black slime. Everything in the room was smashed.

"Where are we?" Tinker looked at the mess, yanked his blade down and around.

"Behind the brother," said Sa'ar.

Wands appeared in hands as Shitar and R-Bar snatched them out.

Messenger yanked her's from her left sleeve. "Bent, twisted, ugly." She stared at the magic strands littering the area.

Fair Morn yanked her cannon from its holster and set levers.

"Most unpleasant a'place," said Chicken, swishing her blade back and forth.

"Which way?" He looked at Sa'ar.

She pointed.

They stepped into a hall.

"Ummmmm?" Tinker held Sa'ar back by one shoulder.

"What?"

"You stay in the back. With Smoke."

She stared at him.

"You are the Heart of the Vander, aren't you?"

"Yes." She frowned at him.

"Well then, I promised a whole bunch of your guys that you would be, ahhhh, well guarded. Can't do that if you are out in front."

"I see."

"DO IT!" snarled Shitar. "Cousin? Please?"

"A strange word for you to use, Cousin. But I will stay safe in the back." She smiled at Tinker. "Just down this hall. We should come up behind him. Aunt did very well."

R-Bar winked at Tinker.

And, ever so carefully, they started down the hall.

Grandeville. Tinker's Place.

"She shouldn't have gone." Rorx looked at his mother.

"The Heart follows her own path." Imdar made them both drink the potion. Szaifeh drank it because Rorx did.

Neither liked the taste.

Ran's sisters sat on the other couch and carefully watched the Vander. They had cast a great crystal clear sphere enclosing most of Tinker's land. Then, after some argument with Szaifeh, had made it fade from sight. It would let through only those selected, none else.

Now they sat, Ran's sisters, on the couch and wondered about such an elseplace as this one. When Ran returned they would have to talk to her about such things.

Rorx stood and walked ever so slowly to the kitchen and back, depositing their cups in the sink. His passage was watched carefully by Szaifeh and Imdar.

He stopped in the doorway between living room and dining room and leaned against the door jamb. "Father said that they would only be gone a few days. It has been longer than that."

Imdar nodded. "Time flows at different rates. As you know." She smiled at him. "Your wife is completely healed and you are rapidly becoming well."

He walked past and stared out one of the picture windows. "I am worried."

Aada slipped over. "They are most capable." And stroked his back.

Magevern. Deep Below.

He sat in the rubble and stared at it and the surrounding mess. Everyone was filthy, clothes torn and tattered.

All were hungry.

Again.

So R-Bar and Sa'ar waved in food.

Everyone ate.

Dark vapors floated in the air, drifted in ugly eddies

puffing toward them from far ahead.

Smoke finished her meal, yanked out her shirt tail and began to wipe Sa'ar's face with it. "You shouldn't have come."

"Had to. My sisters are trapped. This is my home."

Tinker sat slumped against one wall and mumbled, "So now what? This guy seems to have an endless supply of bad news things." He felt how tired they all were, then looked at the entire group.

Shitar sat, sagged against R-Bar as they talked. Smoke was doing something to Sa'ar's face. Fair Morn adjusted the sling on Messenger's left arm while Ran checked the bandages wrapped around Chantal's right thigh.

"My Lord, how fare thee?" Chicken poured disinfectant over the back of his right hand, watching his face carefully.

"Good enough, Princess. But this is taking much too long. Only good thing is that we get some rest between attacks. But we don't seem to be getting anywhere very fast. Any ideas?"

A large piece tumbled from the wall. Messenger and Fair Morn hastily scooted sideways,

Chicken nodded. "Indeed We do. But yon Vander Heart may like it not."

"So?"

She leaned close and whispered softly.

Something far down the corridor snarled angrily.

"Ummmm, I'll talk to her." He heaved himself up, wiped his hand on his pant leg, and walked over, carefully stepping over things on the floor. And sat next to her.

Smoke left them.

"We need to talk."

"What about?" She moved closer and leaned against

his side, holding his arm. Most of the grime was gone from around her eyes. Now he could see the deep fatigue in her face.

"You look like a raccoon in reverse."

Sa'ar managed a smile. "You look pretty bad yourself."

He nodded. "Suppose so. Ahhhh, we need to do something different."

She nodded, turned, and knelt in front of him, legs tucked under. And dropped her hands on his knees. "What, Vander Lord?"

"Ahhhhh, so far all we have managed to do is take care of those things of his, every time he sends them at us. But we are not getting any closer." He waved his hand. And winced. "But we are breaking up your place pretty badly."

"We will rebuild everything." She hitched closer.

He looked into her eyes. "That guy is holed up in the wing where your bedrooms are and that big chamber, isn't he?"

"Yes. The Hall of the Vander Soul." She looked deep, and saw them all, watching her from his eyes.

He leaned and grabbed her forearms. "I want Fair Morn to just erase the whole area. Bedrooms, everything, including that hall."

"Tobtz will die," she whispered, leaning into his grasp, face close to his.

"Merde" The watchers faded from his eyes. He was only Tinker now.

"But she will recover." She kissed him.

"What?"

"A metaphor."

"I want you to aim Fair Morn."

"Yes." She kissed him again

"It is going to leave a awfully large hole."

"Yes." Her lips brushed over his face.

"The rest of your guys out of the way?"

"Yes." Her forehead leaned against his. Her eyes poured into his.

He cleared his throat, and kissed her. "Your place, or mine?"

"Your place. Mine is about to be destroyed." She smiled.

He kissed her again. "I ought to have my head examined.

"I can do that. Afterwards." She stood. "Come, Vander Lord. Let us finish this thing."

He reached out and took her outstretched hand, and heaved himself to his feet. "Right."

They walked over and talked to Fair Morn. Still holding hands.

Fair Morn set her weapon, levers clicking to the appropriate settings.

Sa'ar stepped behind her, grabbed her by the shoulders, and carefully turned her, and faced her exactly where she should be facing. And then reached around and gently pushed Fair Morn's space cannon until it was pointing just so.

Then Sa'ar waited until everyone stood well behind her. She grabbed Tinker's arm and whispered, "Now."

Fair Morn fired.

The silent blast ripped outwards.

A broad, slightly widening emptiness, boring a mirror smooth tunnel out, and out, and out.

They slowly walked into it, watching the far end. Soft witch light illuminated their way.

Sa'ar leaned against his left side and slipped her arm down and around his waist. And sighed.

Tinker swung his great blade up and over as she snatched her arm away, then he threw one arm around her shoulders. "Well, I suppose I could teach the Vander how to bowl. Take their minds off other things."

She halted him, she halted them, and wrapped her arms around him. "We are Vander." And gently, warmly, smiled at him. "And you are The Lord of The Vander Heart."

Crackling violet light erupted from high overhead. A corridor now ended suddenly in space.

"It is Bant." Sa'ar waved.

Bant ducked back. And ran to tell the others.

Chicken joined them. Walking by his other side. They had started forward again. "My Lord, do pear most empty this tube."

Tinker nodded. "Smoke?"

"The rock constricts my sensenet, MindMate, but I see no enemy ahead of us. He is gone."

"O.K. Let's walk down there." He pointed at a depression far ahead. It was all that was left of The Hall of The Vander Soul. "Then go home."

They arrived and stood, stared down into it. Tobtz stood down there, weeping silent tears.

R-Bar grabbed Shitar's hand.

And twisted them away.

Grandeville. Tinker's Place.

They appeared on the rear deck.

A very dirty, very ragged, very tired crew.

And headed inside the house, most turning into The Chamber.

Tinker wobbled into the living room and leaned the great weaponkin in its corner.

"Dad?"

The glow inside the golden jewel that was set in the hilt of the sword slowly faded away.

"Huh? Never noticed that before." He sagged sideways as the long ignored fatigue suddenly hit him.

"Dad, is that you?"

He turned, slowly he turned. "Know anyone else that has a thing like that?" He stepped toward his son, smiling.

Rorx smiled back and stepped close. And was grabbed in a tight hug.

"You were gone so long," gasped his son.

Szaifeh bounded up and grabbed them both, and kissed Tinker's cheek. And leaped back. "Filthy, filthy."

Rorx released him. And looked down at his now stained clothes.

Tinker nodded. "We did get a little dirty all right."

Sa'ar stepped close. "We all did." And slid an arm around Tinker's waist, eyes scanning Rorx. "You look well."

Rorx squinted at her. "Sa'ar? Vander Heart?"

She was almost unrecognizable, hair a matted tangle, roughly shoved back from her forehead, bound with a ragged piece of cloth.

"Yes." She smiled at his expression.

The Vander crowded around them. And bowed to her. And eyed Tinker as her arm tightened around his waist.

"He is dead," announced Sa'ar. "That thing is dead."

"Ahhh, we made a rather large hole," said Tinker to the Vander. "In your, ummm, Tobtz Hall."

Vander gasped with shock, surprise, anguish.

Sa'ar rubbed his side with her hand. "Of little consequence."

Ran dashed past to talk with her sisters, who looked askance at her appearance. And made her stay away, just a little.

Noises came echoing down the hall as the rest of the crew piled their gear, shed their clothes, and turned on the shower room.

"Let's go get clean," said Tinker, turning toward the hall. Sa'ar let him lead her away.

Chicken met them as they stepped into the atrium of their chamber. She had shed boots, socks, and shirt. "Me Lord, do pile vile clothes there. Me'thinks to burn all." Her body had a number of grey blotches on it.

He smiled and sat on the floor and began to yank off his boots. "Looks like the grime went right through our clothes."

She looked down. "Indeed, We do be most besplotched." And tugged off her trousers. "We did fetch in great quantities of soap sweet smelling hair stuff." And hurried away.

Standing, he tossed his shirt on the pile. "You heard her. Everything goes there. Except the boots. I think that we can salvage the boots."

"I may join you in there?" She shrugged off her boots.

He laughed. "Sure, fellow warrior. I will even scrub your back. I bet Shitar was the first one in."

He headed for the noisy gang in the shower room.

Steam was billowing out the entrance.

She followed him.

Shitar growled at him. "I was second." She had heard his comment.

Smoke smiled at him. "She is a little slow." And handed him a bar of soap.

"Tar," gasped Sa'ar. "What happened? Are you all right?" A long red welt ran from Shitar's right shoulder diagonally across her torso.

"Yes. Near miss."

And as the dirt, the grime, and the other stains were slowly washed off and down the drains, Tinker realized that everyone was displaying welts, bruises, cuts, and abraded areas.

"No wonder everyone's clothes were so ragged." He sighed.

"Wash my hair, please." Sa'ar tossed her hair band, mostly grimy black, into the entry room.

"Stand under this nozzle, Vander Heart, and we will see whether you will ever be clean again."

She did. He squirted shampoo over her head.

Messenger's eyes popped open. "I will need help getting out. My arm is really really sore."

Fair Morn surged out of the hot tub. "No problemo, Dude-lett." She reached down and lifted Messenger out and set her on the wooden flooring. "Drain a little. I'll get the towels and robes." And walked into the closet.

"All out." ordered Chicken, looking at Smoke, who winked.

"I am not ready," stated Shitar

"Are now," snapped R-Bar.

"OUCH!"

"Move it, young witch." R-Bar smiled.

Shitar clambered out. And into a large towel held out by Fair Morn. "Why? What's the hurry?"

Fair Morn smiled at her. "Pressing political business."

"Fair wry a'pun, that," observed Chicken, shooing them out the side door, arms heaped with heavy white robes.

Tinker stepped into the hot tub. And wondered. What ever they were up to they weren't talking, their minds had slammed shut. "Now what?" he mumbled.

Sa'ar dropped beside him. "I think that we shall have one of these when we rebuild. We certainly have a large new space."

She looked over the edge at the wet floor, the towels, and the hamper. "Where did they go?"

He smiled. "Up to no good, I suppose."

She stepped in front of him. And stared at him. "Hold me. Please."

"Sure." He did.

Smoke, Chicken, and Fair Morn were busy at the kitchen range. R-Bar and Chantal at the oven. Ran and Messenger set the table and opened bottles of wine.

Aada looked into the kitchen. "What is that you are cooking?"

Rorx slid a finger up her spine as he joined her. "Smells like chili to me. You will like it."

Szaifeh pinched him as she slipped past. "Where do you keep the crackers?" she asked Smoke.

Moonda stood next to Rorx and slipped an arm around his waist. "Where is she?"

Rorx shrugged.

"In our chamber, " said Smoke, nodding at Fair Morn. "We will need lots of grated cheese."

She sprawled on top of him.

And kissed him.

And wiggled, just a little.

And laughed.

A way down, deep in the throat laugh.

"Something funny?"

"Aada will be disappointed."

"Umm," he said.

Sa'ar crossed her arms across his chest and lifted up, just enough to look into his eyes. And smiled. "She wouldn't have to be."

"Oh, no, you don't."

She kissed him again and wrapped her arms around his chest. "Small joke, Vander Lord."

He rolled them onto their sides. "Small favor, Vander Heart?"

"Oh . . . yes."

"Talk to Chantal. She really gets upset with all this Vander stuff."

"I . . . am not stuff."

"You know what I mean."

"Talk later," she growled.

They were scattered all over the living room. Eating. And drinking. It was a sort of an indoor picnic. Messenger had arranged it.

Aada sat next to him and ran her fingers through his hair. "We are leaving after this meal." And kissed the side of his face.

"No need to eat and rush off," said Tinker, brushing the hair back from his face.

"We are leaving the Male and Our Heart here." Her lips brushed over his face and nestled against his ear. "I think that our debt is quite satisfied." She laughed, softly. "Mighty Vander Lord." And sat back.

He sighed.

And ducked.

Chantal had just sailed a cracker at him. "Ask for a hundred dollas," she grumbled.

Chapter Eleven

It Just Keeps On Happening.

Grandeville. Tinker's Place. A Nice Warm Day.

He held her in place.

Pinning her to the ground.

In the thick grass.

Using his body weight.

Her arms, thrown over her head, were trapped by the strong hands that clamped around her wrists.

She swore and thrashed as she heard his assistant, a most evil creature, approaching, dragging an instrument of torture.

"Hee hee hee," cackled the fiendish evil assistant, aiming.

"Dare not, foul wench," she commanded.

He released her as the cackler fired. The blast caught her in the side and washed over her

"What you get," he said, looking down at the body, leaking fluid.

Her rescuers, realizing that they had arrived too late, slowed to a walk. And stood, staring at the body.

"Too late. They got her."

"That shirt is really thin material."

The evil assistant blasted the observers where they stood, cackling happily.

"What they deserve," he said, wrapping his assistant

in his arms, giving her a friendly pat.

She nodded and dropped her weapon, after carefully twisting shut the nozzle on the hose.

"Let's get something to eat. I'm hungry."

She nodded. "Good idea."

They walked off, paying little attention to their victims.

"BOMBS AWAY!"

She released the last three water balloons.

As they crashed down around the pair, he leaned back and yelled up at her. "HEY! You are on our side."

"I know," she said, landing lightly next to the pair. "But you had already killed them. And I didn't want to carry those things around any longer. We going to eat? Now?"

"What I get for using cheap help," he grumbled, heading for the food.

The two cooks, setting out the last platter, watched them approach.

"He is certainly getting familiar with the help," said one.

The other nodded. "Doesn't look like she minds."

"Short people are like that."

"I am not short," snarled the evil assistant, clomping across the rear deck. "And you are just jealous."

"Vertically disadvantaged," he said, slipping an arm around each of the cooks. "We killed them all. They didn't stand a chance."

One cook looked down at his enfolding hand. "Guess he is going to get familiar with all the help."

"Guess so." The other smiled.

"To the victor go the spoils." He kissed them both. "Food looks good."

The one cook looked at the other. "An archaic term

meaning to strip or plunder. Think we are safe?"

"What?" he said.

"Spoils," she said.

"Despoil," said the other. "I am surprised he didn't drag her off."

"Let's eat," he said, stepping around them and taking a dish.

"Spoil sport," said one.

"An awfully literate pun," commented the other.

He passed his assistant a cup. "Do you have any idea what is going on?" And sat on the bench as he dragged over his plate.

"Hee hee hee," she cackled, rubbing the ornate ring she was wearing on her left thumb against her check.

"Ah, ha."

"All mine," she said, patting his thigh as she joined him on the bench.

"Oh boy." The bomber heaped her plate. "Three bean salad." And sat next to his open side. "We won. Fair and square. Although she cheated." And pointed.

The first victim had settled across the table from them and munched on a celery stalk, and stated firmly, "Never."

The cooks joined them.

"How did she cheat?" asked Chantal.

"She wore that really thin shirt knowing that when it got wet and stuck to her, he would be distracted so her foul hench-persons would be able to get him while he was staring."

Fair Morn dragged the salad bowl over to take another serving, or two.

He winked at the wet victim. "Pretty distracting all right, Princess."

"Hee, hee, hee," cackled R-Bar. "Didn't distract me."

"Wench," said Chicken. "Pass fair salad a'Us, please."

Winners, losers, and the cooks ate lunch.

Smoke nudged Chantal. "If we hadn't been cooking, you could have gotten your shirt wet. Bet that would have distracted him."

"Most unkind," said Chicken. "A'jesting pon Our Verra Own under endowment."

"Knock it off,"growled Tinker, attempting to redirect their conversation.

R-Bar smiled at him. "Thought that we'd wait til later."

He banged his cup down hard.

All eyes snapped in his direction.

"Now what is going on?" he demanded.

"Nuttin," said Chantal.

"Nothing."

"Nada."

"Nope."

"Nay."

"Nope-a-roo."

"How come I find that hard to believe?" He looked around at the sea of innocent faces, or trying to look innocent faces.

Chantal grabbed another piece of bread. "What are we supposed to be up to?"

Messenger giggled and nudged R-Bar. "That is his job."

"That does it." Tinker stood. "I will be upstairs. Working. Maybe all you guys ought to take a soak in the hot tub." He left them and went inside.

"Oh my." said Messenger.

"Jolly good idea, that." Chicken stood, grabbed another sandwich, and began to unbutton her shirt with her free hand.

"His Ran is getting a little cool," said Ran, pulling her shirt loose. "Being wet."

Messenger followed them all inside.

"Join you in a little." Fair Morn emptied the salad bowl onto her plate.

Smoke and Chantal began carrying everything back toward the kitchen.

"We weren't doing anything. Different," said R-Bar to Fair Morn. "Were we?"

"Nope. Do you want that piece of bread?"

Three-o-clock.
       In the afternoon.

And came a soft knock on the door, before it was swung open.

"Coffee and cookies, My Lord?"

"Huh?" He spun around in his swivel chair. It complained bitterly, a rust rasp. "Oh. Break time?" His eyes checked the clock on the wall.

"Indeed." She set the tray on top of a cluttered table and poured both cups full. And handed him one.

"Pajamas?" he asked around a mouthful of cookie.

"Most comfortable for a'lounging, Our Prince." She nodded. "We did ourselves soak in great warm hot tub and do talk some."

"About?"

"We do a'loafing then decide whilst amongst much brushing of hair and pedicurial care, sweet smelling lotions, and potions a'plying."

"Uh huh?"

"Fierce warriors do become most lithesome of maidens, My Lord."

"Ummmmm."

"We would hard and rowdy edges smooth away."

He looked at her through his eyebrows. "Is it safe to go downstairs?"

Smiling, she bowed, sweeping her arm toward the door. "Most Great and Fierce Warrior, there do be none but Our Verra Ownselves."

Taking his cup in hand, he started downstairs, reaching out. "Feels awfully quiet."

"Most meek and mild we do be."

"Getting worse and worse."

Smoke and Fair Morn met them at the base of the stairs. Smoke held a thick white robe and his pajamas. Fair Morn held a large towel, soap, and shampoo.

"Clean and pretty, " said Fair Morn.

"Neat and tidy," added Smoke.

"Bathe and relax," added Chicken, deftly plucking the cup from his hands, heading for the kitchen

"Worse and worse," mumbled Tinker, stepping into the shower room. "Where are you going?"

Fair Morn smiled. "Scrub your back? Wash your hair?"

"Massage?" Smoke's eyes gleamed.

He tossed his shirt into the hamper. "If I refuse?"

"We would weep," said Fair Morn, trying to look unhappy.

"Pitifully," added Smoke. Then she took everything from Fair Morn except the soap and shampoo and went around to wait in the hot tub room.

"Baa," said Tinker as he walked through the kitchen.

"Baaa," he said on his way through the dining room.

"Baaaa," he said as he stepped into the living room.

"Tink?" asked R-Bar, rising to her feet.

"Lamb to the slaughter." He stared at her. "Not bad for a witch."

"I am beautiful." They had arranged her hair, glossy black waves over red pajamas next to pale skin.

"Actually," he said. "You are gorgeous, kiddo. May I sit next to you?"

"Yah." She dropped back into the couch.

So did he. "Now what?"

She nestled against his side.

"Maybe you guy ought to do this more often. Hair smells pretty good. It's hard to remember."

"We just thought to be nice."

He threw an arm around her shoulders and tickled her. "Pretty nice, all right." And tugged her around. "Thanks."

She blinked. And slipped her arms around his chest.

They ate dinner by candlelight, windows draped to cause the necessary dimness for the flickering candles.

He dabbed at his eyes with his napkin. And just looked and looked. At them.

"There are times," he said, clearing his throat vigorously. "That are beyond the power of words to describe."

"Let's have dessert." Fair Morn smiled broadly.

"I will get it." Smoke stood, slipped past, trailing one finger lightly over R-Bar, Chicken, and then Tinker. R-Bar stood, walked over, and lightly placed her hand on his shoulder.

He looked over. "What's the matter?" And reached up and wrapped her hand in his.

She hiccuped. "Witches are never, never, ever treated

so . . . wonderfully."

"It is true," whispered Ran. "None would dare. To think to do such a thing."

Chantal slipped an arm around Ran and hugged her. "It is not just witches."

Tinker kissed R-Bar's palm. "Chantal's right." He released R-Bar's hand and stood, holding his glass high. "A toast."

Glasses hastily refilled, floated upward, and eyes turned and watched his face.

"To you. All. Seven times more than any one man deserves." He smiled at them and quickly took a drink.

"Hear, hear," said Chicken, draining her glass.

He refilled it. "But," he said, scanning their faces. "It doesn't mean you get to run amok." He dropped into his chair.

"We wouldn't do that." Messenger eyed the dessert as Smoke set it on the table, handed him the server and shoved a pile of plates in front of him.

"Indeed, Our Prince." Chicken held out her empty glass. "If this fella do require a'running, someone else must do the deed."

Smoke refilled their glasses.

He stopped serving. "What fella?"

"Ah Muck, Handsome Lord." She took a large swallow from her glass. "That Oriental fella."

"Ahhhh." He topped up her glass. "You having dessert, Princess?"

"Indeed." She nodded.

He served. Then slumped in his chair.

And looked at them.

And finished his dessert.

And looked at them.

"John?" Chantal frowned at him, worried. His expression was getting really strange.

"Nothing. It is just that if someone wrote a story and described this scene, I would not believe it either."

"Pish tosh, Our Love." Chicken waggled her fork at him. "Fret thee not. We do be we. And that do most certainly do be that."

"Me too," said Messenger.

Tinker leaned his arms on the table and propped his head in his hands. And smiled at them. "Right."

"Let's watch two movies," suggested Smoke. "You get the biggest couch." Her eyes gleamed. "Me too."

"I demand equal time," snapped Chantal.

"How equal?" demanded R-Bar, frowning at her.

"Two movies at an assumed one point five hours divided by seven per movie is twenty five minutes apiece, plus or minus some small tolerance. R-Bar gets the remainder." Chantal nodded at the short witch.

"I'll get the kitchen timer." Fair Morn jumped up. "First."

He laughed as they headed into the living room. "Awfully organized."

"Damn hard to snuggle with seven babes at once." Chantal stepped to his side. "Second." She kissed him. "Tonight we all want to be held, Simba Leader."

"Right." He threw an arm around her.

So they settled in the living room, ready to watch the double feature, Smoke and Chicken each choosing one.

And their minds flowed together and merged.
And they became one.
And held each other.

And watched movies.

And became more than they had been.

He smiled and kissed the tip of her nose. "Well, what do you think, kiddo?"

R-Bar smiled at him. "You did it, Tink."

"What?"

"Held seven babes at once."

"Kinna hard to believe."

Strong hands grabbed him, lifted him up, and dumped him on the floor. Gently.

"Hey."

Smoke and Fair Morn sprawled next to him.

"More room down here. MindMate."

And he was surrounded.

"You guys up to something?"

"Naught, Me'Lord." Chicken tickled his ear. "'Tis couch small compared to a'being pon floor large."

Ran peered upside down into his face and kissed his forehead. "Most true."

"Just a happy pride of lions." Chantal sat cross-legged, bent forward and tickled the bottom his foot.

He sat up. "Now there is a spooky thought."

"What?" Fair Morn rolled flat and looked over at him.

"Be surrounded by large carnivores."

Smoke smiled at him. And slowly licked her tips.

He stifled a yawn.

"We do not have a big enough bed," said Messenger.

They all jumped to their feet.

Except Tinker.

"Stay there," commanded Chantal.

Smoke and Fair Morn started shoving furniture around.

The rest ran down the hall.

And returned.

Laden with blankets, pillows, and mats.

"Out of the way, Tink." R-Bar nudged him with a knee and dropped her load. And hurried away.

He stood to one side and watched.

Chicken wrapped her arms around him and leaned against his back. "Our Own, we do all feel such a need this even."

Then they were finished. The lights snapped out.

"Crawl in." Chantal tugged at his ankle.

Bottles clinked as things were carried in from the kitchen.

"Party time." Messenger giggled and pushed a bottle into his hand.

"We are being crude," explained Fair Morn. "No cups."

"Just a quiet prelude before sleep." Ran took the bottle from his hand.

"I never cease to be surprised," said Tinker as he wiggled into a comfortable spot.

"You're not the only one." Chantal propped her head on his stomach.

Stepping carefully over various of the lumps, she nudged him with her toe.

"That is positively decadent, Tinker. Good thing that I am your lawyer."

His eyes opened and slowly focused. "Timezit?"

"Almost nine-o-clock. That is pretty decadent also."

"Go away."

"Is that anyway to speak to your very own hard-working, underpaid, and beautiful attorney?"

"Yep."

"You got any coffee?"

"The pots still on the timer. Should be ready. You know where everything is." He smiled up at her. "Bring me a cup?"

She grinned back. "I'll put coffee delivery on my bill." And headed into the kitchen.

He managed to reach the couch before Sandy returned, bearing two steaming cups, and a basket of doughnuts.

She sat and nudged him. "I stopped and got some. Gratis." She poked him with an elbow. "What kind of orgy was it anyway? They haven't moved an inch since I got here. And that is a very robust crowd for one man to tire that badly."

Smoke opened one eye. "Pass the doughnuts down here, please. I drink mine black."

Sandy headed back to the kitchen. "I'll bring the pots and cups."

Smoke sat up and took a big bite out of her doughnut. Bright red filling squirted out.

Ran's eyes flew open. "Is it raining in here?"

"Jelly goo," explained Smoke, carefully wiping up the glob with one fingertip.

Ran twitched. "Tickles."

"He could do it. But would probably get over excited and loose control." Smoke nodded at her. "We have a visitor. Button your top."

Ran moistened one fingertip and rubbed. "Sticky." And licked her finger, carefully watching Tinker's face. "Ummmmm, raspberry. Any more?" And sat up. And buttoned up.

Sandy set the tray on the floor, went back, and

returned with a tray loaded with cups. And pointed at the doughnut basket. "Serve yourself. Everything." And sat in one of the chairs. "Not too bad, two out of seven."

Blankets flew. "I smell doughnuts." Messenger popped up. "Hi, Sandy. Oh boy." She crawled over a lump.

"OOOMP," said the lump.

"Sorry." Messenger sat next to Smoke. "Pass the doughnuts. And the coffee. And the cream. And a spoon. And a saucer. Please?"

"Soooo, how ya doing, Tinker?" Sandy leered at him.

"Well." He straightened up, a little. "Until about, ummm, ten minutes ago, life was quiet, for us. How's married life?"

Sandy laughed. "Wonderful. Of course, with Red, some kinds of decisions are a little different. Everything that we buy is on the large and study size."

Tinker sat up.

Smoke reached over and refilled his cup.

He looked at their visitor. "So, how are you doing, Sandy?"

She leaned toward him. "I need a favor?"

"Oh, oh."

"Sure," said Smoke.

A hand poked up from a tangled mass of blankets. The fingers wiggled. "Sustenance. Else We do Us perish most horribly."

Messenger snatched a doughnut and pushed it into the hand. "Chocolate covered."

"Indeed?" Chicken sat up, shedding blankets. "Pon my soul, tis true. From whence came these, Sweet Kitten?"

"Turn around," mumbled Tinker.

She did.

She smiled. "Fair morn to thee, Sweet Bringer of

Sweets."

A blanket rose into a pyramidal shape. "Thought that we were sleeping late," growled a voice.

Sandy looked at Tinker. "She said that every morning when we were in college."

"Sandy?" asked the pyramid. "What are you doing here?"

"Not much. Just wrestling around on the couch with the big fella."

The pyramid collapsed as blankets fell to one side. Chantal leaned toward them, leaning on a lump with one hand.

"OOOMP," said the same lump as before. "Someone is getting awfully fresh."

"Oh." Chantal sat back. "Sorry."

"That is two different sorrys in one morning," grumbled the lump.

Messenger turned, lifted some covers, and peered under. "We are having doughnuts, Sandy brought them."

"Is that any reason to play with my anatomy?"

"We were not doing that." Chantal shoved at the lump. "Come out of that cocoon and show yourself. Let's see what you have turned into."

"In ugly, out beautiful," commented Tinker.

Fair Morn poked her head out and stared up at the ceiling. "Not true." She blinked her eyes. "Did I hear someone say something about doughnuts?" She licked her lips.

"Trapped," growled another voice. "Who tangled the blankets?"

Fair Morn kicked her legs.

"Watch it," snapped R-Bar as she popped to the surface.

"Reminds me of a circus act," observed Sandy. She

reached down and filled a cup. And touched up Tinker's. "Or have you snatched another one?"

"Somebody file a missing persons report?" Tinker was mostly sitting upright, mostly awake.

"Nope. But Freddie is coming for a visit."

"Ah, ha," said Tinker. "The shoe finally dropped."

"Lots of room," said Smoke.

"Thanks," said Sandy.

Tinker mumbled something.

"Piffle," suggested Chicken.

"I owe you one, " said Sandy.

"NO, YOU DON'T," snapped Chantal. "We had enough of that Vander stuff."

Sandy frowned at her. "What is that?"

"Never mind." Tinker waggled his free hand at her. "It was just the phrase you used about owing a debt that caused the reaction, that's all."

"Right," said Chantal. "Forget it."

"Not really awake yet," added Smoke.

Chantal leaned back against the other couch, holding the cup with both hands. "My partner can take care of things today." Her eyes dropped to half-closed.

"That it?" asked Tinker.

Chicken stood and walked past Sandy. "Do stay for to breakfast have."

"I just did."

"For some," said Chicken, laughing. "Tis naught but mere appetizer."

Sandy smiled. "I forgot."

"Really hungry." Fair Morn rolled over and sat up. "Any left?" And crawled toward Smoke and the basket.

"Yes," said Sandy. "To both questions."

"O. K," said Tinker, as he chewed on the last piece of toast, his toast. Fair Morn bought more from the kitchen. "So Freddie is coming for a visit, and Hotel Mob Scene is giving her a room, right?"

"Indeed, Me'Lord." Chicken nodded.

"Err," said Sandy.

"Ah, ha."He squinted at her. "I just heard the other shoe drop. Spit it out, Counselor. And how many feet do you have?"

"Male or female?" Chantal frowned at her friend. "Janine."

"That it?" Tinker was watching Sandy's face.

"Yes."

He leaned back. And slumped. "S'pose that's all right."

"We have room." Smoke grabbed some of the toast. "Pass the jam, please." She nudged Sandy.

Tinker slumped into an even more comfortable position, and cupped his chin in one hand. "What are you up to?"

"Tinker?" Sandy looked wonderfully blank. It was part of her lawyer skills.

"Let me rephrase the question, Sneaky Pete. What does Freddie or Janine or you want? Huh?"

"Well," sighed Sandy.

"A wet beginning," observed Tinker.

Messenger bumped R-Bar with her elbow.

Ran sat straighter. The coffee pot slid over to her open hand. She refilled her cup and watched Sandy from the corners of her eyes.

"Your silence is making me nervous," said Tinker, staring at his attorney.

Who sat straighter. And smiled. "It is privileged information."

Shoving himself into an upright position, he glowered at her. "No lawyer games." Then he smiled. "O.K., your privileged client and her buddy can stay home. Or they can bunk with you and Red."

Chantal banged her cup down on the table top. "My friends can stay here. And don't you dare glower at me, Simba Leader."

"Whoops," said Sandy.

"Yah," said Messenger.

"What?" asked Tinker.

"Lots of rooooom," added Fair Morn.

"NO," said Tinker.

"T'will Our Verra Own pleasure be," said Chicken.

"We will protect you," said Smoke.

"How come I am always the minority in this democracy?" He frowned in their direction, each in turn.

"Piffle," suggested Chicken.

"I was thinking of a different word," added Chantal.

"Most crude," said Chicken.

"You sure that it is all right?" Sandy looked around the table.

Ran lightly touched her arm, ""He likes to grump."

"Well." Sandy smiled expansively. "What else is new?"

"Germ," mumbled Tinker.

They arrived three days later.

Freddie and Janine in a large glistening silver car.·

Sandy drove up behind them as they parked. Her car was smaller, battered, brown. It didn't glisten.

It was mid-afternoon.

Quite warm.

A pleasant time of day.

Chicken greeted them, dripping water, a large towel wrapped around her waist. "Most welcome. We all do be in most great pool. Bring you suits for swimming?"

Freddie shook Chicken's hand, very formally. "We are very pleased that you would put us up, Princess."

"Where's the grump?" asked Sandy.

"In office, a'working." Chicken smiled. "He do bout this hour finish and descend." She led them over and onto the rear deck, and down toward the swimming pool.

People were crawling out, leaping in, amid great amounts of laughing, and no small amount of swearing.

Smoke and Fair Morn were fighting off the others, who seemed intent upon drowning them.

"Foul beasts," sputtered R-Bar, heaving herself up and over the lip of the pool at the deep end of the pool from where she had just been tossed.

"Damn fresh," snarled Chantal, heaving herself up, stepping into the shallow end of the pool, tying her top. She looked over and grumbled. "Did you bring suits? If you didn't, I am sure that we can find you something."

"Wouldn't want to interfere," said Freddie, taking a chair, beyond splash range.

Sandy laughed. "Can't stay that long."

"Think that I will pass for now." Janine sat so she could watch whatever was going on.

"EEEEEEEK," screeched Messenger. Smoke and Fair Morn had her by the ankles and the wrists and were banging her up and down on the surface of the water, more or less.

"Hi," said Tinker to their guests as he stepped from the side door. He looked at Chantal, then at Chicken. "I think that

I would rather not know." And sat.

Ran joined them. And plopped into Tinker's lap. "Hey."

"It is a warm day," she said, puddling in his lap.

The water war ended And everyone grabbed towels and came over to visit.

Smoke leaned over him, dripping water, just a little from her hair on him, and smiled. "Are we having things to drink?" And looked sideways. "Can we get you something?"

"Root beer?" said Freddie.

"Same," said Janine.

"Coffee?" asked Sandy.

Fair Morn picked up the last of the towels and headed for the laundry room and then the kitchen.

"You are dripping," said Tinker.

"I know," replied Smoke. "It is good for you."

Fair Morn returned and slipped the large tray onto the table top.

R-Bar handed Tinker and Sandy cups. Messenger poured.

"Thanks," said Tinker. And cleared his throat.

Not yet, said Smoke. *Freddie is very nervous.*

See anything?

Very guarded.

All three?

Only one is thinking of telling.

"Need any help with dinner?" he asked whoever was planning on doing that.

"Keep out." Chantal stood and looked at Sandy. "Stay for dinner."

"Can't. Got to get back to work, make a pass at a big cop before he goes to work, and do lots and lots of paperwork." Sandy stood and smiled. "Maybe this weekend?

The monsters are off duty."

Freddie blanched.

Janine took and squeezed her hand. Ran noticed.

"We will roast most large a'turkey," said Chicken.

"Saturday?" asked Chantal.

Sandy thought for a moment, then smiled. "We will be here. With Green."

"Oh boy," said Messenger, who especially like turkey. "I will make dessert. Just lots and lots. Really really."

"I will help," added R-Bar. "With dessert." She especially liked licking the spoons.

"And excitement runs through the house," mumbled Tinker.

"As long as she behaves it will be all right," said Fair Morn.

"Hum." Ran pinched him just above one hip.

"What?" He looked at Fair Morn.

"OUCH." He glared at Ran.

"Brazen hussy," added Chantal.

"Who?" demanded Tinker.

"Bye." Sandy headed for her car, giggling all the way.

"Indeed, My Lord," stated Chicken, gathering up the towels.

Smoke leaned close and breathed into his ear. "So where did you hide her, Sneaky Mate?"

He tried to sit up. Unsuccessfully. Ran wouldn't cooperate. "What are you guys talking about?"

"Excitement, MyTinker. Is she beautiful?" Messenger giggled.

"You are all water-logged."

"Must be very light on her feet," suggested Chantal to R-Bar. "If she is running about the place, she hasn't made a sound. Yet."

R-Bar nodded. "Probably because he wasn't."

"All right, that is just about enough of that." He sighed. And said to their guests. "They get out of control. Now and then. So, how's life in Portland?"

"Yet," finished R-Bar.

"We are going inside and change." Ran stood.

They all did.

Leaving a damp Tinker outside to talk with their house guests.

Late Evening. Same Day.

"Knock, knock," he said, gently rapping with one knuckle and pushing the door open and stepping inside. "Peek-a-boo, I see you."

Her mind clamped down as she yanked the blanket up and over her head. "No you don't."

He sat on the edge of the bed. "We need to talk." And bounced a little.

Her head popped out. "What?"

"About your buddies."

She lurched upright. "Oh no, you don't. It is bad enough with you messing around with those Vander."

He sighed.

Pushing back, she leaned against the headboard. "That bad, huh?"

"What do they want?"

"Beats me. Slip in. It is a big bed."

"You sure you don't know?"

"Cross my heart." She did. And grinned at him. "Or something. Heart isn't in the middle, you know." And frowned at him. "Rumpf. Can't even distract you."

"May I enter?" Ran peeked in through the doorway, pushing the door just open enough to look inside.

"Join the party," said Chantal.

"Oh." Ran stopped. "Maybe I shouldn't." And started to turn away.

"What?" asked Tinker.

Ran ducked her head. "That is not proper, Amtar. And very crude."

"An expression," said Chantal. "Look."

Ran slipped inside Chantal's mind. *I see.* And came over and sat on the edge of the bed. "Hum." And bounced, just a little.

"What?" asked Chantal.

One side of Ran's mouth puckered. "I do not think that he wants them."

"Who?" asked Tinker.

"I didn't either," replied Chantal. "But he is just so easy to tease."

"I just wanted to know what our visitors want, that's all," he grumbled. "And all I get is lip."

"Amtar?"

"What?"

"Would it be acceptable if your Chantal showed me how she gave you lip?"

"Huh?"

"Gave you lip?"

"Oh, boy," laughed Chantal. "Come'mer, Cowboy." And couldn't stop. Laughing.

Tinker sighed. And looked from her to Ran. "Smoke better do something. Our language memories aren't all there, yet."

"Peek." Messenger peered around the door jamb into the bedroom. Ran beckoned her in.

Messenger perched on the edge of the bed next to Ran. "Are we having a party?" And bounced a little.

Chantal shook her head. "I don't think that this bed is that big."

"OH MY." Messenger looked at her, her eyes going all round. "He was trying to get you both in this bed?"

"NO," snapped Tinker.

"Chicken," said Chantal.

"What? Pray tell." she said, stepping into the room.

"Nothing," answered Tinker.

Chicken took another bite from her already bitten egg sandwich. "Then why do We be given most soft call, do tell?" She sat at the foot of the bed, cross-legged and faced Chantal. And bounced a little.

"That looks good." Messenger nodded her head violently. "Really really."

"Indeed, tis most true." Chicken took another bite.

A number of dishes appeared on the bed.

"Heard all the noise," explained R-Bar, sitting on the other edge of the bed. "Pass the bread, please?" And bounced a little.

"I really don't think that my bed is big enough for a picnic." Chantal made a sandwich and yanked her legs around so she could sit cross-legged.

She tapped him on a knee. "Pull your legs around, John. We need more room."

He did. "Pass the toast."

So they had a picnic.
        And they scattered.

"Ahhhhhhh, Simba Leader?"

"Ummmm?"

"The heart is on the other side in case that is what you are looking for."

"Ummmm."

"Ahhhhhhh, Simba Leader?"

"Ummmm?"

"This is a very large bed."

"Uh, huh."

"Sooooooo, how about we wiggle our way back toward the middle. My arm is dangling over the side right now. Ahhh ummm, and I don't think that we want to fall, just now."

"Ummmmmmmm. Right."

The screaming brought them all running. Dragging on robes, dashing down the hallway.

"WHAT?" Chantal banged open the door and charged into the bedroom, hitting the light switch.

Freddie cowered in a corner, on the floor, held in Janine's arms. Janine was whispering softly to her and rocking back and forth.

"Nightmare," said Janine.

Tinker leaned through the doorway, having just put his weaponkin back into its corner. "She going to be all right?"

"For awhile," said Janine.

Chantal nodded. And looked at Tinker. "I get a rain check."

"Only on sale items." He nodded at her as Smoke pushed into the room.

"Very, very, upset," said Smoke, kneeling next to the pair in the corner. She stared at Freddie. And then at Chantal and Tinker. "Strange."

"What?" asked Tinker.

"How strange?" asked Chantal.

Smoke looked at Janine. "Do you know what her terror

dreams are about?"

Janine's eyes jumped from face to face. She jerked her head up and down.

"Even at her home?" asked Smoke.

"Yes," whispered Janine.

"Just her?"

Janine shook her head, face flushing. "Me too. Sometimes."

She stared at Chantal, and began to cry. "I do not understand."

Smoke carefully eased Janine to her feet. "Help me. Sleep with her. We will be in the living room. Talking."

Janine helped Smoke ease Freddie into the bed and then laid down next to her, holding her friend, whispering softly to her.

Shutting off the lights, they slipped away. Into the living room.

The rest had headed back to their rooms. Fair Morn and Chicken carrying snacks.

"You are kidding!" Tinker stared at her.

Smoke shook her head. "You have been attacking them. Horribly. In their dream terror sleep."

"Smoke? Sister Self?" Chantal frowned at her. "While we were . . . ?"

"Yes."

"That is damn Freudian."

"I'll say." Tinker filled their cups. "How is that possible?"

Smoke shrugged. "We always isolate."

"I mean from here to Portland. It is at least two hundred fifty, sixty miles. We can't reach that far. Even Grandeville is out of range."

Smoke shrugged again. Then she grinned at him.

Tinker frowned. "What? I don't like that grin."

Chantal laughed. "I volunteer." She raised her hand. And winked at him. "Besides I've got a rain check. For services . . . interrupted, umm, incompletely rendered, so to speak." She ran her hand over his hair. "So to speak."

Now he was glaring, from one to the other. "What are you two grinning about?"

Chantal kissed him on the cheek. "There are times when you are really slow. Shall I explain?"

"Please do."

"Smoke stays here and reaches out as wide as possible." Chantal glanced over at the wall clock. "Ummm, say at three-thirty, that gives us plenty of time to, ahhhh, get ready. We, you and I, honey bunch, drive to town, check into the Romp and Stomp Motel, and at three-thirty you, as they euphemistically say in certain genres of literature, work your wicked ways upon me."

"WHAT?"

"And Smoke tries to pick us up."

"MERDE."

"It's for the good of science." Chantal grinned at him.

"I will be in Freddie's room," said Smoke. "And I will try to pick up what is happening with her as well. Otherwise you may have to, err, sleep alone for a long, long time."

Chantal jumped up and tugged at his arm. "Let's go, Big Stud. You can pretend that your silver tongue has just talked me out of one of the local pubs."

She dragged him down the hall. Giggling. And began singing in a somewhat minor key, "Hi ho, hi, ho, it's off to work we go. As soon as we get dressed, that is."

Smoke stood in Freddie's room. In the dark. Pupils

dilated wide. Watching the clock. And the sleeping pair in the bed.

She reached out.
And out.
And out.
Minds open in all directions.

Soft sleep thoughts of the rest of herself flowed and billowed. And she felt all the night creatures, predators and prey. Straight forward simple thoughts.
And then Freddie's.
And Janine's.
She pushed and stretched. And watched the minute hand approaching the six.
Freddie mumbled.
And twitched.
Facial muscles jumping.
Her eyes popped wide.
And it surged through her.
Freddie screamed.
Smoke's minds clamped shut as she toppled over. And the rest of them reacted.

Chapter Twelve

Smile. You're On Candid Camera.

Doth Lamex. The Elseplace of Rest and Relaxation.

They sat, the pair did, at the table in their select space, having just finished their meal, sipping their beverages.

He looked across the table at his companion, amazed as always. It happened no matter how many time he looked at her sitting there, hood thrown back. He marveled at the contrast between who she was and what she looked like. He knew that few had ever looked upon one of them and lived to tell the tale. Perhaps this was because if someone did and talked then they would no longer be around to talk again

But he was still alive. It was some sort of thing that he knew not what to call it. So there she sat, quietly sipping her beverage, eyes watching him. Even after all the time that they had traveled together, he was still surprised and startled to be alive and well. He cleared his throat.

"Yes?" She set her cup down.

He indicated the large stack of scrolls, books, sheets of paper, and all the other materials that they had gathered from here and there and elsewhere.

"We have visited many, many elseplaces. And from those many, many elseplaces we have gathered everything. All the tales, however told, together. Now we have to spend the next many days sifting and analyzing all that if we are to make any sense of it and to find the answer to the puzzle that you set us upon and the one that we are trying to solve."

She nodded. "This one has the time. This one has the confidence that the clever Ransapal will find the answer to that which we seek." She smiled warmly at him.

He was amazed again.

Grandeville. The Romp and Stomp Motel.

It was located on the edge of town. Just at the point where the town boundary turned into the county boundary.

It was well known among a certain segment of Grandeville's and the county's population.

He opened his eyes.

Slowly.

He opened his eyes.

And stared. Waiting for his eyes to finally focus. And then he realized that what he was looking at was the ceiling.

Way up there. He was looking up past the edge of the bed at the ceiling.

He was on the floor. In a tangle of blankets and sheets. With Chantal, who was mumbling something in his ear.

"Huh?"

"No more experiments," she rasped. "How did we get down here?"

"Do'n know." He pushed here and there.

"No smart remarks, but I've got a headache."

"Me too." He managed to untangle enough to be able to force himself into a sitting position.

"Let's go to the restaurant next door."

"Good idea." He lurched to his feet, wobbled over and found his clothes. And winced at the throbbing in his temples. "Not a good idea." And made it into the bathroom in just enough time.

After awhile, Chantal leaned in, looked at him, then at herself in the mirror. "UGH." She turned and headed for the door out.

Sipping cold water, waiting for the pain to subside, waiting until they felt like ordering breakfast, they both leaned elbows on the table.

Chantal had found a container of aspirins in the glove box of their truck.

So. They took some.

They sat.

Still. Very still.

And waited.

"Do you know that waitress?" asked Chantal.

"Nope."

"Good."

"Huh?"

"The way she looked at us, your reputation would be ruined."

"Your's too."

"No one would recognize me. I am wearing my dissolute face."

"Not funny."

"Let's get something to eat." She picked up the menu and waved at the waitress.

They were just finishing their breakfast, beginning to feel more or less human again, when the police car slid into one of the parking slots near the front door of the establishment.

The cops strolled inside and held a quiet conversation with the waitress.

"Damn," hissed Tinker.

"Oh, no," gasped Chantal.

The cops were coming their way.

And sat in the vacant chairs at their table.

"Tinker," rasped one. "What have you been doing?"

The other nodded at them. "We have taken healthier looking specimens up to the emergency room."

"Guys, " said Tinker. "You wouldn't believe me, if I told you. What are you doing in here?"

"Chantal?" rasped Red, all coarse whisper.

"Waitress called us in," said Green.

"What?" asked Chantal.

"Wasn't sure that it was you," replied Red.

Green nodded. "She did. You two frightened her." The waitress brought their coffee.

"We are on a break," explained Green. "We saw you through the window." He laughed. "And your truck outside. It is the only rig in the parking lot."

"Something funny," growled Chantal.

"Careful, Red," cautioned Green.

Red sipped at his coffee. And bit on his doughnut. They had also ordered a snack.

"Well?" demanded Chantal.

Red looked at her, all poker face cop face. "Wondered why." Red swallowed. "Tinker would be in here talking with a Portland skid-road hooker." He trapped her arm with one large hand.

Green finished and stood. "Whatever you two did, or were doing, I wouldn't do it again. It doesn't look healthy to me. Let's go, Partner."

Red nodded and stood. "You two need a lift?"

"Nope," said Tinker. "Thanks."

The monster cops waved and headed back to their car.

"Never again," snapped Chantal. "And I don't care what Smoke wants."

"Get no argument from me. Shall we go home?"

"Yep. But." She grabbed her jacket and stood.

"What?" He grabbed the bill.

"My room. And you hold me."

"A deal."

"Now what's going on?"

Tinker and Chantal walked into the living room.

Smoke lay on one of the couches, back propped up by several pillows.

"You look awful," said Chantal.

Smoke rolled her eyes at them. "You look pretty bad also."

"Are you all right?" He sat next to her.

"Tired. Very tired."

"Me too. Both of us." He looked into the great orange gold eyes, now half covered by inner eyelids. "Any idea?"

"Yes."

"So?"

Smoke eyelids dropped down. "Morning. Talk in the morning." She fell asleep.

Chicken pushed him. "My Lord, get thee a'bed."

He headed for the hallway, waggling his hand at Chantal. "Good idea."

"Coming." She followed him.

"You didn't tell him," said Messenger.

"In the morn t'will do. They much sleep require, nay conversation."

R-Bar jerked a thumb toward the guest room. "I spell cast three layers deep. They are safe. I am going back to bed."

She did.

They all did.

Freddie's eyes flew open.

Late morning light flooded into the room.

Janine sat in a chair nearby, brushing her hair. She smiled. "I woke just a few minutes ago. Everyone slept. Messenger popped in just after I woke and said that they were about to have breakfast."

Freddie slipped from the bed and grabbed her robe, "Shall we?"

Janine stood and opened the door. "Sure. I'm hungry."

They were all, almost all, sitting around the dining room table when Freddie and Janine joined them. Various stages of waking up greeted their house guests.

Tinker nodded over the top of his coffee cup as they pulled out chairs and sat.

Freddie directed her eyes elsewhere.

Janine flushed.

Tinker slumped deeper into his chair.

Chantal opened one eye and grabbed her cup, just refilled by Messenger, and settled back, eyes closed again.

"Fair morn, Sweet Prince." Chicken and Smoke brought in dishes of breakfast.

"Everyone is ready to eat." Smoke nudged Tinker in passing. "Decadent and perverted."

"Don't start," he mumbled.

"Wasn't me that frightened a waitress."

"I told her," said Chantal, cutting off his reply.

"After breakfast, we will talk." Smoke filled her own plate. And pushed a platter over to Fair Morn. "There is more in the oven."

By the time they had finished, Freddie was relaxed,

realizing that no-one was looking at her any more than anyone else.

"O.K., what's going on?"

They were all in the living room. Those who wished still held cups.

Tinker slouched in his chair, cup cradled in both hands, its warmth seeping into his stomach through his robe. He looked at Smoke, who nodded.

"R-Bar," she said. "This is your knowledge place. Tell us." She slowly fed her memories of the event to the small witch who stared blankly into nowhere as she lived Smoke.

The air darkened around her. Faint crackling, dull rumbling. "Dim, dim, dim, dim, dim," soft snarling cursing.

R-Bar jerked to her feet. Next to them, her beast snapped, eyes flaring, searching for something to attack.

Freddie thrust herself back into the couch. Janine wrapped her arms around her.

Chantal grabbed them both. "Relax, relax. You are safe."

"I do not feel safe," whispered Freddie. She shut her eyes tight, refusing to look. "Nightmare, nightmare." Tears leaked from tightly clamped eyelids, dripping on enfolding arms. "Worse and worse and worse."

Heavy blows rattled the front door.

Tinker's head snapped around. "Now what?"

Smoke bounded over and threw it open.

A tall man pushed inside and past her, neatly dressed, three-piece suit. And walked over to the couch and stared at them, eyes ending up on Freddie.

"Frederica, it is time to return home." He looked sideways and stared. "Gad, that is certainly the ugliest dog I have ever seen."

Chantal kicked him in the shin. "Beat it, Ralph."

"OUCH." He jumped back.

"This dim-wit is Ralph Andervante," said Chantal, slouching down so she could kick him again.

Ralph moved further back. "'Really, Chantal, do be less unpleasant."

Tinker looked at Freddie who now had her eyes open. "Who is this guy?"

"My fiance. He means well."

"Dim-wit is an understatement," snarled Chantal. "Damn dumb is more like it."

"Ever crude," said Ralph, bending and rubbing a small blemish from the front of one highly polished shoe tip. He jumped further back as Chantal reached for him.

He frowned at her. "Do try to behave." He smiled at Freddie. "Introduce me to your, ahh, friends, Sweet."

Freddie nodded. And did.

Ralph carefully shook hands with each of them. And while he was turned toward Tinker, R-Bar waved her beast away.

"If you are going to hang around, Ralph, sit down." Chantal indicated an empty chair. "You want some coffee?"

Ralph sat, hitched up his pants, just so, and nodded. "Most kind. Cream and sugar, please?"

Messenger handed him a cup. Fair Morn nudged a tray over with one bare foot. "Here, Ralph."

Chantal smiled at Tinker. "Actually Ralph is not a true idiot, he is an idiot savant."

"Chan Tal," said Ralph.

"What?" asked Tinker.

"He is a Stock Broker. Has an intuitive feel for which one to buy, which one to sell. He has even been investigated twice. But no-one can tell how he does it, even while they watch him doing it. Rolling in money. And an absolute twit." Her head snapped around. "Quiet, Ralph."

Chantal hugged Freddie. "Freddie loves him. And, as far as it is humanly possible to tell, he loves her." She smiled at Ralph. "So, we put up with him. Somewhat."

"Quite good," said Ralph, referring to the coffee.

Tinker leaned his head in one hand and stared at Ralph. *Well?*

? they all replied.

"We need to talk," said R-Bar.

"Uh huh." Tinker nodded.

"Privately." R-Bar stood. "They can stay in here with, ummm, Ralph." She headed for the rear deck.

As they trailed out, Chantal stood and turned. "They are staying here until we figure out what is going on." She whirled and glared at Ralph. "YOU GOT THAT?"

He nodded. And daintily licked the sugar from his lips. Ralph had been eating a doughnut. "Yes, Dear."

"And no funny business."

"Of course not." He wiped his fingers on his napkin.

Chantal stomped from the room.

"Frightful person," said Ralph.

"Quiet, Ralph," ordered Janine.

"Please?" asked Freddie.

"Yes, Dear," said Ralph. "She is your friend after all."

"O.K. Now what's going on?"

He dropped heavily into a chair and watched R-Bar as she sat on a bench at one of the tables.

"Demon twist," she said.

Ran sucked in her breath loudly.

"What?" asked Tinker.

R-Bar frowned. "It has been there all along. Just not active."

Tinker exhaled nosily. "Are you telling me that we have been infected with the equivalent of a computer virus? By some demon?"

"Ummmmmmm," replied R-Bar, frantically searching their collective memories.

"Yes," replied Chantal. Computers and that sector of the culture were now her area of interest, next to being a Veterinarian. And from what she saw in R-Bar's mind.

"It never stops," mumbled Tinker. His eyes peered up at R-Bar, his head still tilted down. "Who? What?"

R-Bar leaned toward him, her hands on her knees. "We could send a Gran Maldargon?"

"HORROR!" Ran jumped between them, glaring at R-Bar.

"Take care of the problem," grumbled R-Bar.

"Are the Faan so Ird'apa'ata?" growled Ran.

All around them, the light faded. R-Bar stared at Ran as Smoke's minds roared. She leaped up and caught R-Bar as she toppled forward and slumped over, collapsing Ran into Tinker's lap.

"Had to be done, MindMate." Smoke sat and held R-Bar in her arms.

"So much for that conversation," he mumbled. "Did you see what was going on?"

"Not before the Red Rage."

"The what?" He felt Ran twitch as she mumbled something. A blue crystal sphere appeared, sitting in the middle of the table.

Tinker looked from it to Smoke. "Ran do that?" Smoke shrugged.

Ran jerked upright, twisted around, grabbed his robe

in both hands, eyes blank, face blank, voice hollow resonating. "TAKE IT." The sphere floated over and hung in the air.

Slowly, carefully, he reached out and grabbed it. The sphere was warm to the touch.

She slumped. And smiled weakly at him. "Amtar, your Ran does not feel so good." And turned her head and stared at the thing he held. "How did you get that?" And fainted.

"OOOOOOF." Tinker blew her hair from his face. "What ever is going on is not good."

Chicken knelt by his side. "MY Lord, We her great fear do feel. For thee."

Messenger stood and smiled. "It is pretty. All sky blue soft glow."

Fair Morn leaned on the table top. "Should we put them to bed?"

Smoke shook her head.

R-Bar's eyes began to flutter and open. "DIR TAK ZAZUK."

"Most foul a'sounding," said Chicken.

R-Bar sat up and pointed at Tinker's hand. "Where did that thing come from?"

"Beats me," he said.

"That is Tanpak."

"Ummmm," mumbled Ran. And twitched.

"MyTinker," screamed Messenger lunging toward them.

He jerked violently sideways. "WHAT?"

Messenger reached in. "It is covering you in sky blue."

He lifted his arm and peered at the sphere. "It is?"

Messenger's head jerked up and down. "Really really."

"Emmmmmmmm," groaned Ran.

Tinker dropped his arm and looked over at R-Bar. "Kiddo, what sort of witchy things are you up to?"

"Nothing." She batted at one of Smoke's hands.

"Someone is," he said

"Im dup prog ta," mumbled Ran.

The sphere changed color.

To red.

"Ahhhhh, Tink?"

"Oh my," said Messenger.

Ran tucked her legs up.

"What?"

"It must be Ran," said R-Bar.

"Now you are red," said Messenger.

Chicken's hand felt Ran's forehead. "Most fiery, Me'Lord." She turned and felt R-Bar's forehead. "Most cold." And nodded at Smoke. "Most strange."

Smoke nodded. "Feels like healing."

Fair Morn handed a steaming cup to R-Bar. "Here." She had returned from the kitchen with one of the coffee pots.

"Th . . . thanks." R-Bar grabbed it with both hands, shivering.

Tinker sighed, loudly. "Does anyone have any idea of what is going on, at all? Huh?"

R-Bar nodded. "I told you. Demon twist."

"O.K. What is that?"

"Ummm," she said.

He slumped lower, rearranging arms and legs, his and Ran's, and looked very unhappy at R-Bar. "Gotta do better than that," he grumbled.

R-Bar frowned. "From what I saw in Smoke's memory, I think that those Chan Narh slipped a twisted spell into us.

And it linked out to Freddie and Janine. It should have attached to Chantal and Sandy as well." She shook her head. "I do not really understand demons spells. Too warped for me."

Ran's eyes flew open. "Hum, hum, hum, hum." She smiled warmly at him. And uncoiled. And twisted around on his lap. "Most sorry sincerely," she said to R-Bar.

R-Bar nodded. "You are regaining?"

"So and so."

"Better rest." R-Bar yawned. "Me too."

"Ummm?" said Tinker.

"What?" asked Ran and R-Bar.

"What do we do about it?"

R-Bar grinned. "You could tuck us in."

"Yesssssssss," hissed Ran, slipping a hand inside his robe.

"Twist," stated Tinker.

"Oh, that." R-Bar waggled her arm vaguely. "Just have to go and kill 'em."

"Yep," agreed Ran. And yawned widely.

Tinker shook her gently. "How about you two go take a nap. We can talk about this later."

Ran nodded, stood, turned, and touched the crystal sphere he still held in his hand. It turned yellow. She smiled.

R-Bar slipped from Smoke's arms. "Tuck us in," she demanded.

Sighing heavily, he stood. "Worse than kids." He set the clear sphere on the table top. And followed them into the house.

"I don't like this at all."

He dropped heavily onto the wooden bench, propped his arms on the table top and looked across at Smoke and

Chantal. "Not even a teeny tiny bit."

"Most strange, Our Prince." Chicken nodded agreement.

Messenger sat by his left side.

Fair Morn sat by right side, and winked at Chantal. "Heh, heh."

Chantal walked around and sat next to Chicken. "Me neither."

"Huh?"

"I don't like it either, John. Once was enough." She stared at the table top.

Chicken slipped her arm around Chantal. "Do not, Our Doctor Self." And hugged her as Chantal's silent tears pattered onto the polished wood.

Tinker reached over and held a hand. "Cowgirl . . . "

Her eyes swiveled toward him. "We died. The last time, we died. Those feelings are mine now. Also."

Messenger hurried around and sat by her other side. "Don't. Please?" And hugged Chantal. Also.

They heard the sound of a car stopping in the driveway, the door slamming broke their heavy mood.

"Sandy," said Smoke. "Very upset."

They all watched her as she thumped down the deck toward them.

Chantal wiped her face with a handkerchief.

Sandy dragged a chair to the end of the table, sat, and glowered at them. "I do not know what you are doing, but knock it off."

"What?" asked Tinker.

"Damned erotic dreams," snapped Sandy. "Red is starting to give me strange looks." She banged the table top with a fist. "So, knock it off. YOU UNDERSTAND. STOP IT."

"Your face is getting red and your eyes are bugging

out, Sandermeyer," growled Chantal.

"Anderson," barked Sandy, glaring at her. "Remember?"

"Umm?" said Tinker.

"WHAT?"

"Ahhh, we were just discussing that, ummmm, problem." He sighed. "It is, ummmm, our problem, also."

"What does that mean?"

Fair Morn shoved a cup over to Sandy. "R-Bar and Ran think that it is some sort of demon spell."

"Oh no." Sandy sagged. "Noooooooooooooo. That is over. That is over."

"Ummmm?" said Tinker.

"WHAT?"

"Going to have to go out there and kill them," said Smoke.

"Indeed," agreed Chicken.

"Right." Fair Morn nodded.

Sandy leaned forward. "Don't. Don't go."

She looked from face to face. "Don't," she whispered. "You can't lose anymore . . . anyone." She shook her head

"Ummmm?" said Tinker.

"Ran won't let R-Bar do it," explained Messenger.

Sandy looked blank.

"Ummmm?" said Tinker.

Chantal laughed. "Speak up, Cowboy." And squeezed his hand.

He did.

And told Sandy all that they knew.
And had done.

"WOW." Sandy grinned at Chantal. "Red didn't say anything about that." Her smiled faded. "No other way?"

Tinker slowly shook his head. "Doesn't look like it."

Sandy pointed. "Isn't it a little early for Christmas?"

The crystal sphere had changed color.

Now it was an iridescent green.

"Tis Ran fair bauble," explained Chicken.

Sandy's head turned as she heard footsteps. She frowned. "What are you doing here?"

"Frowning like that puts lines in your face, Sandrew."

"May we join you?" asked Freddie.

"We got tired of just sitting in the living room," explained Janine. She sat at the table.

Ralph waited until Freddie sat, then took a place next to her. He bent forward and nodded at Tinker. "Frederica explained, some. I would prefer staying here until this, ahhh, problem is resolved."

"Ralph will do anything you say." Freddie patted Ralph's arm.

"I will." Ralph sat straight and looked determined.

Sandy stared at Ralph, then at Tinker. "You can't take him with you."

One side of Tinker's mouth twitched. "Wouldn't think of it. That includes all of you."

The crystal sphere rolled down the table.

"Pretty bauble." Ralph touched it with a fingertip. "Sticky."

"OH MY," gasped Messenger.

It swallowed him.

"Ralph?" Freddie stared at the spot where he been sitting.

"OH MY GOSH," gurgled Messenger.

The scream banged through their minds.

Ran hurtled down the stairs and out the side door, glittering silver wand clenched in her right hand. She charged up to the table and banged the sphere on the top with the wand.

It coughed him up.

Ralph stood there, swaying from side to side. His clothes were filthy and ripped. A heavy gash ran from his left temple across his cheek to his jaw line. Eyes glittering wildly, he stumbled forward, one step, two steps, and finally managed to focus his eyes upon Freddie. "Dear?" And collapsed into a heap.

Ran leaped to his side. The house door banged back against the wall as R-Bar dashed outside, snarling wildly. Ran tapped Ralph on the forehead with her wand.

His eyes opened, and stared at her. "Rather strange costume for a nurse."

Freddie plopped down next to him and stroked his forehead. "Shhhhhh, Dear." And looked at Ran.

R-Bar peered over Ran's shoulder. "What happened?"

"It laughed," said Ralph.

"Inspell link," said Ran.

"Him?" R-Bar stared at Ralph.

"Accident," explained Ran.

"Ahhhhhh," said Tinker. "You wanna put on the rest of your pajamas?"

Ran was wearing the bottoms only.

R-Bar hastily buttoned up her own top. And glared at Ralph. "Stop staring, dir dit." She walked over and kissed Tinker. "Ran is."

"Ranfer," said Ran, standing, walking over, and kissing his cheek. "I am Ranfer, Tanpak." She stepped back and waved her top on. And smiled at him. "Your's." Her eyes gleamed.

"Witch, again?"

Ranfer's smile broadened.

"Lookout, MindMate," said Smoke. "She is getting ready to pounce."

"Not out here," snapped Tinker.

Ranfer stepped around, and tapped Fair Morn on the shoulder, and then pushed between her and Tinker as Fair Morn made room.

"Hum, hum, hum," she said, slipping an arm around Tinker and stroking his side.

"That tickles," he grumbled.

"Heh, heh."

"He going to be all right?"

She nodded and tried to sit closer. "He saw our enemy."

"That what happened to him?"

"Shouldn't have touched the sphere."

Tinker turned his head and frowned at her. "Maybe some guys ought to warn people about things like that."

R-Bar leaned against his back, draping herself on him and wrapping her arms around his chest. "We were sleeping."

Freddie helped Ralph stand. And led him back inside the house. Chicken went with them, to fetch the first aid supplies.

"Now what?"

Ranfer kissed him. "My sisters will be happy." And kissed him again. "Feels good to be Ranfer again."

"Ummmm?"

"Amtar?"

"This going to be safe?"

"I have very fine control."

"Not what I meant."

"What?"

He reached back and pinched R-Bar.

She squeaked.

"Two of you."

R-Bar blow warm into his ear. "We are one Tink."

"STOP THAT."

"Hell heh heh." Ranfer smiled at him. "See."

"What?"

"I am smiling. No witch threat."

"I suppose."

"Smiling witches," explained R-Bar, again, wondering why he couldn't remember simple things like this. "Are one step from mayhem." She tickled his chest.

"Except for us. Cause we are us and you." Then she straightened up. "I think that we should celebrate Ranfer's rebirth."

"Good idea," agreed Chantal. "Everyone needs to relax."

Fair Morn stood. "Smoke and I will cook."

"Happy birthday to you," sang Messenger.

Chantal nodded at Janine and Sandy. "Let's decorate."

"Happy birthday, dear Ourself Ran."

As they started for the house, Sandy nudged Chantal. "Can't stay long though. Have a large cop to feed and send to work."

"Happy birthday to you."

Messenger and R-Bar headed for the kitchen and the basement, to select beverages.

Tinker slipped an arm around her waist as Ranfer leaned against him. "Sure you're all right?"

"No. Yes. No."

"Huh?'"

"It is all pouring back. Nervous, nervous. But I am well. Tanpak wealth-thought. Nervous, nervous." She shivered. "Hold me."

He turned. And looked into pale yellow eyes, with brown pupils. Fluttering. "Let's go inside."

"Nervous, nervous, witch nervous." She nodded.

They wound up in her room, in a corner, on the floor, quilts piled around them. She was coiled up, on his lap, inside his arms.

Eventually they ate dinner.
Outside.
On the rear deck.
Everyone.

Ralph was clean and neat again. Wearing a bandage. And a worried look. Freddie held his arm, firmly. He couldn't quite remember what had happened, exactly.

Sandy snatched two birthday cupcakes, Smoke having decided that it was faster than making a cake, kissed Chantal, Janine, and Freddie. And Tinker. And winked at Ralph. And left.

R-Bar poked Ranfer with a fingertip. "Hum?"

"Quite well," she replied. "He is very comforting. I prefer Ran name, still."

"Hum, hum, hum," said R-Bar.

"Better than Valium," suggested Chantal, waving everyone to their places at the tables.

"You all right?" he asked as they sat.

"Mostly there," said Ran.

"Ummmm."

R-Bar sat by her other side. "Indo dedone?"

Ran shook her head. "I will require assistance."

R-Bar nodded and passed the nearest dish.

Ralph cleared his throat and, looked at Tinker. "Tinker? What was that, sssss, thing?"

Tinker shrugged, grabbed a platter, and served himself and Ran, then Chicken who was nudging his other side. "A not nice person."

Ralph stared at him. And hastily served Freddie and himself as Fair Morn thumped a serving dish down in front of him. "Person? A not nice person?"

"Matter of view point," said Tinker.

"Fret you not," said Chicken, smiling at Ralph.

"Right," agreed Chantal. "Don't worry it, Ralphy. And pass that platter down here."

Ralph frowned at her and did. "But."

"Please?" said Freddie. "May we talk about something else?"

"Sure," said Tinker.

"Of course, Dearest," said Ralph.

"Hum, hum, hum," said Ran, pinching Tinker's thigh and rubbing it. "Ran is a fine name."

"Eat your dinner," he grumbled.

R-Bar nodded. "And don't play with your dessert." And burst into laughter.

Tinker sighed.

Smoke winked at him. And pulled an ornate ring from her shirt pocket and tossed it to Ran. "Here. Catch."

She did. And slipped it over her right thumb. And beamed.

"Heh, heh, heh," cackled R-Bar.

"Most kind, Dark Sister," said Chicken to Smoke.

Chantal nudged Janine. "So, how's life in the big city?"

And various conversations started.

The full moon poured white spot bright across the bedroom floor and the far wall. The door eased open, accompanied by a soft knock.

"Tink?" she whispered. "Ran?"

An arm snaked out from beneath the blanket and beckoned her over. The jewel on the ring sparkled in the bright light.

R-Bar knelt on that side of the bed. "You ready?" she whispered as she bent over.

Tinker's bed was set flush with the floor.

The blanket pulled down. Ran looked up into R-Bar's face. And whispered back, "Yes."

She handed R-Bar three crystal spheres.

R-Bar stood, walked around and kicked at the lump with her bare foot.

"Ummmmm?"

"Wake up, Tink."

"Ummmm?"

"Wake up."

"Huh?"

"WAKE UP."

Blankets whipped aside. "What?" He snapped upright. "Oh. Timezit?" And fell back.

"Time to finish Ran," said R-Bar.

His eyes opened. "Do what?"

"I am not complete," explained Ran.

"Yet," amended R-Bar, dropping one of the crystal spheres on her. It flashed. Ran sagged, limp, eyes wide, blank, staring at nothing.

Tinker sat up. "You sure you know what you are doing?" He shook. "I don't feel here . . . there."

"Tink." R-Bar kicked him. "She is there, there, there. Just, ahhhh, disconnected a little."

He bunched his pajama top in both hands and wiped the sudden sweat from his face. Then yanked on the bottoms. "Hurry, will ya?"

"I need your help, your strength."

He nodded.

"If she gets violent, you have to hold her here, so I can use the last sphere."

"I'm ready." He turned and sat, facing the pale form lying so still.

R-Bar began the spell. And dropped the second sphere. It sank into Ran's chest, fumes hissing up around the wound.

In a flash Ran was on her feet, spell flame arcing from her fingers, snarling wildly. A bolt hurtled R-Bar into a corner. Ran advanced on her, growling, fingers curling into claws.

"Grab her, Tink."

He lunged. She dodged and spun, headed for the door.

"GET HER."

He crashed into Ran's back, arms wrapping around her waist. She dragged him toward the door.

"HURRY, DAMN IT, R-BAR, HURRY." He managed to throw Ran onto her face. She thrashed violently beneath him.

R-Bar danced around them. "Other side, other side."

"MERDE." Ran's elbow struck him on the side of the head. "OUCH."

"OTHER SIDE."

Tinker flung himself over, one arm around Ran's neck, dragging her on top of his chest, his legs wrapping around hers.

R-Bar hurtled the last crystal sphere down.

It poured from Ran and enveloped R-Bar. And dragged her across the room. "AAAAAA."

Tinker shoved the dead weight from his chest, rolled

and leaped into the fray, hands, elbows, knees, attacking the thing.

Bright blue flame hurtled the thing and Tinker away.

R-Bar crawled over to Ran, sucking in a deep breath, and punched her in the side. "HELP." And swung her arm up, then down. Her fist thumped in the center of the faintly moving chest. "RAN FER, HELP."

Ran's eyes fluttered open. And blinked. She reached up and yanked R-Bar over.

"Stop that," snapped R-Bar. "Ooooooooo, stop . . . stop, ooooooooooooooo."

A mirror crashed to the floor.

Tinker heaved and tried to escape.

Ran released R-Bar and sat up. And said something. It flashed back and poured inside. She looked around the room.

Tinker was crumpled against wall and floor, legs kicked under a small table, lying on his side. He peered across the surface of the floor at them. "You all right?" he croaked.

Chantal hurtled into the room, revolver in hand. And, stared at them. "I heard screaming."

R-Bar tried to smile. "M'all right."

Chantal knelt by her side and yanked the shreds of her pajamas together. "What were you doing in here?" She glared at Tinker who had finally managed to sit up. Strange stains mottled his chest and arms.

"Put. . . clothes. . . on . . . ," he rasped at Ran.

She crawled over to the bed and shoved blankets around until she found them, her pajamas. And did. And crawled back. And rolled and thumped onto her back. "Fine," she said to the ceiling.

"Bed," mumbled R-Bar.

Chantal heaved her to her feet and helped her over to

it. And eased her down. "You sure you are all right?"

"Yep." R-Bar dragged a blanket up. "Just really tired."

Ran crawled over and nestled against her. "Thank you." And looked up at Chantal. "Fine. All fine."

Tinker stood, leaning back against the wall, having managed to hitch himself up. "Gimme a hand, Cowgirl."

Chantal did. And then violently flapped a blanket open and gently tucked it around them. And kissed each in turn. "O.K., in the morning we can talk."

Chapter Thirteen

Not Another Hunt?

Grandeville. Tinker's Place.

"So what are we going to do about those guys?"

They were all in Fair Morn's room, sitting on the floor. Having a private conference. A place where their house guests couldn't pass by and accidentally overhear.

Those guys, the ones in Tinker's question, were the demons responsible for the problem at hand.

"Go kill 'em," offered R-Bar.

"Given our experience," said Chantal nodding at Tinker. "I'd say that someone needs shooting, all right. That was really . . . nasty."

"Ummmm?" said Tinker. He looked at Chicken.

"My Lord?"

"How do we find them?"

Everyone looked at everyone else. And then at him.

"What I thought," he mumbled. "We ain't going anywhere until we know what we are doing."

"Thought that we were going to Orver," said Fair Morn, leaning back against the wall, shoving her legs straight out.

"And talk to Turtog," added Messenger, poking a finger at a bug crawling across the hard wood floor.

"He found the Chan Narh for us," said R-Bar.

"Bring one here," said Ran.

"Huh?"

"Amtar, bring one here." She nodded.

"How do we do that?"

Ran held an orange crystal sphere from somewhere, and said, as the air crackled and bent around her, "Just take this and . . . "

"HOLD DIT." Tinker leaped to his feet. "HOLD DIT."

The air settled down. Ran put the sphere on the floor. And stared at him. "Dit?"

"This a Tanpak spell?" he asked. "It."

"Yes."

"Knock us all to the floor, things like that?"

She shook her head. "Not a fetch."

"Huh?"

She looked at R-Bar. "A fetch goes out, not in."

"Oh," said R-Bar. She smiled up at Tinker. "Perfectly safe." And tickled his ankle.

He sat. "Sure?"

Both witches nodded.

He looked at Ran. "You are going to, ummmnun, fetch, one of those things here?"

"Yes, Amtar."

"Where you going to keep it?"

"Not in my room," cried Fair Morn.

"Yucko," stated Messenger.

"In a trap, Tink." R-Bar pointed. "Room next to mine."

"No one sleeps in there, Simba leader."

"And you are sure that this fetch is not going to affect us, right?"

Ran hesitated.

"NO," stated Tinker. "Let's work on Plan B."

"Prithee, Me'Lord, do bespeak us pon this Plan B."

"Yah," said Messenger.

"Don't have one," he snapped. "But I do not like the sounds of Plan A."

"Sweet Prince?"

"What?"

"Fair Witch do say naught pon this thing fetch effect."

"Ummmmm," he replied.

"What will it do?" asked Smoke.

"Grab one and fetch it here," answered Ran. "Local area effect. Should not touch anyone." She stood.

"Sit down," he said.

She did.

"You wanna explain should not?" He leaned forward, propping his head in his hands, elbows on knees.

"Amtar?"

"Should not? Or will not?"

"I never did this one before."

He sighed, a long, heavy sigh.

"Tink?" R-Bar leaned toward him. "I will help."

He nodded. And looked back at Ran. "I do not want you hurt again. Or crippled again."

Ran nodded and whispered, "I know. Your Ran will be very very impar, careful careful."

"And I will help," stated R-Bar firmly. Ran nodded.

He cleared his throat. "O.K. We will wait here." He watched her as she and Ran headed for the selected room. And wondered what impar meant.

So. They did.
They waited.
In Fair Morn's room.
And inched closer.
To him.

"Gotcha." Chantal wrapped her arms around him.

"MindMate," said Smoke as she did the same thing from the other side.

"HEY."

"Be for Most Noble of steeds," said Chicken, smiling and kissing the tip of his nose. "Cept we do have beasts naught."

"Heh, heh, heh," gurgled Messenger behind him as Fair Morn stood and walked over.

He twisted his head and watched her approach. "I don't like the look on your face, Winged Stomach."

He struggled as she knelt next to Chicken. "Let go," he said.

"We thought that it was time for you to stop worrying," said Fair Morn.

"What? Me worry?"

"Stop feeding him lines like that, " said Chantal, biting his shoulder, just a little.

"Stop that."

"Just a friendly Lady Lion thing to do, Simba Leader."

Smoke clamped down on his other shoulder.

"Help," he cried softly, so as to not disturb the missing pair.

"Sorry. Forgot." Smoke smiled And licked her lips. Slowly.

The house shuddered to the dull boom.

They instantly released him.

"Oh, oh," said Tinker.

No problemo, Dude, said R-Bar.

We caught one, Amtar.

"Oh boy." Messenger bounced to her feet. "Let's go look."

They all hurried from the room.

"YUCKO."

Grey green oily fumes were being sucked out through the open windows by a faint breeze. Sitting in the center of the rapidly clearing room was a large clear sphere faintly orange colored. The top almost touched the ceiling. Inside stood a very ugly demon.

Tinker wasn't sure what Messenger was referring to, the fumes or the demon.

The two witches turned to greet him. And stepped away from the sphere.

Tinker glared and frowned and violently waved his arms. "You two want to explain how being very, very careful did that to your clothes?"

R-Bar looked at Ran. She stared back. They both smiled. Great patches of their garments were missing.

"Hum," said R-Bar.

"Hum," replied Ran.

"BUG," snapped Tinker.

"Uninjured," said Smoke.

"Most risque," observed Chicken.

"I'll say." Chantal stifled her smile. "Frederick's of Witchdom."

"What is he?" asked Ran.

"Yah," said R-Bar. "Who is this Frederick guy?"

"Funny name for a demon," said Fair Morn.

Smoke nudged him.

"What?"

"You might inspect for damages. Now that things are poking out." Her smiled broadened. "So to speak."

"Oh boy," giggled Messenger. "We had better leave."

"Hum," said Ran.

Tinker sighed. "Not funny."

The witch clothes shimmered. And were whole.

The demon tapped on the sphere wall with one long, jagged talon.

R-Bar whirled around. "What do you want?"

"Let me out, short witch."

She hissed at it, "I am not short, Pez Qat."

"That is vile," said the demon, smiling.

She kicked it in the shin.

"Bibpf," snapped the demon, jerking back. And stared down as her leg easily snapped back outside the wall. "How do you do that?"

"Secret."

The demon stepped close and tried to look sly. "Tell me this secret and I will give you what you want."

"You will?" She slipped an arm around Ran as Ran stepped over to join the conversation.

"Yesssssssss," hissed the demon, drooling on the wall.

"Yuck, yuck, yuck." Messenger spun around and leaned out the window. "UGLY."

"Thank you," said the demon.

"Anything at all?" R-Bar waved everyone away and back.

"Even something for this other," nodded the demon, indicating Ran.

"I need several things," said R-Bar.

Tapping a talon on the wall of the sphere, the demon mashed its nose against the wall. "I do not like it in here." It leered at Ran. "I have a weakness for yellow eyes. Your mother meet a demon somewhere?"

Ran hissed. R-Bar grabbed her arm before she could smash the demon on the side of the head with a blue crystal sphere.

R-Bar yanked a tuft of hair from its belly.

"OUCH."

"Pay attention," she ordered.

"I am," growled the demon. "Why don't you ask your mother to step in here so we can do things?" It licked its lips. And groaned.

R-Bar stabbed it with a silver wand

The demon lurched away, hands covering its groin. "You are witch nasty witch vile horrid child bad witch pooga."

Ran crooked a finger at it. "Come here, thing."

It crept close, one eye watching Ran, the other watching R-Bar.

"Yessssss." And spread both hands against the wall.

"You have been causing problems for that male back there." She indicated Tinker.

The demon looked and squinted. "That is the one. A real demon arpuk. For such an ugly specimen it certainly gastat."

"Why?"

"What?"

"Giving others those, ummm, experiences?"

"Trade for trade."

Ran frowned

"I will tell. You give me your daughter."

"For what?"

The demon pressed itself against the wall. "I want intoodap'ka."

R-Bar growled, deep in her throat.

"Listen," rasped the demon. "She wants me. Uk, uk, uk, uk, uk, uk."

"Why?"

"Because I am handsome. And a real deep arpuk. Eh, eh, eh, eh, eh, eh, eh, eh, eh."

"PAY ATTENTION."

"I want to bite her," drooled the demon. "OW."

Ran had twisted one long ear and yanked it through the crystal wall.

"OW, OW, OW, OW, OW."

And let go. "Tell me."

"What? Oodo yellow eyes? Eh, eh, eh."

R-Bar poked Ran in the side. "Let's kill it. Catch another one."

"Uk, uk, uk, uk," gurgled the demon, slavering across the wall. "I want her."

Ran smashed it in the forehead with her palm, crushing a small green crystal sphere. It stood and stared at her.

"Why do you bother the folk of this elseplace?"

"Chan Narh touch."

"DAMN." Chantal glared at the demon from the other side of the room.

"Shhh," cautioned R-Bar.

"Explain this," ordered Ran.

The demon nodded. "Slow zar ten. Brm tickle. Deep arpuk. Appbzan Riam flicker flicker, eh, eh, eh, eh."

Ran looked at R-Bar. She frowned.

"What is your true name?" asked Ran.

"Zar'gh of Appbzan Riam ar Npkn."

R-Bar readied the cast as Ran released the demon from the spell. It panted at her.

R-Bar rapped on the crystal sphere with one knuckle. "You are mine. Zar'gh."

The demon leaped back and cringed. "Not so loud. They will all hear you." It crept back.

"How may I service you, eh, eh, eh?" It moaned "Deep, deep arpuk, oooo."

"Why are you making others . . . ?" she looked at Ran.

"Flicker, flicker," said Zar'gh.

"Hum," said Ran.

"Exactly," drooled the demon.

"When he is . . . ?"

"Deeeeeeep arpuk great intoodap'ka," groaned Zar'gh.

Fair Morn nudged Tinker and whispered, "That's you."

"Shhhhh," he said.

"Yes," said R-Bar.

"Chan Narh touch. We bought it from the Zang who traded from the Small Qaz who stole it from the Tat Ind who found it in a ruin on Figtl after the Earde War of no survivors. The Small Qaz pitar the touch and it flickers oyhut."

Zar'gh dragged a long arm across its mouth. "Eh, eh. It is a great ooobt when that ugly arpuk luscious."

Messenger's face flushed. She spun toward Smoke. "All these demons have been watching us?"

Smoke nodded. "Sounds like it."

"Most vile," snapped Chicken.

"Zar'gh," said Ran. "We want this stopped. Forever."

Long ears flew straight up. And brushed the top of the sphere. "We traded it for four doarpuk. To the Dark Ump."

Zar'gh leaded closer, eyes bugging. "They are horrible."

"Yesssssss," hissed R-Bar. "Who?"

"The Dark Ump," it gurgled. "The doarpuk were . . . exciting. Eh, eh, eh."

"Can you get this touch back?" asked Ran.

"NOOOOOOO," howled the demon. "We are lovers, not fighters."

"We thought that the a'demons had sealed this place, forever," said R-Bar.

"This did, the aztrok," snarled Zar'gh. "Until the touch activated we couldn't do anything. But, kik, kit, kik, kik, it came first. And we could do . . . it." The demon licked the wall. "But we sold it." The long ears flapped back. "I think that the Dark Ump found a way to make the touch stronger."

"Give me the name of their elseplace," snapped R-Bar.

"Come inside, gulzop. And I will." Zar'gh licked its lips.

She stepped inside. "Done." And nodded. "Tell me the name."

Zar'gh grabbed her. And howled. R-Bar's Fantar released the demon and snapped back, seething around its mistress.

"Name."

"You are witch witch," gurgled Zar'gh.

"Of course. I will know how to find the Dark Ump."

"I will tell only you. And your mother."

"Do it."

Zar'gh did, She tumbled back out of the sphere. "Send it home, Ran."

Ran nodded. The sphere faded and dwindled.

Into nothing.

They crowded around her.

Sitting on the floor.

"Smoke?" asked Tinker. "Can you prowl around inside and find this touch? Take Messenger with you?"

Smoke stared and frowned and slowly shook her head. "Something like that has never been done, MindMate."

"And?"

"I do not know."

He looked at the others. "Well, gang?"

"Try it," said Chantal.

Everyone agreed.

"Lay down and relax, " ordered Smoke, sprawling flat on her back.

They did.

And flowed together.

And heard Messenger giggling nervously. *Oh my gosh. So that is what it is like. We only followed your trace into Chantal. A little. How do you keep from getting lost?*

Skill.

Eyes refocused.

They sat up.

And looked around.

It was dark.

The sun had set.

Everyone was hungry.

"Nothing," said Smoke, struggling upright.

"Nope," added Messenger, leaning against Smoke's side. She stroked the back of Smoke's hand. "Mom, I don't want to ever do that again. Ever, ever."

"Let's go eat," Fair Morn stood.

"Indeed," said Chicken, helping Messenger up.

"Steak," said Smoke.

"I'll second that," said Chantal, assisting Smoke to her feet.

R-Bar and Ran grabbed him as he stood.

"I am tired, Amtar."

"Me too, Tink. Exhausted."

"Think we all are. Let's eat. And go to bed."

"Yep," said Messenger as they headed out the door and down toward the kitchen.

"Thought that everyone was tired?"

"We want to watch a movie, first." Smoke shoved the selected cassette in. Messenger clicked on the TV.

He nodded, stretched out on one of the couches. "Don't mind me if I fall asleep."

Chicken joined him. "We do Us some space require, Me'Lord."

He moved. "Gonna have to behave. Or you'll be in an X-rated movie for the Dark Emp."

"Most ghastly a'thought, that."

"Worse than that," said Chantal.

Freddie and Janine carried chairs in.

"May we?" asked Freddie.

"Sure," said Chantal. "Have a nice time in town?"

"Rather quaint," said Ralph, joining them.

"Not much to do," added Janine. "Nice and quiet and relaxed."

The movie started. And everyone settled down.

His eyes popped open as he jerked awake.

Chicken mumbled something.

They were still on the couch. Someone had thrown a blanket over them.

And he felt them.

They were all there.

"Umm?"

Two bright green spots peered at him.

"We wanted to be together," whispered Messenger. "Freddie and Janine went to their bedroom, Ralph to his."

"Oh."

He fell back asleep.

He woke.

More or less.

He woke.

Bright sun poured through the living room windows. Ran snuggled tighter and kissed him.

"Mup?"

"Your Princess is starting breakfast," she whispered in. his ear.

"Morning," bubbled Messenger, from the floor, sitting up.

An arm reached up, dragged her back, and stuffed a pillow over her head.

"Shhh," said Smoke, yawning and stretching.

Messenger reared up and thumped her with the pillow. "Not nice, mom."

Several arms dragged her back under the blankets, under the moving mound of blankets and quilts.

"Eeeeeeeek," squeaked Messenger. "Help," she gasped. "Stop that."

"Heh, heh, heh," cackled R-Bar.

Ran squirmed against him.

"Tickle, tickle, tickle, " said Smoke, leaning over them.

"Everyone's awake? Right?" grumbled Tinker.

"Murgle," grumbled Chantal, dragging a pillow up and over her face.

"More or less, " said Smoke. She went off to fetch cups and the coffee pots.

Ralph stepped carefully through the living room, trying not to look at the bodies.

"You wanna bring another coffee pot in here," grumbled Chantal.

He nodded. And hurried to the kitchen.

"Good for something," she mumbled.

"He is very nice." Freddie sat in a chair and smiled at them.

Janine flopped on the floor next to Chantal and leaned back against the couch. "Morning. You always this casual?"

"More or less."

"Got room for one more?" She thought that rooming in this sorority looked like fun.

"WHAT?" Tinker snapped upright.

"Steady, Simba Leader," said Chantal. "Nope," she said to Janine. "The place is booked up."

Ralph handed Freddie and Janine cups, and filled them.

Blankets heaved up. "Where's mine?" asked Fair Morn.

Ralph jerked and blinked. "I will get more cups." He spun and hurried into the living room.

Janine nudged Chantal. "Shhhh."

Ralph returned and set a number of cups on the floor.

"Thank you, Dear," said Freddie.

"Morning, morning, morning." Messenger bubbled up. "OOOOOOPS." And yanked a blanket up to her chin. "Buggy eyes," she said to Ralph.

"My apologies," replied Ralph.

Freddie patted his hand. And smiled at Tinker. "We will wait on the rear deck."

"Of course," agreed Ralph.

"Good," grumbled Chantal.

"Shhhhh," said Janine.

"Twerp."

"Shhhhhh."

Freddie and Ralph headed back through the dining room.

"Button your top," snarled Chantal at Fair Morn.

Fair Morn did. "Smoke could have said something."

"YAH," added Messenger, finding her top under the blankets and dragging it on.

"Coffee?" Smoke shoved the pot at Tinker. "I'll pour."

He nodded.

She did.

"Could have said something," he mumbled.

"Breakfast beserved," announced Chicken.

"You sure?" whispered Janine.

"Right," whispered back Chantal. "And don't you dare say anything to him."

"Sure. Who?"

"Him. That guy sitting at the end of the couch."

"Your housekeeper?"

Chantal tugged Janine to her feet. "I think that we have to have a little talk. After we eat. Before we leave."

Chapter Fourteen.

Traveling Again.

Grandeville. Tinker's Place.

Janine sat across the table from her long-time friend and stared at her.

Blinked.

And stared.

At her.

"Him? All of you. With him?" She began to shake her head back and forth. Flashes, images, sounds, smells, and then all the memories flooded back. She began to cry.

"STOP IT." Chantal reached across the table and grabbed an arm. "Stop it."

Eyes blinked away tears. "Shooter, I didn't want to remember any of . . . that. It was horrible. But I just did. Remember. Horrible."

"I know, " whispered Chantal. "I know."

Janine wiped at her eyes and grinned. "'You are making it up, aren't you?" And swiped her hair back from her face, gleaming white streak in startling contrast to the dark brown mass.

"Nope."

"But. How can he?"

Chantal laughed. "We give him lots of rest."

Janine flushed and laughed with her. "I meant inside your head."

Chantal shrugged. "Smoke did it. And I do not know how. I don't think any of us really understand that. It is just how her species does things. And it is strange. Very strange. Was strange. Now."

She tightened her grip on Janine's arm. "Now it is just . . . normal. Sort of like your heart. It is there. You know it is there. But you don't really spend a whole lot of time thinking about it."

"You tell Freddie?"

"Nope. Not gonna." Chantal leaned forward. "And neither are you, Streak. Or, Ralph either. Or him."

Janine bent toward her. "How come?"

Chantal smiled. "He is really a very private person, especially about that. He is afraid people would just gawk at us, treat us like freaks."

Janine sat back and smiled. "And what about shacking up with seven broads?"

Chantal laughed and fell back, releasing her grip. "Hey, that is normal. Every guy's wish come true."

Janine looked past Chantal's shoulder. "Oh, oh."

"What?"

"'Here he comes."

"I know, " said Chantal without turning her head.

Tinker dropped onto the bench next to Chantal. "Hi, there. Hi, Janine. What's up?"

"Thank you," said Janine.

Tinker's eyebrows popped up. "For what?" He bumped Chantal with a shoulder. "We do something that I don't know about? Yet? Huh?"

"Nope."

"For the rescue job," explained Janine.

"Oh." He laid both arms on the table top. "You remembered?"

"We were talking," said Chantal.

"And, uh, so," fumbled Janine. "I just thought that I ought to thank you." She watched his face.

He stared at her. Just stared.

Chantal poked him in the ribs. "Cool it, Simba Leader."

Tinker jerked. And glowered.

"What?" asked Janine.

"It wasn't a Vander offer," said Chantal, jabbing him harder in the ribs.

Janine stared at him, at them. And frowned back at Tinker. "And what exactly is a vander offer?"

His frown disappeared. "Nothing. Sorry. Caught me unawares, that's all." He smiled at Janine. "You are welcome."

"What?"

"For the thank you. You are welcome."

Janine looked from one to the other. "It always this hard to understand?"

Chantal laughed, swung her arm around Tinker's waist, tickled him, and said, "Nope. Not always. He just gets confused. Once in awhile."

Janine nodded, and said to Tinker, "If I give you a box of candy, you going to hit me?"

"What?" Now he did look confused.

"That is the way you are acting, you know. I say thank you and then I feel like you are going to punch my lights out for doing it."

He nudged Chantal, just a little. "Tell her that I am sorry. Really." He looked at Janine. "Really. Sorry. O.K.?"

Janine nodded.

Chantal explained, "He is really sorry."

He smiled at Janine. "So, where is it?"

"What?"

"The box of candy."

And Chantal began to laugh.

And Janine.

And Tinker.

Another Morning. Another Day.

They slipped from the house into the cool dawn quiet and gathered out on the back pasture with Janine, Freddie and Ralph were still sleeping in their separate rooms.

Tinker nodded at R-Bar.

And she turned them away.

Am'Pa'Tar. Dark and Dismal.

The a'demon looked up and grunted.

"It is the crazy Avon Polymorph."

And stood and stepped closer to Tinker. "You have shrunk, Master Boss." A thick nubby tongue licked over fleshy lips. "Were they tasty?"

Another a'demon appeared. And looked at the first. "He is really greedy, eating all those desserts. And not bringing us a taste. Or two?" It burped. And sidled toward Fair Morn.

"We did not do it," said a third as it appeared. "You A.P.'s are really terrible. The Chan Narh are extinct."

"What they get," snapped R-Bar. "Do what?"

"Of course," agreed the a'demons. "Whatever you are upset about."

"Wanna come to my cave," drooled the second, staring fixedly at Fair Morn's shirt, lips curling away from upper fangs.

She looked down at it. It was much shorter, but much wider. Her fingers flicked a lever on her weapon. "Nope."

One smiled at Messenger. It was ghastly.

"Yuck, yuck, yuck," she gasped.

"Thank you." It stepped closer. "Green glowing eyes are a'demon lust hungry." It panted.

Tinker stepped off to one side and beckoned. "Come'mer you guys."

A'demon heads snapped around. "Where?"

"I do not see any," said one.

"Haven't had yoo-eye in a forever," said another.

"Here," demanded Tinker.

"Where?" they chorused, lurching over to him, wobbling from side to side, heads swiveling, looking, searching.

"Never mind." He sighed.

"Of course," they agreed.

"We have a problem," said Tinker.

Three sets of shaggy ears shot straight up.

"And I need your help."

"Oh, oh," said one.

"Maybe he will give us the small treat in black," suggested another.

"Master Boss," said the third. "It is pretty short."

"I AM NOT SHORT," yelled R-Bar, whipping a crackling wand from somewhere.

"Have to cook it four indal," said one. "It looks like a tasty witch."

Another began to polish a great up curving tusk. With a cloth taken from a back pocket. "Rather we got a tender taste." One eye stared at Fair Morn.

"Will you knock it off," growled Tinker.

Three a'demon heads snapped in three directions.

"I don't see anything," said one.

"The A.P.'s are really crazy," said another.

"Maybe it means one of the desserts," hoped the third.

"STOP." Tinker was glowering at them and beginning to mumble to himself.

"Sure," they all said. "What?"

Chicken joined the group. "Me'Lord?"

An a'demon grunted. "Thanks, Master Boss." And reached for her.

She banged it on top of the head with the pommel of her sword.

It stared at her. "You did that the last time."

"Crazy," said another.

"Maybe," suggested the third, "the A.P.'S are not as tasty as they appear."

"That would be terrible terrible ugly evil nasty mean thing to do," said the third.

The second looked at Tinker. And nodded. And folded its ears back. "Master Boss, that is very clever. You want something?"

The loud sigh was Tinker.

"Of course," said the a'demons. "What?"

Chicken laughed.

"Don't be crude," snapped one, glaring at her.

"We need to visit the Dark Ump."

A'demons leaped backward in three directions, growling loudly.

"Now what?" Tinker stared at them.

"Worse than the Chan Narh," hissed one.

"And looked what happened to them," said the second.

"The A.P.'s got them," answered the third, slowly straightening up, its ears rising.

They crept back to Tinker and Chicken.

"Bring us back a taste," said one.

"Never had Dark Ump," said another.

The third carefully poked Chicken just above her belt. buckle. "You sure you are not tasty?"

"How do we get there?" asked R-Bar, stepping close.

The third beamed. "Just peel off the covering and put it in a pot." It reached up and started to undo Chicken's shirt.

She punched it in the right eye.

"Absolutely," it said, stepping back.

"To Estur Nal," said R-Bar.

"Straight through there," said the first. "But do not turn left or right." It pointed at two large stones. "Those turns used to be the way to Chan Narh. But you altered that."

The second inched closer to Tinker. "Master Boss, even if it is not tasty, how about leaving the part with the green eyes."

It panted heavily. "Demon lust green eyes."

"Absolutely," said the third. It stared at Messenger. "Urk, urk, urk, urk."

"Is that part deaf?" asked the first.

"Nope," said Tinker.

"Urk. Urk. URK," warbled the third, leaning toward Messenger.

She stepped behind Smoke and peered back around her to stare at it.

"How can it resist?" asked the first.

"URK URK, URK, URK," cawed the third.

"What?" asked Tinker.

"The lust call."

"Wrong time of the year," explained Tinker.

"My Lord?" Chicken touched his arm.

"Ooooooooeeeeeee," sang the a'demons.

"Time to go," said Tinker, heading for the rocks. The a'demons sat and watched them.

"The A.P.'s are really crazy," said one.

"Look tasty to me," said the second.

"Don't turn," called the third, as Tinker and company faded from sight.

Doth Lamex. The Elseplace of Rest and Relaxation.

He looked up from the ruins of his mid-day meal, past the heaped jumble of papers, scrolls, pamphlets, books, and other materials in the middle of the table, at his companion who sat ever so quietly.

"Yes?" said Lady Fairdeath.

"It has taken a many number of days to separate out the folk tales, the child tell tales, the pure fantasy and wishful thinking, but I think that I have gotten most of the reality out of that mass of odds and ends and all the rest from all that we have collected."

"This Ransapal is most clever a mage," she said.

He shrugged. "I believe that I know the name of their elseplace and how to get to it." He paused.

"Yes?"

"They, umm, are heavily guarded by many."

She nodded. "It is of no concern." One finger lazily caressed the short golden staff lying next to her plate.

"We have to be careful."

"Is there concern?" She looked puzzled into his frown.

He nodded. "There is. For me."

She flowed to her feet. "It is time for me to return to The Lady's House. I must discuss all that we know with my sisters." She nodded at him. "Bring everything."

"Where?"

"With you. With me."

"Is it safe?"

"Are those materials dangerous?"

"Traveling to your elseplace."

"Of course not."

"To me."

She smiled. "The Lady's mark is on your forehead. None may do harm to the clever Ransapal." She turned and walked away, headed for the gateway.

He followed, arms full of all that they had collected, and wondered.

Estur Nal. A Rather Nice Looking Place.

"Well?"

They looked around.

At green fields of very short grass, gently rolling hills, scattered clumps of trees. It was a warm sunny day.

"Well?" He looked at them, having first stared at their surroundings.

"Certainly have a way with words, Honey Buns." Chantal stepped to his side and nodded.

"Think those squat uglies sent us to the wrong place?"

"Nope." R-Bar joined them. "This is Estur Nal. It is just the way that the demon we caught said it would look."

Ran strolled over. "Your R-Bar is correct."

Ummm," said Tinker.

"She is," restated Ran.

"Huh?"

"Your's, Amtar." She nodded.

He sighed. And looked at Smoke."We catch something from those a'demons?"

She shook her head. "Nope." And winked at him. "Honey Buns."

Slowly, very slowly, he looked at each one of them, at each one of himself. Carefully, slowly, he did this. "How about we go home and start over?"

Chantal jabbed him in the soft spot just below the ribs,

just above the hip, with one finger. "Loosen up, Cowboy."

Grandeville. Tinker's Place. Mid-Morning.

"Your cowperson friend is getting even stranger than when she was in college."

Freddie patted Ralph's hand. "Do not worry about Chantal, Dear, she knows what she is doing. She always has."

They were on the rear deck enjoying the mildly warm and pleasant weather.

Ralph reached his other hand across the table and clasped the hand sitting on top of his. "Frederica, something is not right, here."

Janine refilled her cup. And snorted. "Maybe it is you, Ralph. Ever consider that." And refilled his cup. "Thank you. You are welcome." And smiled at him. "That is Cowgirl, not cowperson."

Ralph smiled back. "Where did they go? And how did they go?" He turned back to Freddie. "They are gone, you know. But none of their vehicles are." He looked back at Janine. "You going to tell me that they all just decided to stroll off, to take a walk to somewhere?"

Freddie nodded. And smiled. "Perhaps they did, Dear. Chantal's sister lives out there, in the valley. Somewhere."

Janine banged down her mug. Hard. Splashing coffee over the table top. Ralph jerked his arms to safety. "Does it matter? Really? They are gone. They said they would be gone. And guess what, Sherlock? They are gone."

"Well," said Ralph. "It is strange." He checked his sleeves for damage.

"Et tu," mumbled Janine.

"Everything about them is strange," added Ralph.

"Stick to the stock market," snapped Janine, surging to her feet. And stomping across the deck and into the house.

"Don't upset yourself, Dear. Please?" Freddie patted his hand. Again. Reaching around the wet spot. "Shall we stroll around? I have never seen such complex designs worked into flower beds before."

Estur Nal. A Rather Nice Looking Place.

"Pretty strange."

"Most pretty a'place, Sweet Prince." Chicken nudged him with her shoulder. "What be strange?"

"That it is a pretty place." He waved one hand. "Look at it."

Everyone did.

"That is strange," he said. Again. "Because this is supposed to be demon country. Their elseplaces usually aren't like this, are they?"

"Nope," agreed R-Bar. "At least not the one's that we have seen. Or heard about. Mostly."

Tinker looked at Smoke.

She pointed. "That way is as good a way as any. Don't feel anything around."

So that is what they did.

They walked that way.

Three soft hills later, he halted them and spun around. "Wait a minute, kiddo. I thought, we were going to visit the Dark Ump?"

R-Bar nodded. "We are."

"Then why are we in, ahhhhh?"

"Estur Nal."

"Right. Why are we here, in Estur Nal?"

"The demon we captured told us, Ran and I, how to get to the Dark Ump. We go this way. Even the a'demons knew about Estur Nal."

"Do I look like an a'demon?"

"Too cute for that," laughed Chantal.

"You gonna tell me, tell us, what is going on?" Tinker was glowering at R-Bar. And then at Ran. And now at Chantal.

"Nope," said R-Bar, shaking her head.

"Amtar, your R-Bar dares not." Ran stepped in front of R-Bar, between her and Tinker.

"If she says, the path will collapse."

"What path?"

R-Bar pushed Ran aside. "The one that we are following, Tink. The one that Zar'gh told us to follow, Ran and I." She threw an arm around Ran. "We know where we are going. But we may not speak it."

"Demon spells are most strange, twisted, and anduk," explained Ran. "And this path is very anduk."

"Oh," said Tinker. "Anduk. Why didn't you say so in the first place?"

Chantal kicked him, not too hard on ankle. "Smart ass."

Smoke yanked her away before he could grab her. "Uh, uh, uh," she said. "The Dark Ump are watching."

"Yucko," said Messenger.

"Which way?" asked Tinker.

Ran and R-Bar pointed. "That way," they said.

"Tweedle-Dee and Tweedle-Dum," he mumbled. They walked that way.

"Ever hear of that clan?" Ran looked at R-Bar, who shook her head.

Grandeville. Red and Sandy's Home.

"Certainly been sleeping better."

"Bend down," she commanded.

"The last few days," he rasped in his usual tone of voice.

They were standing in the doorway. The outer doorway. Red was dressed for work. Blue uniform bedecked with the standard policeman gear. He bent.

Sandy kissed him. "Right. It was just some sort of temporary thing."

"Good." He unbent. "I was getting tired of knees battering this or that."

"Especially that."

He smiled. "Especially." The smile broadened. "Green wants to know whether you will release the apron strings. We wanna go bowling Saturday night." The left corner of her mouth puckered.

Outside, a car horn honked.

He stepped backwards, turned, set his cap just so, brim covering his eyes.

Green hastily rolled up the window and banged the door lock down.

Sandy marched down to the curb and rapped on the driver's window. "Open up."

The window rolled down. "Evening Counselor. Got a search warrant?"

"Green," she snarled.

"Said it's fine, Partner." Red had walked around to the other side and climbed in. The patrol car leaned back to level now that he was balancing the weight of his equally large friend.

"I oughta punch you," added Sandy.

"That is battery, Lawyer Person, being politically correct and all that." Green's eyes twinkled.

"Can I come and keep score? I know how, you know."

"Red won't be able to flirt with the waitress if you do."

Sandy bent down and peered across Green. "I am coming."

"Sure, Babe. Let's go, Partner." Red thumped on the dash.

"Night, Sandy." Green eased the patrol car from the curb and headed out on their usual prowl.

Sandy waved. And grinning happily, went back inside.

To the usual paperwork, as always, piling up.

Estur Nal. A Rather Nice Looking Place.

"Still nothing?"

"Nope." Smoke gave him a friendly bump. "Sun's going down. We better camp."

It had been a rather long, a rather dull day. Tinker had finally given up and had stopped counting how many of these low green hills they had hiked up and over. It was just dull. Everything had been the same. And as far as anyone could tell, the monotony stretched in every direction to all far horizons.

So.

They stopped.

    And made camp.

    Dropping their gear in a heap.

"Must be demon country of some sort," mumbled Tinker. "Patterned lifelessness."

Grandeville. Tinker's Place.

Freddie smiled at them. And took a second helping of breakfast.

Janine had cooked.

Ralph poured the coffee and nodded. "Actually, it is quite pleasant, here. Must be the mountain air."

Janine looked at Freddie. "That is three nights in a row."

"I think Ralph is correct," replied Freddie. "It must be the mountain air."

Janine stood. "I think that I will pack a lunch, take a little hike."

Ralph pursed his lips. "I wonder if they sell anything other than the local newspapers?"

Janine laughed. "'Poor Ralph."

Freddie frowned at her.

"O.K.," said Janine. "'I'll help. Ralph, Chantal told me that they have a business computer setup in their corporate headquarters, which is just right around the corner from here. I sure that it will all right if you want to go over there and play. It is connected to everything."

Ralph sat up. "Really?"

"Surprise, surprise." Janine headed for the house, yelling over her shoulder, "Be back in time for dinner."

"We will cook," called Freddie.

Ralph stared at her.

Estur Nal. A Rather Nice Looking Place.

"Amtar?"

"Ummmm?"

She slipped her hand inside his shirt, resting her head on his upper arm, using it for a pillow.

"Huh?" His eyes opened.

It was dark.

Almost.

Three tiny moons, a cluster of small rounds, reflected soft light across the landscape. Scattered stars formed patterns unfamiliar to Tinker.

Ran hitched herself higher and nuzzled his ear. "I

could cast a dark sphere around us?"

"Ummmm?"

"Dark spheres are solid hard no-see reptan."

"Reptan?"

"Yessssssss." She tugged his belt loose.

"What's reptan?" He grabbed her hand.

Hooking a leg over his and rolling over, she sat up, leaned forward, and looked into his face. "Reptan is a quality."

"Yes?"

She yanked her shirt loose, eyes glittering. "Mine."

"Ahh?"

She began to unbutton his shirt. "Nothing escapes, nothing passes through. No thing."

"I see."

Sitting back, she yanked her shirt off and tossed it to one side. "I am your's, Amtar, your Ran."

The dark sphere snapped around them.

Grandeville. Sharp Ridge. On the Edge of Tinker's Place.

Walking along the high, narrow ridge, she met them.

Sitting on large rocks.

Eating their lunch.

They smiled at her, and invited her to join them.

She did, fishing her lunch from the small day pack she wore.

And, as they ate, they talked.

"Oh," said the man.

His wife filled his cup. "We are friends of them. I am Ramp."

"Ahhhh, my name if Alandale Frederico Hardcastle IV. Call me, Hard, everyone does." He reached out and shook Janine's hand.

"Janine," she said.

"Ummmm, ahhhhh," said Hard.

"Husband," cautioned Ramp.

"What?" asked Janine.

"You are Chantal's friend, aren't you?" asked Hard.

"Yes. Why?"

"Your friend told us what happened." Ramp caught his cup as he nudged it off his knee.

"I'd rather not talk about that." Janine stared through them.

"Been here long? Ah, that is, not here, here." Hard waved his arm. Ramp ducked. "But down there, here, ahhh, Tinker's place?" Ramp kept his cup.

Janine shook her head. "Just a few days. Starting to enjoy the quiet."

"You live in Portland, right?" Hard stared at her.

"Uh huh. I asked Chantal if they had room, but she said that they didn't. Are rentals high in town?"

Hard blushed.

"Shhhhhh," said Ramp.

Janine frowned And quickly checked her shirt. She hadn't unbuttoned it that far.

"You are very pretty," said Ramp. She handed him his cup back. Filled.

"They all are, " said Hard, face trying to get redder. It couldn't.

Ramp touched his cheek. His color changed back to normal. "From what we understand," she said to Janine, "they are complete. Did Chantal explain?"

Janine nodded. "Sort of." And carefully looked at this calm woman. "Is it true?"

Hard choked on his coffee.

"Yes, it is," said Ramp. "But it would be very hard for

folk from this elseplace to understand."

"Certainly is." Janine stared past them at the two people who were hiking up the back slope. "Did they go this way?"

Hard turned to look. "Who?"

"Them," said Janine. "Tinker. And them."

He turned back. "What?"

"No," said Ramp.

"That is our son and his wife," explained Hard.

Janine stared at them. And at their son and his wife, rapidly approaching.

"Hard to explain," said Hard.

"I'll bet," said Janine.

"What?"

"Never mind," she said.

Ramp stood, and pointed. "We are walking out to the point. Join us?"

Janine nodded.

So. They turned.

And that is what they did.

Estur Nal. A Rather Nice Looking Place.

Creeping up over the far horizon came the sun. The bright light flowed over deep green and bumped, tickled, and nudged the sleeping forms.

And they woke.

One by one by one by one by one by one.

Smoke began to gather up the breakfast ingredients.

R-Bar came over and sat beside her. "Never mind." And waved in their breakfast. And stared over at the dark half-dome rising above the tight grass carpet. "Tanpak."

"Completely cut off," said Smoke. "But it feels all right."

"Strange."

"What, pray tell?" Chicken joined them.

"That Tanpak sphere, Princess." R-Bar took a piece of toast and nibbled on one corner of it.

"Indeed. Most dark."

"Morning, morning, morning," bubbled Messenger as she sat by them. "Oh, boy, omelets." She served herself and Chicken.

Chantal yanked a blanket over her head. "Shhhh."

"Ooopsy," said Messenger, ducking her head.

Fair Morn crawled over and became part of the ever expanding breakfast circle. "Smells good." She arched her back and stretched. "Sun feels so good." And balled up her shirt and tossed it over to her sleeping bag. "Anyone around?"

"Nope," said Smoke.

Chicken yanked off her shirt. "Most true. This fiery ball do offer most gentle warm soft a'caress." She cut another piece of omelet and smiled.

"Think he'll mind?" asked R-Bar.

"Nay. Tis omelet most elegant." Chicken took another slice.

"Thank you. I meant shirtless." R-Bar began to undo her shirt buttons.

"Praps aye, praps nay. We do be but most alone. And tis naught but what Our Verra Own Sweet Prince do have peered pon many a'time afore." She refilled R-Bar's cup. "Tis true."

"Well," said Messenger, carefully folding her shirt and setting it beside herself. "We can always put them back on."

Everyone agreed.

Grandeville. Tinker's Place. Corporate Computer Room.

"You have been in here for just hours and hours, Dear." Freddie slid a tray onto the desk top. And poured tea.

Ralph swung around in the plush swivel chair, eyes sparkling. And leaned back. "Tea. How wonderful."

"Why, thank you, Dear." Freddie sat. "You do look happy."

"I am. Oh, I am." Ralph sipped from his cup. "Did you know that this Tinker fellow is linked into the Morgan Enterprises system?"

"No, Dear."

"I had quite a chat with Morgan himself when I first logged on? In real-time images and all?"

"You did?"

"I most certainly did. I required his permission to do what I wanted to do. This system is heavily guarded."

"My."

Ralph leaned close. "Frederica, did you know that this Tinker person is, to put it in vulgar parlance, rolling in it?"

Freddie shook her head. "I met Mr. Morgan once. He is married to one of Chantal's sisters. What?"

"Money. Wealth. Morgan manages it for him."

"My."

Ralph grinned. "Morgan is coming up here tomorrow. We are having a meeting." He reached out and took one of her hands.

"Yes, Dear."

"Frederica, if we can come to an agreement, Morgan and I, guess what?"

Freddy smiled at him. "You know that I do not have a head for business things."

"This . . . is . . . not . . . business."

"How unlike you, Dear."

Now he held both of her hands, tightly. With both of his. "Dear, I firmly believe, that if Morgan and I come to an agreement, that your Father will no longer stand in our way."

"OH," gasped Freddy.

"OH," she cried.

"Oh. Dear," she wept.

"Please don't do that."

Blinking frantically, she nodded. And stopped. "I knew you could do it, Dear Ralph."

"Now he will also," hissed Ralph.

The large screen flickered and beeped. Fred peered out at them. "Oh, hello Freddy. Just confirming the meet," he said to Ralph.

"I," stated Ralph, "will be here."

"Good." Fred smiled. "Tomorrow, then."

The screen went blank.

"Let's go to town. Have a good meal. Celebrate." Ralph stood.

"Dear, I have already cooked something. Let's do that tomorrow. After your meeting."

He nodded.

They walked outside and toward the main house.

She held his hand.

Tightly.

Estur Nal. A Rather Nice Looking Place.

Suddenly.

It was gone.

They walked over.

For breakfast.

"Now what's going on?" He sat down to eat.

"Hum hum," said Ran, taking the plate handed to her by Chantal.

"We were not," snapped R-Bar.

"Never mind," said Tinker. "I don't want to know."

"Take it off, take it off," cooed Messenger. "Take it all off."

He glared at her.

"Ooops." She ducked her head. "I meant shirts."

He sighed.

"Tis most pleasant, My Lord."

"Amtar?"

"What?"

"Your . . . "

"What?"

". . . permission."

"What?"

"One would not dare without permission."

"Oh? Ah, go ahead."

"Amdo intok, Amtar." Ran started to undo her shirt buttons.

He looked at R-Bar. "How come you didn't ask?"

"Different clan values. She is Tanpak." R-Bar grabbed another piece of toast. He ought to know that.

Chantal shoved out her hand. "Hand it over, Cowboy."

"What?"

"Your shirt."

"We get to ogle your bod," said Fair Morn.

"In return," said R-Bar.

"Yah," drawled Messenger. "Dude."

"We are still alone," said Smoke, shaking off her shirt.

Tinker nodded. "Everyone sleep all right?" And began slipping off his shirt.

They all nodded.

He smiled. "Takes care of that. Let's go home."

"Wench," said Chicken to Ran.

"Hum, hum, hum," hummed R-Bar.

"No escape," said Ran. She nodded at R-Bar.

"Rah-ther, sneaky, that." Chicken stared at her. "Mayhap this device around us each night be placed?"

Ran nodded. And handed the ornate ring to Smoke.

Smoke rolled her eyes at Tinker. "Eat some more, MindMate."

"Not going home," stated R-Bar. "Not until we fix those Dark Ump."

"How come?" asked Messenger.

"We can not have Our Self Ran place dark spheres all the time." R-Bar frowned. "It would be bad for her health."

"Not to mention his," laughed Chantal.

"Ha. Ha. Ha," said Tinker. "We ready to go?" He stood.

And soon they were.

Headed for the only thing that they could see that was different. A dark spot on a far horizon.

Grandeville. Sharp Ridge. Near Tinker's Place.

"They left. Three days ago." She pointed down at the house.

From out here, on the point, they could see the house. Tinker's place.

Way down there.

Way over there.

"That is, they are not home. We are."

Ramp nodded. And watched Hard carefully. This was not the place for one who tripped over things that were not there. "I felt my sister leave."

"Sister?"

"R-Bar is my sister."

Janine took another look. And nodded. Now that Ramp had mentioned it, it was obvious. Their faces were similar. Large dark eyes. High cheek bones.

Ramp smiled. "She was often call The Runt, being so short compared to the rest of us. She is very sensitive about her height."

"She growls," said Hard, stumbling over something. A small stone rolled over the edge, and fell. It was some time before they heard it hit.

Tajaar had a firm grasp on Shem's arm. "Walk back back," she ordered.

"What?"

She pulled him, firmly, steadily, back from the edge.

Then they all started walking back along the narrow bare rock ridge.

And, after Shem and Tajaar were well ahead of them, Janine said softly. "You do not look old enough to have a son his age."

"Oh, that," said Hard.

"It is . . . hard to explain," said Ramp.

"Oh?" said Janine.

"Um," said Hard "Ahhhhhh, yes."

Janine laughed. "Sorry. But it must be a local thing. I keep having conversations that don't make sense."

"I think that when they return, you should talk with them," said Ramp.

"I see," said Janine.

"What?" asked Hard.

"Shhhh,"said Ramp.

"What?"

She grabbed him and kissed him. "All mine."

They hurried to catch up with Shem and Tajaar.

Grandeville. The Burger and Bowl.

Sandy snorted, hissed, swallowed hard, and burst into loud laughter.

"Partner," said Green. "I always thought that lawyers, of either kind, M or F, were polite, well-mannered, and in general, a model of good behavior. In public."

Red emptied his glass. It was one of the large pitchers. And picked up his bowling ball. They were halfway through the second game. "I think that this is some sort of subtle editorial comment." He turned and bowled.

Green waited until after Red's second try to ask, "Don't you know? You are cohabiting with her."

Red waved over the waitress and ordered, for them all. "There are aspects of the female psyche beyond human, that is, male, ken."

He handed Sandy her glass. He left the two pitchers, one for himself, one for Green. "Besides, I think she is getting sloshed."

"I am not." Sandy sat straighter. "It is just that I have never thought that watching bowling, up close and personal, so to speak, could be so entertaining."

Green stepped up to the line. "We bowl for fun." He managed to get three pins. And then, three more.

Sandy tittered.

And belched.

Green bent and peered into her eyes. "Good thing that we are driving."

Red watched his ball wobble down the lane. "I think that I am going to win this game."

"One up," announced Sandy. "Gentlemen?"

They both looked at her.

"Must mean us," said Green.

"Babe?" asked Red.

"You two been bowling long?"

"Second time," said Green.

Estur Nal. A Rather Nice Looking Place.

They were walking along, in the same direction as before.

"Good question." Chantal ran a finger up his spine. And snickered as he twitched, and grumbled at her.

"Most dour a'cloud, Me'Lord."

"Too far," said Smoke.

"Bletch," added Messenger. She smiled at Tinker. "Ogle, ogle, ogle."

He sighed. "Bug-nuts."

"You have an insect fetish, Simba Leader?" Chantal tilted her head to one side and waggled her eyebrows at him.

"TINK," gasped R-Bar.

Ran nodded at her. "I could cast kinquar."

"Hold it," he said.

"Per-verted," said Messenger.

"Buzz, buzz, buzz," buzzed Fair Morn. "Course I'm the wrong gender for that." She grinned at him. "But the closest thing to a bug that you have."

Grandeville. The Burger and Bowl.

"Impressed, right?" asked Red.

Sandy giggled. And waved back the waitress.

"Guess not, Partner." Green ordered food. For all three of them. He nodded at Sandy, but spoke to Red. "If she doesn't eat something you'll be able to pour her through your front door mail slot."

The third game struck Sandy as even funnier than the first two.

Estur Nal. A Rather Nice Looking Place.

"Passing strange, Our Prince, this thy insect interest."

"Knock it off," he growled.

Smoke leered at him. "This evening."

He jolted to a halt. "O.K., now what?"

"Naught, Our Love," explained Chicken.

"Then?" he demanded.

"Fair word play, Our Prince."

"Fair maid play," added Messenger.

"That's us, all right." Fair Morn beamed at him. "And me. Fair maid, Fair Morn."

"I am not a maid," grumped R-Bar.

"We are not for sale," hissed Ran.

"WHAT?" He stared at her.

"Fair," intoned Fair Morn. "A festival or carnival where there is entertainment and things often sold."

"Ergo, fair maids are maidens sold at fairs." Chantal winked at him. "Ask for top dolla."

"Ran is not a thing," stated Smoke.

"Most fair," said Chicken, running a finger over Ran.

"Yum, yum, yum." Smoke licked her lips. "For a non-insect."

"Lepidoptera certainly are. Shall I lie down?" Fair Morn beamed at him. "Spread my wings?"

"That's it!" He waved his arms wildly. "Shirts on. "You are all getting sun poisoned."

"Pish tosh." Chicken shook her head. "Tis naught but deep boredom in this most dull green a'place."

"Yah," said Messenger. "And besides, you thought that I was a boy."

"You're kidding," gasped Chantal. "How young were you?" She turned toward him. "Were you cradle robbing?"

"Way she was dressed," growled Tinker. "And she

wasn't that young."

"MindMate. It moved."

All heads snapped around.

To stare at the darkening.

It was suddenly closer.

And getting even closer.

"Oh, oh," he said.

In moments, shirts were on, buttoned, tucked in, and weapons readied

Grandeville. Red and Sandy's Home.

"You and that other moose are not very nice people."

Sunday morning light filtered into the kitchen. Sandy was slouched in a chair, head in hand, watching Red fix breakfast.

He shoveled in the diced potatoes and other ingredients. And watched things cook in several pans. "Root beer's good."

"Orange juice," she replied. He refilled her glass.

She looked up, and licked the juice from her upper lip, "Was that deliberate?"

"What?"

"Plying me with all that non-root beer?"

"T. 5 A."

"What?"

"Take the fifth amendment." He began cracking eggs into one of the pans. "Certainly put away a lot for a little person."

"I am not a little person."

"T. 5 A."

"Taller than average."

He sat. And served. "Eat. Maybe. We're not very good at it, you know."

"It was fun." She started to eat.

"Three weeks before we can get Saturday night off again."

"O.K.," she mumbled.

"You can keep score."

"I will try not to laugh."

"T. 5 A."

Chapter Fifteen.

Surprise, Surprise.

Estur Nal. A Rather Nice Looking Place.

"Wonder what it is?"

It was a cloud.

It looked like a castle.

Sorta. Or, thought Tinker, maybe it really was a castle. But then.

Maybe not.

Now it looked like a cloud.

Sorta.

Smoke shook her head as her minds reached out. "Coming our way," she gasped. And sagged.

Chantal grabbed her.

Smoke looked up through eyebrows at Tinker. "Twisted, turning, changing."

"Let go, " he snapped.

Something was coming out of the front door of it. Something.

It walked toward them.

And stopped and stared.

At them.

They stared back. He looked mostly human.

Except for the red eyes, long ear lobes, and dark colored, very pointed teeth.

"Who?" he asked.

"No one," replied Tinker, guessing at the question. "We are strangers here."

"True name," he demanded.

"Don't," snapped R-Bar.

"Alamaedur," answered Alamaedur. He walked closer and stared at Fair Morn. "Strange." And stepped carefully around her, staring intently. "Who power wonder do." He seemed to be having trouble speaking their language.

Tinker heard the sharp click as Chantal cocked the hammer on her revolver. So did Alamaedur. He finished his inspection of Fair Morn and turned.

"Your's?" he asked Chantal.

"Our's," said Tinker.

"Set?"

"Most true ," said Chicken. Her left hand clenched the top of her sword's scabbard.

"Strange." Then he stared at Smoke.

Suddenly the air sizzled around Alamaedur. "QUINQUIKZL."

Smoke jerked the 45 from her shoulder holster and fired past his left side.

Alamaedur lurched stumbling backward, purple stains splashing, flowing from his side.

Two figures hurtled from the castle cloud entrance, ran up, grabbed Alamaedur, and dragged him back inside.

"He wasn't where he appeared to be," explained Smoke, straightening up. "They attack by indirection."

"A Quinquikzl?" asked Tinker.

Smoke shrugged. "Nothing like that ever visited us. He was after Fair Morn." She stuffed her pistol back into the shoulder holster.

R-Bar stepped closer. "Tink, he saw something, some after effect of Big Red."

"Your R-Bar is correct," said Ran, stepping up to R-Bar's side. "He identified your three gift's."

"Gifts?"

Ran nodded at him. "Your Princess, Your Dark Smoke, and Your Winged Fair Morn."

Chicken frowned. "We do Us forget. Tis true. Mere bit of fluff released from toy box small."

"Princess," said Tinker, softly. "Please?"

She looked at him, eyes moving up. She had been staring down at nothing. "My Lord?"

"No toy. No gift. Just real live person."

She dropped to one knee. "As thee do wish."

Tinker whirled and jabbed one finger at Ran, snapping angrily, "One more word about gifts and you are in deep trouble."

She leaped sideways, away from that pointing finger. "AMTAR."

"Watch it, Tink," hissed R-Bar. "She is triggering."

"One is coming," called Messenger.

Dark eddied around Ran. Everyone turned to face the direction Messenger was pointing.

The woman stopped and stared at them. "Ahamaezur."

"Sure," said Tinker, nodding. "Whatever."

"Alamaedur heals."

"Good."

Dark crackling startled them all. Ahamaezur winced. Ran growled.

Another had stepped out and walked over to them, joining the first.

The pair stood and looked the group over. Especially Smoke, Chicken, and Fair Morn.

Fair Morn cradled her cannon in her arms and stared

back.

"Who the set?" asked Ahamaezur.

"We told whozizt," said Tinker. "No one did."

Ahamaezur nodded. "Dontt."

Tinker looked blank.

That's you, Tink, explained R-Bar.

"Aandanleleptark," cried the pair, leaping backwards, making warding off signs with both hands at R-Bar. Sharp blades leaped into their hands.

R-Bar's beast snarled and crouched by her feet.

A small sphere hung in the air above Ran. It quivered.

"Now what?" Tinker looked from pair to pair.

"She, they, heard, felt me," cried R-Bar.

They ran from the castle cloud. Men. Wearing dark glittering costumes. And a wave of women similarly dressed. All held sharp blades in their hands.

Chantal stepped away from Tinker. Making room. Finding a clear field of fire.

"WAIT, WAIT, WAIT," yelled Tinker.

Fair Morn reset levers. "Taking no chances, One."

"Right, Simba leader," agreed Chantal.

"Kiddo?"

"Yesssssss," hissed R-Bar.

"Any idea?"

"NO."

Ran slipped up next to him and touched his arm. "Amtar?"

"Yes?"

"Zar'gh called these, Tark," she whispered.

"And?"

She leaner closer, very close, and spoke low. "The demon said these are multi-twisted bent eaters."

"Uh huh?"

"What?"

"That it?"

"Yes, Amtar."

He sighed. "Not a whole lot of help, is it?"

"No, Amtar."

R-Bar stomped over to them, Ran and Tinker, dark ugly terror creeping at her side. "They know the way on."

He frowned at her. "Them?"

"Yesssss."

"Zar'gh say that?"

"Shhhhh," cautioned R-Bar. "The Guk'demon feared these."

"The Tark?"

"Them," replied Ran, nodding.

"Either of you have any idea what we should do?"

"Nope."

"No, Amtar."

"Ah, ha," he said. "Ah, ha. Standard problem, like always. SNAFU."

"That is not nice," said R-Bar, her lower lip beginning to push out.

Ran nodded, looking equally put upon. "I agree with your R-Bar."

"Ah, ha," he said, turning to face the other pair.

The Tark pair stepped closer, and closer.

"Ah, ha," said Ahamaezur.

"Gesundheit," replied Tinker.

"Hist, My Lord," gasped Chicken. "Tis nay time for levity."

The two Tark eyed him.

"Let's talk," he said.

Ahamaezur nudged her companion who looked at Tinker and said, "Amamaedur." And rubbed her hand over her lips.

"No souvenirs," snapped Chantal.

"She is pretty," whispered Messenger to Chantal.

Fair Morn joined them. "If you go for red eyes and pointy teeth."

Chantal snorted. "I suppose he could always put a sack over her head."

"Most crude," snapped Chicken.

"Will you guys knock it off?" Tinker's head snapped around, glowering at them. And turned back to the Tark.

Ahamaezur beckoned to him. He walked closer.

"GET OUT OF THE LINE OF FIRE," yelled Chantal.

He nodded.

And ignored her.

Grandeville. Greater Downtown. Chen's Chinese.

"I will house sit."

They were in the last stages of finishing their dinner.

They were in a private room at Chen's Chinese, having Chen's Special Number One dinner.

Janine had phoned Sandy and she had suggested this as the best place in town.

So, now, they sat around the table, and finished the meal. Freddie, Ralph, Janine, and Sandy. Red was working.

"I will do it," said Janine. "We can't just walk off and leave the place empty."

Freddie had announced, earlier that day, after lunch, that she and Ralph were returning to Portland. To speak with Freddie's father. Ralph had been wearing a dazed look on his face ever since yesterday afternoon.

"You will be all alone," gasped Freddie.

"Perfectly safe out there," said Sandy. "Nobody will bother anyone up there."

"I'm not worried," said Janine.

Ralph sipped his tea. "We could stay."

"No, Dear," stated Freddie firmly. He nodded.

Janine leaned sideways and kissed his cheek. "Thanks, Ralpho."

Ralph blinked.

Sandy handed him a fortune cookie. "Here."

The door opened and Master Chen leaned in. "Good grub, right?"

Sandy smiled at the small, slight figure. "Wonderful."

Chen nodded. And said to Freddie, "When you return, I will have a special wedding feast prepared just for you." Then he winked at Sandy, backed out, and shut the door.

Freddie stared at the closed door, half turning in her seat. "How did he know that?"

Sandy shrugged a shoulder. "Must be the expression on Ralph's face. What did you do to him?"

Freddie blushed. "Nothing." And sipped at her tea. "Ralph will be opening a special office for Morgan Enterprises in Portland. Investments and things like that."

Sandy stared at him. "Really? Wow, Ralph. Did you need a job?"

Janine laughed. "Freddie made him an offer that he couldn't refuse."

Sandy pretended to be shocked as she looked at Freddie. "Tsk, tsk, tsk, tsk."

Freddie blushed again and played with her napkin. "Ralph will have four assistants and a secretary. And may come and go as he pleases. And even work from home."

"Telecommuting," said Ralph. "It was Morgan's suggestion."

"And a car and a driver," said Freddie.

"That ought to impress your Father," said Janine.

Sandy nodded. "Ought to."

Freddie smiled at them. "And he may call upon the corporate jet whenever he has to travel." She reached over and squeezed Ralph's hand. "Not even Daddie has that."

"Just passed Go," said Janine.

"Bet he collects more than two hundred dollars," laughed Sandy. "Congratulations, Ralph, Freddie."

"Me too," added Janine. "Never thought that it would happen."

Freddie leaned against Ralph, a little. "We are going to the company chalet in Switzerland for two weeks. Then we are coming back. Ralph will start doing business things after that. I think that I will ask Daddie for the right wing of the house. It has a large room for entertaining." She smiled happily.

Ralph nodded. And said to Janine, "Do thank John Tinker and the rest, ermmmm, when they return from, ermmmm, their travels."

Janine nodded. "I'll do it."

Sandy stood. "Gotta go. Just let me know when the big occasion is. We will all come over."

"Of course," said Freddie.

Ralph stood. "We will."

And then.

They all headed in their respective directions.

Estur Nal. A Rather Nice Looking Place.

Ahamaezur squinted at him. "Not strange."

They were both standing close to him.

"Thanks," said Tinker. "Ahhh, we need your help." He could feel the heat radiating from their bodies.

She reached out and touched his cheek with one finger. And looked at her companion. "There."

"Crippled?" asked Amamaedur.

"Nope." He reached out. His hand passed through Ahamaezur. Then he moved it to the left, and bumped into warm, soft flesh. And jerked his hand back. "Now that is strange."

She smiled at him. "Kek."

Amamaedur nodded. "Kek."

"I suppose," he mumbled, shifting his feet. "We were just passing through, looking for the way to the Dark Ump, when you," he pointed at the castle cloud, "appeared."

"Dark Ump," echoed Amamaedur, inching closer.

"Tokark," stated Ahamaezur, inching closer.

"Pretty bad, huh?" Tinker was beginning to feel fairly nervous with this pair.

"Steady on, My Lord," called Chicken.

"Show way," said Ahamaezur.

"For this," stated Amamaedur. "To us." And rubbed her hand over her lips.

"WHAT?" Chantal stepped further sideways so she could get a clear shot at them.

"What?" asked Tinker.

"Tartakle bluestone give." Ahamaezur stepped to one side and close to him. He could feel her touching his chest.

Tinker cleared his throat. "Ahhhh, don't you guys ever appear where you are really are?"

"Safe," said Amamaedur.

"Do." Bright red eyes stared into his. Ahamaezur stood in front of him, leaned against him, both arms draped over his shoulders. "Do? Strange male."

"Ummmmmm? Bring this bluestone? From the tartakle? Correct?"

Her nose touched his. "In do."

Everything went black.

Then white.

Grandeville. Tinker's Place.

She heard the noise.

And rolled her head over to see what it was.

And screamed, leaped from the lounge, and ran inside the house.

"What are we doing home?" He stared unbelievingly at the house. "And who was that?"

"Sounded like Janine to me," answered Chantal. "I'll go inside and see what the problem is."

"Excited," said Smoke.

"Nice bod," said Fair Morn.

"Most athletic," added Chicken.

"Now what?" Tinker sat on one of the benches.

He beckoned at Ran and R-Bar.

They took seats across the table from him.

"Does the Dynamic Duo have any idea about what is going on?"

"Not exactly," said R-Bar, slowly.

"It is so." Ran nodded.

"Very witchy replies," observed Tinker. "So, how about this question? What, or who, is or are, the tartakle?"

R-Bar frowned.

Ran looked blank.

"Wonderful," he sighed. "Just wonderful. How come it always goes like this."

Smoke sat next to him. "This elseplace has blue stone, MindMate." And slipped an arm over his shoulders.

"Think that's it?"

Chicken sat by his other side. "We do be home, My Lord." And slipped an arm around his waist.

"Ummmmm?"

"I think that I'll make us a little snack. As long as we are home." Fair Morn headed for the kitchen. Messenger went with her.

Chantal came back outside and joined the group at the table. "Sun bathing. We have been gone for six days. She was surprised."

"Huh?" He twisted around to look at her.

Chantal leaned on the table and stared back at him. "Cowboy, we have been gone for six days. That little excursion cost us six days, our time. And Janine was sun bathing when we turned up. Unannounced. Sort of a surprise."

Shoving arms away, he stood. "I am going into town. See ya later." And headed for the driveway. "Gonna purchase some blue stones."

"She will be all right," said Chantal to Smoke.

"Nice bod," said Smoke. "Athletic."

After dinner, they lounged in the living room. Everyone had showered, dumped their dirty clothes, and repacked their gear.

Messenger leaned against one side, R-Bar sat on the other. Tinker slumped, his arms around them and said to Janine, sitting in one of the chairs. "Sorry."

"Ts'all right. It has just been so quiet that I was really surprised when you snuck up on me like that. Chantal explained."

"Ummmmmm," said Tinker.

Janine smiled at him. "Really. All right."

Smoke winked at him.

"Do you mind watching the place some more? We are leaving in the morning."

"For how long?"

"Hard to say."

"Wellll," drawled Janine. "O.K." She grinned. "But it will cost you."

"Oh my gosh," said Messenger.

Tinkers eyes jumped from face to face. "Ahhhhhh?"

Chantal laughed. "You can have almost anything," she said to her friend. "Almost."

Messenger cupped a hand around her mouth and whispered in his ear. "She is really pretty."

"Kitten," he cautioned.

"Certainly nicer than those Tark," mumbled R-Bar.

"They weren't doing anything," he mumbled back.

"Heh, heh, heh," replied R-Bar.

He sighed. "I think that it is time for bed." And struggled to escape. "Now what?"

"Nothing," said Messenger and R-Bar, sitting back.

"Goofy," he replied, heading for the hall.

"I'LL TELL YOU MY PRICE WHEN YOU RETURN," called Janine at his back.

"Anything takes a lot of thought," she said to Chantal.

"Almost," cautioned Chantal. "Anything."

"Well, she is your buddy."

Tinker was grumbling as they walked past the flower beds and out into the first pasture.

Chantal tossed an arm around his shoulders. "That's right, Cowboy, she is." She bumped him with a hip. "And besides."

"What?"

"I already told her how you were."

"What?"

"How we were."

"WHAT?" He jolted to a halt.

"So she can wave goodbye, if she feels like it." She pinched his cheek. "Cutie."

He sighed "We can always put up a billboard, I suppose. Down by the highway."

"Grump, grump, grump," said Chantal. "Sandy knows. Morgan knows. Anything happen? No. So, now Janine knows."

She grabbed him and spun around, peering into his eyes.

"Besides, she remembered, lots of what happened. Before." She kissed the tip of his nose. "You are safe."

R-Bar joined them and poked him in the side of the ribs. "Absolutely, Tink. Besides, if she talks, I will send a gat to visit her." Her eyes gleamed at the thought.

Ran gasped. And growled. At her.

R-Bar frowned. "Well, only if you say so, Tink." She looked disappointed.

"We ready to go?" he asked.

"Yep." R-Bar swung away. And gathered everyone together.

Messenger waved gaily at Janine.

Who started to wave back.

Only there wasn't anyone to wave to.

Only the empty pasture.

And a wisp of black.

Far Corner.

It was mid-morning and they were sitting and discussing yesterday and what they had learned.

In a soft puff of black they were there. One stomped over and punched. And glared down at the sprawling body, then knelt next to her. "I, we, will not be casually thrown to our rooms, Anaza Natanada."

Turintor watched Abadoda carefully.

"No harm intended," stated Abadoda, watching the man and woman.

Rbat helped Natanada stand and rubbed her palm over the discoloration on her forehead. "Heal works, shadow cousin." Something crackling left the room.

Natanada waved in cups and a jug. "Sit with us, shadow cousins. We have much to discuss. I have a special request."

"Hum." Rbat sat and looked at Turintor.

Turintor nodded. "Speak tell."

Bahn Duhr Tohr.

The many armed Narmot, native to the steaming dense growth of the elseplace named by the settlers, Swamp Ugly, had grabbed her and dragged her down. Snarling and growling, she tried to free herself. In the raging struggle, her blouse had been yanked loose and was being slipped away. The beast pressed her down.

"Enter!" demanded a voice from somewhere.

"Ptar nar nar," she snapped, sitting up, her blouse shifting back into place. "Enter!"

They appeared. In the middle of the room.

"Hayou, sister."

Ripple stood and stared. "Who are these, sister?"

"Hayou, Rbat. And Turintor and Motaiss." Hanred stared at the group.

Rbat gestured. "Natanada. Abadoda."

"Humble greetings," said Turintor. She gestured at Natanada. "She is Elixa of the Anaza. Clan head."

Ripple stared. "Strange title. Never heard Anaza clan."

Natanada stared back. "We call Phylota, not clan."

Hanred gasped.

Ripple's head snapped around. "Husband?"

He cleared his throat. "I read, in a small rare book, about some that used such a word." He stepped closer and looked at these strangers. "I thought that it was just a small tale. But here you are."

"What?" snapped Ripple.

She bowed. "Anaza sorceress Natanada."

"We must talk," snarled Ripple. She pointed at the table, now set with refreshments. "Sit."

Estur Nal. A Rather Nice Looking Place..

They were very close to the castle cloud.

When they appeared.

Amamaedur leaped one way, Ahamaezur the other.

"Ah, ha," said Ahamaezur, recognizing them. She beckoned at Tinker.

He headed over to her. "Here's hoping," he mumbled.

Amamaedur walked over to join them. Both stepped close to him.

Tinker carefully reached out. And touched them. They were right where they appeared to be. "Thank you," he said.

And took a small, oblong box from his shirt pocket. "Certainly hope this is what you guys are looking for." And handed it to Ahamaezur. He thought. They were hard to tell apart.

Gingerly she took the box from his hand and looked at her companion. Amamaedur looked blank. So Ahamaezur bit it.

"HOLD IT. WHOA." Tinker held out his hand. "Gimme that."

Slowly, carefully, she did. One corner of the box was sheared of. Cleanly.

He stared at the damage. "Bet Red Riding Hood

would really like to meet you two."

"Redridinghood," said Amamaedur. She stepped closer. And ran her fingers over his forearm and shoulder.

He held the box in one hand and carefully eased off the top with the other, and moved the tissue aside with one finger. "This what you are looking for?" He tilted the box so the pair could easily see the contents.

Amamaedur carefully picked up one of the brooches. The silver surrounding the blue sparkled. Holding it close to her mouth, she gently touched the stone with the tip of her tongue.

She spun, clenching the jewelry in one tight fist, and ran. And leaped on one of the four watching males, bowling him over.

Two of them dragged her off and carried her inside the castle cloud, followed by the selected one.

"Worse than catnip," observed Tinker.

"Ah, ha," said Ahamaezur, stepping closer to him.

"Guess that's the correct blue stone, right?"

She removed the other brooch from the box and held it tightly in one clenched fist. And stepped up against him, clacking her teeth softly. "In, ah ha."

"Ummmmm?"

"Passage, ah ha."

"Oh." He let out a held breath.

"You strange strange." Red eyes stared into his. "Strange strange." She slid her free hand over his chest and rested the palm against his cheek. "Tarkhabkae."

"O.K., I suppose. Passage?"

Stepping back, she took one of his hands in her free one, and tugged him into motion. "In." Toward the cloud castle.

The rest followed.

Staying close.

And walked into . . .

Riotous color.

Splashes of color.

Walls.

Floor.

Ceiling.

Everything was a different color.

"Oh my gosh." Messenger stared at it. A great pulsating blotch on one wall.

"Passage," said Ahamaezur, pulling his hand to her face, brushing her lips over it.

"That?" Tinker pointed at the blotch with his other hand.

"Ah, ha." She stepped to one side, releasing him.

He glanced over at R-Bar. "You think that thing is safe?"

She shrugged.

Ran looked blank.

Messenger walked up to it and poked it with one finger. And giggled.

"Guess that it is safe," he said, and nodded, and smiled at Ahamaezur. "Well gang, let's step through."

They did.

"Thanks," he said, following them.

Grandeville. Tinker's Place.

Janine stepped back onto the rear deck, wearing one of the thick white robes and admired the quiet of the place. Then she shed the robe, stacked it on a small table next to the lounge, and sprawled out, skin glistening from toe to hair line.

They had left this morning, so she figured that they

wouldn't be popping back in right away.

Turning the portable radio to soft classical music, she exhaled, and relaxed.

And relaxed.

Enjoying the sun warm on her skin.

"By George, Me'Lady, I do believe me Our Lord taint here."

Janine's eyes flew open and wide as she snatched her robe over and dragged it up to her neck.

The man standing there, near the swimming pool end of the deck, looked as startled as Janine, spun around and faced away.

The Chinese woman by his side walked over and bowed to her. "I am Chen, a thousand thousand pardonsss."

Janine stood and shrugged on the robe. Tugging the belt tight, she turned around. "Who are you?" And called, "O.K., you may turn around."

He did, smiling broadly. "Be Our Lord about?" He bowed to her. "Prince Goose, at your service. Me'Lady Chen does be fair niece of Master Chen."

"They're gone." She stared at them. "Prince Goose?"

"Indeed. Brother to His Queen," replied Goose.

"Chicken?"

"Most true." Goose frowned. "Be somethin' amiss?"

"No, not at all." Janine waved an arm. "Please sit."

Goose dropped into a chair. "Delighted."

Chen walked around and stood behind him, resting her hands on his shoulders. "Well," he said.

Janine sat, clenching her robe at the neck. "You pop in like this a lot?"

"Most randomly." He smiled. "Praps we might your name know?"

"Janine. I am house sitting."

Goose giggled. And reached up and patted one of Chen's hands. "Fair Dragon, tis most unusual a'game for to play, a'sittin' pon great house."

"Care taker," corrected Janine. "I fetch the mail, water the flowers, things like that."

"I see." Goose smiled happily at her. "Be thee also?"

Chen hissed loudly and pinched his shoulder.

Goose looked sheepish. And stood. "Wouldst tell Our Lord pon his return we did pass through?"

"Sure."

Goose bowed. "Fair thee well, then." And giggled. "Great noise shall we make when next we do Ourselves visit."

Chen bowed, and walked with Goose to the swimming pool end of the rear deck, and around that end of the house, back the way they had come.

Then it appeared as if a great cloud eddied there, one edge just visible past the corner of the house.

After a moment's hesitation, Janine walked to the corner and peered around it. They were nowhere to be seen. Nor was the cloud.

"Fast walkers." She headed inside, for one of the upper balconies. Nobody should surprise her up there, three stories above the ground.

Angok Goblok.

"Yuk, yuk, yuk, yuk, yuk, yuk."

They were standing ankle deep in something soft, smooth, glistening.

"Barf ugly," added Messenger to her first description of the stuff.

"That way." Tinker pointed toward the higher ground, just off to their right.

They plopped that way.

Chantal nodded at Messenger. "Yuk is right. Do you think that the Tark broad was unhappy with us cause he didn't jump her?"

Messenger giggled. "He could have licked her brooch."

"I think she wanted him to," said R-Bar.

Chicken stomped her feet, kicking off the stuff as she walked up the slope. "Most solid." She looked over at Tinker, "My Lord?"

He looked up at her as he made it onto dry land. "What?"

"Exactly which portion of fair anatomy do be brooch?"

Tittering and giggling broke out all around him.

"Ha. Ha," he said. "Ha. Ha. Ha." And frowned at them all. "Where are we?"

"This should be Angok Goblok," said R-Bar.

"That is what Zar'gh told us," said Ran.

"He leave out a few details?"

Ran nodded.

R-Bar smiled. It was a witch smile promising things better left undescribed. "We will talk with that demon after we finish our business with the Dark Ump."

Tinker waved an arm at the undulating grey surface stretching into the distance. "What lives here?"

"Demons," replied Ran.

"Yep," said R-Bar.

He beckoned them over with one crooked finger. "Tell me something."

"Sure," said R-Bar.

"Of course, Amtar." Ran nodded.

"Back there." He jerked his thumb over a shoulder. "Why didn't the Tark attack us? Smoke shot one of them.

They didn't do anything."

"They made goo-ga eyes at you," suggested Messenger, stepping close. "And rubbed all over you."

"They wanted blue stones," added Fair Morn, standing by his side.

"So they could pounce." Smoke huffed warm air against the back of his neck.

"Indeed, My Lord. It do seem so." Chicken stood behind R-Bar and nodded at him.

"Demons are hard to figure, Tink." R-Bar slid her hands into her belt. "And the Tark were really hard to figure."

"Probably your winning smile, Simba Leader," suggested Chantal. "Was she soft and warm?"

"Let's walk. You all are making me nervous."

"That way." Smoke pointed at the bright spot on the far grey horizon. It was the only bright spot. The sky was as grey as the ground.

She slipped an arm under his as they started walking. "I think that they saw Big Red traces and backed off. They were the first creatures we have ever met that could do that."

"Except for Messenger."

Messenger stepped to his side, hopped to get her stride in pace with his, and punched him on the hip with the side of her fist. "I am not a creature."

"HEY. Stop that." He glared at her. "I didn't say that, Smoke did. Walk on the other side and thump on her."

He lengthened his stride. And mumbled, "Maybe if we walk faster."

"I am a young female person," stated Messenger, keeping in step with him.

"I am taking a vow of silence," he grumbled.

"Most beautiful," called Chicken as the group began

to spread out.

"Cuddly curvaceous," suggested Fair Morn.

"Yah," said Messenger. "That too."

"Beautifully short," added R-Bar, walking alongside Messenger.

"Taller than you," replied Messenger.

"Only by less than an inch," snapped R-Bar.

"Not too bad," laughed Chantal. "For a boy?"

"As the Tark said," interjected Tinker. "You are all strange strange."

"Certainly bent the boy form all out of shape," said Fair Morn, winking at Messenger.

"Heh, heh, heh," said R-Bar, giving Messenger a little poke with one finger.

"Knock it off," he growled at one and all. And wondered how lion tamers managed to keep their charges in line. Maybe he could got a whip. Or a fedora.

They walked on in silence.

For a little while.

"O.K., Short Stuff, you have dodged the question for long enough."

R-Bar growled.

Ran strolled over to walk next to her.

"Well?" he asked.

"What question, BIG TALL STUFF?"

"Who lives here?"

"Told you," she grumbled. "Demons."

He sighed. "Like pulling teeth from chickens."

"Our chickens do not have teeth," said Messenger.

"Must mean our Princess Self," suggested Smoke.

"I DID NOT." He glared from side to side. Everyone looked somewhere else. "Faan witch R-Bar, answer my question."

"Oh, oh," said Messenger.

"Demons, dir dit."

Ran clamped a hand over her mouth and glanced sideways at R-Bar.

"That all you know?"

R-Bar nodded. "All we were told, Master Boss, Mighty One, Maltreater of Helpless Females." She gurgled way back in her throat.

"Stud," added Messenger.

"That to," said R-Bar, clearing her throat.

He looked sideways at Smoke. "What's going on? Something in the air here?"

Smoke shook her head. "Just a healthy cohort." *Burning off nervous energy. Everyone thought that the Tark females were going to cause a problem.*

"Oh." He nodded. "I see."

"Pretty slow," said Smoke.

Fair Morn walked over to stroll alongside Chicken, glanced back over at Tinker, and said loudly, "Princess, a brooch is also called a breastpin."

"Whoops," laughed Chantal. "Skewered again."

"And on and on and on," sighed Tinker.

"Most vigorously be'pinned," agreed Chicken. She stopped and waited until he caught up with them. "Most dour a mein, Sweet Lord. Be thee vexed?"

"Silence is golden," he grumbled.

Messenger and the two witches stepped around them.

"Wouldst have this, thy Verra Own pride, drift wraith silent cross soft most dingy a'ground?"

He smiled, and threw an arm around her. "All the kids keep picking on me." And tugged her into motion.

"Noble Lord, praps tis required this?"

He tickled her ribs. "Not gonna protect me, huh?"

She twitched. "Cease."

He did it again.

"Our Prince, it be not thee do protection require." She jerked. "Desist. Leave off Our Verra Own Ribs, Pesky Lord."

Fair Morn peered around Chicken and smiled at him. "I think that he is looking for your brooch." She winked at him.

"Try higher." Chantal joined them. "Probably developing a new wrestling hold."

"Indeed?" Chicken looked at her, peering back around Tinker.

"Yep. The brooch."

"Forsooth?"

Chantal started laughing. "Also called the breast pin."

Messenger turned, looked at them, giggling. "Oh, that is not new."

"Ho, ho, ho," stated Tinker. "Hee. Hee. Hee. Giggle, giggle. Tee hee and titter titter."

"Heh, heh, heh," cackled R-Bar.

"I do not think that is funny," said Ran.

"Wry pun, that," observed Chicken, looking at him.

"What?" asked Smoke.

"Do not say anything!" He yanked his arm away and waved at them. "SHOO. SCAT."

No one moved very far away. They just kept walking parallel to his path, staying a small bit beyond Tinker's arm length.

"I am hungry," said Fair Mom. "Let's have something to eat."

R-Bar waved in something comfortable to sit on.

Ran took care of the lunch.

Grandeville. Greater Downtown. The Wash House.

"I've decided to stay here."

They were having lunch. At the W̶A̶S̶H̶ ̶H̶O̶U̶S̶E̶, an updated ca. 1880 dwelling not far from the main drag, turned into a restaurant.

Sandy and Janine sat at a small table in a corner.

"Up there?" asked Sandy. "With them?" She grinned across the table at her friend.

Janine shook her head. "Somewhere in town. Know any place that is available? Cheap?"

Sandy laughed. "As a matter of fact, I do. Got a job?"

"Ahhh, no, I don't."

"Hard place to find work, out here on the frontier."

"You did."

Sandy smiled and sat back, dabbing at her mouth with a napkin. "Hey, lawyers, doctors, and undertakers can always find work. You don't qualify in any category."

"I can always wash dishes."

"Er um?" said Sandy.

Janine stared at her. "Sander, you have that sneaky lawyer look on your face. What?"

"My secretary is moving to Seattle. Pay is not too bad, hours are mostly regular, location is handy, to your apartment."

"What apartment?"

"The inexpensive one. Just down the hall. Empty, but available."

Janine leaned forward. "How do you know that?"

"Sneaky lawyer trick."

"Oh?"

"I used to live there. I know the landlord. And the manager. And I know that it is not rented."

"You said inexpensive?"

"Sure did. Ready to go take a look?"

"Uh huh."

Sandy grabbed the check. "My treat. Let's go."

Angok Goblok.

"Either the clouds are getting thicker or we got here late in the day."

Smoke looked up. "Late in the day."

"Might as well camp right here."

Tinker looked around.

At the picnic crowd.

Everyone agreed.

So they did.

Ran and R-Bar cast heavy protection all around.

R-Bar grinned. "Anything that comes by to bother us is in for a big surprise." She banged him on the forearm. "Big stuff."

Ran nodded. "Your Faan witch R-Bar knows wonderfully dark nasty."

"Heh, heh, heh." R-Bar cackled witch happy.

Smoke tapped him on the shoulder and stood. "Step over here, MindMate." She walked to one side of the camp site. He followed

"What?"

Ran nodded. A large dark sphere snapped around them. "His Smoke has the ring."

Grandeville. Greater Downtown.

"WOW. I mean like wow, wow, wow."

"Guess you like it, right?" Sandy handed Janine the door keys.

"Sure do."

"My office is the other set of doors down the hall.

Open at nine, close at five." Sandy grinned. "And I only yell once in a while."

Janine laughed. "I remember. Freddie always tried to hide."

"Can you start tomorrow?" Sandy laughed. "You make the coffee."

"Em, sure. But I'll sleep up there until they return."

Sandy turned and looked out the window, down at the main street, watching what little traffic there was, go by. "You're not messing around, are you?"

Janine grabbed one of her shoulders and spun Sandy around. "Look, news-snoop, even if I was, it wouldn't be any of your business. But I am not."

"I am not in the newspaper business anymore, Streak. And it is my business. I am their attorney. And friend."

Janine released her grip. "O.K. Sorry. But I probably would, if he wanted to. Hard to explain, having that kind of a debt. What he did, what they did. For me, for you, for Freddie."

"I know."

Janine laughed, softly. "But I think that Chantal would drag out her hog-leg and blow me away if I did."

Sandy nodded. "Probably right."

"Anyway, I think that she gave me a subtle warning away. She said that they were complete, whatever that means. And so, all that I am doing is house sitting up there. Period."

"Ever go bowling?"

"No. Why?"

So, Sandy told her.

Angok Goblock.

"Yum, yum, yum." Her lips nibbled their way across

his chest. And eventually, found his lips.

"Don't get any Tark ideas, " he grumbled, rolling them onto their sides.

"My teeth are not pointed. And besides, you have been displaying Tarkish habits for years."

"They really made me nervous."

"Me too. I shouldn't have shot him."

"No harm done. Apparently."

Smoke reached over and touched the wall.

The light dimmed to soft candle glow.

She began to purr.

Portland. The Hensler Estate.

"That Morgan?"

She nodded.

He stood, all burly energy and motion. Walked over to the cabinet, set three glasses on the counter, snatched out a dark purple glass decanter, poured, and handed one glass to each of them.

"Don't believe in drinking alone." He took a mouthful, nodded, and swallowed. "Good stuff." And dropped into one of the large, overstuffed chairs.

"So, now you are An Associate, an Investment Manager for Morgan Enterprises?"

"Yes, Sir," replied Ralph, taking a sip from his glass.

"'Nice title." His eyes bored into Ralph's. "What exactly does it mean?"

Freddie frowned at her father.

Ralph look another sip. And then he carefully explained.

Angok Goblock.

Messenger sat up and looked around and felt the soft

relaxation sleep of the others.

Beginning day cast diffused shadow from the dark sphere.

Standing, she carefully stepped over her other selves. A hand clamped around her bare ankle.

"Did I step on you?"

"Nope." Fair Morn looked up at her. "Time for breakfast?"

"It is still early."

"Never to early to eat."

"I suppose that we could."

Fair Morn tossed her bag open, sat up, and stretched.

"Better put a shirt on," said Messenger. "It is sorta cool here."

Fair Morn rummaged in her sleeping bag, found her pajama top and yanked it on. "Let's eat." And stood. She carefully stepped over the double bag that was Ran and R-Bar. Now that Ran was fully Tanpak again, the two witches had taken to sleeping together.

Messenger knelt by the stack of back packs and began to rummage in their gear.

A hand crept from the sleeping bag next to her, slithered up her leg, and tickled the back of her knee.

"EEEEK."

"Hist, Our Kitten, be thee not so loud. Else fair grumbling will descend itself pon our Verra own heads." Chicken yanked her hand away. And sat up.

"Why are we up so early?" R-Bar sat on the end of Chicken's sleeping bag. She waved in breakfast.

Messenger shrugged a shoulder. "Just woke up."

"Hungry," said Fair Morn, sitting, reaching and dragging over one of the steaming platters. "Smells good."

"Of course," acknowledged R-Bar, nodding. She

stared. "Kitten? What is wrong?"

Messenger sat hunched over, not looking at anything, eating quietly.

"I don't like it," she mumbled.

R-Bar nodded. "Tell me what and I will bring it in."

Messenger looked up at her. "The food is good." She pointed behind herself. "That."

On the far horizon, a bright spot in the dismal grey.

R-Bar sat straighter. "What do you see?" The air grumbled low rumble around her.

"Nothing."

"Then what is the matter."

"Nothing."

R-Bar hissed.

Chicken grabbed Messenger's shoulder. "Sweet Kitten Ourself, how does thy answer nothing nothing cause such distress?"

Messenger turned her head and blinked. "Because I cannot see anything there."

"Oh, oh," said R-Bar. "Kitten, turn around and look at it. And let me look. Please?"

Messenger hitched herself around and stared at the bright spot. "Good ahead."

R-Bar slipped inside and peered out, seeing what Messenger was seeing. And left. "Dim, dim, dim, dim, dim, dim." The air crackled and snapped all around them.

"What see thee?"

"Princess, there is nothing there. Just a vague spot where something should be."

"Most strange."

"Pass the toast," said Fair Morn.

Chapter Sixteen

Just Another Surprise Among Many

Grandeville. Red and Sandy's Home.

"Is Herr Doctor Frankenstein home?"

She had walked to the house, a mere four blocks from her apartment, having first stopped to unload some of her belongings. She had borrowed Tinker's pickup truck to make the run into town.

And, having decided to stroll over, to see the sights, so to speak, she stepped up on the front porch and rang the bell.

And the door had opened.

And he had filled the open space.

And now nodded at her question.

"Herrn is in the kitchen dissecting one of the recently deceased neighbors. Come on in, I'll get you a lab coat." He backed up.

"Anyone I know?"

"I doubt it. Just someone we dug up for the occasion." He moved her in the direction of the kitchen. And as she slipped past, and into the kitchen, he said, "Sandy, your bud is here." All rasp rough voice.

Sandy waved her into a seat by the kitchen table. "You are a little early."

Red leaned in through the doorway, hands on either

side the opening, and looked at their visitor. "You must be Janine. Or Frankie's wife."

He gave Janine his professional cop stare. "You run away from an abusive husband with a bolt in his neck?"

And examined both sides of her head. "Guess not. His wife had a white streak down either side. Don't look like Elsa Lanchester either."

"What started all this?" asked Sandy, reaching behind herself and snapping the last tie onto her pony tail.

"Startled me," explained Janine. "Your letter said big. But not how big." She fished around in her bag, yanked her hair back, and fastened it in place.

Sandy nodded. "Right. You didn't get over for the wedding."

The front door chime bing-bonged.

"I'll get it." Red ducked back. "Better warn him."

"Who?" asked Janine. "Needs warning?"

"Green," said Sandy. "His partner in crime, in a manner of speaking."

"Another cop?"

"Yes. They are a matched pair."

"What?"

"Hunker down," said Red, entering the kitchen first. "She is kinda flighty."

"Who is?" demanded Janine, turning around. "GOD Zilla."

"Nice racing stripe," said Green, reaching out and enveloping her hand in his. "You ever go bowling before?"

Janine stared at her hand, completely hidden by his. "No." And smiled up at him. "How's Bambi doing these days?"

"Not bad." He released her hand. "For a little flat guy."

He looked at his partner. "Do you think that it is safe, taking these two into a public place?"

Red shrugged. "We could always call for back-up. Two Gun's on duty at the Sheriff's office."

"Better leave him out of it. He'd get so excited he'd probably shoot himself in the leg."

Janine looked from one to the other.

Sandy stood, shoving her chair back. "Time to go. What are we going in?"

"Green's truck."

Sandy stared at Green.

"I bought a new one," said Green. "Extended cab. You'll fit."

They did.

Red and Green in the front seat, Janine and Sandy in the back. On the way to the bowling alley, Sandy made the introductions.

Angok Goblock.

"Five foot two,
> Eyes of blue,
> And, oh what that five foot two could do.
> Ubee do dah!"

It was well after breakfast.

And they were well on their way toward the bright spot.

"Put me down."

"Hell, heh, heh," he said. And started to spin around and around. And finally stopped, breathing heavily.

"Messenger doesn't see anything there."

"And you are worried, right?"

"Yes. I am." She slipped an arm around his neck. "I am four feet eleven and three-quarters of your inches tall." She grumbled softly at him. "And my eyes are black."

"Three and black don't rhyme."

"We have to be careful."

"Four foot three, eyes so free?"

"There is nothing there."

"Four foot three, eyes so faerie?"

"I am NOT," hissed R-Bar.

"What do you mean, nothing?"

"Faerie are bantz arp zat," she growled.

"Doesn't look like nothing to me? Awfully bright."

"Sneaky little meddlers," she mumbled.

Chantal nudged Smoke. "How long can this go on?"

Smoke rolled her eyes. "Some time."

Ran joined them, watching the pair ahead. "His R-Bar is starting to crackle."

"No problemo, dudette," said Smoke in her best Arnold manner.

"Witches, right?"

"TINK!"

He patted her on top of the head. "Sneaky little meddlers."

The air darkened around them. "Ik tik prak prak," she rasped.

He stopped walking, making a shocked face. "What are terrible thing to say. Good thing our daughter or son isn't around to hear their mother say such shocking things like that. Gosh oh gee whiz."

"Dek dak," she snapped.

He jostled her up and down. "You putting on weight?"

"What are you doing?"

"Not much. Arms are full." And jounced her up and down. And managed to tickle her. She wiggled.

"Hold still," he cautioned.

"Your fault. Let's camp here, now."

"Rather get a lot closer, first."

R-Bar plucked at a button on his shirt. "Can't get much closer than we are."

"To the nothing."

"Set me down."

He did.

R-Bar snatched a gleaming golden wand from somewhere and slashed the air open.

Grandeville. The Burger and Bowl.

"Must be because she is a lawyer."

"What?" Red made a mark on the score sheet. Sandy had just sent her second ball down the alley.

"Weird friends. Not counting you, of course. You're her husband."

Red nodded. "They're winning the second game, also."

Green waved over the waitress. "I think she snuck in a ringer when we weren't looking." He ordered for them all.

"Natural athlete." Sandy peered around Red's shoulder at the score sheet as she joined them. Checking.

"She play football?" asked Green.

Janine made a strike. Another of many already marked down. And walked back, smiling happily.

"Nope," said Sandy.

"Good," replied Green, heading for the lane. "Figure she'd show us up."

"What's the problem?" Janine looked puzzled.

"Nothing," said Red. He paid the waitress.

"They are losing." Sandy took a sip.

Red emptied his glass. "At least you're not laughing

this time." He walked over to talk to Green before he launched his second ball in the general direction of the pins.

"From a distance they don't look so huge." Janine started on her hamburger. She and Sandy had moved back to the row of tables for visitors.

Sandy smiled. "Gentle giants. Having a good time?"

"Sure. Bowling is fun. I ought to do better in the third game."

"Ummmmm, Streak?"

"What?"

"How about we lose the last game?"

"Lose?"

"Sure. Make 'em feel good."

"Oh." Janine grinned. "How close?"

"How about a squeaker?"

"Sure. You're score keeper. Just tell me how many each time."

"NEXT," called Red.

"Start now," whispered Sandy. "Five."

Janine nodded.

And did.

Later Evening.

The were in Big Darlene's when it happened.

After the third game, won by Red and Green, barely, they had decided to stop, for some chili and stuff.

So, there they were, sitting at one of the tables, way in the back, near the pool table, having a quiet conversation, enjoying the chili in large bowls, and the stuff in large mugs.

Janine blew her nose. "It's good." She was referring to the hot chili. Mainly.

And then it happened

It did.

He came in and announced in a loud voice. "Everyone just be cool, just be calm, just be collected, and hand over your money. I am the Tax Man."

He waved a large pistol wildly around and began to herd the patrons toward the far end of the bar.

The large bowl of chili crashed into his face. His arm jerked, his pistol shot a hole in the ceiling.

And Red was suddenly there and hit him in the stomach. And watched the Tax Man as he slowly folded over and collapsed.

Red turned and nodded at his partner. "Aim is as good as ever."

Green nodded back. "Fast as ever, partner."

Red heaved the gasping holdup man to his feet, swiped at his face with the bar-towel, and draped him against the bar. "You are under arrest, Tax Man." He kicked the pistol away and began to read him his rights while Green phoned the station for a patrol car.

Then Red walked over to watch out the front window.

And two hundred and fifty angry pounds burst through the front door, having just hurtled down an interior staircase and out onto the sidewalk before spinning and crashing into the bar.

"WHO JUST SHOT A HOLE IN MY FLOOR?" screamed Big Darlene.

The barman pointed at the crumbled figure hanging onto the bar, sucking in deep breaths, making strange sounds, and now staring at her.

"NOBODY DOES THAT IN MY BAR." She kicked him.

And before she could do it again, Green slid up, grabbed her by the forearms and lifted her to one side and gently set her down. "He is our prisoner. Leave him alone."

"Oh. Officer Green. I didn't see you." Big Darlene batted her eyes at Green, then stared down at the Tax Man, now curled into a tight ball, singing a low moaning song. "He's got chili all over his face and head."

Red stepped over to them and looked down. "Probably safer down there. However." He bent and lifted their prisoner to his feet and handed him to the two policemen just entering the barroom. "All your's. We'll write up the report later."

Green ripped a page from his pocket notebook. "Here. List of charges. Have a good night."

"Who hit me," mumbled the Tax Man as they dragged him out the door, one cop on either side.

"You on duty?" asked Big Darlene, sidling closer to Green.

"No, " said Green. "We just came in here to eat a little chili."

"It's on the house, then." She bustled behind the bar and shooed the barman over to replace their orders.

Green and Red picked up their chairs and sat. And nodded at Sandy and Janine.

"Have some chili," said Green, pushing his bowl over to Janine. Her's had been the missile.

"What if you had missed?"

Red laughed. "Never happen. That was a T. D. for sure, for sure."

Janine frowned. "T. D.?"

"Touch down," explained Red. "Right on the button."

"Oh. I see."

"High school and college," said Red. "Never missed."

Janine stared at Green. "You were a quarterback?"

"Sure," he said. "Red helped." Green began to mash crushed crackers into his newly arrived bowl of chili.

"We played both ways, offense and defense," said Red. "More fun that way."

Janine stared at Sandy.

"All too true," she said. "From what I hear."

Green refilled their mugs. "Drink up, B.D.'s buying."

More chili arrived.

And pitchers.

"Glad we went bowling tonight," said Red. "Lotta fun."

Green nodded.

And winked at Janine.

Angok Goblok.

"That is nothing?"

They stood not too far from it, from the blotch that was nothing.

It was a great splotch of bright, a half-sun, half-set into the ground.

Messenger faced away from it. "Yes. It is nothing."

R-Bar grabbed him by the belt, dead center, in the small of the back. And leaned against his side. "I looked out and saw what she saw. There was nothing there. Just a dark blank spot."

"Ummmm?" he said.

"Tink," whispered R-Bar. "She has never seen nothing before."

"Exactly. How could there be nothing to see?"

"I do not know. But I saw it."

"Nothing?"

"Yesssssss."

"Sort of a paradox, seeing nothing." He glanced sideways at her as she hissed again.

"Kinna cute when you get that wild witchy look on

your face, kiddo."

"I should have married a gargoyle," she grumbled.

"Look at all the fun you would have missed." He waved one arm, the only one free. "Travel to exotic places. Doing neat paradoxical things, like seeing nothing. Having gay, happy companions. Ho, ho, ho, ho, ho, ho, ho."

"Gim dit."

"And," he continued, "let's not overlook . . . expanding your vocabulary." He grinned at her. "Let's give the little lady a gold star for picturesque language. Whoop, whoop, whoop."

"I . . . am . . . not. . . that . . . either."

"Gold? Or star?"

"CRETIN."

"Yah, sure George," he drawled, trying and succeeding, in looking idiotic.

"MY LORD," called Chicken. "WE DO US SET CAMP HERE."

"Well, my little chickadee, my little pigeon, shall we sashay over there and inspect what the galley slaves are doing?" It was W.C. Fields leering at her

"Pith, pith," she snapped.

"What are you now? A cat with a harelip?"

The corners of her eyes turned up. She began to shimmer and change.

Ran screamed.

"OOOP." R-Bar was herself. "Forgot that there was another witch nearby." She looked over at Ran. "Sorry sorry, Ran self." Ran gestured.

"OUCH."

Tinker's head snapped back and forth, from one to the other. "Now what?"

"Nothing, Amtar." Ran shook her head.

"Are both of you all right?"

"Yesssss."

"Yes, Amtar."

Smoke joined Tinker and R-Bar. "We would like to eat. And then decide what we are going to do about that." She indicated the bright spot.

"Sounds like a plan." He threw his arm around R-Bar's shoulders. "What's for dinner, witchy-poo?"

"By now," said Chantal. "I would have probably punched him."

Fair Morn nodded. And flapped her sleeping bag vigorously.

"Turn about is fair play, Doc," said Tinker, as they walked over to the group. And gave her a little pat. "Puttin' on some weight?"

Chantal whirled around and glared at him. "Don't you start on me, Cowboy. And I am not."

He nodded, dropped to the ground next to Messenger and wrapped his arms around her.

"What's the problem, kitten?"

"Nothing."

"Yah, I know. But other than that." And held her close. "Scared."

"Me, too," he whispered into her hair. "Me too."

Fair Morn joined them. "We are going to be very, very, very careful."

"Absolutely," stated R-Bar, pushing into the middle of the several arms. She kissed Messenger on the forehead.

And, one by one, the others nestled around.

And eventually.

They had dinner.

Grandeville. Tinker's Place.

Dumping the mail onto the dining room table, adding to the pile already there, she smiled to herself and decided that a good soak in their very large hot tub would be just the thing before eating dinner.

And so.

She did.

And eventually, she came back to the living room, wearing one of the thick white robes, gathered up her clothes, and carried them into the bedroom she was using.

And, after reheating yesterdays leftovers in the microwave oven, she sat on one of the couches and ate her food. As she did, she idly looked around and admired the large and somewhat cluttered space that was the large living room.

She set her empty plate on the small table, stood, and walked over to inspect one of the bookcases, searching for something to read. And noticed the odd collection of things occupying an open space on one of the shelves.

Picking up the red cube, she turned it around and around, thinking it was one of those clever puzzles, except this one was absolutely smooth. Every side was smooth. Not a sign of a joint anywhere. She rubbed one side, searching for a clue. And ran her fingernail across it, feeling for the crack.

"May I help you?"

Janine spun around. And stared at the empty room.

"No one has asked for help in ever so long a time."

Stomping angrily into the connecting hall, she glared down its length. Then she tromped into the kitchen, through the dining room and back into the living room. And demanded loudly, "All right, come out, whoever you are."

"I am not hiding."

She set the cube back on the shelf and dropped to her

knees to peer under things. "You are really pissing me off."

"I did not intend to do that."

Now the voice was above her. She leaped to her feet. And carefully scanned the room. "All right, say something." She peeked over the back of the couch. "You are not funny."

"What?" The voice was behind her.

Janine turned and stared at the bookcase, "Do it again."

"What?"

She leaned forward and poked at the cube.

"What?" repeated the cube.

"You talk?"

"Of course," said the cube.

She stared at it. "Bonkers. I am going bonkers."

"Never heard of that elseplace."

"What?"

"I am unable to provide directions or information for your planned travel to elseplace Bonkers."

She nodded. "Wireless mike, right? You guys are home and playing games, right?"

"No," replied the cube. "That is not true. They are not home."

"Dumb joke," she snorted. And picked up the ornate ring lying next to the cube. And stared at what looked like an eye carved into the face of the ornate gem.

It stared back. And knocked her to the floor, sprawling flat on her back.

"You are not my Great Master," stated something small, standing on her face, peering into her eyes.

Janine couldn't move anything. Arms, legs, fingers, toes. Nothing would move. So, she did the only thing she could do. She screamed.

Angok Goblok.

"Well, shall we sleep on it?"

They had settled down, relaxed, and organized their camp. And had eaten dinner and discussed what to do about nothing.

"Sure," said R-Bar. "I am it."

"Pretty crude," said Fair Morn.

"Damn crude," added Chantal.

"Worse and worse," mumbled Tinker.

"Unrefined," stated Chicken.

"Barbarian?" suggested Messenger.

"All of the above," suggested Tinker.

"Who is?" growled R-Bar.

"Amtar?" Ran looked past Smoke at him.

Tinker turned his head back and forth, from Ran to R-Bar, and back again, and again.

"Gee, I wonder who? Which witch did twitch?"

R-Bar hit him in the chest. With one of the several dinner rolls Fair Morn hadn't eaten. Yet. R-Bar was sitting across their dinner clutter from him.

He threw it back. And missed. It sailed toward the bright spot. And disappeared.

"Gimme another roll, kiddo."

R-Bar pitched one to him.

He pegged it past her head, at the bright spot. The roll disappeared.

Smoke leaned forward. "MindMate, they disappear before they get there."

He nodded. "That's what I thought I saw also. More rolls, please." He stood.

R-Bar handed him a basket full of rolls and remained close to his side as he walked around the dinner dishes and toward the bright spot.

"Careful," she hissed, glittering orange wand clenched in her right hand.

He waved the rest of them back, behind.

"O.K., everyone watch carefully." And gently rolled a bun across the ground, just a little way. The next one rolled a little further. And the next. And the next. And soon, he had a ragged line of dinner rolls stretching from them toward the bright spot.

"Ummmm, so far so good."

The next roll bounced, rolled past the furthest roll in the line. And disappeared.

"Ah ha." He tossed another at the same place. It disappeared.

"Whatever it is, it starts right there." He looked over at Smoke, then at Messenger. "Well?"

"Something flickered," said Smoke.

Messenger stared, and nodded. "Soft." And gasped. "GOSH."

"WHAT?" He jerked.

Messenger squinted, and smiled. "That is really, really sneaky."

Fair Morn jerked her cannon free and flicked two levers. "High power."

"Hold it, hold it." He stepped over to Messenger. "What is it?"

"Hiding. All this time, hiding."

The air ripped around them. Ran and R-Bar swirled protection around, stronger and stronger.

"Who?" asked Tinker. "What?"

Messenger shook her head. "It looks like nothing." She slipped her long black wand from her left sleeve. She turned her head. "Let's go poke it."

R-Bar looked at Ran, who shook her head.

Ran stepped over to Tinker's side. "Amtar, Tanpak have no knowledge of things like this."

"Me neither, Tink." R-Bar shoved her wand somewhere. And yawned.

"We safe, kiddo?"

"Yep."

Ran yawned widely. "Your Ran is tired, also." And pointed. "Over there."

R-Bar grabbed his arm and tugged him in the indicated direction. "Mine."

The dark sphere swallowed them as they stepped into the indicated space.

Ran crawled into her sleeping bag. And instantly fell asleep.

Smoke nodded "I will watch." And stretched out on her bag. "While we sleep."

Grandeville. Tinker's Place.

"Don't do that."

"Get off my face."

"You are not My Great Master. I do not have to."

"Who is your Great Master?"

"The one called Tinker by his houris."

"John Tinker is your Great Master?"

"They bought me for him. At the Foregather."

"Then you are in great trouble, sprite."

"Why?"

"Cause when he returns I am going to tell him about you abusing me and he is really going to be angry, that's why."

Suddenly Janine could feel her arms and legs and toes and fingers. She sat up. The tiny figure tumbled to the floor, landing on her feet.

And glared up at Janine. "I am not a sprite. I am a beautiful indjinn." She ran her hands over her upper torso. "See?"

Janine leaned forward. "Where did you come from?"

"The ring. Do you know how to make cocoa?"

"Why?"

"I like it."

Janine stood and started for the kitchen. "Your Great Master and I are really going to have a talk when he returns. No one mentioned talking boxes and pixies that jump on people's faces."

"You going to make me walk?" yelled a tiny voice. "And I am not a pixie. Nor a sprite either."

Janine whirled around and snapped, "What do you want?"

The figure stared up at her, balled fists jammed on her hips. "A ride."

"I must be crazy," mumbled Janine. "O.K. You have a name?"

"Dat."

Janine bent and grabbed her.

Dat squeaked, "Not so tight."

"Well," said Janine. "If I am hallucinating, it is pretty graphic."

Dat squirmed in her grasp.

"STOP WIGGLING. Or you'll get dropped."

In the kitchen, she set Dat on the counter top. "Happy?"

And started to gather together the ingredients to make cocoa. "I wonder how many other secrets they have lying around? Do you know?"

"No." Dat leaned back against the wall and watched as Janine stirred the cocoa over a low flame. "I bet he really enjoys playing with your body?"

Janine's head snapped up. "WHAT? What was that?"

"I'll bet that he says yum, yum, yum, yum, yum, yum."

"Enough of that, Dat." Janine shook her wooden spoon at her, spattering brown dots everywhere, including on Dat.

"Dik, dik, dik," snarled Dat, wiping at them. "Bad rhyme."

"Oh. Sorry." Janine grabbed a paper towel and shoved it at Dat. "Here. But you knock off that kind of talk, O.K.? That is not going on. With me."

"All the others do." Dat wiped away from the cocoa spots, walked over and peered over the edge of the pot.

Janine snatched her away. "CAREFUL. You'll burn yourself. I am not all the others."

Dat squeaked.

Janine hastily set her down.

"You squeezed me." Dat glared up at her. "Again."

"You almost burned yourself, dummy."

"Indjinns do not burn." Dat walked back and poked one bare foot into the blue flame. "It tickles." And pulled it back. "Cocoa almost done?"

Janine gave the liquid in the pot another stir. "Almost. You are real, aren't you? Not some wild dream, or something else? Spoiled food that I ate?"

Dat nodded. "Certainly real." She leaned over the lip of the pot and dipped her cup in the steaming cocoa. "Don't you like my Great Master?"

Janine fetched her own cup and poured. "He's all right. Let's sit at the table."

Dat ran up her arm and stood on her shoulder, free hand clenching Janine's hair. "Then how come he doesn't play with you?" She leaned forward and peered down. "Certainly formed well enough."

"Dat?" Janine tugged her robe closed.

"Yes?"

"Change the subject, will you." Janine sat at the dining room table.

Dat leaped down and sat cross-legged, facing Janine, and sipped from her cup. "To what?"

"Indjinns. Tell me about indjinns."

Dat smiled "We are very nice. And beautiful." She stood and turned slowly around. "See?" And preened.

Janine nodded, and suppressed her smile. "Beautiful."

"He doesn't appreciate that." Dat sat.

"Maybe he needs glasses. You are fairly small, hard to see the details."

Dat sat and propped her head on her hands. "Probably it. Of course, I did become large once. But I couldn't hold it."

"Oh, too bad." Janine leaned forward, head on hand, elbow on the table top. "What else do indjinns do, other than look beautiful?"

"Cast spells, protect our Great Master from almost anything, do their bidding, things like that. Standard indjinn stuff." Dat looked up. "You ought to get one of your own."

"Hard to do that around here."

"A male. Even harder to find." Dat stood. "But if you did, he could come and visit."

"I will keep my eyes open." Janine pushed her chair back and stood. "I am going out on the rear deck and lounge. You coming?"

"No." Dat vanished.

Shaking her head, Janine headed for the outside.

Angok Goblok.

"Uh?"

She poked him again.

"Ummm, huh?" And dragged the heavy comforter up and over their heads.

"I am awake."

"Ummmm?"

"Hold me."

"Zzzzz'matter?"

"I want to be held."

He rolled over. And gathered her into his arms. "O.K."

"Kiss me."

"Kinna bossy for a short kid witch." He did.

And after awhile she whispered, "Nervous, nervous."

"What about?"

"Nothing."

"Ummmm?"

"It. The nothing. Or something."

He tilted her head up, pushing gently under her chin with one finger. "Messenger saw something hiding. Finally. We will run a little experiment tomorrow. You and Ran will help." His lips brushed her's. He smiled.

She jerked her head back. "Something funny?" And wiggled. "Hum, hum."

"Did you know that witches have really smooth skin?"

"Yesssssss."

"O.K.?"

Everyone nodded. They had eaten breakfast, packed everything and now stood in a curved line facing the bright spot, or nothing, or something.

R-Bar handed him a dinner roll.

"Safe to touch?"

"Yesssss."

She and Ran fixed another one.

"Well," said Tinker.

"Toss it," snapped Chantal, cocking the hammer back on her revolver.

He did.

A slow, high arc. So they could easily watch it. The roll sailed up and started down. And disappeared.

"We will wait a bit," said Tinker, slowly counting to himself.

". . . and thirty. Reel it in."

R-Bar nodded. And jerked on a green wand. Ran snatched a green crystal sphere from somewhere.

And something was slowly dragged toward them. Thrashing and snarling. Something large. Something grey.

"Bigger than a bread box," said Tinker.

Whatever it was, it appeared to have been assembled by someone who had lost the instructions. The thing was larger than them. Warped, bent, all odd angles and joints. Straight slit for a mouth. Eyes glittered at them from rows of puffy flesh. Long claws ripped furrows in the grey stuff of this elseplace.

"Not too close." Tinker swung his weaponkin around and down. It sang soft kill song.

R-Bar stopped the pull. And nodded at Ran. She hit the thing with the green crystal sphere.

It began to melt.

Messenger spun away, gagging. Chantal whirled and grabbed her by the shoulders. "You all right?"

"To soon after breakfast," murmured Messenger.

R-Bar hissed.

Ran growled.

"BY GEORGE," gasped Chicken.

A very unhappy looking man stood there, frowning at them. Dressed in flowing grey clothes.

"Release me," he snarled.

"Who are you?" asked Tinker. He swung his weaponkin up and over, back into place on his back.

"What are you?" came the reply as the man tried to step back. And spit at them. It splattered against Ran's shield. And sizzled down to the ground.

Chicken jerked back. "Most foul." She stared at the bubbling spots, leaking soft fumes upward. "My Lord?"

"Uh huh." He stared at the spot on the ground. "Glad we were prepared."

"Release me."

"Hose no, Joe," replied R-Bar.

"That's certainly different," said Tinker. "Ummmm, we can talk about it later. For now, what are we going to do with him, it, or whatever?"

Ran nodded at R-Bar who nodded back.

"HOLD IT!" Tinker threw an arm around each witch.

Something dark and vague snarled overhead. Dark clouds were forming.

Their captive looked up and folded his arms over his chest.

"Doesn't look very impressed," observed Tinker.

Messenger walked around and stood next to R-Bar. Chantal stepped up to Fair Morn, her arm down by her side, still holding her revolver. Smoke joined Chicken, staying on her left side.

Chicken was swishing her sword back and forth.

"A grey guide," stated Ran.

"Think so?" replied R-Bar.

"What?" asked Tinker.

"It is what our captive told us," explained Ran.

"True," agreed R-Bar.

"What?" asked Tinker. He pulled, tugged them around and close.

"Hum," said Ran.

"Hum," echoed R-Bar.

"Nuff of that," grumbled Tinker. Two blank faces looked at him.

"Tink?"

"Amtar?"

"That guy a demon of some kind?"

Ran nodded. "Yep," said R-Bar.

"How are we gonna control him? Can't have him spitting on anyone." He sighed. And waited. And sighed. "You mean to tell me that here I stand, holding armfuls of mean, black-hearted nasty witch and all that I am going to get for an answer is two pale-faced black eyed blank looks?"

"Not our fault." R-Bar plucked at a lower button on his shirt.

Ran inched closer.

"What? Leave my shirt along." He twitched.

R-Bar was rubbing a finger inside his shirt. "Tink?"

"Too sneaky for words?"

"Amtar? We want to catch the other one."

"There is another one? Demon?"

"Yep," replied R-Bar.

"You have a plan?"

"Yessssss, Amtar." Ran's eyes glittered.

"Not sure that I like this."

"We will be careful, very careful." R-Bar pinched him.

"Hey! O.K. Let's try it."

"Heh," replied R-Bar.

"Heh, heh," replied Ran.

They spun out of his arms. R-Bar handed him another

dinner roll. Then she and Ran stepped further away and readied themselves.

He tossed the roll as close to the first spot as he could remember.

The roll soared up, down, and disappeared.

Grandeville. Chen's Chinese.

"So, how do you like your job?"

It was Wednesday, the mid-point of the week. And the boss and the employee were eating downstairs, having lunch at Chen's. They had just finished the Wednesday Special, and were now sipping tea.

"O.K., more or less. Pay is all right, demand is high. But the commute to work is short." Janine refilled Sandy's cup. "Standard boss. Secretary makes the coffee in the morning."

Sandy grinned at her. "Should have hired some cute guy and had a real role reversal."

"Pass me a fortune cookie, Boss."

Sandy did. "They have been gone an awfully long time."

Janine nodded. "Uh huh."

Sandy leaned forward, both forearms on the table top. "Streaker, I am worried. From what little that I understand they usually are only gone for a few days."

"That is what Chantal told me." Janine reached out and held one of Sandy's hands. '"Not much we can do about it, is there?"

"No."

Janine released her and sat back. '"Right. I doubt we know anyone that could." And sipped her tea.

Sandy jerked upright. "I saw that."

"What?"

"You just thought of something. You are up to something."

Janine frowned.

"Can't lie to me," stated Sandy. "I know that expression. Tell me. Hey, I will be your attorney. Now it is privileged communication. I will even come and get you out of jail."

Janine shook her head. "Don't think I should." She smiled. "Besides, it probably won't work."

"If it does, you'll tell me, right?"

"Maybe."

"Close enough for legal work." Sandy stood, grabbed the check, and winked. "And speaking of which."

"Slave driver," said Janine as they walked toward the cash register.

Angok Goblok.

She spit at them.

It didn't do any good.

"O.K. So now we have a pair of them. Now what?"

"So now we get him to cooperate." R-Bar spun around and faced Tinker. And whispered, "And don't get excited either. We know what we are doing. It will just look worse than it is."

Ran nodded and walked over to the cage of the male demon. And spoke softly to it. He spit at her. She said something. He leaped at her. And bounced off the shield and hit the ground with a heavy thud.

The female watched R-Bar approach. R-Bar nodded, looked at Ran, and called it. Inside. With the female.

"BANNED," howled the male. "BANNED INTO NEVER." He crashed into the wall.

The female pressed her back against the far wall.

Multi-eyes fastened upon her, mandibles clacked.

"MY LORD." Chicken ran up to them. "What manner of hell beastie be this?"

"I think that it belongs to R-Bar."

Fair Morn ran over. "One, if I shot from that side, I would probably miss her and him."

He grabbed her. "No." And glared at Ran. "Tell them before everyone goes bug-nuts." Fair Morn jerked free and stepped to one side.

Ran reached out and told them, carefully not touching R-Bar who was maintaining control over the Ravenoi.

"Be this safe?" Chicken grabbed Tinker's forearm.

"She said that it was," he whispered. "Shhh."

The Ravenoi inched closer, extending feeding tubes.

"ARPAZ," screamed the male as the female readied herself to attack. "AN NAH!" He whirled and spoke rapidly to Ran. She nodded.

"Whew," sighed R-Bar, collapsing back against Tinker, who hastily wrapped his arms around her. The thing was gone.

"Hum, hum, hum," said Ran as she stepped over to join them.

"You are just jealous because he is not fondling you," said R-Bar.

Tinker jerked his arms away. "Trouble with short swooners."

"Heh heh," said R-Bar.

One corner of Ran's mouth pulled down. "Amtar, the grey demon male, Txquar, agrees to help us. Your rangle sneak Faan witch R-Bar garbatak is very clever. Also."

"All your's, Tink," gurgled R-Bar, collapsing sideways.

Ran leaped, grabbed her, and wrapped them in red flame.

Everyone else leaped in various directions. Away from the pair.

"Now what?" he demanded.

Ran tumbled out against his legs. "Fine, Amtar."

He helped her to her feet. "If you say so."

She leaned against him, wrapping her arms around him.

"What was that thing?" he asked.

Ran swallowed. "A Demon Ravenoi. Long, long ago that spell was banned and they were banned. It all occurred during the Thirty and Nine Demon Witch Void War."

The flames flickered out.

R-Bar stared up at them. "Fine, Tink."

Chicken knelt by R-Bar. "We will here ourselves make camp. And pon the morrow bespeak ourselves with demon grey." She helped R-Bar sit up, then stand.

And they did what Chicken said.

Grandeville. Tinker's Place.

"You really want to do this?"

It was Janine. Talking to herself.

She had eaten a large dinner, washed the dishes, made everything very neat, and steeled herself. Now she stood in front of the bookcase. And stared at the ornate ring.

Sucking in a deep breath, she reached out and tapped it with one fingertip, on the jewel.

"Dat! You in there?"

The jewel glowed, pulsated, and went out.

"What do you want?" Dat stretched. And kicked the side of the red cube. "Move over."

It did.

"I want to help John Tinker."

"Are you a magician? You do not look like a witch."

"No. Neither."

"Did you make cocoa?"

"I will make some." Janine headed for the kitchen.

"Hoooooooo," yelled Dat.

Janine spun back. "I forgot." And snatched the indjinn off the shelf.

Dat squeaked.

"Hush," said Janine.

And then, while Dat watched, Janine made cocoa.

"I do not like being squeezed."

"Tough it out." Janine banged a wooden spoon on the edge of the pot. "It's ready. Help yourself." She pulled a kitchen stool over and sat.

"Yum, yum, yum, yum," said Dat, sipping from her cup. "That really you?"

"What?"

"Blouse filling."

"Yes. And knock off the comments. Drink your cocoa."

Dat dipped her cup back into the steaming liquid, and took another sip. "It is yum, yum, yum, also." She leaned on the pot and idly kicked a bare foot through the blue flame of the burner.

"You said that you cast spells, did his bidding, protected him from almost anything."

Dat nodded. "Standard indjinn behavior."

Janine leaned forward, her face getting close to the small figure. "Then it is time to go to work, dinky."

Dat frowned at her. "I am not dinky. I am as well, more well, developed than you are. But much nicer."

Janine leaned back. "That is not what I was referring to. Pay attention."

"Of course. Say something."

"I think that we should go find Tinker and help him."

Dat refilled her cup. "You are not properly dressed to do things like that."

Janine jumped up. "Don't go anywhere. Be right back."

"Look in the hall closet," called Dat.

Angok Goblok.

"Now what?"

He had been sprawled on his sleeping bag, thinking about tomorrow, drifting off, when a sleeping bag was dumped by his side. And then, another on his other side.

"Nothing," said R-Bar, nestling along his side.

"Nothing," whispered Ran in his other ear.

"Then why do I feel like a piece of salami between two hungry dogs."

"Nervous tired," said Ran.

"Tired nervous," said R-Bar.

"Me too," said Tinker. "Both." He yawned.

They fell asleep before he did.

Grandeville. Tinker's Place.

"O.K., let's go."

Dat was sitting on the edge of the counter top, kicking her legs back and forth. "You look just like his other houris."

Janine was wearing sturdy boots, jeans and a flannel shirt. "A little dirty, but O.K. I found the duds in the laundry hamper."

"Where is your weapon?"

"What weapon?"

"They all carry weapons when they go out there."

"Right. Don't go away. I know just the thing. Saw it in a closet." Janine spun and headed for the hall.

Grandeville. Red and Sandy's Home.

"Green thinks we ought to go bowling again."

"Oh?"

They were sitting, eating their meal, in the kitchen. She was having dinner. He was eating breakfast.

"Pass the hot sauce, please. Yes."

"Ugh." She wrinkled her nose. He dumped some over his eggs.

"Try it, you'll like it."

"Nope. When?"

"Umm," he said, mouth full, pointing at the calender. A date had a large red circle around it.

"Looks good," said Sandy. "Think I should invite my new secretary?"

Red swallowed And shook his head. "Thought you might like to ask your jock friend again."

"My new secretary."

He stared at the table. "She really know how to bowl?" And checked his watch.

"Big Lump, my jock friend is my new secretary."

He stood. "Lawyer sneak." And bent and kissed her and headed for the door. And kissed her again as she joined him. He reached for the door knob. Outside a car horn honked.

"See ya, babe." He opened the door and headed down the walk to the patrol car.

"Night, Red. No noise. I am working late."

He waved as he got into the car.

So did Green.

Wave.

Grandeville. Tinker's Place.

"O.K., let's go."

Janine smiled at Dat and grabbed her.

Dat squeaked.

Angok Goblok.

"You sure that this is safe?"

They both nodded.

The grey demon male stood and watched them approach.

Fair Morn stepped to one side, flicked a lever, and aimed. "Ready."

Tinker wiped his palms on the sides of his jeans legs. "O.K."

R-Bar nodded. Ran took the sphere away.

"What are you," demanded Txquar.

"Ummmmm," said Tinker.

"Avon Polymorph," said R-Bar.

Txquar cleared his throat. Everyone twitched.

"The destroyers of Chan Narh." Txquar wobbled his head. "Unbalanced balanced."

"We need some help," said Tinker.

Txquar stared at him. And pointed at Ran with his chin. "Your Impta spoke so." He indicated R-Bar. "As your other did unspeakable."

"We are just passing through," said Tinker.

"Your other should zakatk be."

"AN NAH!" shouted the other grey demon, leaping, crashing into the wall, sliding to the ground.

"Release Arpaz," said Txquar.

Tinker looked at Ran. She nodded.

Arpaz ran toward them.

Tinker heard the click as Chantal cocked, aimed, and tracked her.

Arpaz stopped next to Txquar. "Na." And cleared her

throat. "Tandal Chan Narh."

Txquar touched her shoulder and looked at Tinker.

"Here's the problem," said Tinker. He began to explain.

Chapter Seventeen

Surprise, Surprise, Surprise.

Am'Pa'Tar. Dark and Dismal.

"What are you?"

Said the a'demon and Janine simultaneously.

"Dat?" Janine looked at the indjinn.

"What?"

"Did I shrink?" Janine's face blanched as she stared at the indjinn standing next to her.

"I am large." Dat looked embarrassed. "I forgot the ring."

The a'demon wobbled over and gave Janine a poke with one talon tipped finger. "Tasty taste."

She slapped its hand. "Watch it."

Its head snapped around. "Where?"

"Your father a demon?" asked a second, sidling up to Dat. "Lovely claws."

Janine stopped staring at the a'demon and then stared at Dat. She did have claws. On hands and feet, flat curved claws. "I think you ought to wear more clothes."

Dat was wearing a pair of baggy trousers. And a sparkling necklace. She ran her hands over her bare torso. "See. I told you that I was beautiful."

The third a'demon hastily polished one of its up curving tusks. And poked the small cloth back into a rear pocket.

"Oooooo," it moaned, trying not to drool too heavily, rolling one eye wildly at Dat.

The second grabbed the indjinn, hands circling around her narrow waist. "Dessert."

"That is not fair," grumbled the first. "I found it first."

Dat yanked one demon hand free and bit it, sinking one long canine into the back of the knobby hand.

The a'demon leaped away. "Not me. Try Fith." It pointed at the first.

Fith poked Janine again. "Look tasty to me."

She punched it in the eye.

"Of course." It stepped back.

"She acts like those Avon Polymorph," said the third.

"This part doesn't." Fith slid a long talon over Dat. And jerked its hand back before she could bite. And peered at Janine. "You steal your own dessert from elsewhere?"

Janine frowned at everything. "Dat, will you please put on some clothes so these, these things will stop all that drooling."

Dat shrugged on a shirt. "Shouldn't have to cover up beauty. And I am not going to wear foot coverings." She flexed her toes and made little cuts in the soil with her claws.

"O.K., no shoes," said Janine. "But you keep your shirt on. Buttoned up."

"Now we will have to unwrap it first," grumbled Fith as Dat fastened her shirt.

"Gorgeous," cooed the third, staring at Dat's feet. "Run away with me." It panted at her.

"SHUT UP!" yelled Janine.

A'demon heads snapped around and stared at her. Shaggy ears jumped straight up.

"You part of our Master Boss?" asked Fith.

"It went that way," said the second, pointing at several

tall stones.

"Don't turn," said the third, running crooked fingers over Dat's hip. "Special occasion dessert."

Janine started for the stones. "Let's get out of here." She stopped and turned. "DAT!"

Dat patted the a'demon on top of the head. "Demon ugly."

It panted. "Thank you. Hurry back."

They sat and watched as Dat joined Janine. And disappeared with her.

"Delicious," agreed the second.

The third panted heavily.

Grandeville. Red and Sandy's Home.

It rang.

And rang.

And rang.

He strangled it.

And said, "What?"

"Red, I want you to go up to Tinker's place and find out why Janine hasn't come to work."

He sat up. "All right. Right away."

"Sorry."

"Don't worry, babe."

"She doesn't do things like this. Didn't answer the phone, either."

Holding the phone under his chin he changed into his clothes, and said, "Uh huh," in the proper places. "Twenty minutes. I will phone from there. Bye."

"Thanks."

He hurried out the door, thinking that there was no reason to wake up Green.

Angok Goblok.

"What need we from you?" Txquar looked at Tinker, then from face to face, watching them.

"Good question," said Tinker. "How about peace and quiet?"

Arpaz edged behind her mate, who gurgled deep inside his throat.

"Well then," said Tinker. "What do you want?"

"Canx."

"How many? How much?" asked Tinker.

"My Lord?" Chicken lightly touched his arm.

"Beats me. I have no idea."

"Aaaaa z'taz." Txquar held up both hands, fingers splayed wide, talons gleaming darkly.

Tinker held up one hand. "Five."

Txquar showed seven fingers. "Zzzz on'tpz."

Tinker held up one more finger. "Six."

Arpaz nipped Txquar on the side of the neck. Txquar held out his hands, cupped together.

"Ummmmm," said Tinker. "There is one small problem."

Both grey demons stared at him. Tawny eyes blinked.

"Ahhhhh, we do not know what Canx is, are."

Txquar yanked Arpaz around to stand by his side, slightly in front.

"Better not be what I am thinking," grumbled Chantal.

"Could be a long night, all right," observed Fair Morn. "He agreed to six."

Arpaz opened a baggy side pocket on her lower garment and took it out. It was a light brown color and badly smashed.

Smoke stared at the thing. "Looks like a dinner roll, MindMate." Smoke held out her hand and indicated that

Arpaz should let her have the object. Smoke held it close and sniffed. "Yep." And gave it back.

Arpaz quickly stuffed it back into her pocket.

"Passing odd, that, Our Prince." Chicken chewed on the corner of her mouth. "Tis naught but dinner roll."

"Exotic cuisine, I suppose," said Tinker.

"Canx," stated Txquar.

"Half now, half when we get to the way out of here. Pay them, kiddo."

Ran handed R-Bar a small basket. R-Bar handed it to Txquar. Now it held three dinner rolls.

Txquar carefully handed the basket to Arpaz. She clenched it to her chest. And cleared her throat.

Txquar pointed. And started walking. Arpaz stayed close to his side.

Tinker and company followed them.

"Could always open a bakery here. Make a fortune." Tinker ruffled R-Bar's hair. "I thought those rolls were all right, but nothing to get excited about."

Estur Nal. A Rather Nice Looking Place.

"Aaaaaaaaaah." She spun to one side, stomach heaving.

"I think he played with you."

Janine straightened up, wiped her mouth, and turned. "Those three things were horrors." Then she frowned. "What?"

"Not too bad. For demons. Of that type." Dat nodded. "I understand."

"What do you understand?"

"Females of your species often empty their stomachs."

"I NOT PREGNANT. AND JOHN TINKER HAS NOT BEEN . . . doing anything . . . to me." Janine glared at Dat. "So you can just knock off that line of conversation too."

Dat smiled. "Even though you are not, I can make you some food."

"Ah, maybe later. Thanks." She looked around. "Any idea of where we are?"

"Following my Great Master." Dat pointed. "He went in there."

On the far horizon lay a grey cloud.

"Long way. Let's get going."

Dat grabbed Janine's wrist and yanked.

Grandeville. The Sandermeyer Law Office.

"Hello, babe."

The telephone had rung as she had been working on a final draft. Sandy snatched it up and checked the clock on the wall. She was due in court in thirty minutes.

"How is she, Red?"

"Nobody home."

"WHAT?"

"Found a note. It was sitting on the dining room table, next to a pile of mail. Addressed to Tinker."

Sandy sighed. "Well?"

"It said that she and someone named Dat went off to find them and that if they, Tinker and group, get home first, not to worry. You know anyone named Dat?"

"No. That it?"

"Yes. She washed all the dishes so it doesn't look like a rush job. Note doesn't look hurried either. All very planned, all very normal."

Sandy nodded. "Sounds right for Janine. Thanks. Go home, go back to bed." She had heard him yawn.

"Sure thing, babe." He hung up.

So did she. And sat back and sipped on her tea. And

wondered. Then she jumped up, grabbed her brief, and charged out the door. Headed for the court house.

Angok Goblok.

"Come'mere, you two."

He beckoned. Ran and R-Bar walked over and strolled on either side of him.

"You guys sure that we are in demon country?"

"Why?" asked R-Bar.

Ran waited.

"Think about it. Everything from that branch we have ever met before that been horrible beyond belief, ugly as sin, and dark as nightmares. Right?"

R-Bar nodded.

Ran waited.

"Gut wrenching terrible," he added.

"Yep," agreed R-Bar.

Ran waited.

"So," he said looking from one to the other. "These guys do not took that way. Mostly."

R-Bar shrugged. "Hard to understand demons. We really do not know much about them."

"Ummmm." He stared at Ran. "Well, Susy Silent, nothing to say?"

She looked off to the side. Then back. "Amtar?"

"No ideas?"

Ran nodded. "Tanpak myth legend speaks of a second type of demon race."

"Uh huh."

"Terrible terrible."

"Pretty bad, huh?"

R-Bar hissed at him.

Ran looked at her.

Tinker sighed.

"Amtar?"

"That it?"

Ran frowned. "It is hard to translate. Tanpak myth legend speaks of The Others, removed and hidden. Strange strange. Not people, not demons. Not described."

Tinker watched the pair ahead of them, leading them somewhere. "I see."

"Tink." R-Bar edged closer to him. And lowered her voice. "I think it is because we look like we look and not like the demons we have seen elseplace."

"Ah ha."

"More or less," added R-Bar. "It must be why they didn't try really hard to kill us. They must have thought that we were some of the other types of demons."

"Ummm," added Tinker.

Ran nodded. "I think that your R-Bar is correct."

"And I think," he said, throwing an arm around each of them. "That a certain ugly you guys captured tried to see to it that we got killed."

"Hum," said R-Bar.

"Hum, hum." said Ran.

The air began to crackle faintly around them.

"Careful, careful, " he whispered. "We don't want to excite our grey guides."

"I think that I will kill it," said Ran.

"Me too, Ran, me too," agreed R-Bar, smiling. It was a pure witch smile.

He laughed. "That demon have a lot of lives."

"Not any more," grumbled R-Bar.

Ran nodded.

And told the others,

Estur Nal. A Rather Nice Looking Place.

"Neat trick. Looks like a big house."

Janine smiled at Dat. They were standing in front of the castle cloud. Dat had put them there.

Right in front.

By the entrance.

The Tark overwhelmed them.

Red eyes stared into Janine's as she was pressed flat, back against the damp ground. Tark teeth clattered loudly in front of her face as very warm hands tore garments to shreds and ran over her body.

She screamed.

Grandeville. Red and Sandy's Home.

"We will cruise by and take a look, once a night. Even though Tinker's place is outside the city limits."

Sandy nodded.

Red pushed his plate away. "What do you think she is doing?"

"What she said, looking for Tinker." Sandy reached over and refilled his cup.

"Must be walking." He poured some coffee into his saucer and blew on it. "All of Tinker's rigs are still there. Pretty odd behavior. She have any problems."

"There is nothing wrong with Janine, Big Cop."

He nodded. And poured the coffee back into his cup. "We still going bowling?"

"What?"

"Even if she doesn't turn up?"

"Oh." It was a low whisper moan. Sandy blinked fiercely.

Red stood, moved around the table and wrapped her in his arms. "Sorry, babe. But, well, we see things like this happening all the time."

"I am all right, Red." She sniffled loudly. "Green's late."

A horn honked outside.

"Nope." He headed for the door. '"We will check after we get off, also."

Sandy nodded. And stared into space as the front door softly closed. And wondered.

Angok Goblok.

Txquar stopped, turned, and gestured them forward. And pointed down into a deep hollow.

In the center of the hollow, four green columns framed a square, paved floor. Everything was made from stone. Everything gleamed soft polish smooth.

And, after they had all gathered near the edge, the grey demon pointed down at the structure.

"Otkz ark'demon. They aid Dark Ump." He spit on the ground.

Tinker nodded. "So, we go through that thing to the ark'demon and they know how to get to the Dark Ump? Right?"

Arpaz looked around her mate at Tinker. And curled her upper lip. The upper canines curved sharply back.

"Ahhhhh," said Tinker. "These ark'demons are not very nice, right?"

Arpaz cleared her throat.

"Well, thanks for the help."

He looked at R-Bar. "Pay them kiddo."

R-Bar handed the grey demons another basket, a large basket. It brimmed with dinner rolls.

"Here," she said, shoving it at Txquar. "Erm, thanks for the help." Ran stared at her.

"Txquar," said Txquar.

"Arpaz," said his mate.

"Oh," said Tinker. "Just call me Tinker." He smiled at them. "But I doubt we will be back this way."

He waggled one arm and pointed. "Come on, gang. Down there."

They headed down the gentle slope.

The grey demons watched them walk down and step into the structure. And disappear.

Txquar held a roll in front of Arpaz' face. She snapped it from between his fingers, fangs gleaming in the soft light.

Estur Nal. A Rather Nice Looking Place.

"Ah ha."

Fingers radiating heat peeled away more strips of her shirt and ran over her bare skin while other hands held her in place. Something sniffed loudly. Hot breath puffed against her skin.

"Do you require assistance?" asked Dat, tossing aside the last of the males.

"HELP!" bellowed Janine.

The rest of the bodies were yanked away and thudded heavily here and there.

Janine wiped at her face and glared up at the indjinn. "What were you doing, just watching the rape scene? You some sort of pervert? Like to see people eaten?"

"Would you like a new shirt?"

Janine nodded and sat up. Then she stood and snatched the garment from the indjinn's hand. "You are not much help." And jabbed it back at Dat. "Here, hold this. While I shed my shreds. What are these things?"

She dumped her gear, then the remains of her shirt. "Stop staring at me." And snatched the new shirt and yanked it on.

"Yum, yum, yum," said Dat. Then she added, "They are returning."

"WHAT?" Janine spun around. "Why didn't you kill them?"

"Should I have?"

The two females stepped close and stared at them.

"Ahamaezur," said one.

Janine nodded and clenched the hilt of her dagger. "Stay back."

The other stepped closer and tugged the left side of her blouse forward. The brooch gleamed silver and blue. Then the other one did the same thing. And four red eyes stared at Janine's dagger handle.

She looked down. The end of the handle was ornate silver work encasing a blue stone.

"Ah ha," said Ahamaezur.

Janine gasped. "They are the same thing. Their broaches and my dagger, the same blue stone."

She glanced at Dat. "But I found this knife in the hall closet."

Dat nodded.

Red eyes snapped in her direction.

"Fine food," said Ahamaezur. She beckoned at the males. They began to circle around and approach, cautiously.

"STOP THAT," shouted Janine. "She is not fine food."

"What it?" demanded the other. "Not demon?"

Dat glared at them. "I am a beautiful indjinn. Who are you?"

"Tark."

"Tark?" echoed Janine.

"Ahamaezur ar Tark," stated Ahamaezur firmly. She ran a finger over the blue stone of her brooch. "Passage." She rubbed her lips with her hand.

"I am not fine food either." Janine edged back.

"Indjinn," said Amamaedur.

"No," replied Janine. "Human."

"Beautiful," said Dat.

"Did Tinker come this way?" Janine picked up the rest of her gear and kicked her ruined shirt to one side.

The Tark watched her, the demon set shifting slightly from place to place.

Janine held up one hand. "Tall guy?" And described Tinker. "With a whole bunch of women, ahhhh, females."

"Ah ha," said Ahamaezur.

"Which way did they go?"

Amamaedur beckoned.

Janine looked at Dat. "Don't wait."

"For what?"

"To help, Dat, to help."

Dat nodded.

"Come on." Janine started after the Core Pair who were walking into the castle cloud, as the demon set opened a passage for them.

Hmp Zat.

The stone lined path wandered into the thick mist.

Tinker smiled. "If anyone hears howling I'll bet that it is the Hound of the Baskervilles."

"Indeed, My Lord? Be this England?" Chicken looked at their surroundings.

They were standing in the middle of a structure similar to the one they had left. Only this one had brown pillars.

"A joke."

"Most poor a'jest."

"Anything around?"

"No, MindMate." Smoke shoved her pistol into its shoulder holster.

Everyone relaxed.

"Only one way to go." He started down the path.

"What's that?" Chantal grabbed his arm.

He jerked.

Weapons appeared and poked in every direction. "Where?"

She pointed, just ahead of them.

Tinker approached it and bent to take a closer look. "I'd say that it is the remains of something, mostly eaten. With long legs." He straightened up and nudged it with his boot tip. "Not very fresh."

Chantal stepped to his side. "John, I am really getting worried."

"Ummmm?"

"First we meet lady sharks with red eyes. Next a couple of acid spitters, or whatever that stuff was. Now this." Chantal pointed at the remains. "The chewed upon remains of something ugly, something demon ugly, that was something else's meal."

"Uh huh."

"You listening to me, Cowboy?" She banged him on the shoulder.

"Sure. But."

"But, what?"

"But what can we do about it? Seems like this is the only way to the Dark Ump." He brushed the hair back from her forehead. "And nothing bad has really happened so far. Much. Has it?"

"That is why I am worried."

He nodded. "I know. But, so far, bribery has paid off."

He leaned close. "And two black hearted witches." He kissed the tip of her nose. "Got any plans for tonight?"

"The Princess has the ring, Simba Leader."

"We could always sneak off into a fog bank."

"DUCK," shouted Smoke.

Those in front dropped to the ground as Fair Morn fired over them. And removed ten acres of fog and mist, sheared away parts of the landscape, and eliminated a number of things that had been racing toward them.

Chantal shoved him aside, revolver flying up, hammer cocking.

Smoke looked over at them. "They were attacking. Seemed to know we were here. They were already racing toward us when they entered my sensenet."

Tinker looked into the space slowly filling with drifting mist fog. "Think we ought to get off this path?"

Smoke shook her head. "Clearing not far ahead. They thought of it, came from there."

He nodded. "O.K. Maybe if we hurry."

Everyone nodded.

And held their weapons ready.

And hurried.

Up the path.

Up the incline.

Angok Goblok.

"They were not so bad."

Janine nodded at her own comment and released a loud breath. "If you ignore red eyes and those teeth and a certain interest in eating one alive. And a zeal for poking and prodding."

"They thought that we were fine food," grumbled Dat. "Anyone can see that I am a beautiful indjinn."

"It wasn't you that they were preparing for their picnic," snapped Janine. "And enough with the beautiful indjinn comments."

She waved at their surroundings, a seemingly endless grey. "Which way?"

Dat pointed at the bright spot on a far horizon. And looked at Janine. "I can understand their interest, Fine Food."

Janine grabbed one of Dat's wrists. "Let's go. And don't get any funny ideas."

Hmp Zat.

"I wonder what ark'demons are going to look like?"

They had walked up and out of the mist fog. Behind them, below them, was a deep bowl filled with grey that lapped at the upper edges.

Ahead, and all around, sunny stark open desert hills, with thick patches of tall trees and undergrowth, all yellow brown. And that one deep puddle of grey.

The path shot into a place of jumbled pillars. The collection appeared haphazard, almost, this strange arrangement of stone pillars.

Tall.

Short.

Thin.

Fat.

Upright.

Canted, in every direction.

Some were lying flat.

Tinker looked at Smoke. "Think that they are in there? Should we enter that mess?"

"The path goes there."

"See anything?"

She shook her head. Then her eyes flew wide.

"Suddenly they are there. Many many."

He stared into the pillar maze.

Fair Morn stepped to his side. He grabbed one of her arms as she aimed. "Hold it, Killer Moth. Let's see what they are up to, first."

Everyone spread out, a long line facing the stones. And readied themselves.

"Smoke, watch our backs, please." The great black sword danced lightly in his hand. He could feel its eagerness. "We will just wait out here and see what they do."

Angok Goblok.

"What is that thing?"

Dat shook her head.

They both stared at the bright spot.

Janine stepped closer and carefully, ever so carefully, reached out to touch it. Her finger slipped through. "Nothing there."

She shoved her arm through.

She was yanked in.

Something coughed.

Twice.

Hmp Zat.

"Standoff."

Tinker looked at his watch. "It has been almost a hour." He nodded at Fair Morn. "Mothra, think you can just take out just one pillar?"

"Sure. No problemo, Dude."

He sighed. And pointed. "That one way over there on the right, sorta by itself. Zap it. Let's see if that does anything."

Fair Morn nodded.

And fired.

Angok Goblok.

The female quickly dragged the body to one side as the male leaped for the other.

He was thrown backward, rolling and tumbling.

She joined her mate as he hurtled forward, spitting and coughing.

Hmp Zat.

"Well, that didn't do any good."

They had been waiting, thirty minutes this time, by Tinker's watch, and nothing had happened.

Again.

One pillar was missing.

"Time for Plan B." He shrugged off his pack, retrieved his weaponkin, and gestured for Fair Morn to come with him.

"Let's go and talk with them."

"MY LORD." Chicken started forward.

"Taking no chances," said Fair Morn.

"Right," agreed Tinker. He turned and glowered at the rest. "And you guys stay right where you are. Understand?" He stared from face to face. "Good." And spun away.

Fair Morn walked by his left side as they walked slowly toward the pillar maze. She cradled her cannon in her arms, watching for anything to move, finger resting lightly on the trigger.

"And I do not care how much damage we do." He glanced over at her. "O.K.?"

"Yep."

"Close enough." He halted.

They were well away from the apparent entry to the jumble.

"Ready?"

"Yep." She stepped a little further to one side and aimed down the path into the opening. And flicked a lever. "High power, wide angle."

Tinker nodded And sucked in a deep breath.

"HALLO IN THERE. ANYONE WANT TO TALK?" He waited. And mumbled to himself. "Or anything?"

Fair Morn reset the levers on her weapon.

Short swift movements. Things approached. Hiding, pillar by pillar.

Angok Goblok.

Dat chained them to the ground. And threw a lid over them. And walked over and sat on the ground next to the still figure.

And stared at the ragged holes.

And leaned closer.

She touched the shirt.

It disappeared.

She touched Janine's forehead.

Her eyes popped open.

"Good," said Dat. She smiled. "I am going to have to fix the mess."

Janine tried to look down.

"Do not move." She stared into Janine's eyes. "Sleep now."

Both eyes banged shut.

Dat started working. Periodically she wiped her hands clean, and patted away the tears leaking from beneath Janine's tightly closed eyelids.

Then, smiling to herself, she sat back and thumped Janine sharply on the sternum with a kunckle and watched.

Janine moaned and opened her eyes and looked up at

her. "I'm hurt, Dat. Something shot me. Am I gonna die?"

Dat shook her head.

"Don't lie. Please?"

"You are fixed," said Dat.

"Fixed?"

Dat nodded. "Indjinns have many skills."

Snapping her legs up, Janine rolled into her side, and moaned. "Then how come it hurts so bad?"

"Must be healing." The indjinn gently touched Janine's shoulder. "I used all new parts."

"Aaaaaaaaaaaah . . . what do you mean?" Janine shivered. "New parts?" And curled into a tight ball.

Gently the clawed hands rubbed down the bare spine, stroking the pain away until Janine unfolded, and rolled over onto her back and stared up.

"You were very messy," explained Dat.

Janine licked dry lips. "Thirsty. Maybe we ought to go home."

Dat helped her sit and held a cup of cool water to parched lips. "My Great Master is not too far away. I can tell."

"We are not doing too good."

Dat nodded. And stared at the ground. "I will try to do better." And looked up. "But you are not my Great Master, so it is hard."

She smiled. "But now you are beautiful."

Janine frowned and looked down at herself. "What did you do?"

Dat reached over and gently poked with one finger, curving the claw down. "I had to replace this one. And all these ribs. And around to here."

"Tickles."

"And things inside."

Dat admired her handiwork. And ran a soft palm over Janine. "And I changed this one to match. And narrowed the width of the rib cage. And the waist. Then made this a little larger. Softened the shoulder line, here and here. Tightened these muscles a little. And made your legs a little longer."

Janine stared at her. "Is there anything of me left?"

Dat nodded. "Most of the insides. Head. Hands. Feets. Now you are almost as beautiful as me."

"Help me stand."

Dat eased Janine to her feet. "Your color is returning. You must be done."

"Done what?"

"Healing."

"That fast?"

"Yes."

"How much taller?" Janine looked down.

"Some of your inches." Dat picked up Janine's gear. "Ready to go?"

"Clothes."

Dat set down all the gear. "Too nice to cover up. There." She pointed at a pile of neatly stacked and folded clothes sitting next to Janine's boots. And stood quietly while Janine dressed.

"This is really going to be hard to explain." Janine held out her arms and rotated her hands. "You mess with my arms too?"

Dat looked indignant. "Everything has to be in the correct proportions."

"Well, thanks," mumbled Janine, still inspecting her arms. "I suppose."

Then she spun and grabbed the indjinn and kissed her. "Thanks, thanks a lot, a whole bunch. I would have died, right?"

"Yes. You were messy."

Janine stepped back and grabbed her gear. "I really feel good." She looked over at the lid.

"What about those things?"

Dat looked blank.

"We can't leave them under that thing, they will die."

"You told me that my Great Master would be very upset if someone abused you." Dat folded her arms over her chest.

"Can't you talk to them? Make them understand?"

"Should I?"

"Yes."

Dat walked over, tossed the lid aside. And did.

Murklan Obscuratan. A Place Never Visited.

In a forest black as shadow the palace sprawled casting no reflection from the few points of light that penetrated the dense vegetation over and around it. One narrow path wandered sinuous trail to a distant open meadow, startling green in all the midnight growth.

In the center of that meadow a dark spot formed. And she stepped out, a tall figure dressed in a forest green robe almost as black as the surrounding forest. She clenched a short gold staff in one hand. Turning, she strolled across the meadow and into the near tunnel of the only path. And soon stepped through the dark smudge that was the entrance to the large structure. Blood red flame cast flickering light on the polished stone of floor, walls, and ceiling.

She strode the remembered corridors and finally arrived at her destination and announced herself as she walked into the main temple. The great open space was dominated by the altar stretching before the statue of The Lady of Death. Peering up at the shadow hidden features, she stated firmly, "Lady Fairdeath returned from the Lands Beyond. This one begs release." She waited, patient as the death she asked for. Then she turned and spoke to the silent figure sitting on the stone throne of Thantos. "This one has heard tales of one dark as death. That one brings The Release even to The Final Darkness that opposes The Light of Life."

She becked her companion forward, hovering in the shadows of the entrance. "This one is the learned and ever so clever Ransapal, Sluba mage. We have traveled long and long and have learned much and all. Many has already been sent here. We have solved the last part of this long ago and long ago puzzle." She bowed her head.

Ransapal walked in and over to her side, arms still clenching all the materials that they had gathered and analyzed.

Lady Fairdeath looked up and slid her hood back and off, the soft folds folding back and around.

Lady Grimtouch, Glimmer of the Divineal of Thatala, shook her hood back and peered at the pair, and nodded. "He has the Lady's Mark."

"A debt paid," replied Lady Fairdeath.

'This is an interesting moment," stated Lady Grimtouch. "This mage is the first to take more than two steps from the entrance place before being greeted by death itself."

Ransapal swallowed loudly and worked very hard to not stare or try to flee for his life.

"We owe this one all that we have learned." Lady Fairdeath gently touched his shoulder.

Lady Grimtouch rose, stepped over, and stood in front of Ransapal. "The Face of Death is rarely seen. Which is as it should be. The Voice of Death is but a passing whisper. Which is as it should be. The Touch of Death is but a light caress. Which is as it should be. The Passage of Death is but a soft shadow. Which is as it should be."

She reached out and gently touched the tip of one finger to the black mark on his forehead. And stepped back. She smiled a warm gentle smile.

"You are welcome, Ransapal mage of the Sluba Guild, as the silent shadow that all will eventually find. You are welcome, Ransapal mage of the Sluba Guild, consort of Lady Fairdeath."

He stared at her. And fainted. The materials spilled over her feet.

Hmp Zat.

"COME OUT, COME OUT, WHERE EVER YOU ARE."

Tinker dropped his cupped hands from around his mouth and stared into the pillar maze.

Something was hiding behind various of the pillars. They cast misshapen shadows.

"Or whatever you are," he mumbled. "Seem to be a lot of them in them."

Smoke nodded. "Many many." And looked at Chantal, who counted what Smoke could see in her sensenet. "...Twenty-two, twenty-three." Chantal took a speed loader from a pocket and held it in her left hand. "Twenty-three, total," she told Tinker.

Fair Morn flicked a lever with her thumb. "Maximum width."

"We need survivors," said Tinker. "Won't do us any good if there is no-one left to talk to."

Fair Morn pushed a lever to a new setting.

The ark'demons attacked.

Springing high into the air.

"Kangaroos?" Tinker and his weaponkin waited, watching one of the things sailing in a high arc in his direction.

And then everyone did something.

Ark'demons died.

Came apart.

And disappeared.

Tinker saw the one he was watching suddenly go limp and tumble. It crashed nearby, bounced and lay still. Something poked from its forehead.

He ran forward, great sword clearing away a few survivors, and bent over to take a look. "An arrow?"

Chicken charged up. "My Lord, be thee injured?"

He pointed. "That is an arrow." And straightened up.

Chicken nodded. "Indeed. Tis that." She kicked the dead ark'demon onto its back, stepped on its throat, and yanked the arrow free. And handed it to him.

R-Bar ran over. "We got two. Alive. Ran and I. Where'd you get an arrow from?"

"Most dead thing," said Chicken, scraping her boot back and forth in the dirt wiping it clean.

Chantal joined them, tossed an empty cartridge box aside, and finished reloading. "Those were strange critters. Really long legs. Where did that arrow come from?"

"Ummm," replied Tinker.

Messenger trotted up. "They certainly do leap high in the air." She poked him in the side with her wand. "Why did you bring one of my arrows along?"

Everyone looked at her.

"What?" asked Messenger. She looked at Smoke.

Smoke shrugged a shoulder. "MindMate?"

"Your arrow?" He handed it to Messenger. "Take another look."

Messenger shoved the wand into her left sleeve, grabbed the arrow and did. And nodded. She rubbed a section of the shaft clean, and shoved it at his face. "See? Little green dots. That is mine."

He took it.

"MindMate."

"How did your arrow get here?"

"MindMate."

"My Lord, someone do shoot," stated Chicken firmly.

"MindMate."

"That doesn't make any sense."

"WE HAVE VISITORS, MIND MATE!"

They spun and looked behind them. And at the two figures walking toward them.

"That is a compound bow," said Tinker.

"That is my bow," cried Messenger, yanking her wand from her left sleeve.

"Hi," said the one holding the bow.

"Great Master," said the other.

"Janine?" gasped Chantal.

"Dat?" Tinker stared at them. "Janine?"

R-Bar whipped a bronze wand from somewhere and leaped in front of him. "Demon trick."

"I am not," snapped Dat. "I am a beautiful indjinn."

"Right," said Janine, walking up to them, smiling at Tinker. "She is your very own beautiful indjinn. Large."

Dat nodded.

Tinker glared at them. Over the top of R-Bar's head. "What is going on, Dat?"

Dat scuffed one toe in the dirt, looked embarrassed.

"We came to help," explained Janine.

"You do not look right." Chantal yanked her revolver free, cocked and aimed at Janine. "Everyone step away.

Something is not right."

Dat nudged Janine. "She is just jealous because you are so beautiful."

Tinker sighed. And sat. On a convenient short pillar stump. "I am getting fairly confused. You guys shouldn't be here."

He looked at Ran. "This some sort of illusion? An ark'demon trick?"

Ran shook her head. "The indjinn is the indjinn.

"Smile, Dat." Tinker watched her.

She did.

Tinker nodded. "Long canines all right."

He pointed. "Now you, smile."

Janine bared her teeth at him.

He nodded. "Standard Homo sapiens."

"This is ridiculous," snapped Janine. She stomped over to him. "Gimme my arrow back."

Messenger glared at her. "That is my arrow. You stole my bow and arrows."

Janine glared back. "Dat said I needed a weapon."

Chantal nodded. "Number one on the Archery Team."

"Nothing else handy. Gimme that." Janine grabbed the arrow from Tinker's hand.

"Go home," said Tinker.

Janine shook her head. "You have been gone for a long, long time. I got worried. You said that you would only be gone for a few days. And then I found Dat and then I told Dat to do it, to bring us here, to you. So, that's our story. What's your's?"

"You are taller," said Chantal. "Different."

"Crazy," mumbled Tinker. "This is all getting crazy. Maybe it is the air here in ark'demon land."

Chicken threw an arm around him. "Steady on, My

Lord."

Smoke nudged his other side. "They are Dat and Janine." She bent and whispered in his ear. "She has been horribly injured."

"Dat?"

Janine, replied Smoke.

Janine stepped away and over to Chantal and kissed her on the cheek. "I'll tell you later about, ahh, everything. What were those flying things? They looked really ugly."

Dat stepped close to Tinker. "Great Master, shall I take off her clothes so that you may admire her, she is almost as beautiful as I am." Dat began to unbutton her own shirt. "Now."

"HOLD IT." Tinker glared at the indjinn. "You behave." And looked over at Janine.

Chantal glared at him. "Don't you even think about it. She is keeping her clothes on."

"Go home," said Tinker. "Go home, go home, go home."

Dat looked unhappy.

Janine pushed around her. "NO." And threw her arm around the indjinn. "After all that we have been through, we are staying."

She looked sideways at Chantal. "Can't we?"

Chantal looked at Tinker.

He sighed. And stood. "Let's go talk to those ugly kangaroos. They will probably make more sense."

Grandeville. Red and Sandy's Home.

"Think that I ought to file a missing persons report?"

It was Sunday afternoon. And they were relaxing in the small backyard.

Sandy was lounging. Red was doing something in the

small flower bed.

"No."

"Why not?"

He carefully patted the soil around one of the plants. "Cause she is not missing. She is off running around with some person named Dat."

Sandy looked at him. "You think that it is some guy, don't you?"

Red shrugged. "T. 5 A."

Hmp Zat.

"Sorta like very oversized kangaroo mice."

The ark'demons watched them. They were almost as tall as R-Bar. Short round ears on elongated skulls. Thin bodies. Great long, bent legs.

"Only uglier," added Tinker.

"We really are not much tasty," said one, wringing its hands, hoping to convince these horrible beasts that it was a true statement.

It tried a winning smile. Rows of tiny teeth glistened in the bright light.

Janine spun around, staggered a few steps, and was sick.

Chantal jumped to her side and grabbed her. "What's the matter. You catch the flu before you left?"

"It is them," mumbled Janine. "Every time. I keep remembering . . . being grabbed, and pulled, and poked, and carried to that, that awful place."

She straightened up. "I didn't realize . . . that nightmares . . . could be real."

She glanced from the corners of her eyes at Chantal. "One has stopped. Since you left."

What one?"

Janine's face flushed. "The one with, ummm, him."

"Oh." Chantal rubbed Janine's back. "We found a way around that problem."

She frowned at her friend. "Go home. Everything says that the ones that we are after are even worse than anything you have ever seen."

Janine shook her head.

"This is really dumb, you know."

"I know. But we came to help."

"Then we will have to do something." Chantal reached out. *Smoke.*

NO! His scream staggered them all.

Smoke and Chicken banged inside. *Calm, My Lord. MindMate, calm.* Their arms encircled him. And held tight.

Smoke huffed warm his ear. "You are safe. We will protect you."

"Indeed, Sweet Prince. Do ever that athletic body in warm bed drag thee, We will, with great speed and dispatch, skewer most fair anatomy through and through."

"Ha. Ha." He looked at her. "We are not adding any more. No more."

Dat stepped close. "Great Master, is it true that females of your species often lose their meals in the morning when they are?"

"Huh?" Tinker stared at her.

"DAT!" Janine stormed over, red-faced. "Damn it, I told you to knock it off." She jerked her head sideways. "Gimme that gun, Shooter." She held her hand out.

Chantal jumped further away. "Cool it, Streak."

Tinker looked from person to person. "Now what's going on?"

The rest gathered around.

Janine glared at Dat. And spoke to Tinker. "This, this

person, has a one-track mind. She keeps insisting that we are screwing around and that I must be pregnant."

Chantal stared at him. "Better not be."

He sighed. And frowned. At Dat.

"Great Master?"

"Go home. Take her with you."

Dat shook her head. "I may not."

"What?"

"She does not want to go."

"Merde." He sat. On the ground. "Double, triple, merde."

R-Bar crouched close to him. "Ran and I can do it." She grinned. "Whether she wants to or not."

Janine sat in front of him. "I make my own damn decisions, damn it." She tapped him on the knee. "And I do not like damned interference either."

R-Bar yanked a glittering silver wand from somewhere. The air darkened and thickened around them. The ark'demons began to howl. Ran sucked in her breath.

"Hold it, kiddo." Tinker looked at Janine. "Awful lot of dams around here. For a desert, umm, of some sort."

Janine's eyes jumped around "What's that stuff?"

Dat joined them. "I will be very, very sad if you send me home, Great Master." Tears rolled down her cheeks as she knelt next to Janine.

"Indjinns are supposed to do what they are told to do," he grumbled.

Dat sniffed. "We do not have to like it."

Smoke leaned on his back, arms curled around his chest. "I can bury her nightmare trace." And hugged him. "And nothing else will be changed. That is what Chantal wanted, nothing else."

He looked up at Chicken who was standing near.

"Promise?"

She nodded.

Smoke rubbed the back of his head with her chin. "She has no need. We have no need."

"You're sure?"

"Of course, MindMate. Want to look?"

"NO."

Smoke stood and gave him a hand up as he stood. Then she and Chicken and Chantal led Janine far to one side, away from the ark'demon cage.

R-Bar waved away the dark.

Ran relaxed. Some.

The ark'demons quieted down.

"What's going on?" asked Janine. She didn't like the way Smoke was looking at her.

"Relax," said Chantal. And she explained.

Tinker, R-Bar, and Ran walked over to talk to their prisoners, who were sitting on their haunches, watching these ugly things approaching them.

Everyone else scanned their surrounding.

"Still really horribly ugly," said Janine, staring at the ark'demons. "But at least my stomach is behaving."

"Takes care of that." Smoke walked over to Tinker. "Buried deep."

Chantal slipped her arm around her friend. "We really don't need any help, honest."

Janine nodded. "I saw what happened, what you did, to those things."

An ark'demon came close to the edge of the holding cell. "We do not want to be eaten."

Janine twitched. "Wouldn't think of it."

"Something did." Chantal jerked her thumb up and over one shoulder. "Back there."

The ark'demon looked right and left. "Did you see some?"

"What?" Chantal stared at it.

"Tark."

Janine gasped.

"What?" asked Chantal.

"Tark," repeated the ark'demon.

"Almost got me," whispered Janine. "Me and Dat, called us fine food."

"You also?" asked the ark'demon. "You had better hop carefully, they are sneaky."

It nodded. "With ugly legs like that you will never be able to leap fast enough."

Smoke stepped up behind them and peered over Chantal's shoulder. "Wonder what they taste like?"

The ark'demon hurtled away. And crashed into the far wall of the cage.

"Twitchy, " observed Chantal.

Everyone hurried over to see what was going on. Dat stood next to Smoke, and slid an arm around Janine.

"STOP THAT." Janine slapped at Dat's hand.

"Just checking my handiwork," said Dat.

"Knock it off, " growled Janine.

Tinker frowned at Dat and snarled, "Things were bad enough before you two got here. I don't need any more agitation."

"Damn right," snapped Chantal. "Seven is enough."

Janine looked at her friend.

Tinker exhaled loudly. And beckoned to the ark'demons. "We need your help."

They scuttled over, keeping wary eyes on Smoke.

"Bargain?" asked one.

"Sure," said Tinker.

"What do you want?"

"We want to visit the Dark Ump. And not take any more detours."

He glanced over at R-Bar. She frowned back.

"What do we get?"

"Freedom," said Tinker.

The ark'demons suddenly pressed themselves against the cage wall directly in front of Tinker. And began to shiver. And tried to make themselves small.

"Sssssssssss, save us," cried one.

"Ah ha."

The loud voice came from behind them.

People spun around.

Ark'demons crouched lower.

"Holy crap," gasped Janine. "It's them."

"The Tark broads," said Chantal, yanking her revolver out and up.

The Tark Core Pair approached them, eyes watching the ark'demons.

"Hi there." Tinker stepped toward them.

"Ahamaezur," said one.

"Amamaedur," said the other.

They stopped in front of him. And stood close. Very close. He reached out and touched one. She was right where she appeared to be.

"Tik ar Er," said Ahamaezur.

Amamaedur looked at Janine, then Dat. "Fine food." And clacked her teeth softly.

"Ahhhh, Ladies," said Tinker. "Can you go somewhere else? We were trying to talk with these ark'demons."

"Talk," said Ahamaezur, patting his lips. Behind them, the secondary males began to slip from the grey pool. They fanned out. And began to gather up the ark'demon bodies.

"Waste not, want not." Tinker looked at Ahamaezur. "How did you know my name?"

"My fault," said Janine, from behind him. "I asked them where you'd gone. After they had finished mauling me."

He looked around. "What?"

"Tell you when we get home. I'd rather not talk about it now." Janine swallowed hard and stared at the males. They were carrying arm loads of ark'demons into the grey pool. One or two of them taking a quick bite as they walked down.

"Tik ar Er," said Ahamaezur, reaching up and touching one side of his face.

Amamaedur touched the other side of his face. "Tik ar Er."

They both stepped back, spun, and bounded after the secondary males.

Tinker blew out his breath, and sighed. "Always feel like they are about to do something. Violent."

Chantal eased the hammer on her revolver back down and jammed the weapon back into its hoister. And looked at Janine. "You don't look so good. Why not go home?"

Janine shook her head. "No. Staying."

Chantal nodded. "Always stubborn. Just aim away from me when you get sick."

"ARE THEY GONE?" One ark'demon was standing on fully extended legs, peering at the grey pool.

Tinker turned around. "Looks like it. How come you, ahhhh, guys built your village so close to that . . . pool?" He pointed at the grey swirling fogmist.

The ark'demon settled back on its feet, rocking back and forth. "What's a village?"

"Ummm, homes."

It rippled its upper lip. "Those are not homes. Those are . . . "

"Bargain, bargain," pipped the other, kicking the slightly larger one.

"Deeeeeeee," squealed the one just kicked.

"Fellas. Hey, fellas. You going to bargain or what?" The ark'demons stared at him.

"How do we get to the Dark Ump?" demanded Tinker.

"Freedom?" asked the larger.

"No eat?" added the smaller.

"A real deal," said Tinker.

"In there." The ark'demon pointed at the pillar maze. "Two tall, two short, one flat, and two close." It held one clawed paw close to the ground. "Entrance to Dark Ump."

The other pressed against the cage wall. "Do not tell, do not tell."

Tinker nodded. "We won't. Let 'em go, Ran."

Ran nodded and tapped the cage with a dark wand. The holding cell disappeared. She sagged against him.

The ark'demons leaped away, bounding high, traveling as fast as they could go.

"Tired, Amtar," mumbled Ran.

"Better camp right here. We can go on after we all rest up." He looked for a good, flat spot.

After they had finished their meal, and as the camp was being set up, Janine grabbed Dat and pulled her to one side.

"We don't have any camping gear."

"I do not require camping gear," said Dat.

"Well, I do."

Dat pointed. "There." A sleeping bag, mat, pillow, sat

on the ground, next to Janine's feet.

"Thanks."

Dat smiled. "You going to become one of his houris?"

Janine frowned, exhaled loudly, and snatched up her gear. "NO. I am not." And stalked over to where Chantal was laying out her stuff. "Kin I sleep over here, next to you?"

Chantal nodded. "Sure. Lots of room."

Janine knelt and began shoving things into place. "He isn't going to get mad at me, or anything, is he?"

Chantal sat on her bag and yanked off her boots. "About what?"

"My sleeping here? With you? Getting in the way?" Janine's face flushed.

Chantal smiled. "Don't worry about it." She watched R-Bar swirl dark around and overhead.

Janine jerked. "What's that stuff?"

"Protection. Keeps the bad guys away while we sleep."

"Oh."

Chantal loosened her clothes, stretched out and flapped her bag closed. "Don't worry. You are safe." She laid her revolver next to her boots, just above her head. "Relax."

Janine laid down and stared up. Dark red eyes peered down from the swirling black clouds. "Weird."

"Belongs to R-Bar. Sort of a pet."

Janine rolled onto her side, reached over and touched Chantal. "Maybe I should have stayed at home."

Dark grey-green eyes stared at her as Chantal rolled onto her side. "Kinna late for that." She threw her bag back. "These things zip together."

And after they had rearranged everything and settled down, Dat walked over. And peered down at them. She smiled at Chantal. "Are you going to inspect my handiwork?

It is really beautiful."

"Go away, Dat," mumbled Janine. "We are trying to sleep." She glared up at the indjinn. "And that is all."

Dat nodded, and smiled at Chantal. "She is really nice." And stepped over them and laid down next to Fair Morn.

"Isn't that uncomfortable?" asked Fair Morn.

"No."

"You can share my bag."

Dat touched the bag and the mat. They became a double. "You are welcome." And slipped inside. "Who put you together?"

"Long story." Fair Morn grabbed Dat's hand. "Stop that."

"Pretty nice."

"You ever get punched in the nose?"

Dat lay back. "That is not nice."

"Go to sleep."

Dat nodded. And did.

And one by one by one by one.
Everyone else did.

Chapter Eighteen

Things Just Never Work Out As Expected.

Hmp Zat.

"O.K. We all ready?"

They had eaten, packed their gear, and were standing, ready to go.

He looked around.

At them.

At their surroundings.

And at the pillar maze.

"Guess so." He pointed. "Fair Morn, left side. Ran and R-Bar, right side. Smoke, Chantal, in the back. Chicken, Messenger, and I go first. Janine, you stay with Chantal. Dat, you stay out of the way. O.K.?"

He heard seven say "yes."

And looked at Janine. "From this moment on, you do exactly what anyone, except Dat, tells you to do. Understand?" He whirled away and started walking into the pillar maze.

Janine looked at Chantal.

"For your own good," said Chantal.

"He angry about something?" Janine shifted the bow to her left hand.

"Nope. Nervous. Ahhhhhh, Streak?"

"What?"

"Don't be surprised by anything that you see. And stick real close to Smoke. Everyone else may be too busy to keep an eye out for you."

Janine nodded, and looked at Smoke.

Smoke winked at her.

Dat walked close to Tinker. And grumbled at him.

"Shhh," he said.

And pointed.

The path turned between the first pair of pillars.

And turned again.

And again.

Tinker reached up and around. And swung the great black sword down. He nodded to himself, always amazed at how easy it felt to do that. And how easy the weaponkin made it feel.

His arm tingled. The old familiar tingle. Of the sword taking control. Ready to begin killing things.

He felt them all, all of himself, getting ready. Being ready.

He stepped in.

Into the world of the Dark Ump.

Tang Lerg.

It leaped at him.

From one side, it leaped.

All dark shadow and angle spines.

And crashed into a loose limbed heap.

The explosion echoed from nearby hills. One single sharp explosion.

Chantal had blown away half its head.

Janine stared. At her friend.

"Lots of practice. Every Saturday. Rain, shine, snow,

or sleet. Just me and the mail man." She laughed.

"I blew it, didn't I?" Janine stared at the ground.

"What?"

"You don't need any help."

"Right. Keep your eyes peeled. Smoke?"

Smoke looked at Chantal. Great orange gold eyes grew wide. Then wider. Larger and larger.

Suddenly her pupils dilated, crowding the color into a thin edge. "Uhhhhh." Liquid trickled from the corners of her mouth. Her fingers jerked as she lurched toward them. "Uhhhhhhh."

Chantal leaped forward. And punched. Her fist caught Smoke on the side of the jaw.

Smoke crumpled.

Janine screamed, "HELLLLLPPPPP."

Chicken spun and ran back toward them. The rest stood in place, watching everywhere.

"Frothing." Janine pointed at Smoke. "Frothing at the mouth, making horrible noises."

Chantal rubbed her hand. "Decked her, Princess." And carefully flexed her fingers. And watched Chicken as she knell and carefully began to check Smoke.

"Most strange. None do feel this thing."

Fair Morn joined them. "I will carry her."

"I will do that." Dat stepped up, bent and lifted the limp form in her arms. And looked at Chicken. "Shall I take her home?"

"NO." shouted Chantal, grabbing one of Dat's arms.

Chicken touched Chantal on the arm and spoke to the startled indjinn. "Sweet Dat, separation t'would most fatal be. Praps for us all."

Dat nodded.

Janine whispered to Chantal, "What is she talking

about?"

"Not now, " said Chantal.

Tinker pointed. "Over there. On top of that hill."

They looked. A low structure squatted there, half-hidden by trees and thick underbrush.

Fair Morn nodded. And took aim.

"HOLD IT." Tinker shook his head. "Not yet." He beckoned over the two witches.

"Can you guys do something for Smoke?"

They stepped over to Dat.

R-Bar tapped Dat on the arm. "Better set her down. Don't want spell splash to touch you."

Dat did. And stepped back.

The witch pair sat on the ground next to Smoke and began to poke and prod her with glistening purple wands.

"Must be them," growled R-Bar.

Ran looked up at Tinker. "Dark Ump."

They set to work.

It leaped at her.

From behind, it leaped.

All dark shadow and angle spines.

And wrapped around her.

And dragged her backwards, kicking and struggling, mouthing words no-one could hear.

"SHOOOOOOOOTER!" Janine screamed and ran, legs pumping hard.

To one side.

After them.

She stopped, whirled, and fired.

The first arrow smacked into its side. The second smashed through the skull and out the other side.

Chicken hurtled past Janine, snatched a knife from her boot, and began to hack away some of the stuff still clenching wrapped around Chantal. Chantal heaved violently, twisting free, eyes jerking. And sagged.

Chicken tossed a large piece of the thing to one side, cleaned her knife and stood, stuffed the blade back into her boot. She bent over, her palm making a loud crack as it banged against Chantal's face.

"Obscene," mumbled Chantal.

"Shooter?" Janine leaned over and stared at her friend.

"Wench," snapped Chicken. "Watch for more of them?"

She knelt and wiped Chantal's face with her sleeve. "Sweet Doctor of Animals, how fare thee?"

Chantal's eyes focused on Chicken's face. "Those things need killing in the worse possible way," she rasped. "Princess, there is something wrong. With me." And collapsed.

Tinker stepped over to Fair Morn. "O.K., Killer Moth, sterilize this area. Hundred feet or so ought to do it. For now. All the way around."

Fair Morn did

They stood.

In the center of a bare circle. And watched all around the outer edge. Dark swirled and rumbled around the three figures in the center, totally obscuring them.

Dat crouched over Chantal and touched the thing still tangled stuck around her. It disappeared.

Chantal sagged flat on her back.

Dat reached over and began to unbutton Chantal's shirt.

"Fair Dat?" Chicken frowned at the indjinn.

"Not too messy," said Dat, yanking the garment open.

"You screw with my . . . my anatomy, and I'll blow your butt off," mumbled Chantal.

"I thought that you people could take care of yourselves." Janine stared at Chantal, tears running unattended down her cheeks.

Tinker walked toward them. He stepped carefully around the grumbling clouds in the center, slapped the great sword onto his back, and looked over Dat's shoulder as she set to work on Chantal. Chantal stifled a groan.

"Time for Plan B," he said.

Janine whirled around and slapped his face.

He stared at her. "We done having hysterics?" He blocked her second attempt. "We don't have time for this right now . You can beat me up after we get back home."

He turned his back on her. "Dat?"

"I am done, Great Master. Your houri is fixed."

He peered down at Chantal. "Looks about the same to me. Yum, yum, yum."

"Lech," grumbled Chantal. "Help me stand. And get me another shirt."

He helped her up. "Really. Looks pretty all right. Never know anything was done. Mostly."

Dat nodded. "Not bad. Not as beautiful as me, but not too bad." She handed Chantal a new shirt.

"Indjinns always this egocentric?" Chantal shrugged on her new shirt.

Tinker nodded at Chantal. "Hollywood starlets would pay a fortune to have that treatment." He nodded again, bent, grabbed the two arrows lying there, straightened, turned, handed them to Janine. "Here."

He spun away. And hurried over to the black chaos in

the center of their bare space.

"Nothing wrong with that," mumbled Dat.

"What are you guys doing in there, having a party?" Tinker peered into the black, and then walked over to Messenger.

"Heartless creep," snarled Janine.

"Button it up," grumbled Chantal. She stomped away to speak with Fair Morn.

He fluffed Messenger's hair. "See anything out there, kitten?"

"My Lord do most vexed and worried be." Chicken thumped Janine on the chest with the hilt of her sword. "And do himself wish us not to know of such concern."

"Yucko," replied Messenger. "Black, twisted. Spinning straight up." Her eyes flickered toward Janine. "She should not slap you." Even in the bright light, he could see the green glow, fluxing in her eyes.

He slipped an arm around her shoulders. "Just worried about Chantal, I guess."

Messenger leaned against his side.

Behind them the black covering flared blue. And disappeared.

"Dim, dim, dim, dim, dim, dim," growled R-Bar as she leaped to her feet and glared up the hill at the structure. Somewhere something rumbled.

"NO," shouted Ran, mashing a deep red crystal sphere into Smoke. "NO."

"How is she?" Tinker and Messenger had walked over to them.

Ran stood. "In this demonplace we can do no more. "

Dat joined them. "Great Master," she said, bending and lifting Smoke in her arms. "I will carry her. And protect her. For you."

Tinker nodded and hurried over to Fair Morn. He pointed at the path wending up the side of the hill. "Looks like it leads up to that building. Clean everything from both sides of the path. Once we get to the front door we can decide what comes next."

Fair Morn nodded. "Right as rain, booby-duck."

He stared at her.

"Minor levity, One." She poked him in the stomach with one fingertip. "You putting on some weight?" And laughed.

"Let's go," he grumbled.

She nodded, turned, and fired.

Twice.

"Well, do we knock, or blow it in?"

They stood in front of the building, in front of the large, they hoped main entrance door, they stood in the clearing, and looked at the door.

A few moments earlier this space had not been a clearing. But Fair Morn had taken care of that.

"Praps, Me'Lord, some small thump pon great door might be in order?" Chicken kicked a small cobble lose and picked it up. It had one mirror-smooth flat surface. She approached, door-knocker in hand. And smashed it against the front panel.

The door thumped.

A dull hollow thump.

She struck it again.

From the other side they could hear faint noise. The door swung inward.

Very, very slowly, it swung inward.

Chicken backed up until she stood near Tinker and tossed the rock to one side. And rubbed her hand across her mouth.

"Princess?"

She bent and yanked the blade from her boot, and watched the entrance, sword in one hand, knife in the other, face grim.

He looked at the rest of them.

Weapons and weapon users appeared ready. He nodded at Janine. She stood near Chantal and held the bow, arrow already resting in place, in her left hand.

She nodded back.

They waited.

"Pretty dark in there."

He leaned in and backed up. "I suppose we could shoot a hole in the roof."

"No need, Amtar." Ran tossed a small crystal sphere through the open door. The interior glowed with softlight.

Tinker sucked in a deep breath and slowly blew it out.

"O.K., let's go in and visit."

His hand snapped around and pointed. "Dat, stay outside. Ummmmm? Should someone else stay out here with you and Smoke?"

Dat shook her head. "No need, Great Master. I will protect her."

He nodded. And waved. And stepped in through the door, Chicken on one side, Fair Morn on the other.

They walked into a long, curving hall. It bent, twisting to their right.

"Not good." He stopped. "Chantal, you and Ms. Hood watch our backs. Ran, can you keep pitching light balls or whatever those things are ahead of us?"

"Yes, Amtar."

He looked at R-Bar. "What do you think, kiddo?"

"Bad place, Tink. Magic dampened." She shifted uneasily.

"Ummmm. Let's go. But carefully, O.K.?"

They started walking, slowly, carefully, watching everything. There was nothing to see.

The hall kept twisting around. And down. And inward.

Chantal and Janine kept checking behind. Janine touched her friend on the arm. Gently.

"How does he do that?"

"What?"

"Carry that huge sword that way?"

"It has something to do with the nature of that thing."

"Shooter, when we get back, you and I have to have a long, long talk."

"Bout?"

Janine snorted. "Lots of things. That sword. Smoke. Dat. A red box that holds strange conversations. Here. There. And everywhere."

"O.K." Chantal spun around. "Hear something?"

"Uh huh."

"Bout time," said Tinker, as they stepped into the chamber, suddenly illuminated by Ran.

Large dark forms clustered around some other large dark thing at the other end of the chamber.

Tinker and group could see images moving on its surface.

"Probably Lucy reruns," mumbled Tinker.

But as they walked closer, they could see what it really was.

"It's us. On candid camera." He stopped.

And waited.

And waited.

And waited.

And then he nodded.

To himself.

And called. "LET'S MAKE A DEAL." And looked at Chicken. "Think I should try Wheel Of Fortune?"

"Tis nay time for to make jests poor, My Lord."

"I suppose ." He checked everyone. "O.K., then." And stepped a little closer to the things.

"Hey there."

Dark Ump slowly turned and looked at them.

"We are from the FCC," called Tinker. "We are here to cancel your broadcasting licence."

One sprang at him. Two pieces thrashed violently on the floor. The black sword sang a song of violence and blood thirst.

"Next." He pointed. With the weaponkin. "Mothra, shoot that TV set."

"STOP!" A Dark Ump pushed through the cluster, sent slither at them.

Lightening flashed. R-Bar slumped. Ran grabbed her and held her up. Dark Ump recoiled.

"Tink," gasped R-Bar. "Can't do that much in here."

The demon stepped closer. "Go back, go back."

Suddenly the monster flew backward. And crashed to the floor.

Fair Morn had drilled a hole through it, the image device, and out. Daylight poured through the hole.

And was pinched out. Everything repaired itself.

"Now what?" Tinker stared at the things.

"Go back," they said.

He shook his head. "Nope. We came to get the touch left on us by the Chan Narh." Tinker waggled the great sword at them. "The one traded to you by . . . ummmmm?"

"There are no Ummmmm," stated the largest of the Dark Ump. "They were oku z'mu by Zqtor."

"Appbzan Riam ar Npkn," hissed R-Bar.

It snarled at her. "Who told you?"

"None of your business, mak plak."

It stalked forward. "None of your feeble spells, or other strangeness, can affect the Dark Ump." It glared down at her. "We have your touch."

Chicken stabbed it in the side. Her hand and knife passed through.

"Go back," it said. "We would have arpak."

Tinker stared at the demon he had cut in half. It stared back at him.

"Go back," it said, standing, whole again.

"Time for Plan C," said Tinker.

"My Lord?"

He shrugged. "Haven't thought of it, Princess. Yet."

"Great Master?"

He whirled around.

Dat walked across the open space toward them. She still held Smoke cradled in her arms.

"Told you to stay outside," he grumbled.

"Do you require assistance?"

Janine stomped over and slammed the indjinn on the shoulder. "What kind of a dummy are you anyway?"

She glared at Tinker. "I'd find other ring if I was you."

And spun back to Dat. "OF COURSE WE NEED ASSISTANCE." She turned and shot an arrow at the Dark Ump. The arrow passed through and banged off the far wall. "See?"

Dat nodded. "Someone will have to hold Smoke."

Fair Morn shoved her cannon into its holster, stepped close and slipped her arms under Dat's and lifted Smoke free.

Chantal yanked Janine away. "Cool it, Streak."

Dat shook her head.

Tinker sighed.

"Someone," said Dat softly.

Tinker stared at her. "Someone?"

Dat nodded. "Shall I bring them here?"

"Sure. Who ever." He held up one hand. "Not yet." And turned back. And back again, grabbing one of Dat's hands. Then he tugged her over to the Dark Ump spokes thing.

He looked up at the demon. "This is Dat, my very own personal indjinn."

It stared down at Dat. "Go back, you can do nothing here."

"My Great Master wishes to retrieve the touch."

"Go back."

"We will bargain," stated Dat firmly.

"We have the touch. You have nothing. Go back."

"You will die."

The Dark Ump laughed And crowded closer to them. It glared down at Dat. "You can do nothing here, little indjinn."

She glanced over at Tinker. He sighed. And looked up. "Let's bargain."

"Go back."

"Go ahead," said Tinker, yanking Dat backward, making space between them and the demon.

She nodded. "It will be as you wish, Great Master." She made an opening.

And they padded through.

On soft silent feet.

They padded through.

Coming through.

Dark Ump screamed. And ran. And were kept from leaving the great chamber as the Core Pair and the four Prime Males sprang. And bore down the Dark Ump speaker.

Janine spun away, stomach heaving up and down, barely in control.

"YUCKO," cried Messenger, hiding her face against Fair Morn's side.

"MY LORD!" shouted Chicken, leaping to his side.

"AH HA," called Ahamaezur as she stood and wiped the gore from her face, turned and smiled at Tinker.

"You?" He stared at the pair.

"It's the Tark broads," said Chantal.

Ahamaezur waved the Prime Males over. And tapped a bent over figure on the back. She straightened, turned around, and wiped her face clean.

"Tik ar Er," she said. "Ah ha."

"Hi," he said, stepping over to them. "Don't kill everything. They have something we came for."

Ahamaezur snarled at the secondary males and fringe females who had poured into the space and who had begun to feed. They hastily backed away, dropping bits and pieces.

Moaning softly, Janine spun away from the sight.

"Most ghastly," said Chicken.

Ran wrapped R-Bar in her arms and began whispering in her ear. R-Bar nodded.

Smoke twitched and mumbled something.

Tinker stepped toward the Dark Ump, who were crowding back, watching the Tark demons. Tinker was flanked by the Core Pair. "Someone want to bargain?"

A Dark Ump stepped forward. "Bargain?"

Tinker swung his great sword up and over his left shoulder, onto his back. "Right."

"How bargain?"

"We want the touch. Hand it over."

"What bargain?" demanded the demon.

Tinker leaned forward. "You give us the touch. And we keep you from becoming Tarkburgers."

The Dark Ump stared at him. "Tarkburgers?"

"Eaten," snapped Tinker.

"Nothing controls the Pla Dar," stated the demon. "You have no bragindark."

"Umm." Tinker looked and reached out. Ahamaezur was exactly where she appeared to be. He snaked an arm around her waist and yanked her against his side. And then be pulled Amamaedur over against his other side.

"Let's go over that again," he said to the Dark Ump.

The demon stared down at him. "What are you?"

"Just someone who doesn't like being spied upon. Shall we bargain?"

Ahamaezur looked at Tinker. "Barghan."

"Ah ha," said Amamaedur.

Chantal nudged Janine. "You can turn around now. The feeding frenzy is over. I think."

Janine did. And whispered. "What is he doing?"

"Beats me. Since we've been here in Dark Ump land, we have been closed off from each other."

Dat walked over to them. And glared at Janine. "You are not nice. I am sorry that I made you so beautiful."

Janine blinked. "Sorry Dat. Really." She touched the indjinn's shoulder. "Really."

Chantal threw an arm around Janine. "She really is, Dat. She just gets a little excited, that's all."

"I accept your apology." Dat smiled at Janine. "When we return to my Great Master's house, are you going to . . . "

"Come on, come on, come on." R-Bar grabbed Chantal and Dat by an arm and yanked them over to the tight cluster standing not too far behind Tinker and the Tark.

"You too," she snapped at Janine. Ran was pushing all the others close together.

"Bargain," said Tinker to the Dark Ump. Ahamaezur nuzzled the side of his face and clacked her teeth softly against Tinker's ear, her lips lightly tickling.

Chantal reached for her revolver.

"Careful," hissed R-Bar, grabbing Chantal's arm.

"Bargain," demanded Tinker.

Amamaedur gestured angrily at one of the males. He jerked and quickly threw back the Dark Ump he had just grabbed.

"Bargain," said the demon.

"Good," replied Tinker, releasing the two Tark, slipping his arms free. "I want that touch."

The demon turned and walked to the back wall, touched the viewing device, and removed something. And walked back, holding out its arms. A golden rod gleamed and flashed sparkled in its hands.

"This is the Chan Narh touch bought from the Appbzan Riam ar Npkn worthless one."

Tinker gently pushed the Tark Core Pair further away and held out his hands. The Dark Ump set the touch in his open palms.

And all of them jerked. Smoke's eyes had just popped open.

R-Bar yanked out an orange wand. Ran threw and leaped and grabbed him by the belt.

Tinker yelled as he was snatched backward into the crystal sphere.

And. Then.

They.

     Were.

Gone.

Chapter Nineteen

Well, It Is Always Good To Be Home.

Grandeville. Tinker's Place.

Dat squeaked as Janine hastily snatched her up out of the deep grass of the first pasture as Janine stumbled sideways and sagged against Chantal.

Tinker staggered and crashed into Chicken who grabbed him. "Steady on, My Lord. We do be a'home."

"We are not doing too well," he mumbled, clenching the touch in one hand as he threw an arm over her shoulder. He looked at them.

Smoke hung limply in Fair Morn's arms. Both witches were sprawled loosely in the grass.

And Janine was weeping in Chantal's arms as Dat stood on Janine's shoulder and growled into her ear.

Two figures leaped up from the lounge on the rear deck and charged toward them. One ran. One lumbered.

She pounded up to him, her eyes checking his face carefully. "DAD! What have you been doing? You have been gone for over a long time."

Then she stared at them. "What is wrong with my Moms?"

And then she noticed Janine. And started to laugh. "Oh, Father? You didn't? Not again."

She quickly counted.

"NO!" Tinker shook his head. "Tell you later."

He nudged Chicken. "We have got to get them all inside. Get some help." She nodded and stepped away.

"Oh, Daddie, I will take care of that."

Chantal turned Janine around and walked her over to them. "Sedeem, this is Janine, an old friend of mine. She came to help us. Big mistake. Janine, this is our daughter, Sedeem, and her husband, Farth."

R-Bar mumbled. And sat up. "It worked."

She shook Ran. Ran wobbled limply. R-Bar shook her again. "Tanpak witch, it worked."

Ran rolled over and batted weakly at R-Bar's hand. "Just fine," she mumbled.

Messenger and Chicken walked over and helped them stand.

Smoke jerked violently, startling Fair Morn.

Sedeem stepped away from Tinker and walked over to Fair Morn. "Better lay her down, Mom."

Fair Morn did, and jumped back as Smoke's eyes flew open and wide. Smoke bounded to her feet. "MIND MATE!"

"We're home," said Tinker. He held out the long rod and waggled it at them. "And we've got the Chan Narh touch. Let's go sit on the deck."

Sedeem walked by his side. "Dad, what have you been doing? This time? Everyone really looks awful."

"Later," he mumbled.

Dat leaped from Janine's shoulder to Chantal's. "I am small again."

"Dat?"

"What?"

"Big or small, I am glad that you were around. You saved our butts back there. Thanks."

"I did, didn't I?" Dat sat and kicked her legs happily, clenching the collar of Chantal's shirt.

"Everyone owes you thanks," said Janine. "Especially me. So, thanks Dat. For everything."

"You are welcome."

"You want some cocoa?"

Dat jumped up, leaped to Janine's shoulder, and kissed her on the cheek. Then, grabbing a handful of hair, she leaned forward and peered down. "They are very beautiful. Yum, yum, yum, yum, yum."

Janine laughed.

They sprawled in the living room.
Clean.
Relaxed.
Sipping this and that.
Everyone wore pajamas.
Except for Dat.

The indjinn was sitting on top of the back of one of the couches, still grumbling about being small again, dressed in her preferred costume, or lack of costume. She was watching Tinker.

He was sitting on the edge of the same couch, tickling Smoke, who was sitting with her back against the arm, legs stretched out and over his lap, back propped up with large cushions.

"I am not ticklish."

"Spoil Sport."

"Giggle, giggle."

"Much better." He checked her glass. "How you feeling?"

"I am well. Our daughter has many skills."

Sedeem plopped down next to them. "Thanks, Mom." She grinned at Tinker. "So, where did your new babe go, Pop?"

He frowned. And sighed. "She is not my new anything."

Chantal leaned over the couch back, avoided Dat, and refilled Smoke's glass. "I loaned her our truck. She'll bring it back tomorrow." Then she ruffled Tinker's hair. "So you can just relax, Simba leader."

He grumbled at her. "I wasn't not relaxing. Where is that touch?"

"I put it . . . away, Dad." The blue flared and quickly faded in her eyes. "Tell me how to find those Dark Ump."

Dat barked at Sedeem. "You do not want to go there." She shook her head violently back and forth.

Sedeem looked at the indjinn. "Yes, I do." Her eyes flared again.

"NO!" Dat leaped up, ran to the end of the couch, jumped onto Smoke, crawled up and huddled in the space between Smoke's head and the couch back. And stared at Tinker.

He stared back.

"Do not sell me," cried Dat, pushing one arm deep into Smoke's hair.

"Dat?" asked Tinker.

"Promise," wept the tiny figure crumbling into a dejected heap, hands now covering her face.

Messenger carried a chair over and sat close by. "Why are you abusing Dat?"

"I am not."

"She is crying."

"Nothing that I did."

Chicken walked in from the kitchen via the dining

room. "Sweet Prince Our Own, for why do our most fair Dat weep so?"

"He has been abusing her," replied Messenger.

"Dad," gasped Sedeem, stifling her giggle.

Chantal walked around and massaged Tinker's shoulder muscles. "Yah, pick on someone your own size."

He reached back and tickled her.

Dat peeked at him through her fingers.

R-Bar banged down a chair as she joined the group. "You may not sell her, Tink. She is a gift."

"Yah," added Messenger.

Dat sat up, arched her back, and nodded at him.

"Ah ha."

Everyone jerked, heads snapping around.

"OH." Fair Morn stared back at them. "Sorry. I just saw Ran bringing the cocoa."

"Thank you," said Dat, jumping upon the arm rest so she could dip her cup in the pan that Ran held low.

Tinker waited until they were all settled down. Then he leaned forward. "O.K., what did you do?"

"Made cocoa, Amtar." Ran looked at the pan, then at Tinker. And frowned

"Dat," said Tinker.

Dat held her cup in both hands. "Your black houris did it." She took a sip.

"Huh?" He stared at the indjinn. Then shifted his gaze to R-Bar and Ran. R-Bar shrugged one shoulder.

"We left too fast," said Dat, resettling herself between Smoke's head and the couch.

"What is that supposed to mean?" growled R-Bar, leaning sideways to stare around Smoke's head at the indjinn.

Dat walked across and down Smoke's chest and stood on her stomach, and looked up at Tinker. "I did not have a chance to close the hole I made."

"What hole?" He stared at her. "Where?"

Dat nodded. "The one that the Tark used."

"Oh," said Tinker. "I see." He sat back, and sighed.

Chantal's hands tightened on his shoulders. "The Tark babes. They will be able to run back and forth whenever they feel like it." She patted his shoulder, leaned forward and kissed the side of his neck. "Well, all I can say to that, John, is . . . bon appetite. That bunch of perverted peeping demons deserve it. Or deserved it. As the case may be."

She straightened up and wrapped her arms around him.

He sighed, heavily, and leaned against her.

Sedeem gently touched his knee. "Dad?"

"We are gonna rank right up there with the S.S.," he grumbled.

Chicken leaned on the back of the couch, arms crossed, and shook her head. "Pish tosh, My Lord, tis nay fault of thine."

R-Bar leaped to her feet. "That reminds me." She smiled. And looked at Ran. "Ran, we have a certain demon to talk to."

Ran nodded.

The two witches walked out the front door, arm in arm.

Fair Morn smiled at Smoke. "How do you feel?"

"Like a steak, or two. With all the trimmings."

"Me too," said Fair Morn. "I'll cook." She handed Smoke a large, ornate ring. "You owe me."

Smoke leered at Tinker.

"And," cautioned Fair Morn as she headed for the kitchen, "don't wear him out."

The loud sigh was Tinker.

Smothered by everyone's laughter.

Grandeville. Red and Sandy's Home.

The pounding, thumping, door-bell chiming, clanging, and banging, interrupted their dinner.

Red looked at Green, and headed for the front door.

Green waved Sandy to stay where she was and slipped out the kitchen door and headed out and around the house.

Red waited, hand on the door knob, counting to himself. Then he nodded. And yanked the door open.

Janine screamed. And blushed. Then she jerked. She had just felt Green's presence behind her.

"Find Tinker?" asked Red.

Janine started to shiver. "Lemme in."

Green touched her shoulder. With one finger. "You all right?"

"Yep. Sure. Fine. Peachy keen. All right. O.K." She wiped the sweat from her forehead. "Actually. Not so good." And started to sag.

Green scooped her up.

"Nice catch, " said Red, stepping back inside the house.

Sandy pointed at the couch. "There's fine." She knelt next to Janine as soon as Green moved away. "Hey, Streak, you wanna tell us where you've been?"

"Uh uh."

Red dropped a blanket on Janine, then carefully straightened it out. "Stay there."

Green pulled a chair over and sat. "I suppose this means we lose at bowling again."

Janine tried to sit up. "You bet."

Green's forefinger centered between her eyes on her forehead held her down, She rolled her eyes at Sandy.

"What?"

"No Doctor."

Sandy nodded. "Sure?"

"Right. I am fine. Really. Just a sort of delayed shock." Janine smiled at them. "Go eat. I could smell it through the door. Curry, right?"

Green stood. "You hungry?

"Sure."

"Stay there. I'll get you a plate."

The three of them went back to their dinner in the kitchen.

Green heaped a plate full. "Big eater as I remember." He looked at Red. "She look different to you?"

Red nodded.

Sandy smiled at Green.

"Can't you control your attorney, partner?" Green headed for the living room, carrying the plate, holding a fork in his free hand.

"Well?" asked Sandy, looking at Red.

"T. 5 A., babe."

Individuals Of Note

Grandeville.

Tinker's Place
John Tinker -- the individual used as an intermediary by Big Red in his ongoing activities to maintain the balance of the universes. During his initial time on Mirk Wild Weald, Tinker was told by The Thought that he is The Chosen One of legend. Now merged telepathically into an entity with the rest following the cultural values of Smoke's people.
Smoke of the Velvetmist - a gigantic, telepathic carnivore, now transformed into a human shape by Big Red. She was selected from her home, a hidden and never visited elseplace, to be one of the original companions to aid and journey with John Tinker. Now MindMate to Tinker, Chicken and the rest.
Princess Chicken - an Easter Season fluffy chicken toy from an Easter basket, transformed by Big Red and placed as a traveling companion and aid for John Tinker.
Messenger - Once "The Messenger" of her people but joined with Tinker and the rest when she began to fold inside herself believing Tinker and crew were monsters and demons from her folk's mythology come alive.
Fair Morn - a one-time mythological jest created by the magical force, Big Red. Messenger severed her magical bonds changing Fair Morn from jest to an alive person.
R-Bar - a witch of The Faan clan, now joined into the polyorganism of Tinker and the rest by Smoke.
      Sedeem - her daughter, a magician.

Farth - her mate-for-life, a Silver Ranger.
Ferrelden - of the Risshar, a Night Runner from Zhorndar'h. (Deceased).
Flar - one time owner of a Magical Items Shop. (Deceased.)
Chantal Baire - a Veterinarian with a clinic near Grandeville.
Ran - witch of the Tanpak clan. Prefers to be called Ran.

Chantal's Friends
Frederica Hensler - "Freddie" - lives in Portland.
      Ralph Andervante - her husband
Sandrew Sherl Sandermeyer now **Anderson** - "Sandy" - Tinker's Attorney.
      Red - her husband, a member of the Grandeville Police
      Department.
Janine Teacate - "Streak" - Sandy's secretary.

Chen's Chinese - The Building.
Adam Lieu Chen - Master Chen owns and operates *Chen's Chinese,* a restaurant located in Greater Downtown Grandeville. He also trains Tinker in the martial arts.

Dragon Ranch - not far from Tinker's Place.
Prince Goose - a windup plastic toy transformed by Big Red into a traveling companion for John Tinker. Goose commands The Guard, a number of warriors vaguely reminiscent of Grenadier Guards. He is a brother of Chicken.
Chen Gum Lung - The Golden Dragon of the House of Chen. A sometimes amulet gifted to Tinker by Master Chen.

Doc's Home
Kappa "Doc" Heckmann - anthropologist and adventurer. A friend and neighbor of John Tinker's.
J. C. Smith - one of Tinker's close friends. He works for Doc

in many capacities.

      Reep - of the Faan witch clan, married to J. C.

          Szaifeh - her daughter, a witch.

Membrane - one of Doc's "associates." He run Doc's stores, *Cactus Spine*, specializing in cacti and succulents.

Badnews Treefalls - another of Doc's "associates." He is Doc's constant companion.

The Hardcastle Residence.

Alandale Fredrico Hardcastle IV, known as "Hard" by all his friends.

      Ramp - of the Faan witch clan, a magician, his wife.

          Sa'ar - her twin daughter, a magician.

          Shem - her twin son, a magician, also known by his parents and grandparents as Alandale Fredrico Hardcastle V.

              Tajaar - his wife.

Grandeville Police Department (GPD)

Red and **Green** - two very large men who once played football together on the local college team. They function, usually, as the late night patrol. They are good friends of Tinker, J. C., and Hard.

The Elseplaces

Paradise.

Big Red - a pure force of magic personified. He is primarily concerned with maintaining the balance and order of the universe of universes. And, more often than not, has some influence over the events that plague Tinker.

      Dancing-All-The-Day - Big Red's wife.

Silly-All-The-Day - their son.
Treena - the wife of Silly.

Various - depending upon mood.
Dram - an individual often called The Evil One. He began life on Murk Wild Weald as a magician-in-training. But after long and secretive study in The Library of Arcana he slowly was transformed by his knowledge and his ambitions into one of the few pure forces in the universe of universes. Dram has a tendency to work at living up to his title.

Stumpf.
The-Mountain-That-Walks - an individual most often addressed as Mountain by his traveling companions. He is one of the original companions, selected from Stumpf, to aid John Tinker.

A Place Unnamed.
Macabre - who specializes in killing things. He is usually accompanied by his pets: The Vipers, and the Sparkling Tigers.
Gyre - his female companion, created by his vessel, Gyreship.

The Six Lands.
Sorrowful Mistidings - a professional Teller of Tales, selected from The Six Lands, as one of the original companions to aid John Tinker. He lived with his wife and sons. Now deceased.
Tears Trimblechin - his grandson, a growing Teller of Tales, trained by his grandfather.

Clear Bandler - The Land of Magicians
The $1.98 Magician - trained by Big Red and told to aid Tinker in whatever manner he could.

Plum Duff - a magician and consort to $1.98.

Bahn Duhr Tohr
Willawa, The White Warrior, Queen of all the lands.
Toucan, The King - he is the brother of Prince Goose and Princess Chicken and once was Tinker's advisor.
Hanred, Ripple's mate-for-life - he is a Master Illusionist who once traveled widely through the universe of universes and is also known by many of the folk as "Old Hanred."
Ripple, Advisor to the Royals - she is the Clan Head of the Faan witch clan.

> **Shitar** - her daughter, a witch.

Dol Spar - Headquarters of The Monetary Control and Mirf's home.
Mirf - The Special Chief First Inspector, often sent on special assignments by The General, the overall director of The Monetary Control and her boss.

> **Fred** - a suk-dragon, her Assistant.
> **Quan** - Fred's mate - Mirf's Assistant.

Magevern - home of the Vander mage Guild.
Sa'ar - the Heart of the Vander, who made Tinker The Lord of The Vander..

Clans, Guilds, and Other Organizations.
(known individuals listed)

Anaza sorcerer Phylota located in Far Corner.
>**Netanada** -- Elixa (Clan Head), Sorceress.
>**Abadoda** -- Three Rank Sorceress.
>**Hatopa** -- Three Rank Sorcerer.
>Important Artifacts.
>>The Ancient Book of Songs.

The Divineal of Thantala located in Murklan Obscuratan.
A Place Never Visited.
>**Lady Grimtouch** - The Glimmer (Clan Head) of The Divineal of Thantala.
>**Lady Fairdeath** - traveling with Sluba mage Ransapal.
>**Lady Dawnmort**
>**Lady Softtouch**
>**Lady Nightreaper**
>**Lady Final Kiss**
>**Lady Lastgift**
>Clan robe color - forest green almost black; carry a short gold staff.
>Important Artifacts
>>The Book of Death.

Potri witch Clan
>**Turintor**
>Clan robe colors - grape and green design.

Faan witch Clan - scattered widely throughout the universe of universes.

> **Ripple** - Clan Head - The fifth Born.
>> **Hanred**, the Illusionist, her Mate-For-Life.
>>> **Shitar**, their daughter, a witch.
>
> **Ranna** - The First Born
>
> **Riz** - The Second Born.
>
> **Rekel** - The Third Born.
>
> **Rbat** - The Fourth Born. At one time thought by many to have gone far.
>
> **Reptar** - The Sixth Born.
>
> **Rumtah** - The Seventh Born. Known as The Lucky One.
>
> **Reep** - The Eighth Born. Known as The Silent One. Married to **J. C.**
>> **Szaifeh** - their daughter, a witch.
>
> **Rotak** - The Ninth Born.
>
> **Raft** - The Tenth Born. Known as The Fast.
>
> **R-Bar** - The Eleventh Born. Called The Runt.
>> **Tinker** - her Mate-For-Life
>>> **Sedeem**, their daughter, a magician.
>
> **Ramp** - The Twelveth Born. A Magician. Married to **Hard**.
>> **Sa'ar**, their daughter, a magician.
>> **Shem**, their son, a magician.

Important artifacts.

> An immense collection of volumes dealing with the arcane collected by Hanred during his many travels through the universe of universes.

Talair witch Clan - located on Tanadra.
>Motaiss - a warlock
>Mendurra - a witch.
>Clothes colors - black with just a hint of faint grey in an ornate design that runs dwn the outside of each sleeve.

Sluba mage Guild, one member located in Three Trees Town.
>Ransapal- studied the Dark Under and ancient witch history. Traveling with Lady Fairdeath.

Vander mage Guild - located in Magevern.
>Sa'ar - the Heart of the Vander.
>Tobtz - the Soul of the Vander.
>Cazor - mage warrior.
>Moonda
>Aada
>Imdar - the Healer.
>Bant
>>Rorx - Vander warlock - her son by Tinker.
>>Szaifeh - his Mate-For-Life.
>Clothes color - they are always dressed in garb of the faintest purple. It is from the color of their garments that folk often call them "The Purple Magicians."

The Wood With located in Newlar, relocated from Blurratha. Hidden. In Plain Sight.
>Fairlan - Cluster Head
>Ringlan - Cluster Head
>Clearlar - Cluster Head
>Faerlar - Cluster Head
>Flerlan - The Observer

The Wood With are always accompanied by their beast. When the Wood With are present one might notice the smell of blooming flowers on the air.

The Garden Gnomes located in Growing Green.
>**Phineas Grass**
>**Hiram Toadstoll**
>**Franny Waxflower**
>**Franelken Vetch**
>**Tiny Rosebud** - the emissary
>**Rose Perrywinkle**

Monetary Control - located on Dol Spar.
>**The General** - Head of Monetary Control.
>**Mirf** - Head of the Special Investigations Office.
>>**Fred** - a suk-dragon - First Assistant.
>>**Quan** - Fred's mate - First Assistant.

Bits and Pieces of Cultural Data
(From the files of Monetary Control)

The Garden Gnomes.

The Garden Gnomes are a small folk, perhaps the smallest of all the folk. As their name implies they are fascinated by gardening and frequently visit those gardens that they recognize as being above the average in terms of arrangement and care, whether ornamental or functional.

At some point, in their past, one of them had been seen while visiting a particularly well designed ornamental garden. This kind of happening was not something that they liked to happen nor did they like to talk about it. This garden, as things seem to happen to this folk or that folk over their histories, belonged to a sculptress of some skill and very fast eyes. She made a statue of what her eyes saw as just a fleeting glance and set this statue in and among a artfully organized patch of flowers.

And as things so often happen, a visitor saw this statue and asked the owner to make one for him. And so it went. And so it went. Much to the consternation of the Garden Gnomes.

And eventually an entire industry sprang up around these statues and their production. People even wrote fanciful books about the culture of these things. They were all wrong, of course. None of the authors had ever talked with one of these small folk or had ever visited a Garden Gnome village.

The end result of all this was that the Garden Gnomes retreated deeper and deeper into areas where they would not, or could not, be observed.

Young Garden Gnomes, every once in awhile, on a dark, a particularly dark night, would steal one of these statues and hide them away.

Of course, it had no effect on the overall population of these fake garden gnomes. The industry was to well intrenched.

The Divineal of Thantala.

In time before time almost before memory it is told that the Divineal were there, passing through the universe of universes upon business that none dared ask about and few would dare challenge. The few that did, died. This rare occurrence, challenging one of them, and the result of that challenge, was told one to the other, and thus was the tale spread, and The Divineal were left to pursue their own interests. Most of these interests appeared to have something to do with Death. Death as a being, not merely as the end of something.

All the folk of the elseplaces recognized them as none else would dare to wear a deeply hooded robe of dark forest green that was almost black. And none else would presume to carry a short gold staff.

It is said among the many cultures in the universe of universes that few have ever seen the face of the individual hidden in the blackness of the deep hoods. It is also said that to see that face is to die. But, if one had ever done so and survived, none had ever so stated.

It is known and understood by most folk that one does not approach one of The Divineal and start a conversation. One does not watch one of The Divineal closely. One tries as much as possible to ignore their existence. One hopes to stay alive. It was this understanding that brought into being the label used far and wide for them, "The Sisters of Death." But it never, ever, was used when of them could hear it.

None knew where their elseplace, their homeplace, was located. None knew which of the many elseplaces, numbers beyond counting, would be the one wherein they resided. And even if one could find out, in some mysterious way, none would dare chose to go to such an elseplace.

The Divineal were polite and very soft spoken, if and when they might chose to speak to someone. And all, but the foolish and soon to be dead, would do all that they were capable of doing, if asked to do something. That is what the folk in the universe of universes believed. And none knew of anyone that had been asked and who had refused and survived.

None knew how many Divineal there were. None knew why or what they were about and most folk felt that the best place to be when one of them was around was to be somewhere else.

The Divineal were like a pebble dropped into a still pond whose action caused ripples to flow out in all directions. And like that pebble, they were totally unconcerned about those ripples.

The Witch Clans.

The Potri witch clan came into existence, as did all the witch clans, during what all the clans call "The Great Migration." From where this migration came is a great matter of debate and argumentation, but not why.

The ancestral clan, or clans, also a matter of intense debate and argumentation, had, through arcane knowledge, come to understand that a disaster beyond the control of any user of magic was about to happen to their homeland.

So they fled out into the universe of universes and over time the witch clan, or clans, splintered and grew into the myriad of clans that are now present.

The long ago seen disaster happened in a single violent explosion that removed their homeland as their sun erupted and ate everything within reach.

Some thing, some event, during that long ago migration and scatter brought into the witch culture a sense of authority coupled with a powerful magic that each clan cultivated. Each clan developed their own clan interests and evolved their own unique concept of magic. The end result of this was a somewhat provincial sense of proper witch attire and proper witch behavior. The pairing of these beliefs with their sense of authority meant that the folk living in the many elseplaces in the universe of universes knew that any witch tended to be rather short-tempered and had a predilection toward violent behavior when the behavior of other folk, witch, magician, or non-magical user, was felt by the witches to be engaged in improper behavior, undesirable behavior, or were just plain irritating.

Most witch clans dressed in wardrobes of midnight black, the exact style of their clothing varying widely. Some of the clans, in the long before before, had, for reasons they chose not to reveal, settled on wardrobes of other colors.

The Faan witch clan is unique. Among all of the witch clans scattered across the universe of universes, they are the only one that does not maintain a clan house. And, unlike all the other clans, the members are all and only generationally linked. The magic of the Faan flows down the female line from mother to daughter.

The Faan clan, unlike the other clans, are trained almost exclusively by their female relatives, mainly by their mother and their aunts. But if a sister has learned some new and unique twist, it may be shared, sister to sister. It is due to this multi-generational sharing and training that has made the Faan noted throughout the witch clans as being the most powerful clan and to be avoided if at all possible. And some few understand that at some point in the long ago long ago, in their mating with their chosen mates-for-life, from other witch lines, that something unusual happened that twisted and transformed their genetic material.

The result of this event was that, at times, their offspring are born with new and unique abilities. This tends to explain why the Faan do not maintain a clan house. Members of their clan, most often, prefer to wander mostly by themselves and to study and collect magic and magic spells. And other things.

The Mage Guilds

The mage Guilds apparently came into existence in the long ago long ago in a manner none understand or thought to record as this event was in a time when such occurrences were not seen as being important enough to warrant special note.

Magicians are, in one sense, at the opposite end of the magical spectrum from the witches. That is why the magicians and the witches tend to avoid each other whenever possible, especially physical contact. The magics of each tend to be unstable in contact, often resulting in fatal results. However, there is the fact that, at times, in a manner none truly understand, that magicians and witches may have close association, even mates of the others, without dire affects.

The **Vander mage Guild**, as written in the *Histories of the Arcane,* was once a sub-Order of the Fanderlaine mage Guild. Little is known of the Fanderlaine and what they thought to specialize their skills upon. The Vander sub-Order eventually split away from the Fanderlaine and pushed deep into the arcane knowledge that was of particular interest to their members. The Vander became the most radical of the experimenters of the mage Guilds and explored many areas of interest to them. This was considered most strange in the mage communities as the Guilds tend to be extremely conservative in their outlook and mage knowledge. Unlike most Guilds, the

Vander are almost exclusively female, each member carefully selected for skills and aptitude.

The Anaza Sorcerers.

The Sorcerers were, and are, a small clan and have forever lived in small isolated elseplaces rarely relocating. Small isolated elseplaces were more common in the universe of universes than most of the folk realized. And that suited the Sorcerer clan quite well.

Why they preferred to live this way is lost in the dim reaches of an ancient history begun in a time almost before time itself. Various of the First Sorcerers at numerous points in time in their long, long history had searched their book of lore and learning, The Book Of Songs, for clues as to why this was the way it was. But each had failed. None of them realized, or knew from the oral traditions of the clan, that the Book Of Songs had come into existence long past the time when the reason why could be remembered.

So, as these things happen, the Sorcerer clan has remained reclusive and unknown to the larger universe of universes, not really hidden so much as just being very remote and private.

There was one piece of information known to the clan, a piece of information never allowed to be transmitted to anyone not a member of the clan. And similar to the reason for their preferring small, isolated elseplaces, the acquisition of this piece of information, the how and the when and the why of it did happen, was lost in the time long before before.

Someone, way back then, had learned to recognize the presence of a folk never seen and poorly understood. This recognition was not visual but rather a matter of odor, the odor of blooming flowers. With such an olfactory clue, this small clan of magic users, the Sorcerer clan, knew when the Wood With were around. They had never seen one but the delicate and pleasant odor told them when these folk were about.

The Wood With knew of this strange thing. So they tended to keep a watch on this small group more from a matter of curiosity than of any fear of what that clan might do.

The Sorcerer clan, of course, knew when these other strange folk came and went so they, the Sorcerers, tended to keep Sorcerer business very carefully hidden from these others. And in some strange and subtle way, the clan felt that the Wood With were not to be trusted. It was a cultural tradition, never to be questioned. The reason for this was also lost in the dim historical past. And, of course, they would never attempt to affect the behavior of the Wood With. Tradition also stated that this was not to be done.

The Wood With.

The Wood With are a small folk. If anyone saw one of this secretive group from a distance, an event so unlikely as to be in the realm of never, it might be thought that what was seen was a very young human child of ten or twelve years of age. Of course, few human children are accompanied by a beast as tall as they are.

The Wood With, from a time before forever, have remained unobserved and unknown, which is exactly what they wish. As a group they are, for the most part, uninterested in the affairs of other sapient beings in all the universe of universes. But, every so often, there occurs a one that attracts their attention. This event is a rare, but not unusual, happening.

The Wood With prefer to live in and among the big trees, taking comfort one from the other. They and the environment blur together where ever they might be. This skill, this cultural attribute, is the main reason, but not the only reason, why they remain unseen and unnoticed.

Their beasts are as unique a species as the Wood With. From an early age one finds the other and from that instant the pair are inseparable. The beasts blend into their surroundings with the same ease as their constant companions.

It is a peculiarity of the Wood With that their presence leaves a faint odor of blooming flowers in the air. In all the time of their existence only one small group have ever realized this fact. But that group's mythology and cultural values are such that the fact that they know this is all that they know. Every thing else they believe, everything else are tales from antiquity with all the error that derives from that.

The Kingdom and Kingdoms of Bahn Duhr Tohr.

The Kingdom of Bahn Duhr Tohr had been, until its most recent merging into a whole, a series of large and small kingdoms, each with a unique name and a unique color scheme. These color schemes were relegated to their Royalty and to their armies. It was very useful to combatants to be able to recognize friend from foe in the chaos of massed combat.

Many of the kingdoms, but not all, could trace their existence back into the dimly remembered past. Some even argued that they existed long before written records came into use. The kingdoms large and small, frequently merged, or broke apart, as the normal political intrigues and royal wheeling and dealing created large kingdoms out of smaller ones, or as so often happened, smaller kingdoms out of larger.

But, in spite of the usual turmoil over boundaries and royal household alignments, all the kingdoms were dependent upon each other as no single one had all the resources necessary for true self-sufficiency.

The bonds between the rulers and the ruled are tight and mutually advantageous. Rulers who did not keep the needs of their folk foremost did not last long. Of course, the occasional battle with a neighbor was accepted as just part of life. Battles were, for the most part, short. This was due to the usual approach to warfare that assumed that most of the fighting would happen between the royalty of the houses in contention. The knights and lessor troops often suffered nothing worse than broken bones. Most of the time this occurred during the first melee and charge.

Grandeville.

Grandeville is a small, rather isolated, rural community of 8,000 population (more or less) tucked away in the mountainous corner of northeastern Oregon. It survives in a provincial unawareness of many things, being overly conscious of the ancestors who settled the place long after the westward migration brought California, Washington, Oregon, and Idaho into statehood.

The town sprawls down from "The Bench," a shallow bench along the edge of the next door mountain slope, to The Blue River, named after the color it has after the first snow melt surges from the canyon and out across the valley proper, always threatening to jump its banks and flood the surrounding farm land.

There are two newspapers published in town, a weekly and a daily (except for Sunday). The Daily, The *Grandeville News*, tends to ignore anything happening outside the edge of town. The weekly, *The Mountain View*, tends to ignore anything happening in Grandeville and prints whatever the publisher happens to feel like publishing.

There are a number of local establishments of note:
- The Two Bags Full - a grocery store.
- The Railroad Bar and Grill - also known as The Rail.

- Big Darlene's Bar - the home of the Annual Chili Cookoff and Arm Wrestling Championship Event, All Comers Invited.
- Johnson's Everything Shop.
- Chen's Chinese Restaurant.
- Leonard's Outdoor Supply Shop.
- The Always Open Gas Pump.
- The Romp and Stomp Motel.